**Nadine Gonzalez** is the daughter of Haitian immigrants, born in New York City. She was raised both in New York and Port-au-Prince, Haiti. A lawyer by profession, she lives in Miami, Florida, and shares her home with her Cuban American husband and their beautiful son. Nadine writes joyous contemporary romance featuring a diverse cast of characters, American, Caribbean and Latinx. She networks on Twitter but lives on Instagram! Check out @_nadinegonzalez. For more information, visit her website, nadine-gonzalez.com

A born-and-bred New Yorker, **Nicki Night** delights in creating hometown heroes and heroines with an edge. As an avid reader and champion of love, Nicki chose to pen romance novels because she believes that love should be highlighted in this world, and she delights in writing contemporary romances with unforgettable characters and just enough drama to make readers clutch a pearl here and there. Nicki has a penchant for adventure and is currently working on penning her next romantic escapade.

# SCANDAL IN THE VIP SUITE

## NADINE GONZALEZ

# INTIMATE NEGOTIATIONS

## NICKI NIGHT

MILLS & BOON

First Published in Great Britain 2020
by Mills & Boon, an imprint of HarperCollinsPublishers,
1 London Bridge Street, London, SE1 9GF

*Scandal in the VIP Suite* © 2020 Nadine Seide
*Intimate Negotiations* © 2020 Renee Daniel Flagler

ISBN: 978-0-263-28279-5

0121

**MIX**
Paper from
responsible sources

**FSC** www.fsc.org   FSC™ C007454

This book is produced from independently certified FSC™ paper to ensure responsible forest management.

For more information visit: www.harpercollins.co.uk/green

Printed and bound in Spain
by CPI, Barcelona

# SCANDAL IN
# THE VIP SUITE

## NADINE GONZALEZ

Sincere thanks to my editor, Errin Toma. It has been a pleasure working with you. Here's to a long, productive relationship!

Shout-out to Roxanna Elden, best writing buddy, and the Miami Book Fair and Writers Institute for their unwavering support.

With regards to craft, I would first like to thank my husband, Ariel. You are always my first story editor. Special thanks to my sister Martine for the unlimited brainstorming sessions that resulted in the perfect meet-cute. To my "creative consultants," Ian Midgley and Julia Taylor, you have breathed life into my first Jamaican British hero.

To my sisters Martine and Murielle: your support means everything to me.

A special shout-out to TEAM 12! You are the best #bookstagram helpers a budding author could have.

Finally to Ariel and Nathaniel, let's dream on!

# One

It seemed to Nina Taylor that she'd been traveling forever. Her flight was delayed at JFK, and the plane had spent an eternity in the queue at Miami International Airport before reaching its gate. Outside, she slipped on dark sunglasses to block out Miami's Technicolor brightness and settled into the back of a cab. It was unreasonably hot—even for July—and the fake leather seat stuck to her bare arms. The driver loaded her bags into the trunk and slipped behind the wheel. "Where to?"

"Fifteen ten Ocean Drive."

"Sand Castle? Good choice." He adjusted the rearview mirror. "What brings you to Miami?"

A simple enough question. Most people wouldn't have to lie. "Meeting a friend."

"Nice! Nice!" The driver nodded. A bald spot on the back of his head revealed a patch of shiny brown skin. He eased into traffic. "I tell my grandkids to have fun! Take chances! Enjoy their youth!"

"Sounds like you're a good grandpa."

He glanced at her in the rearview mirror. "You look like my granddaughter. Which island are you from?"

The question didn't surprise Nina. People from the islands had a sixth sense for this stuff. But Nina's Caribbean roots were so deeply buried, Manhattan was the only island she could legitimately claim as her own. Just then, a massive SUV sped past them, cutting them off. A honking match ensued. The driver returned his attention to the road, saving her from having to answer his question. It was better this way; her family tree was more of a twisted, brittle vine.

As the AC kicked in, Nina got comfortable. This was not her first trip to Miami, but the memory of the last trip was blurred in a Jell-O shot glaze. She was twenty-three at the time and on assignment for *Belle*, a women's magazine. She was thirty-one now, and her taste in cocktails had greatly evolved.

Nina lost herself in the view. Miami was one big, bloated suburb. One strip of highway connected to the next with a few well-placed palm trees to maintain the illusion of paradise. Soon enough they reached a causeway soaring above the dazzling bay, and everything changed. Suburban sprawl gave way to waterfront mansions and glass condo towers. Traffic was at a crawl when they inched past the iconic Welcome to Miami Beach sign. Nina snapped a photo with her phone, excitement bubbling inside her. By the time they veered onto Ocean Drive and pulled up to the hotel's glossy black gates, Nina's outlook on life shifted. Maybe this solo trip wasn't the worst idea she'd ever had.

The mansion-turned-private boutique hotel stood proud in the sun. It had all the trappings of classic Mediterranean style: chalk-white walls and an angled terra-cotta tile roof, randomly placed windows—some arched, some not—and French doors opening to Juliet balconies. But it wasn't until she entered the courtyard that Nina hit all-time Zen. The villa soared three stories above an interior garden complete with a fountain, each floor opening onto balconies with iron rails as fine as lace.

*Mom would have loved this.* The thought escaped her like a leaf caught in a breeze. But it assured her that she was in the right place.

Nina approached the front desk, gave her information and helped herself to a complimentary mint.

"I'm sorry, Ms. Taylor. There's an issue with your reservation."

The words no weary traveler ever wanted to hear.

"What's the issue?" Nina asked. "I booked my stay a month ago."

"Not sure. The manager will tell you more."

The clerk offered her a mini-bottle of water, but Nina would not be placated. The sharp click-clack of high heels on tile announced the arrival of the manager. Nina readied herself for a fight.

"Welcome to Sand Castle, Ms. Taylor! I'm the general manager, Grace Guzman."

Despite the circumstances, Nina winced at the hotel's generic name. It wasn't suited to a Mediterranean-style mansion, and Nina had half a mind to let this Guzman woman know.

"Come with me. Let's get you sorted."

Nina followed the manager along a cloistered walkway to a small office that might have been a butler's pantry in another era. A nameplate read simply, "Graciela Guzman." The stark white walls were cluttered with charcoal sketches framed in gold. She sat behind a desk that was free of all clutter and got down to it. "Ms. Taylor, the suite you requested is no longer available."

Nina dropped into an empty chair and stared at her. "I don't understand. I booked the Oasis spa getaway package one month ago."

"Sand Castle has no official spa suite," Grace said. "All our rooms are suited for relaxing stays."

"Not according to your website."

The spa package had included the two-bedroom top-floor suite. Jackie Onassis had called it an oasis when she'd spent a night in February 1988 and the name had stuck. *Belle* magazine had ranked it among the top ten hotels for the sophisticated traveler—a list that Nina had curated without ever stepping foot on any of the listed properties. It was her late mother's dream to spend the night there.

Nina was here to fulfill that dream. If that weren't the case, Nina would have picked a less expensive, less pretentious hotel. Even as the thought crossed her mind, she knew it wasn't true. The instant her cab pulled up to the gates and her luggage had exchanged hands, she had succumbed to the old mansion's charm.

"Ms. Taylor, try to understand. The Oasis is our equivalent of the presidential suite. It's subject to availability."

"Is the president coming?" Nina asked. "Because according to CNN, he's expected to give a speech in Johannesburg."

Grace's eyes narrowed. "We've had to make it available for an important guest. It's all last-minute, and I apologize. Since you're traveling alone, would you settle for a superior room instead?"

What? She wasn't going to settle for some single-lady-traveler downgrade! "I'd mind very much."

Grace smiled coolly. Nina noted the lovely creases at the corners of her eyes. In her midfifties or so, she was a beauty and knew it. Her foundation makeup didn't blend well into her olive complexion, but otherwise she was perfect. Wearing a belted yellow dress and heels, Grace had the advantage of style. Nina felt plain by comparison in her go-to travel uniform: T-shirt, skinny jeans, don't-mess-with-me shades and ballerina flats.

Prepping for this trip, Nina had scrubbed, peeled and waxed. On the plane, she'd slathered serum on her face; as a result, her matte brown skin was dewy, but not in a good way. Her hair hung in a limp braid down her back. And now it was clear that in her zealous preparation for her Miami getaway, she'd neglected all the smaller moments leading to it, like arriving in style at a luxury hotel, dressed to kill and prepared to confront the arrogant staff.

Grace checked her gold watch. "Your stay is important to us, I assure you."

Nina's anger spiked. "Not as important as this person you've given my suite to!"

It was probably a lost cause, but there was no way she was going to make this easy on management.

"We think you'll be happy in our Garden Room."

Nina shut her eyes. A tingling sensation spread from her chest to her throat, a sign that things were going to get loud and ugly. She thought it best to warn the other woman. "I'm sorry, but I'm about to throw a fit."

The flutter of Grace's unnaturally thick lashes was the only hint that Nina had gotten under her skin. "Naturally, your account will reflect the change in price."

Nina remained stone-faced. Grace tried a different tactic. "What if we offered a complimentary in-room massage? Would that make up for the inconvenience?"

"No, it wouldn't." She was so brittle with exhaustion, if anyone laid a hand on her, she'd snap like a twig.

"How about an extra night's stay on us?" Grace proposed.

That would round up her trip to seven nights. But why stop there? "Make it two nights."

Grace made a show of checking her computer before tossing her reading glasses onto the glass desktop. "That'll work."

Nina nodded. She was disappointed, to be sure. The point of this trip was to honor her mother with the sort of Jackie O experience she'd deserved, but even the most unhinged traveler had to yield to reason. The Garden Room would do for now.

Grace pressed an intercom buzzer and called for a porter. Rising from behind her desk, she said, "Let's get you settled."

Nina followed Grace out the office just in time to witness the commotion in the courtyard marking the arrival of new guests. Grace promptly abandoned her and, in a state of agitation that didn't suit her, went off to greet the new-comers. A hostess trailed behind her with a tray of champagne flutes. Nina wondered where the welcome committee had been when she'd arrived only moments earlier. Then it dawned on her—she'd been booted out of the Oasis to accommodate the excessively attractive people making their entrance.

A power couple if she'd ever seen one. The man was stunning. Nina hated to admit it, but there was no tap-dancing around the obvious. Tall, broad and with a pro-file that matched the marble busts hidden in the mansion's many alcoves, he was hard to ignore. His complexion was raw honey, taking on a golden patina in the sun. His eyes were concealed behind smoky glasses, and he wore his long, wavy hair tied neatly at the nape of his neck. Given three guesses, Nina would go with soccer player, baseball star or prizefighter—middleweight division. He looked important, even though his appearance was somewhat di-sheveled in a black blazer worn over a wrinkled white T-shirt paired with faded jeans. The woman was obviously younger, still in her twenties, but that was how those things sorted themselves out. She was blonde and wore the equiv-alent of Nina's travel uniform, elevated by a pair of black pumps. Nina imagined the couple getting settled in *her* suite, sipping champagne on *her* balcony before having sex on *her* custom double king bed—the absolute best sex in the world. That image alone prompted her to move all her resentment from Grace Guzman to the power couple with a simple mental balance transfer.

Nina hid behind a pillar and watched as Grace, clumsy with giddiness, gushed over the couple. The man laughed at something she said, the full, throaty laugh of a man who had everything going for him. Something about it sent a ripple down Nina's spine.

A porter approached, startling her. "Ms. Taylor, my name is Jim. Please come this way."

She followed him up a grand, winding staircase, that unnerving laugh licking at her ears. And because she couldn't let a damn thing go, Nina tossed a final look over her shoulder. To her surprise, Mr. VIP was at the bottom of the stairs staring up at her without the filter of the smoky sunglasses. Mortified, she held his gaze a beat longer than necessary for no other reason than to prove that she wasn't. Their eyes locked, and for a split second it was just the two of them in the courtyard. Nina grabbed the handrail for support. Jim the porter called out, "This way, Ms. Taylor." Good thing, too, because for a moment there, she'd forgotten who she was and where she was headed.

On the second-floor landing, Jim turned to her. "Sorry about the commotion. You know how it is when Hollywood comes calling."

Nina knew something about that. The daughter of a Broadway actress, she'd witnessed firsthand the frenzy the arrival of a Hollywood player could provoke. Her mother's friends would enjoy a collective orgasm whenever a film actor signed up for a play. So… Hollywood? She'd been wrong on all three guesses.

"I shouldn't say this, but it's a madhouse down there. Glad my shift is over." Jim stopped abruptly and checked the key in his hand. "You're in Oasis? Really? I thought…"

"What?" Nina skipped a step and nearly tripped.

"We could have taken the private elevator," Jim said glumly. "Sorry about that."

"Uh…no worries. I could use the exercise."

"All right. Only one more flight to go."

The stairs wound up to the third floor. Nina looked over the rail down at the courtyard. The VIP couple was still chatting with Grace. She had time. To do what exactly? As she tried to puzzle that out, her gaze lingered on *him*. She had the luxury of staring at him unchallenged and took full advantage. An athlete would have had rough, rugged edges, but he was Hollywood beautiful: solid, symmetrical, smooth. His casual clothes looked expensive, and he wore them with effortless cool. His smile was like the sun. Nina's core turned to jelly, and it had nothing to do with the languid heat.

"Ms. Taylor?"

*Damn it! Busted again!*

Nina swiveled around and followed Jim, her heart racing. On the third floor, potted lavender plants lined the way down a hall to a pair of carved mahogany doors. She was at the threshold of paradise, but what was the plan here? Take a quick look around. That was all. And why not? She'd been robbed of the experience.

Jim punched a code in the keypad and explained that a new code would be sent to her via email. Then he inserted a hefty skeleton key in the lock and turned it until the lock clicked. Sweat beaded at Nina's temples, and she wondered about the maximum sentence for trespassing. The door swung open to reveal a Greek key tiled floor that seemed to go on forever. Jim ushered her into a sitting room furnished with antiques. A crystal chandelier hung overhead, and French doors opened to a wide balcony. Nina's anxiety gave way to a rush of excitement.

Jim stacked her luggage on a loading table in the foyer. "Would you like a tour?"

"No, thanks. I'm beat."

"Very well. The master suite is to your left, and the guest room to your right. Each room has a private bath."

Nina tipped Jim handsomely to better send him on his way. She preferred not to get him mixed up in this. As soon as the door shut behind him, she wasted no time storming the master bedroom suite, only to stand frozen at the threshold.

*This* was the famous Oasis. The space glowed. Honey oak furniture, gold leaf accents and yellow silk drapes all helped to spread the sunlit luster. A mural of hand-painted flowers crawled up the walls. The bed was a sea of blue silk anchored by four wood posters—and it called out to Nina. She went over, sat at the edge, bounced a bit to test the mattress, then she spilled onto her back. "Oh, yes," she murmured, staring up at the ceiling. A fresco depicted angels floating on tufted clouds. They looked down at her knowingly.

She made a mental note for her journal: *Elegant, opulent and a little too much! I love it!*

Only one more box to tick: a selfie. For good measure.

Nina sat up, pulled her phone from her pocket, smoothed her hair, selected a photo filter, tilted her head, pursed her lips, grimaced, attempted a smile and—

"Does the bed feel just right, Goldilocks?"

The phone fell from her hand. The masculine voice had a blunt British accent. It punched her in the gut and left her winded. Nina folded forward, squeezed her eyes shut and prayed that the angels frolicking on the ceiling would do her a favor and summon the angel of death.

*God, please! I'd rather die than live through this. Amen.*

# Two

The first thing he noticed was a flock of birds flying past the bell tower at the end of the courtyard. Julian Leroy Knight, better known as JL Knight, felt that he could've been anywhere in the world—Mexico, Spain or Cuba, where a similar estate stood. He'd done his research. This mansion was an exact replica of a villa in Havana's elegant suburb of Miramar. The original currently housed an embassy.

Julian exchanged pleasantries with the property manager, declined a glass of champagne and left his assistant, Kat, to handle the details of his stay. He ventured deeper into the yard. A central fountain stood as tall as him and struggled to mute the street noise. Day or night, Ocean Drive was a party. He should know. At nineteen, he'd left his home in England seeking adventure in the United States. He'd stayed with a family friend in Miami for a week before making his way down to South Beach. For six months, he worked for Sand Castle as a valet attendant, and during that time he never stepped foot past the iconic black gates. Access to the "main house" was denied to low-level staff. Fast-forward to today, and they were throwing him a parade.

The fuss was a balm to his bruised ego. Julian wasn't the celebrity that he had been five years ago, when his action films dominated the box office. In Hollywood, the whiff of failure was poison gas, and it followed you everywhere. Add to that a very public breakup and the public outcry over the portrayal of women in his latest release, and Julian was practically persona non grata everywhere. Except here in Miami, which was nice.

A grand staircase curved up to the second floor. He wandered to it and tested the sturdiness of the oak handrail. He'd worked carpentry for a while and appreciated the craft. A woman was making her way up the stairs. Tall, slim, light on her feet, cocoa-brown skin, body beautifully packaged in a pair of fitted jeans. She wore her coffee-black hair in a long braid that snaked down her back. When she glanced over her shoulder, looking directly at him, her long lashes veiled her eyes. But nothing could shield him from that scorching glare.

Fair was fair. After all, she'd caught him staring. Ogling women wasn't a habit of his, and this wasn't the time to start. He'd been labeled the poster boy for toxic masculinity; he couldn't afford any slipups. Only nothing about this felt like a slip. It felt pointed and personal. She held his gaze, and Julian couldn't break away. He watched, fascinated, as her cheeks turned the shade of wine. Who knew how long they'd have stayed like this if a porter hadn't called out to her?

With an imperious flip of her braid, she continued her ascent, turned a corner and disappeared. Julian fought back the impulse to give chase. What was the matter with him? He was here on business.

In the end, it was Kat who saved him from himself. She linked her arm around his and dragged him away. "Come on! I'd like to see the pool before we head upstairs."

They made their way to an open veranda overlooking the pool below. The manager explained that a previous owner had purchased the neighboring lot just to make space for it. Julian had to admire the audacity of a man who thought, *Screw it! I'll knock down a house and put a pool in its place.* But once he saw it, he was on board.

The pool was the true oasis, not some stuffy bedroom

filled with antiques. It stretched one hundred feet wide and was paved in thousands of tiny gold tiles. Each corner was punctuated by urns set high on pedestals. A fountain spit water down the middle, sending ripples along the crystal surface. Julian yearned to dive in, but for now he'd settle for a photograph. He pulled his Nikon out of a well-worn, well-loved travel bag.

"Look at it!" Kat exclaimed. "Julian, isn't it gorgeous?"

He adjusted the lens of the camera and raised it to his eye. "Gorgeous."

"Would you like a closer look?" Grace offered.

"No, this works."

Julian framed the shot in his mind. He pictured a woman in a bikini floating on her back, eyes closed against the sun, hair like a halo around her head. Act one, scene one. He snapped the photo and put away the camera.

"Our annual Independence Day pool party is the most exclusive on the beach," Grace said. "It starts tomorrow at four. We'll end the night with fireworks."

Julian relied on his acting skills to fake interest. "Sounds great."

Grace nodded, pleased. "Now I'll show you to your private elevator."

As he, Kat and the manager squeezed into a rickety lift that led straight to his floor, Julian wondered if he might run into the woman on the stairs again, if only to apologize.

The lift opened to a wide, sun-filled walkway leading to a pair of sturdy doors. Grace ushered them inside, all the while entertaining Kat with the highlights of the mansion's storied past. In her excitement, she missed the luggage stacked neatly in the entrance. The Louis Vuitton weekender bag and matching tote did not belong to him. He was not a fancy-luggage type of guy.

"Come see the view from the balcony," Grace said.

Kat followed Grace. Julian swiveled on his heel and took

off in the opposite direction. The master bedroom was be-hind a pair of thick wood doors. He drifted over, quietly turned the heavy brass knob and peeked through the crack. There she was. Taking a selfie on the bed.

Shit. This was not the second encounter he'd hoped for. Now instead of apologizing, he'd have to call security.

He entered the room. "Does the bed feel just right, Gold-ilocks?"

At his words, she stiffened and dropped her phone. He took no joy in her reaction. He didn't like seeing her so defeated where earlier she'd been so defiant. *Come on. Where's that fighting spirit?* When she finally stood to confront him, her eyes were wild with panic. Julian tried to muster something stronger than amused annoyance but came up short. If it were up to him, he'd let her escape and pretend this incident never happened. This wouldn't be the first time a fan tried to sneak into his hotel room. He was blasé enough to shrug it off. But it wasn't up to him. She didn't know it, but the countdown had begun. Before too long—

"Ah!" Kat screamed in Julian's ear. "What's going on? How did she get in?"

The manager stormed the bedroom. "Ms. Taylor!"

The porter arrived with Julian's plain black logo-free luggage and offered to call security.

Julian stepped forward to cover Ms. Taylor from the incoming fire. She may be an intruder, but she was *his* in-truder. But she stepped out of his shadow and addressed the room.

"Settle down," she said. "This is just one big misun-derstanding."

Her voice was calm. Julian liked that.

"Someone get Jim up here!" Grace yelled.

"Leave Jim out of it," she said. "It was a mistake. Prob-ably *your* mistake. I bet this suite is still under my name."

"Ms. Taylor, we have an agreement. This suite is not yours, and you know it."

"What agreement?" Julian asked, and Ms. Taylor got him up to speed.

"The agreement we reached after she kicked me out to accommodate you."

Julian turned to Grace. "Is that true?"

She went pale. He had his answer.

An assistant arrived, flanked by security guards and trailed by poor Jim. The comedy of errors checked out. The suite was still reserved under Ms. Taylor's name. Jim was given the wrong key at the front desk. To complicate matters, the hotel had no vacancies.

The assistant clutched an iPad with a white-knuckled grip. "We're fully booked for the holiday."

"I thought the Garden Room was available," Grace said, her voice thin.

"Full, ma'am." An elderly guest had thrown out his back and couldn't be moved until his pain medications kicked in. "Our hands are tied."

Grace switched to Spanish to vent her frustration. Julian glanced at Kat. She was chewing on her bottom lip the way she did when she was anxious. All this turmoil over a hotel room was ridiculous to Julian. People liked to treat him as if he were a descendant of the royal family, but he'd stayed in hostels and motels that he'd like to forget. He'd slept in his car for a month when he first moved out to Los Angeles. He'd gladly give up the suite, but unfortunately, he needed the buffer the private floor provided.

"That's enough," Julian said. "Ms. Taylor and I will figure this out. We'll draw straws or something. Please wait outside."

"Julian, it's not your job to figure this out," Kat said.

"I agree, Mr. Knight," Grace said.

"Even so, I'd prefer you clear the room."

After he ushered the delegation out the door, Julian turned to the crafty Ms. Taylor. She stared at him with a vacant expression, and he worried that she might have suffered a stroke. "Hey! Are you okay?"

She uncurled an index finger and pointed at him. "You're JL Knight!"

*Here we go.*

Julian cupped the nape of his neck and rubbed out the kinks. He could speak up now or let the madness run its course. He decided to let it run.

She continued to launch accusations. "And you're *British*?"

"Jamaican and British," he specified. "Is that bad?"

"I don't know! Malcolm Brown was from the South Bronx."

For two seasons, Julian had played paramedic Malcolm Brown on *Riverside Rescue*, a long-running network police procedural. Very few people remembered his early work. "I've been in a few projects since then."

"I wouldn't know," she said. "I binge-watched *Riverside* last Christmas, and Malcolm was my favorite."

"Thank you," he said. "And sorry for this mix-up. My assistant handled the travel arrangements. Usually she'll call, drop my name and—"

"And people drop everything?"

"Something like that."

"Must be nice," she said.

"You know what? It is."

"Well, I handle my own business. You should try it sometime."

"Want it back?" he offered. "I'll go elsewhere."

Sand Castle was central to his presence in Miami, but he wouldn't have insisted on staying here had he known the suite was booked. There was no shortage of five-star hotels on the beach. And in retrospect, showing up in Miami on a holiday weekend was a stupid idea.

"Keep it," she said firmly. "The manager will poison my food if you walk out. You're too *important*."

"How about we share it? There's no reason you can't stay here until the Garden, Fountain or whatever opens up."

"You're wrong." She folded her arms over her chest. "There are about one hundred reasons. Top of the list—stranger danger."

"Never played that game. Sounds fun."

What was he doing flirting with the woman he'd caught taking a selfie on his bed? Talk about stranger danger.

"It would only be for a night, maybe two," he said. "This place is huge. We could go for days and not run into each other."

"There *is* a second bedroom with a private bath," she said, speaking more to herself than to him.

"Look how much you know," Julian said.

"I wrote a piece about this hotel long ago," she said. "Also, the porter told me."

"Good old Jim?"

She looked uneasy. "I hope I didn't get him fired."

"If it helps, I'll put in a good word," Julian said. "So, you're a writer?"

She raised her chin. "I am."

"What do you write?"

"Books," she said. "Well… I wrote one book, but there are several formats."

"Okay."

He must have hit a sore spot. She was suddenly less sure of herself, stumbling over her words. But she was no less beautiful. The light from the windows washed over her face, warming her bronze skin and adding specks of gold to her brown eyes. Julian itched to reach for his camera.

There was a double knock on the door. He moved away from it. "They're getting restless. Time to decide."

She let out a sigh. "Well, what about the blonde?"

Her question left him confused. "Which blonde?"

"The one you're traveling with," she said. "She won't want me around. Three is a crowd."

"Blondes are people with parents and pets and feelings. They're objectified enough without you piling on, Ms. Taylor."

She wrapped her arms around her waist as if to control the spread of a full-body laugh. "I apologize, Mr. Knight. Thanks for shining a light on the plight of the blondes."

"You're welcome," Julian said. "Her name is Katia Wells, and she's my assistant."

"The one who booked your travel?"

"The same." Kat was in Florida to attend a family re-union. She'd gladly abandoned her seat on a commercial airline to fly private with him. A car was waiting outside to take her to her grandparents' house in Boca Raton. "If we were together, do you think she'd be waiting on the other side of the door?"

"I don't know anything about you or how you live your life," she said. "Which brings us back to stranger danger."

"Yeah? Of the two of us, only one has demonstrated a disregard for social norms."

A triple knock rattled the door. Kat called out to him. "Julian! I can get you a suite at the Fontainebleau."

That was timely information. He liked having options.

"We could both leave," he suggested to Ms. Taylor. "I'm sure there's more than one available room at the Fontaine-bleau."

"Or we could both stay."

They fell silent and, in that silence, they reached an agreement. Still, there were some wrinkles to iron out. "Are you traveling alone?" he asked. "You booked this entire suite for yourself, or are you expecting a full bachelorette party?"

"Did anyone question you for wanting a suite to yourself?"

"It's mainly for privacy reasons," he said. "Which brings me to my one caveat."

"Just one? I have a few."

"You're a writer," Julian said.

"And you're an actor."

"You can't write about me or anything that happens while you're here."

She eyed him with suspicion. "What do you think will happen?"

"Not much," he said with a shrug. "I'm going to dive into bed as soon as everyone clears out. What are your plans?"

For the first time ever, she relaxed. Her rigid posture loosened, and her arms fell to her side. "Same. I'm exhausted."

"All right, then."

He went to open the door, but she stopped him. "Wait! Why are you being so nice?"

"This is not about niceness," he said. "It's about fairness. If I hadn't showed up, you wouldn't be in this position."

"I got a good deal out of it," she said.

"Yeah? What's the deal?"

"Two free nights."

"Not bad."

"Right?"

Another loud, imperious knock, and the manager scolded him from the other side of the door. "Mr. Knight! This is not how we do things at Sand Castle. Let us handle it."

This summit had to end. Julian was seriously sleep-deprived and all that knocking was drilling into his skull. He turned to her for confirmation. "Are we doing this?"

"Sure," she said. "I'll stay until my room becomes available. And don't worry; I have no interest in writing about you. A, I don't find you that compelling. B, I'm only really qualified to write about myself."

"Not compelling?"

There were feature stories dedicated to the rise and fall of his career. A talentless hack to some, an action hero legend to others, but nothing if not compelling.

She rolled her eyes and murmured something about fragile Hollywood egos.

"Excuse me," he said.

"Open the door before they call the cops."

"Fair point." He'd sweep up the shards of his ego later. "Let's face the firing squad."

# Three

*Ha! Joke's on me! The second bedroom is actually a tidy study with an attached bath. All this opulence and I'm spending the night on a pullout couch.*

Nina put aside her journal and closed her eyes. She'd kept a diary since childhood. An only child, her diary was often the guardian of her deepest secrets. When her fiction had failed to sell, she'd turned a year's worth of old journals from her late teens into a memoir—a decision she now regretted. Regretting important life decisions was becoming a pattern.

She never should have come to Miami. What had she hoped to achieve? Closure? *I mean...come on!* This was life, not the Oprah show, and this trip was one big, unmitigated disaster.

Oh, but that wasn't entirely true. There was one tall, dark and handsome mitigating factor.

Nina grabbed her phone and googled JL Knight. A torrent of results crowded the small screen. She started with the facts:

*Julian Leroy Knight is an English actor. He is best known for his starring role in* Thunder, *directed by George Kirby.*

Then she searched for the fluff. There was so much of it: fan art, photographs, video, essays and articles. Nina swiped through photos of the actor posing on the red carpet to snapshots of the man stretched out all but naked on a beach. However, the most recent photo was of him, hunched low, handing a handsome black cat to an ecstatic little girl. It had a clever little caption: *JL Knight literally saves the cat!* There were batches of cheerful on-camera interviews and one grainy thirty-second clip of a young JL Knight, drunk at a Hollywood party, with a message for the critics who'd panned his debut feature film: "Kiss my ass!"

Celebrity gossip sites provided relationship status updates (*Love Is Dead: JL Knight and Bettina Ford Have Split*) and chronicled professional setbacks (*JL Knight—of "Kiss My Ass" Infamy—Gets His Ass Kicked at Box Office*). A few more clicks and Nina landed on a blog dedicated to the film industry that put it all in context. JL Knight's ex-girlfriend and former costar, Bettina Ford, had spearheaded a boycott of his latest release after most of her scenes were cut in postproduction. The movie had flopped.

And, to top it all off, she came across a devastating profile of the actor in *Vanities*, titled *Nite Nite, JL Knight*.

*The star's brand of toxic masculinity should have gone the way of the Hummer. His bloated films glorify violence, celebrate hypermasculine culture and belittle women. The actor is famous for his portrayal of an assassin for hire (code name "Thunder") in the film adaptation of a once-popular video game. In the films, he stops at nothing to fulfill a contract, sometimes destroying entire cities to wipe out one target. Having not made much of his talent, content to feed from the bottom of the Hollywood swamp, JL Knight ought to retire.*

Well, damn.

Nina, a reader, writer and theater geek, was not one to line up for a big Hollywood release. A regular at her neighborhood's art house movie theater, she preferred her movies with subtitles. All this fuss about an action movie seemed a bit much. A fast-paced, high-voltage action flick served a purpose and had a place on the entertainment spectrum—particularly at the end of a long, hard day. On the other hand, why cut the scenes of a female character? Who'd made that call? Representation mattered, and she would've supported a boycott.

A new-message alert popped up on her phone screen. It was a much-awaited email from her literary agent.

Had lunch with editor today. She passed on the short story collection BUT expressed great interest in a follow-up to Backstage Diva. This is promising. Let's have lunch next week and discuss.

Nina moaned. Another memoir? She was done with all that. *Backstage Diva* chronicled her experience growing up in Manhattan, the daughter of a Broadway actress. The book tour had been torture. She'd had to crisscross America answering intrusive questions from strangers that she would have never entertained otherwise. That was the price she had to pay for offering up details of her family life for public consumption. She'd vowed never to do it again.

"Ugh!" she cried up to the ceiling. The vaulted ceiling was fresco-free, not one rosy-cheeked angel to be found— a disappointment.

Nina kicked off her shoes, stacked a couple throw pillows under her head and sank into the couch. *Thunder* was available for streaming, and because this qualified as a long, hard day, she slipped on her headphones and hit Play.

The best room at Sand Castle didn't guarantee rest. Julian was stretched out on his back on the comically large bed, staring at the painted ceiling and wondered who, in their right mind, would want to have sex with angels staring down at them.

He closed his eyes, desperate for sleep. Two days ago, he'd woken up in California to the threat of wildfire overtaking his neighborhood. The view from his bedroom window was walled off with smoke. On a clear day he could see as far as the Pacific.

He'd turned on the television and checked his phone for information. The news headlines were short, capturing the general state of panic. *Brush Fire Erupts. Brush Fire Doubles in Size. Fire Changes Course.* An evacuation order was in effect for the Hollywood Hills. His landlord sent him a text message in all caps to reinforce it. GET PACKING! Since his landlord was also his neighbor, he couldn't ignore the directive.

It had irked him to abandon his house, only it wasn't his to stay and defend. The modern home, nestled in the Hollywood Hills, was a rental. He'd moved in after his breakup. The house had come fully furnished. Most of his personal belongings were still in storage, which made packing a breeze. Julian folded his clothes into two large suitcases and tossed in his toiletries. He gathered his laptop, tablet, camera, personal phone and burner phone. He emptied the contents of his file cabinet into a messenger bag. The only thing left to do was return the cat.

Wasabi, his neighbor's green-eyed cat, would be asleep under his car. As per their routines, Julian popped open the trunk of his black Ferrari and the cat sprang out. He scooped him up. It would only take a minute to deliver him to Rosie, the neighbor's nanny.

The night he'd moved into the neighborhood, Julian had caught Rosie lighting a cigarette in the gazebo. At his approach she'd leaped to her feet, knocking a planter on its side. She hid the hand with the cigarette behind her back, but a curl of smoke rose above her head.

"Are you supposed to be here?" he asked.

Her eyes widened. "Holy mother! You're JL Knight!"

"I know who I am."

"I'm not trespassing, sir," she said. "I'm the nanny from next door. I come over once a week to do some light housekeeping."

She was older than him by a decade—and a Brit. Julian asked her to drop the "sir."

"Please don't tell my employer you caught me smoking. He doesn't hire smokers."

Her employer was his landlord. Julian told her to relax. The day he caused a hardworking woman to lose a job was the day his mother would turn in her grave—she who only wanted to rest in peace in her homeland of Jamaica. He and Rosie had been friends ever since. He would not have wanted to evacuate without first checking on her, and Wasabi gave him the perfect excuse.

Julian accessed the neighboring property by a side gate. If not for the threat of flames and the low-hanging clouds of smoke, it was a peaceful morning. He made his way to the front door, passing a U-Haul truck parked in the U-shaped driveway. Rosie threw open the door before he had a chance to ring the doorbell. "JL Knight, you're my hero!" she exclaimed. "You've saved me the trouble of mounting a search party for that cat."

"Next time check my garage," he said. "That's where he'll be. Do you still have the code?"

While Rosie checked to make sure her information was up to date, a little blonde girl came barreling into the foyer, squealing with joy at the sight of Wasabi. Julian knelt until they were almost eye level and put the cat in her arms.

Rosie plucked her phone from her uniform pocket and snapped a photo. "How precious! Samantha, say thank you to Mr. Knight."

The little girl offered a shy smile. "Tanks."

Julian ruffled her hair and unfolded to his full height. Then he asked Rosie if she planned to evacuate with her employers.

"We're heading to the house in Palm Springs," she said. "It's a fixer, so we'll be roughing it. How about you?"

"I'm ready to roll out." Julian had no definite plans. There were calls for donations to the fire department— water bottles and eye drops, mostly. He'd see to that and then possibly check into a hotel until it was safe to return. He had no place to be, really.

Rosie asked Samantha to find Wasabi's favorite toy and accompanied him down the front steps.

"I've been meaning to talk to you, JL Knight," she said. "Now seems like the right time."

Julian winced at her use of his stage name. He'd asked her one hundred times to stop calling him that, but with Rosie it was either "sir" or "JL Knight." This confirmed what he'd known to be true for some time. For some people, no matter what he did, he'd be indistinguishable from his acting persona. For years, he hadn't minded. He was best known for his role in *Thunder*. The character had served him well and made him rich, but now he couldn't shake him. Not that there would be any more *Thunder* movies. The third had bombed so badly at the box office there was no talk of a fourth installment. One day they'd reboot the franchise with another, younger actor and he'd be forgotten.

Rosie linked her arm through his, and they walked down the path to the side gate. "I'm in no position to give you life advice."

"I wouldn't be so sure," Julian replied.

Rosie was a practical-minded woman. In England, she'd run a playgroup in her home, but she'd found that looking after of the kids of the Hollywood elite was more financially rewarding. "They think I'm Mary bloody Poppins," she'd confided one night. She planned to retire in five years once she had enough saved away to buy a cottage in her hometown. Her life was in order. By comparison, his life was a mess.

"All this free time is not good for you. Get back to work."

"It's not that simple." Julian's agent wasn't returning his calls.

"It is, actually. You're too smart and talented to waste your time."

They'd reached the end of the path, and Julian felt a wave of relief. He recognized the truth when he heard it, and the truth wasn't something he was equipped to deal with right now. He was running from an actual fire—no time to run from existential ones, too.

He faced Rosie and rested his chin on the top of her head. "Tanks."

She pushed him away and called him a softie. Julian marched home and blamed his stinging eyes on the smoke that thickened the air. He loaded his bags in the trunk of his car and went back inside the house for one last thing. From a bottom dresser drawer, he pulled out a dog-eared copy of a screenplay well into its ninth revision. *Midnight Sun.* He flipped it open, thumbed through it, shook his head, then tucked it under his arm.

While he locked up the house, Julian got his assistant, Katia, on the phone. "Hey, Kat. Heading to Miami in the morning. Could you charter a plane and book a suite at Sand Castle?"

"Only if I can bum a ride. I'm heading to Boca for the holiday."

Oh, right. Independence Day. "I'll be there for a bit longer, but I'd welcome the company on the flight out."

"How much longer?" she asked.

She needed this information to book the hotel, only he couldn't give her exact dates. "A month or so."

"You're not retiring to Florida, are you?"

"No. The opposite."

She let out a grumpy sound. "Okay. Fine."

His next call was to an independent film producer who had once expressed interest in his project. When Julian had finally backed out of his garage, he didn't get far. A police checkpoint at the foot of the Hills slowed the flow of traffic, but he felt as if he were going places.

Julian grabbed his phone and played a few rounds of the sort of game that would have solidified his reputation as a warmonger. He lost the final round, slipped off his headphones and listened for sounds of the woman locked away in the adjoining room. Ms. Taylor. She claimed to be a writer. Time to find out. He typed "female author Taylor" in a search engine and filtered the results by image. He swiped through dozens of photos of Taylors, including Taylor Swift, but there was only one professional headshot of a dark-skinned, brown-eyed beauty.

In the photograph, she looked straight at the camera with a measured smile. She wore red lipstick and her black hair fell straight and loose, framing her face. The caption read: *Nina Taylor, memoirist, NYT Review of Books.*

*I'm only really qualified to write about myself.* He recalled her words. They hadn't made sense at the time. They did now. Julian reached for a second pillow and wedged it under his head. He was about to jump down the internet rabbit hole and might as well get comfortable.

One hour later, he'd read several reviews of her memoir, *Backstage Diva*, and listened to snippets of podcast interviews. He'd watched a panel discussion on memoir writing on Book TV. She was one of three panelists, but by far the most remarkable. He'd learned the following:

A) Nina Taylor was the daughter of a deceased stage actress celebrated for her Tony-nominated portrayal of Beneatha Younger in a 1999 Broadway revival of *A Raisin in the Sun*.

B) Nina was a respected artist in her own right with a bestselling memoir and several published magazine articles.

C) Nina was single, lived in New York City and was working on a collection of short stories.

There was only one thing left to do. He purchased *Backstage Diva*, the audiobook, with one click. Then he adjusted his headphones and hit Play.

# Four

Nina had dozed off on the couch halfway through the movie. She woke up to the sound of screeching tires, a car chase in full swing. She sat up and massaged a kink in her neck. If the Garden Room was still unavailable, they had better find her something! She had no intention of spending the night on a sleeper sofa while JL Knight slept in luxury. If Sand Castle couldn't accommodate her, she was leaving. She'd arrange a ride to the airport, hop on any flight and get the heck out of the Sunshine State. *Sorry, Mom. I'll light a candle or burn sage and celebrate your life...at home.*

Her room opened to the hallway. Nina slipped out and took the stairs to the courtyard. The front desk clerk had no answers, so she marched to Grace Guzman's office. When her knock went unanswered, Nina was certain nothing would be resolved tonight. Angry and aimless, she wandered along the cloisters, coming across an enclosed garden. It was small but lush. Mesmerized by the fairy lights creating the illusion of a starry sky, she traveled down a gravel path and somehow missed the bronze statue at the center of the garden. She struck her foot against the granite pedestal, fell to the ground and yelped like a dog.

She choked on a sob. Had she flown to Miami just to make a fool of herself?

Rhythmic applause, sharp and slow, rose up from deep in the garden. Nina scrambled to her feet and wiped away the blades of grass stuck to her cheek. When she was presentable, she scrutinized the shadows and saw, quite clearly, Grace Guzman staring back at her. Grace sat in a rattan chair, hair loosened from the bun she'd sported earlier. Besides her was a low table with a pitcher of red sangria and a couple of wineglasses. Say what you want, the woman had style.

"You're quite the performance artist, Ms. Taylor."

Off-duty Grace was even bitchier than on-duty Grace. How was that possible?

Nina pointed to the statue. "This thing is a hazard."

"The goddess is not a hazard."

"Goddess?"

"Aphrodite," Grace said, as if it were obvious.

Nina examined Aphrodite. Hunched low to the ground, her demure pose struck Nina as unnatural—Aphrodite being the goddess of love and beauty and all. Shouldn't she stand tall?

"Have a seat, Ms. Taylor," Grace said. "That statue will be here long after you've gone."

Those words put everything in perspective. This mansion had seen war, economic depression and ecologic catastrophe. Aphrodite was no stranger to drama.

Her chin held high, Nina hobbled over to the offered seat. Grace poured a glass of sangria and handed it over as if it were the cure for all things. Then she folded her hands on her lap and waited for Nina to explain herself. If there was a goddess in this garden, it wasn't Aphrodite.

When Nina wasn't forthcoming, Grace broke the silence. "I like to sit here in the early evenings. The guests are getting ready for dinner and the hotel tends to be quiet."

The hotel was as quiet as could be expected with the street noise drilling through the wall of high shrubs. Nina raked her brain for something to say. "This is a beautiful garden. The lights are a nice touch."

"We were supposed to host a wedding here tonight. It was canceled."

"That's awful."

"The couple was eloping," Grace said with a sigh. "Never a good sign."

Nina disagreed. "Not every bride needs an entourage."

"Yes, but for some it takes a village," Grace said. "They need a nagging mother, a dozen bridesmaids and a minimum of fifty guests to get them to the altar. I know I did."

"My mother is dead."

The words spilled out without warning. Fragments of her mother's obit surfaced in her memory. Estelle Taylor, star of *A Raisin in the Sun* and *Porgy and Bess*, died of pneumonia in New York City on July 3. She was sixty.

"I'm sorry to hear it, Ms. Taylor."

"Oh, never mind." Nina dabbed at the corner of her eyes. "It's been a year. I don't know why I brought it up."

"Does it matter if it's been a year or ten?" Grace asked.

"No."

"Please don't take this the wrong way," Grace said, "but you look exhausted. Get some rest tonight."

"I don't have a room!" she reminded Grace. "I'm on a sofa bed in the study! How restful will that be?"

"You and Mr. Knight came up with this solution on your own."

"I didn't think it through," Nina said.

"Had you let me do my job, I would have offered you accommodations at any one of our hotel partners."

Had Grace done her job, she wouldn't have given away Nina's suite to JL Knight. But she was too exhausted to belabor the point. "Is that still an option?"

It was a holiday weekend, and she assumed most hotels were booked solid.

"It is. But you should know the sofa bed is very comfortable. It's imported from Italy." Grace stood to leave. "I'll leave instructions with the front desk. Whatever you do, don't delay."

"Because of the holiday?"

"Because of the rain."

As soon as Grace spoke the words, a gust a wind swirled through the garden trailing the scent of rain. A clap of thunder had Nina jumping to her feet.

Nina was out of breath when she made it back to the third floor, just narrowly escaping a downpour. She entered the suite through the sitting room. The doors to the balcony were wide-open and there he was, standing with his back to her. Without the added layer of a jacket, she could plainly see the contours of his muscles under his T-shirt, and it was impressive—not that she cared.

Nina drew a breath for courage and joined him on the balcony, leaning against the rail. He smiled down at her, and she noticed that his soft brown eyes were flecked with gold. How had she not noticed before?

"There you are, Goldilocks."

Nina cringed, but only on the inside. On the outside, she remained cool. "I spoke to the manager. They can put me up at another hotel."

"You'd head out in the rain?"

"I love rain." It was Miami! Summer showers were part of the package.

"What do you love? Singing in it? Dancing in it?"

"None of the above." The sound of it was enough.

"Hate to *rain* on your exit parade, but if anyone is leaving, it's me."

"I just think—"

"Stop thinking," he said, interrupting, and yet his voice was gentle. "We agreed to make the best of this. Don't flake on me now."

Her gaze fell to his hands gripping the rail. In the movie, he'd gripped the steering wheel of his sports car in the same way. To take her mind off the soft color of his eyes, his gentle voice, firm grip and sculpted arms, Nina turned away and focused on the view. The palm trees swayed in the rain. Below, a cluster of tourists stood outside the hotel gates. Once dubbed the *Playboy* Mansion of the South, it was a Miami Beach tradition to pose on the stone steps—even in the pouring rain.

"Did I ever tell you about the time I worked here as a valet attendant?"

She had read about that online, but she couldn't tell him that. "When would you have told me, JL Knight? We've just met."

"Call me Julian," he said. "Trash this hotel suite if you like. I don't care. But I insist you call me Julian."

"In that case, *Julian*, I insist you call me Nina," she said. "Call me Goldilocks one more time and I'll throw you off this balcony."

"I'd like to see you try." He stretched lazily. "Nina is a pretty name."

The unexpected compliment threw her off guard. She felt herself softening and couldn't allow that. "We're off topic, *Julian*. I'll stay the night, but I'll probably leave in the morning."

"Tomorrow's the Fourth," he said. "Won't that ruin your holiday?"

Her holiday was ruined. There was no use pretending that it wasn't. "I'll buy a hot dog at the airport. That should do it."

"You'll be missing the pool party," he said. "Grace says it's not to be missed."

This day had been so draining, so bizarre, that she hadn't even made it to the hotel pool. How sad was that?

Julian's phone rang in his pocket. He reached for it and answered right away.

"I know, I know," he said, laughing at whatever the caller had said. "Soon! Promise! But tomorrow won't work. How about the day after that? Would you be up for it?"

Nina turned away, pretending as if she weren't listening. The winds picked up and tossed her braid about like threadbare rope. Julian wrapped a hand around her elbow and steered her inside, still carrying on his conversation. "You don't have to sell me on it. I want to come, and I miss your cooking." He shut the door behind them. "All the flowers you want. Promise."

Nina crossed the sitting room to her door. Julian's conversation was taking an intimate turn, and it made her uncomfortable. But when he spoke up again, she knew he was addressing her.

"Have you eaten?"

She turned in time to see him pocketing his phone. "I'm not hungry."

She had a couple protein bars and airline pretzels stashed in her purse. She'd make a meal out of it. More than anything, she wanted to lock herself in her room, fold out the bed and sleep for twelve hours straight. She wanted to say good-night and disappear behind a shut door, but a nagging feeling kept her rooted in place. She had something to get off her chest.

"Julian, I'm not a crazy person in real life."

"Okay," he said. "You just play one on TV?"

"Something like that."

Nina might never be able to correct his first impression of her. Back in Hollywood, he'd likely entertain his friends with the story. "Did I tell you about the time I walked into a hotel room in Miami to find a woman taking a selfie on my bed?" And they'd all laugh.

He sat on the arm of a wing chair and leveled those golden-brown eyes on her. "Why did you do it?"

"You mean sneak into your room, climb on your bed and pose for a selfie?"

He nodded. "That sums it up."

"Who wouldn't? It's a gorgeous room, don't you think?"

"No. Not really," he said. "Too many gold knickknacks for my taste."

She agreed. There were way too many knickknacks, period. She wished she could leave it at that, but the truth was clawing at her throat. It would choke her if she didn't speak up. Nina had to share the burden with someone. Julian was right there, watching her, waiting for more. She might as well tell him. "It was my mother's dream to stay at this hotel. She'd go on and on about the Oasis. Her idols had all spent the night here—Elizabeth, Marilyn, Diana, Aretha… My mom had extravagant dreams."

Nina had planned this trip to mark the one-year anniversary of her mother's passing. She had wanted to do something to honor the late actress's life, something other than showing up at her grave with flowers.

Julian's gaze softened. "Want to switch rooms?"

"No," Nina said firmly. She'd gone too far with this already. "And don't argue with me. I'm too tired."

"Want to come in and take that selfie?"

Nina smiled despite herself. "No, thanks."

She opened the door to her room. The brass doorknob jammed, so the movement wasn't as smooth as she would have liked. "Good night, Julian."

He was still watching her with that same unwavering interest, as if she fascinated and confused him all at once. "Good night, Nina."

She shut the door and collapsed against it. She was hungry and a little light-headed. That was all. However, the feeling stayed, even after she'd eaten, showered, detangled and braided her hair.

Nina pulled out the bed and sat up cross-legged. A minute later, she got up and poured herself a glass of water. Outside, it was raining still, and the wet windowpanes glistened in the moonlight. She picked up her phone from the charger and took it to bed with her. Earlier, she'd skipped past the more revealing photos of her roommate online. Now she believed they were worth a second look. She found a trove of glossy photos taken on location in Italy's Amalfi Coast for a *British Vogue* editorial. Some of the photos were candid shots taken during breaks. Nina tapped on one to enlarge it. Wearing dark sunglasses and a towel flung around his neck, skin baked to a golden brown, Julian stood palling around with the crewmen. In another, he was stretched out on the hard, flat sand, one arm across his eyes shielding them from the sun. He looked thoroughly relaxed, not pressed for time, not pressed for anything. His long limbs looked heavy.

Nina hoped his skin tasted like salt.

# Five

Julian's car pulled up the drive to the Coconut Grove estate. Nestled among mature oaks was the modern home of Francisco Cortes. Julian asked his hotel-appointed driver to come back around in a couple of hours, then climbed the steps leading to the porch. A housekeeper greeted Julian at the door and led him to a back patio. The silver-haired man with the profile that ought to be minted on coins steered forward in a motorized chair. His lips split into a smile. "This is an honor. Welcome to Miami."

Over lunch, they discussed the California wildfires, at last under control. "With the sea levels rising," Julian said, "you must worry—"

Francisco interrupted him midsentence. "You and I are not going to solve climate change, not today. So why don't you tell me why you're here?"

Julian took a gulp of water. This would be the first time he discussed his project with anyone, and he was nervous. "I'm here to shoot my first film."

"Going independent," Francisco said. "JL Knight Productions… That's got a nice ring to it."

Julian didn't dispute it, but he'd settled on Knight Films.

"Good luck to you," Francisco said. "I mean it. In my day, when the business spit you out, you were done. So I admire what you're doing. But here's the thing—if you've come to offer me the role of the grandpa with the heart of gold, you can forget it. I've retired. I don't play grandpas. I sure as hell don't play characters with hearts of gold."

Julian sat back in his chair and considered the clear-eyed

man opposite him. He'd come to the right place. "I've come to ask you to direct."

"You might have inhaled a little too much smoke in the fire," Francisco said, deadpan.

"Back in '91, you made a short film that debuted in Toronto."

Francisco dismissed his words with a wave of a hand. "That was just for fun."

"Fun is what I'm after," Julian said. "I watched it five times. As I've watched all your films."

"Not all of them, I hope," Francisco said with a chuckle. "Some of them were trash."

Francisco Cortes had played the quintessential Latin lover in countless films. He was magnetic on camera, commanding every scene he was in. But a near-fatal car accident had left him disabled and killed his career.

"Wouldn't you have liked to direct given the chance?" Julian asked.

"Well, now." Francisco ran his fingers along his well-trimmed goatee. "If anyone had predicted that I'd be having this discussion with JL Knight, I wouldn't have believed them."

"That's 'cause you're not." Julian felt compelled to reintroduce himself at every turn, like some parody of James Bond. "I'm Julian. You can forget JL."

"Don't wipe out your legacy. On winter nights we screen movies out here." He made a gesture capturing the world within the coral rock wall surrounding the estate: his home, the garden with its tangles of tropical plants, a kidney-shaped pool and a hot tub fitted under a pergola. "*Thunder* is always a crowd pleaser."

Julian clasped his hands together. "Happy to hear it."

"Tell me about your project."

Years ago, a UCLA film school student and waiter at one of his favorite taco spots had pitched Julian a story based on a true crime set in LA. The half-baked pitch was a non-starter, but it had planted a seed in Julian's mind. On and off, he'd worked on a script of his own set in Miami. *Midnight Sun* was a heist film loosely based on the story of a Miami heiress who fell victim to her con-artist boyfriend.

"Yeah… I read about that," Francisco said. "He stole her jewels during a solar eclipse."

"Hence the title."

"And you'd play the con artist."

"That's the idea," Julian said. "It's a supporting role. This heiress is the lead."

"Very smart. You plan to film here in Miami?"

Julian relaxed into his chair. Francisco was asking all the right questions. "Can't do it convincingly anywhere else."

"Florida doesn't offer tax incentives," Francisco said. "Broward County has a program. You might want to consider filming some scenes there."

Julian was open to anything, so long as he could shoot some scenes at Sand Castle.

"I'll make a few calls. Find out what kinds of incentives are out there," Francisco said. "Meanwhile, send me the script."

"Thought you'd never ask." Julian pulled a copy of the screenplay from his leather messenger bag and handed it over. "If you'd like an electronic copy, just give me your email address."

Francisco flipped through the pages. "You wrote this?"

Julian mumbled his answer, fearful of Francisco's reaction. What if he thought it a joke and withdrew his support? But the older man chuckled good-naturedly. "You surprise me, Julian."

For the next couple of hours, they discussed financing and distribution options. Julian had reached out to a production company and had secured some financing. Francisco had not committed to the project, but he promised to help raise more funds and support Julian in every possible way.

"What are your plans for today?" Francisco asked. "I'm having a family cookout. You're welcome to join us."

"Thanks, but I'm meeting with friends."

With that lie, Julian ended the meeting. He was not in the holiday cookout or party mood. His driver, a young guy who went only by Pete, was waiting outside. Kat had secured his services for the duration of his stay. On the drive back to the hotel, he asked question after question until Julian slipped on his earphones to signal the Q&A session was over. The rest of the ride was blissfully quiet and, by the time he got back to Sand Castle, he'd received good news and bad news via text message.

The good news was from Francisco. He'd immediately reached out to friends at a local arts foundation and put in an informal request for grant funding. "They won't turn me down." The bad news was from Kat. A photo of him and Nina Taylor had surfaced on social media. It was a grainy cell phone pic of the two of them on the balcony.

In the photo, they were staring at each other. Julian was dropped back in time to the moment Nina had threatened to toss him over the balcony if he called her Goldilocks again. She was looking up at him with a glint of defiance in her eyes. He'd loved the display of bravado and it showed on his face. The social media caption read: *Kiss Already!*

Julian let out a sigh. He only had himself to blame. He knew better than to stand on an open balcony within cell phone camera range in the company of a woman. The cover of darkness plus a veil of rainfall was no cover at all. He'd have to warn Nina. He did not want her to be blindsided.

This gave him the perfect excuse to knock on her door. Every cloud, a silver lining…

He knocked, but there was no answer. The famous pool party was raging downstairs, and he decided to check it out. Not because he thought it would be fun to celebrate the Fourth with a bunch of drunken strangers, and not because he enjoyed being passed around like a photo booth prop, which was sure to happen, but in the vague hopes that she might be there.

Downstairs, he was ushered without question beyond the velvet ropes. He ignored the assortment of vodka on display at the bar and ordered a gin and tonic. Out of the corner of his eye, he spotted a woman elbowing her way toward him, and he readied himself. Holding up her camera, she begged for a photo. "My boyfriend will die. He's your number one fan." Women seldom admitted to liking his films. It was always a husband, boyfriend or brother who got them to the theater.

The bartender volunteered to take the photo. He was a fan as well. With so many fans, Julian wondered how his film had flopped. Then he grabbed his drink and moved away from the bar. From his vantage point on the veranda, he scanned the crowd below. It was possible that Nina had done the reasonable thing—checked out of the hotel and flown home. But then he spotted her on the dance floor, and it was clear to him that reason wasn't the fuel she was running on.

Julian didn't make a move—he couldn't. In the short time he'd known her, he'd seen her angry, distraught, threatening and resigned. But here was a side of her that he hadn't guessed existed, and he was riveted. Nina was playful, dancing freely and having fun. But then he noticed the tight set of her jaw. Her movements were forced. He recalled what she'd told him the night before. He'd lost his mother years ago and knew exactly what she was going through. He'd been in Hawaii filming a special crossover episode of *Riverside Rescue* when he'd learned of his mother's untimely death. The loss had sent him reeling for months.

Julian lost sight of Nina. When he spotted her again, she was standing dangerously close to the edge of the pool, throwing back a shot of the night's signature vodka. She wore a little white dress held up by thin straps. Her hair fell in loose waves past her shoulders. Her dark skin gleamed in the soft light of the setting sun. She was so bloody beautiful.

He raced down the stairs and forged a path toward her despite mounting doubts. *Leave her alone. She doesn't need you.* Then a few things happened to erase his concerns. A rocket exploded overhead, causing the crowd to compress and swell. Nina lost her balance and tipped backward into the still waters of the pool and vanished. It was possible that he was the only one who'd seen it, and now there was no question that she needed him.

*He's not my type.*

Nina had spotted Julian the moment he'd entered the upper-level VIP veranda, the same she'd been turned away from an hour earlier. She'd had to access the party at the general population entrance by the lower-level pool. Although the whole ordeal had irritated her to no end, her irritations were washed away when a hostess presented her with an array of fruit-flavored vodka shots to choose from.

She'd slept well the night before—either the sofa bed was surprisingly comfortable or she'd been too exhausted to notice the difference. In any case, she woke up with a clear head and realized that attempting to travel on the Fourth of July was plain dumb. She had the suite to herself. Julian had set out early—she'd heard him fumbling around in the sitting area actively trying not to make noise. Once he left, Nina ordered room service and sat at the antique desk to write in her journal. But she'd refused to stay cooped up in her room while a party was in full swing outside.

Nina was relieved that Julian had not yet returned when she left the suite in her made-for-a-Miami-(or Vegas)-pool-party minidress. And yet she was doubly relieved when she spotted him on the VIP veranda. She'd enjoyed the quiet in the suite, but there was such a thing as too much quiet. She had missed his voice. And then she watched as he pulled a bikini-clad beauty into a hug. Her mouth went dry, and she turned away in search of more fruit-flavored vodka.

*Whatever. He's not my type.*

She went for clean-cut lawyer/stockbroker types. Men who couldn't bench-press anything heavier than a laptop but still managed to wear suits beautifully. Julian Knight in his jeans and tees worn mostly to show off his sculpted body was the opposite of that.

Assessing the attractiveness of one action hero on the scale of lawyer to stockbroker was an insane waste of time. She was at a party crowded with men! Nina infiltrated a squad of women on the dance floor. The DJ played the summer hits, and above them the sky was turning purple. She laughed at the crazy moves of her new friends and matched them with moves of her own. Soon, though, the crowd swallowed her up. She searched around for the others, but the group had dismantled.

The dance floor stretched alongside the pool, and Nina danced her way toward it. She took a breath. *I'm tipsy,* she admitted, and scooped another glass from a passing waiter's tray. *Might as well get good and drunk.* She sent coconut-flavored vodka down her throat in one gulp then clutched the empty shot glass to her chest. Still, the words crawled across the ticker of her mind. *He's just not my type.*

The first rocket of the night surged into the sky and exploded; the sound ripped through the night. While everyone welcomed the burst of sound and color with cheers, Nina startled, lost her balance and toppled cleanly into the deep end of pool. It was a relief, frankly. The news ticker in her brain went dark.

# Six

Nina stood shivering in the chilly marble bathroom. From the other side of the door, Julian asked whether she was decent. She tightened the towel around her torso and the one wrapped around her head before answering yes. He handed her a hotel robe and slippers through a crack in the doorway. All she could think was: *This man has seen me naked.*

This man had also dived into a pool to fish her out, carried her through the party crowd guided by the flash of hundreds of camera phones and whisked her up to their suite via private elevator. All the while, she'd coughed up water on his chest. Once in their room, he'd helped her out of her dress. The zipper gave way easily enough, but the soaked fabric had clung to her like suction wrap. Then he'd assisted her into the shower.

Nina attempted to blow-dry her hair. The noise aggravated her pounding headache and she gave up, letting her hair fall damp down her back. And since she could not think of anything more to do to stall the inevitable, she slipped on the robe and stepped out to face him.

He was waiting just outside the door, his face soft with concern. "Hey. Come lie down."

"Here?" Nina flatly refused. "That's fine. I'll head to my room now."

She bolted toward the bedroom door, but her tortoise's pace made it easy for him to block her. All he had to do was step in her path. "I'm going to order tea and soup and whatever else you like. It'll make things easier if you camp out here."

That sounded reasonable enough. Not the part about

the soup, though. That sounded terrible. Nevertheless, it felt wrong to give in to him. "My things are in my room and…" She winced with pain. Her headache intensified with each word of false protest. Between the drinking and the drowning, she had no energy left to argue.

He linked an arm around her waist and assisted her onto the large, inviting bed. Tonight, it was covered in a hunter-green bedspread embroidered in gold.

"What things do you need?" he asked. "I'll grab them for you."

She wanted to ask for her journal. Instead, she asked for her bag of toiletries on the bathroom vanity. Julian left and returned in a flash with her toiletries, her phone that she'd left charging in her room, her monogrammed slippers from J. Crew *and* her journal. She thanked him enthusiastically, and yet he didn't look pleased.

"What's the matter?" she asked.

"Don't tell me you slept on a couch last night." His voice was flat.

"The couch converts into a bed." When his eyes widened in disbelief, she added, "Don't worry. It's imported from Italy and very comfortable."

He placed her slippers at the side of the bed. "You said this suite had two bedrooms. That's not a bedroom. That's a study."

"Shows you how much I know."

He stood over her, a frown tugging at his lips. Nina wasn't comfortable with him handling her journal, so she pried it out of his hands. "I'll take this. Thanks."

"You're spending the night here," he said. "It's my turn on the couch."

"Don't be ridiculous." Nina checked her phone to better give the impression that she was fine and everything was good. There were a few social media alerts, but she ignored them.

"If it's so comfortable, what's the problem?"

"I'm not putting you out of your bedroom. And that's that."

"Why not?" He poured her a glass of water then riffled through a leather case on the dresser for a bottle of Tylenol. "You have a stronger claim to it than I do."

"Yeah, but you're paying for it," she said. "You *are* paying for it, right, JL Knight?"

He handed her the glass and two pills. She lifted her head off the pillow, but that was all she could manage.

"Need an extra pillow, Goldie?" he said with a smirk. But seeing that she was truly struggling, he stepped forward and scooped the back of her head in his palm. "Lean on me," he said. "Now open wide." He dropped the pills in her mouth, and Nina wondered why her imagination was running wild with those two simple commands. He held the glass to her lips. "Swallow."

When he lowered her onto the pillows, there was no question where she was spending the night.

He ordered food: mint tea for her, a veggie burger for him and extra fries for them to share. He hung up and looked at her intently. "You okay?"

"I'm fine," she said. "This is a lot of fuss. I fell into a pool. That's all."

Her words did not seem to reach him. "Don't get out of bed. I'll open for room service when they get here."

"Don't tell me what to do."

"Don't be difficult." He left to take a shower, waving goodbye.

As soon as the bathroom door shut behind him, Nina reached for her journal out of habit. A hotel logo pen was tucked in the pages. She chewed on the cap for a minute, then jotted the first thing that came to mind.

*Welcome to Rock Bottom! Hope you stay awhile.*

It killed her that she'd had to be rescued by JL Knight

like some damsel in distress. How did she get to this place? She had not been herself these last few days. It was as if she were on an emotional roller coaster: throwing tantrums, sneaking into hotel rooms, crashing into statues and now this!

She listened to the sounds of the shower. When Julian came out of the bathroom in a clean T-shirt and soft sweatpants, he looked fresh. She likely looked as bad as she felt, because he rushed over.

"Oh, come on, love. Don't do that." He sat next to her and stroked a lock of hair away from her wet cheek. "Don't cry."

Nina jerked away. His touch hadn't startled her, but his words had. Was she crying? Julian recoiled from her in one smooth ripple of muscle. She caught him by the hand before he got away. "It's okay. You startled me, that's all."

He nodded but stayed quiet. She gave his hand a little squeeze. "Thanks for rescuing me and…stuff."

God knew she owed him a debt of gratitude for all the "stuff" she was too embarrassed to mention now.

He shrugged. "Anyone would have done it."

"No one else did. Just you," Nina said. "So, thanks."

"You're welcome." His face remained impassive, but she caught a glint in his eyes. The room went warm. Nina fought the impulse to shed the plush robe as images of him half-naked on the coast of Italy flooded her mind. She blinked the images away as he went to sit at the far end of the bed, as far from her as he could manage without falling to the ground.

"Listen, Julian, I have something to say, and it's important."

"I'm listening."

"I don't want to have sex with you."

"You're in good company," he said. "The queue of women who don't want to have sex with me goes around the block."

"Okay, then. I'll get in line."

"And take a number," he added. "I like to keep things orderly."

JL Knight was self-deprecating and funny. Why hadn't any of this gotten into the *Vanities* article?

"All this is to say, we can share this bed," Nina said. "It's as large as a continent. There's room enough for the both of us."

"We could build a wall, line pillows from top to bottom?" he suggested.

She nodded in agreement. "I've heard walls are super effective."

And they laughed like kids until room service arrived with the food. Julian prepared her tea and set up a tray with her fries—the only effective cure for drunkenness. Nina's headache was dissipating. How could she feel bad when she was receiving such excellent care? Her eyes drifted up to the angels floating above. She'd drowned, died and gone to heaven. That was the only explanation that made sense.

Julian dragged a wingback chair over to the bed and settled in to eat his burger. Between greedy bites, he explained that he'd been raised vegetarian. He only ate meat on occasion.

"What's your deal?" she asked. "Are you here to film a movie?"

"That's classified information, Nina Taylor."

"You don't trust me," she said. "Even now. After everything we've been through. I trust you with my life."

"That's because you've seen me in action," he said. "You know what I can do."

He had a point. "Here's the thing—I don't have the energy to keep up this tit for tat. I trust you…enough. Could we just be friends now?"

"My friendship is a complicated thing." He picked up

his phone, scrolled for a bit and handed it to her. "I'll show you what I mean."

Someone by the handle @TheAimlessDayTripper had posted a photo of her and Julian standing on the balcony, facing each other, gazing into each other's eyes. Caption: *Kiss Already!* The post had 5,470 likes.

She returned his phone. "That's not so bad."

He tapped the screen and showed her a video of him lifting her out of the pool, water pouring off his back. Her face was buried in his chest, and for that she was grateful. Caption: *#RescueMeJLK*

Nina passed him the phone with a nervous laugh. She couldn't look at the photos or video without cringing. There was something about them, something indefinable. Everyone was picking up on it.

Julian fell back into the chair and read her a tweet. "'JLK sliced through the crowd, dived into the pool and emerged the hero cradling the drowning woman in his arms. #RescueMeJLK.'"

Nina repeated the hashtag. "Like from that time you saved the cat!"

He looked up at her from the screen, brows drawn in confusion. "What cat?"

Nina stuffed her mouth with fries. She couldn't answer that question without admitting that she'd googled him.

"I didn't rescue any cat," he said. "Does that even sound like me?"

"How would I know?" She reminded him, again, that they'd just met.

"You keep reaching for that tired excuse."

"Anyway. There's a picture of you returning some little girl's cat."

"Wasabi? That old goat didn't need saving."

He sounded genuinely offended on the cat's behalf. Nina grabbed her phone off the bedside table and searched the hashtag. The video had been shared thousands of times. Someone posted a screenshot with the caption: *She's all long brown legs and dripping hair. I see you, girl!*

Nina's cheeks were burning when she tossed her phone onto the mattress beside her. Great! She was a *New York Times* most notable author and a bona fide damsel in distress. Fun times!

He got up and loaded their plates onto the room service tray table. Nina scooted out of bed and took her case of toiletries into the bathroom.

"Hey, Nina," he called after her.

"Yes?"

"I'm going to be the best friend you ever had."

Nina shut bathroom door with a flourish. Cute, clever and overconfident—not at all her type.

# Seven

Julian had hoped to keep a simple routine until things picked up. He planned on staying close to the hotel and out of the spotlight. He intended to fill his days with early workouts, late swims, light meals and hard liquor. But here was Nina, attention-grabbing Nina—a lightning rod of a woman—sleeping on the other side of a pillow partition, her face soft, her long, brown fingers clutching the blanket and strands of black hair stuck to her cheek.

Typically, he was the guy who slipped out of a woman's bed before dawn, so waking up next to Nina felt intimate. The kind of thing you did with a girlfriend. Not that this was a hookup—far from it. She'd made her position clear. There'd been no funny business. Instead, they stayed up swapping funny stories and laughing in the dark as fireworks burst over the mansion and cast a colorful glow through the windows.

He'd made her admit to having looked him up. How else would she have found Rosie's photo of him returning Wasabi? Even Kat had missed it, and she received Google alerts for even the slightest mention of his name. Julian had asked her what had drawn her to writing. She told him about the journals she'd kept since childhood. He recalled how she'd pried the red leather-bound notebook from his hand. Then she asked him to tell her about the time he worked as a valet at the hotel.

"You remembered!" he said, teasing.

"Oh! Just get on with it!"

So he told her about the time that he'd spotted soap opera actor Tony Cash on the same balcony that he and Nina had stood on the night before. She recognized the name of the soap star. "He played a gambler on *Set the World on Fire*."

"That's the one."

He had just started his shift when the actor stepped out to soak up the last rays of sun and the adulation of his fans pressing at the hotel gates. He flashed a smile, waved then turned his back on the growing crowd. Julian was then dispatched to retrieve a Land Rover and ran off with the key jangling in his pocket. Up until that point he had never considered acting. He was no artist. The summer he'd worked building sets for a local theater company in England had convinced him of that. But he was also convinced that the man on the hotel's balcony wasn't setting the world on fire with his acting abilities. If the bar was set that low, couldn't he step over it?

"How did you get your start?" she asked.

"It wasn't easy."

It took leaving Florida for California, sleeping in his car for weeks, forgoing expensive acting classes and attending cheap matinees instead, getting laughed out of auditions then slowly, eventually, receiving callbacks and an offer to play the recurring role of a paramedic on *Riverside Rescue*. It was something. It was a start.

"Ah, Malcolm!" She twisted onto her side, facing him. "I loved him."

Pride sparked in Julian. "And he loved the ladies."

She laughed. "He sure did!"

And they talked like that well into the night.

Out of habit, he fumbled around for his phone to check the time, weather and news. The phone rang in his hand, rousing Nina from sleep. Julian fought the urge to reach over the pillow partition and soothe her. The last time he'd touched her without warning, she'd leaped out of her skin. She was a bit jumpy. He silenced the ringer but couldn't ignore the call. It was Amelia Chin, longtime family friend and his former landlady for all of one week. He'd promised to take her to the orchid market in Homestead. Was that today? Crap! That was today!

"Hey! Amelia! Good morning." Nina squirmed next to him and disappeared under the bedspread. Amelia suggested he pick her up before ten to avoid traffic and heat and all the rest. "Sounds reasonable. What time is it now?" Nina slipped out of bed and tiptoed across the room to the bathroom. Did she think he was talking to another woman? He was, of course. But Amelia was old enough to be his grandmother. And it was precisely because she reminded him of his grandmother that he was taking her out flower shopping. "Eight thirty? I better get a move on, then. See you soon."

Julian kicked back the sheets and rushed to knock on the closed door between them. She opened almost immediately, her toothbrush in her mouth, something hard in her eyes.

"What? No good morning?" he said, teasing. "I saved your life last night."

She pulled the toothbrush out of her mouth. Again, he had to fight the urge to wipe at the smudge of blue toothpaste on her lower lip. "You were on the phone. And how long are you going to keep that up?"

"Until it gets old, and it hasn't yet," he said. "Want to go orchid shopping today?"

She stared at him, confusion marking her sleep-creased face. But she didn't say no.

Julian sent for his car and driver for the trip to Homestead. When it arrived, he waited in the back seat of the Escalade for Nina to come down. Pete, the driver, sat drumming the steering wheel, humming a tune, as the wait dragged on. Julian was just so relieved that she'd said yes that he didn't mind. No question, this outing would be more fun with Nina. They never seemed to run out of things to talk about or, more accurately, to tease and taunt each other about. And the long trip to Homestead promised to be tedious. He loved Amelia, but shopping for orchids wasn't his idea of a good time.

Finally, the gates parted and Nina stepped out in a pair of denim shorts and a cotton halter top, sunglasses on top of her head. Both he and Pete reached for their door handles. "Not so fast," Julian said, stopping him. "This is my job." He sprang out of the black SUV and held the door open for Nina.

"Sorry I kept you waiting. I don't do well with last-minute invitations," she said. "I'm not that spontaneous."

He helped her climb in, taking a moment to admire the curve of her bottom. She might not want to sleep with him. He could make no such assertion.

"I gave up on you," Julian said, sliding in next to her. "Pete here kept me going."

"Hi, Pete," she said, tugging the seat belt across her torso. "I'm Nina."

"Good morning," he said, and pushed the start engine button. Julian had previously given him the itinerary. They'd make one stop in the neighborhood of El Portal before heading south to Homestead.

Nina arranged her tote bag on her lap then eyed him with suspicion. "Orchids, huh?"

"Okay, you got me," Julian said. "We're location scouting."

She brightened at this. "For a film?"

He nodded. "I need a clear field to land a helicopter. In the scene, I jump out and fight ten men. I take them all out, but a grenade detonates and the helicopter explodes, sending me, or my stunt double, flying. I haven't committed to doing my own stunts this time around."

"Can't you make a movie without explosives?"

"And disappoint my dwindling fan base? Not on your life."

She tucked a lock of hair behind her ear. Today she wore it wavy and loose and still a little damp. He caught a hint of her perfume and wanted to lean close, so he did the opposite, leaning back and folding his arms across his chest.

"Your fans will evolve as you evolve."

"Aren't you a fountain of wisdom this morning! You must have slept well."

"It's the truth," she said. "You deserve the truth."

"And so do you," he said. "We're going to Homestead to shop for orchids. And that's all."

"Okay. But who with?" she asked.

"You and your questions…" he said, mocking.

"Look. I agreed to be your friend, not your wing person."

"Are you always so easily riled up?" he asked. "You really need to work on that."

She bit back a quick response. "You know what? You're right. I'm on vacation. I need to chill."

"You've decided to stay."

"Might as well. What do I have to rush back to?"

"Work," he suggested.

"No." Her shoulders slumped low. "I'm on sabbatical."

He would have liked for her to say more, to open up about her life down to the nitty-gritty, but she clammed up.

"I've been on sabbatical a year," he said.

"That long?" she said. "Is it liberating?"

"It's soul crushing."

"Oh." Her eyes flooded with concern. She blinked a few times and offered him a crooked grin. "Breeding orchids is an interesting choice, but I support you."

"You mock me, but it's a billion-dollar industry."

"Is that a fact?"

"Oh, yeah. Easy money."

Pete cleared his throat, reminding Julian that they were

not alone—much as it felt that way. "Traffic is light. The destination is ten minutes away."

Nina leaned forward to ask Pete a question. "What's ten minutes away?"

He glanced at her in the rearview mirror. "It's not for me to say."

"Smart man," Julian said.

"Are you here from California?" Pete asked Nina, expertly changing the subject.

"No such luck," Julian replied.

"We can't all be California girls," Nina said with a sigh.

They arrived at Amelia's house. Pete pulled up to the curb. Nina turned to look out the window, studying the modest yellow house sitting on a generous lot.

"We are at the home of my mother's childhood friend Amelia Chin," Julian said. "They grew up in Jamaica together. Amelia gave me a place to stay when I got off the plane from England and didn't know a soul. So today I'm taking her orchid shopping."

Nina was now studying him. "Julian Knight! I could kiss you, that's so sweet."

He could not stop a foolish grin from spreading. "Please do."

She punched him in the shoulder instead.

"Before you think too highly of me, I'm only doing it for the food. She always cooks my favorite meals after I take her out. You'll see. She'll invite us in for lunch afterward."

"Now *that* makes sense," she said, grinning.

Amelia, not one to wait, had come out of her house and was standing on the sidewalk. Julian hopped out of the car and pulled her into a hug. "What are you doing? I was going to ring your doorbell like a proper gentleman."

"You're no gentleman," Amelia said. Turning to Pete, she said, "And you're parked near the hydrant."

"Leave the man alone," Julian said. "I can afford the ticket."

"You'll get towed! Can you afford the aggravation?"

Amelia looked the same as she did when he last visited, five years earlier. Her fine features were bracketed with deep and fine lines, but she was still as vibrant and energetic.

"All right, then, why are we wasting time? Let's get out of here before the tow truck arrives."

At the orchid market, Nina stayed behind with Pete, allowing Julian and Amelia to wander the stalls alone and catch up for a bit. The market was a field large enough to land a helicopter but dense with palms and bamboo. She leaned against the car and watched him assist the older woman, her frail hand locked in a death grip around his thick forearm. Nina was inexplicably moved.

Pete had gone off to buy refreshments, and he returned with chilled bottles of water. "Mr. Knight says you're an old friend. How far back do you go? Since before he was famous?"

"Not that far back," Nina said.

"I read that he and his girlfriend broke up."

Nina took a sip of water. She didn't like the turn of the conversation. She supposed anyone who'd stood in a supermarket checkout line had read all the details of the Julian and Bettina seismic split. Still, she was not going to discuss it with Pete.

"If you're going to make a move, now is the time."

"Excuse me?"

"Just saying."

Nina went still. Back home in the city, she could silence a chatty cab driver with one sharp glance before things went too far—and things had officially gone too far.

"I think it's time to catch up with Julian and Amelia."

Nina slipped on her dark glasses and marched down the makeshift aisles lined with tables crammed with orchids in various state of bloom. The Florida heat weighed on her shoulders like a damp blanket. She couldn't shake the feeling of being watched and glanced over her shoulder to check on Pete. He was on his phone, his back to her. The feeling persisted. And then she caught it—the flash of a camera.

A photographer was hiding behind a cluster of palms, camera lens pointed at Julian and Amelia. She stiffened with anger, torn between wanting to attack the photographer and rushing over to shield Julian from view. The flash of the camera snapped her out of her inertia. She ran to Julian.

At her approach, he held up a potted orchid with milk-white petals peppered with purple dots and a splash of yellow. "Look what we got."

"It's a Mystic Isle," Amelia said. "My favorite."

"Lovely!" Nina took care to position herself in the photographer's line of sight, obscuring his shot. Under normal circumstances, she would have found this exchange about flowers delightful, but unfortunately some shady paparazzo was documenting every second. She glanced over her shoulder to confirm this, and the flash went off again in the distance.

Nina waited until Amelia was out of earshot to alert Julian, out of fear of rattling the older woman. Even though, to be fair, Amelia did not seem like the type of woman who was easily rattled.

"Listen up," she said. "There's a photographer in the bushes. Twelve o'clock."

Julian wasn't rattled in the least. "I spotted him a while ago, and that's six o'clock. Not twelve."

"Who cares about his coordinates?" Nina snapped. "This is still a gross invasion of privacy."

"I'm used to it," he said. "Did you fly across the field to protect me?"

"I… I…" Irritation and embarrassment clogged Nina's throat. She was not so jaded to shrug off the presence of a lurking photographer.

Julian pinched her cheek. "You're a true friend, Nina."

Amelia returned with two more plants. "I'm done. We should go now. I'll get dizzy in this heat."

Nina was relieved. They didn't have to kick the photographer's ass, but they also didn't have to linger and give him a show.

Paparazzi presence at the orchid field had pissed Julian off—and justifiably so. He'd played it down to reassure Nina, who'd seemed genuinely upset. Plus he hadn't wanted to rattle poor Amelia. As to be expected, Katia wasted no time calling. They were on their way back to the hotel when his phone rang.

"Here's a tweet for you," Kat said. She went on to read it, hashtags and all, adding emphasis wherever needed for drama. "'Shelve this under #shamelessactsofselfpromotion: JLK buys a little old lady a bunch of flowers then helps her across the street. Like…really? That's piling it on thick! So now he suddenly respects women? #notbuyingit #RescueMeJLK is a sham.'"

Julian switched the phone from one ear to the other. "Thanks for the update. You don't have to call for every little thing, you know."

"You're wrong!" she exclaimed. "This is major. I love where you're going with this."

"Not going anywhere with anything," Julian said. "I took a family friend on an outing."

"You saved a cat. You saved a drowning girl. You helped a little old lady across the street. See a pattern yet?"

"That's nonsense."

"That's gold! That photo of you kneeling before the little girl is the kind of thing that rehabs an image. You can't buy that kind of publicity."

"Clearly, not everyone is buying it."

"Don't worry about that. We need the naysayers. They're useful."

He looked over to Nina, a potted white orchid on her lap. At some point, she'd gathered her hair in a knot on top of her head. He wished he could snap a picture of her. "Katy Kat, I've got to go."

"Sure, but do me one favor—think up some more heroics. Let's get #RescueMeJLK trending."

"All right. Hanging up now."

He ended the call and tossed the phone from one hand to another, hot potato style.

"Everything okay?" Nina asked.

He'd let her decide. He searched for the tweet and showed it to her.

"Wow, that was fast," she said.

The attached photo showed Julian carrying a cardboard box overflowing with paper-white orchids. Amelia walked beside him, her arm linked around his. Nina walked a step ahead, leading the way. He loved the way she walked—always light on her feet and with those long, sure strides.

He'd helped Amelia carry the flowers to the car, but it was Nina who paid attention to her lengthy instructions on how best to graft an orchid onto a tree. Back at Amelia's house, Nina ate most of the ackee and salt fish that she'd prepared for him. When he protested, she reminded him that he was a vegetarian.

"*Mostly* vegetarian."

"Then you won't mind if I eat *most* of this."

He smiled remembering the afternoon. Just as he'd predicted, Nina had made his day better. Still, she wasn't over the incident.

"Is it normal for paparazzi to follow you around like this?" she asked.

"Not lately."

"Hmm…" She pulled out her own phone and tapped on the screen. *"You're gonna eat those words."*

The words were spoken in Julian's voice, but an octave lower and without a trace of a British accent. The musical score to *Thunder* swelled in the car. Nina turned ashen and stabbed the phone screen with her fingers, desperate to silence it.

Julian let out a shout. Kat, the tweet and the meddlesome paparazzi were forgotten. "Naughty Nina Taylor, what have you been up to? Are you binge-watching me?"

"Don't flatter yourself!" she said. "Thought I'd get familiar with your work. That's all."

"In that case…" He pulled up her audiobook, and her words flowed from his phone. *"My mother played dress up and make-believe for a living. She wore makeup and costumes and performed on stage. We did not go to church. On Sunday mornings, when she wasn't performing, we attended matinees."*

"Oh, God, no!"

She ripped off her seat belt and lunged forward to wrestle the phone from his hand. He let her exhaust herself awhile, holding his phone out of her reach, just to enjoy the feel of her body. Her top might as well have been cut out of tissue paper. He felt everything, and everything felt wonderful. Her round breasts crushed against his chest, her bare thigh slid against his.

"Settle down," he murmured in her ear. "And buckle up. Safety first."

She moved away from him, her cheeks flushed. When she was settled, she returned her attention to the orchid, the only near casualty of their tussle. A long time passed before she spoke up. "I don't think you play make-believe for a living. I have a lot of respect for the profession."

Warmth spread through Julian's chest. "I knew that," he said. Although it was good to hear her say it.

"In those early journals, I'm such a brat," she said. "I went on and on about how horrible it was to be the daughter of a struggling actress. Only it wasn't so bad. It was special and unique, and I wouldn't trade it for some cookie-cutter upbringing in the suburbs."

"Did your mother have a chance to read it?" he asked.

She let out a bitter laugh. "I don't have to tell you that she hated it. She thought it tarnished her image, and she's probably right. Then she died before I got a chance to publish anything else. Now my publisher wants another memoir, and I can't bring myself to do it."

Julian wished they could get to the hugging stage of this relationship, because he desperately wanted to pull her close. "Hey, listen," he said. "Your mother wasn't objective. You do a good job showing her humanity."

"She didn't want to be human, Julian. She wanted to be a star."

"Stars burn out."

She turned to him, eyes brimming with questions. Good thing Pete pulled up to the gates of Sand Castle. Julian helped Nina step out of the car, hyperaware of the glances and phones angled their way. He rested a hand on the small of her back and ushered her up the stone steps and into the courtyard, heading toward the lift.

"I smell like a horse," he said, close to her ear. "Shopping for flowers is hard work."

"I smell like roses," she said.

"Of course."

"But I'm grimy," she admitted.

"I'll race you to the shower."

"You can have the shower," she said. "I want to soak in a bath."

The front desk clerk chased them down. "Ms. Taylor! Wait! There's news!"

Nina turned to him expectantly. Julian had a feeling that he wouldn't like the news. When the doors to the lift parted, he wanted to stuff Nina inside.

"Your room will be available in the morning. I wanted to tell you myself."

Nina cleared her throat. "That's great. Thanks."

On the ride up, her mood flattened. She stood fussing with the plant.

Julian leaned against the back wall. "If this is going to be our last night as roommates, maybe we should order in."

She looked up at him. The spark had returned. "I'd like that."

# Eight

Nina woke up alone in the large bed. The note on the pillow beside her was short. *Morning workout—J.*

The night before, she and Julian had stayed up late. He'd recommended they watch *Thunder* on a large screen in high definition and with surround sound. "It's not the type of movie you can watch on your phone."

They ordered dinner, tossed silk pillows and a blanket onto the antique rug, and camped out on the bedroom floor. They watched the movie, and when the credits rolled, Nina grabbed the remote control and hit Pause.

"Straight talk?"

"Absolutely."

"It's not trash."

"Think so?" He stretched out on the pillows. "That's a three-star review in my book."

"And you're hot in it," she said. "Really, really hot."

His eyes flashed. "Are you trying to start something tonight?"

"Only a conversation," she said. Although she couldn't deny that being this close to him sent waves of warmth through her body. "Ever heard of the Bechdel test? Two named female characters in a film discuss something—anything—other than a man."

"I've heard of it. I'm not a caveman," he said. "And I know it doesn't apply here."

"How could it? None of your female characters have names." Nina pointed to the screen frozen on the list of characters by order of appearance. "Girl in Yellow Bikini… Ferrari Girl… Casino Girl Number One… Casino

Girl Number Two… Girl at the Bar… All you're missing is the Girl with the Dragon Tattoo!"

Julian doubled over with laughter. His T-shirt bunched up to reveal a patch of taut brown skin. Nina sat on her hands to keep from reaching out and discovering more.

"Now repeat after me," she said. "Representation matters!"

"Don't blame me. I had no say in the matter."

"But you were the star!"

Nina would not let him off the hook. Some actors had inclusion clauses in their contracts to improve representation of women and minorities on film sets.

"I got the job because I looked the part," he said. "If I made noise, they'd have kicked me off the project. I was no one and I had zero clout. I got that job on my headshot alone."

"Really?"

He winked. "It was a good headshot."

Such a modest man! "Okay, but later—"

"Later, the criticism caught up with them. That's when they brought in Bettina to play a computer scientist."

Nina reached for her glass of wine and took a swallow. "And that's where they went wrong. The one woman with any agency is a computer scientist in a film populated with assassins and criminal masterminds. What's lacking is a female crime lord, assassin, bomb expert… You know… the type of character that is central to the plot."

His expression clouded over, and Nina knew she'd touched on something. "Aha! I love it when I'm right!"

He reached out and brushed a lock of hair from her cheek in a surprisingly tender gesture. "What do you love about it? The ego boost?"

"Maybe," Nina replied in a whisper. "You may not be the only egomaniac at the Sand Castle."

They'd stayed up late, talking. But in the morning, she

awoke in bed, on her side of the pillow partition, with no idea on how she'd gotten there.

The lines were blurring fast.

"We serve breakfast anywhere. Our guests love to lounge by the pool."

"Where would I go if I wanted to avoid the guests?"

"The rooftop deck is deserted at this hour."

"So that's where I'll be."

Nina took a stack of magazines up to the roof. An attendant promptly brought her a mimosa and a platter of fruit. She took a seat at an umbrella table with a view of the pool. Just as she got settled, her phone chimed with a text message.

Hey there! Just checking in.

It was her cousin Valerie Pierre. She never checked in; they weren't close. Valerie was the one relative on her father's side whose contact information she'd bothered to save. Nina's parents were only together long enough to conceive her. They were two New Jersey kids who met, predictably enough, at a party in the city. Her mother was the aspiring actress who'd caught the acting bug from performing in church. Her father was the son of practical-minded Haitian immigrants, who dreamed of writing poetry. Nina's mother had never encouraged her writing; it was the one obvious trait she'd inherited from her father.

The timing of the text was suspect. Her cousin lived somewhere in South Florida—that much Nina knew. If she'd kept up with celebrity gossip this past weekend, it was possible that she'd spotted Nina in a viral video or two.

*Enough! Just answer the message!*

Nina had the terrible habit of overthinking everything. It was just a text, and Valerie had always been friendly.

Nina thought of an appropriate answer and riddled it with exclamation points. Hey there! All is good!! Happy holiday weekend!!!

The response came quick.

I know it's a difficult time for you... With the anniversary and all.

Nina read the message a few times. It was possible that her cousin was checking in out of sincere concern. Why hadn't she considered that? Her eyes glazed with tears as she punched a response. Yes... Thank you.

Of course! We're family. Call me whenever. Okay?

Nina set the phone aside and gazed down at the pool, seeing it for the first time without the hordes of partygoers. The word *pool* was deceptive, evoking the smoke of coal barbecues, overcooked burgers and cheap beer. This wasn't so much a pool but *the* fountain of youth hidden in a garden of tropical flowers. The morning sun beat down on the diamond-clear surface. The surrounding grounds were immaculate. Grassy patches were cut into geometric shapes and laid out like stained glass. Where vegetation lacked it was hand-painted onto the walls. A half a dozen guests were lounging half-naked on sun beds, working off hangovers or working on their tans. The men came in all shapes, colors and sizes. The women were uniformly slim. They offered their bikini-clad bodies to the sun but kept their faces hidden under wide-brimmed hats. There were no kids among them. Sand Castle had a no-child policy, solidifying its reputation as an adult playground.

Nina hummed a tune. *Heaven. I'm in heaven.*

A man peeled himself off a bed and made his way to the edge of the pool. He dived in and swam a lap in slow, smooth strokes. He moved freely, as if he didn't feel the weight of the eyes pinned on him, and climbed out the other end. Water swirled down his broad back and golden-brown limbs.

Something short-circuited in Nina's mind.

She got up from the table, approached the deck rail and watched, transfixed, as Julian grabbed a towel off the back of a chair and wiped himself down. He dropped the rumpled towel in a basket and stood still a moment, hands on narrow hips, head back, face offered to the sun.

~~Heaven~~. *I'm in hell.*

Nina's breath went shallow as need and want coiled inside her. She ran through the *not my type* argument one more time. Some women preferred men who could change a flat tire or handle power tools. Nina didn't own a car, plus she had a competent handyman on speed dial. She liked brainy guys, the type who could review her tax returns, give her investment advice or draft a cease-and-desist letter in a pinch. Practical stuff. And there was one more thing: she didn't date actors. Never had. Never would. She had a lot of respect for the profession; that was the truth. To get sucked into that world again, all that drama, she'd sooner jump out of a plane just for kicks. But Julian... Oh, God, Julian... Was he worth it? Was she overthinking it? Their future together was capped to the five nights she had left on this vacation. Then it was back home to a life that did not include buff movie stars splashing around in pools.

Now the buff actor was staring up at her, grinning and waving, doing his best to grab her attention. It was cute because he didn't have to work so hard. He had all her attention, all the time.

Moments later, he joined her on the deck. She stood and smoothed down her linen shirtdress.

"Don't move," he said. "Sit."

She eased back into the chair and watched him drop his gym bag to the ground, pull out a camera and raise it to his eyes. "What are you doing?"

"You are so beautiful in the morning. I want you to see what I see."

Nina laughed off the extravagant compliment. While he snapped a few photos, she lost herself, watching him. He had a healthy post-workout glow. He wore a loose T-shirt, but his muscles were taut and glistening from his swim.

"Sit down. I ordered breakfast," she said. "Want anything?"

"I'll grab a protein shake," he said.

"Of course you will."

"Believe it or not," he said, "maintaining this body requires discipline and sacrifice."

Julian was not as bulky as in his films. She imagined that physique required months of intense training to achieve and the discipline of a pro wrestler to maintain. He kept to a strict diet and workout regime. As a result, he was lean and toned to an inch of his life. Generally, Nina avoided this type of guy, jocks and gym rats and the like. She wanted her man fit but miraculously so. Maybe he played ball with his friends on weekends. Maybe he built muscle chopping firewood or whatnot. Either way, he ate real food, didn't obsess over protein powders or stock up on power bars.

That was before she met Julian.

The rooftop attendant arrived with her food. She'd selected the Cuban breakfast, consisting of scrambled eggs, sliced avocado, *pico de gallo* and crusty bread. Julian eyed her plate lustfully. Still, he ordered a protein shake with added greens.

"Any preference of greens, Mr. Knight?"

"No preference. Just toss everything in."

"Yes, Mr. Knight."

"Mmm." Nina patted her belly. "Sounds delicious."

He flashed a smile, displaying a row of perfect white teeth. "Don't mock me, Nina."

She grabbed her fork and loaded it with eggs and avocado. "Try this," she said, holding it up to his lips.

"Don't tempt me, Nina," he said. "I'm trying to be good."

"Come on, Julian," she whispered. "Live a little. I won't tell your personal trainer."

He locked eyes with her. Then he took the fork in his mouth, his teeth scraping the prongs as he pulled away. The desire to kiss him was so sharp it cut her appetite.

She dropped the fork and picked up the bread. She ripped a piece and bit into it, buying some time. It was light and chewy and delicious. "I work out and eat right and all the things," she said. "Just not on vacation. It's against my religion to be so disciplined at a five-star hotel."

He relaxed in his chair and stretched out his legs, brown skin over taut muscle. "What church is that? Can I convert?"

"Sorry. We only let in true believers."

The attendant returned with his shake, topped off Nina's mimosa with champagne, then discreetly backed away.

Julian stirred the thick shake with a glass straw. "I'm going to miss you tonight."

Those few words undid her. She cleared her throat. "How about we continue our marathon with *Thunder II*?"

"You've been through enough," he said. "Plus, I have a thing tonight."

"Oh!" She had to grip the bread or risk dropping it. "I… Oh."

Of course he had a thing—whatever that meant. He hadn't flown across country to swim laps in a fancy pool. Unlike her, he had a life. Nina scarfed down her eggs, aware that he was watching her. He was such a keen observer. Nothing was lost on him. She'd pay cash to know what he was thinking.

"It's a work thing," he said. "The last time I met with this person, we spoke for hours. I have no idea how it will go tonight, but I'm hopeful."

She reached for her glass and raised it. "Good luck."

"Thanks." He continued to stir his shake, in no apparent hurry to drink it. "What are your plans for today?"

"There's the move to my new room, and that'll take all of ten minutes."

He offered to help, and she turned him down. "I'm good. Thanks."

"What else?"

At this point, she should initiate plan WWMD: What would Mom do? "The point of this trip is to celebrate my mother's life. So I'm going to do the things that she'd like to do, given the chance."

"Which are?"

"Lounging at this fabulous hotel, drinking, flipping through magazines… I'll have to book a manicure." She shrugged, failing to come up with anything better. "She took relaxation very seriously."

"What are the things that you like to do?"

"Me?" Why had the question stumped her? "Honestly, I don't vacation well. I work a lot of the time. So I'd read or revise a manuscript or use the trip to research a setting."

The straw clinked on the sides of his glass as he continued to stir. He was mulling over something. Nina held her breath until he came out with it.

"Why don't you come with me tonight?" he said.

"To the work thing?"

"It's a dinner."

"I don't know," she said, suddenly uneasy.

"You might enjoy it. And you'd be doing me a favor— I'm the third wheel."

Nina immediately considered what she might wear and

missed it when he lifted his gym bag onto his lap. He pulled out his phone. "What's your email address?"

"Why?"

"I'm going to send you some reading materials," he said. "You might want to study up for tonight."

"Oh? Okay," she said. "Send it to *Hello@NinaTaylor. com*."

He narrowed his eyes, tapping away at his phone. "I don't have to remind you that anything I share with you is confidential."

"Should I remind you that friendship is based on trust?"

He put the phone down. "Is that what this is? A platonic friendship?"

"I don't know what this is," she said. And that was the honest truth.

He seemed to like her answer. Concealing a smile, he drew the straw from the shake, set it down on a napkin and drained the glass with a few gulps. His Adam's apple bobbed when he swallowed.

Nina's mouth went dry.

He rose to his feet. "I need a shower."

"What time is dinner?" she asked.

"Seven. I'll come get you."

"See you then."

He turned to walk away, hesitated, then returned to his seat. "Nina, I'm nearly done with your book."

She groaned. He raised a finger. "Let me say this one thing. You don't have far to go to connect with your mum. You saw her clearly for who she was, and that's a lot."

Nina shook her head, regret and sorrow churning in her gut. "She didn't see it that way."

Her mother had read an early excerpt of *Backstage Diva*. She wept and accused Nina of distorting facts to paint herself in a positive light.

"Why do you think I insist that you, that everyone, call me Julian?" he said.

"It's a beautiful name," she said.

"Most people can't separate me from the person they see on screen. It's annoying, for one thing. And it's isolating."

"Oh, Julian…" The name escaped her lips, now full of meaning.

"You were not her *fan*. You were her daughter. She had something real with you, and it's a shame she couldn't see it."

He got up and slung his gym bag over his shoulder. Nina watched him leave, speechless. Every time she thought she had this man figured out, he revealed another facet of himself. Curiosity as to what he might have sent her in the email took over. She grabbed her phone and clicked on the message. The attached document was titled *Midnight Sun*.

Nina finished her breakfast and took her drink over to a lounge chair. It was time to hit Pause on plan WWMD. She had a fresh drink and new reading material. This was *her* idea of fun.

# Nine

Julian stood at Nina's door in a steel-gray suit that his stylist had had delivered after he put in an emergency call. He'd wanted to look good for their night out, only they were staying in. Francisco had agreed to meet at Sand Castle. Actually, he'd insisted on it.

Nina looked stunning in what couldn't be dismissed as a little black dress, because the long bias-cut skirt had a high slit and the bodice was completely backless. Julian went stiff with want. He yearned to take her in his arms, and it took effort to suppress the urge.

"Don't just stand there," she said. "Come in! I have something for you."

He stepped into her room and cast a look around. The Garden Room lived up to its name with hand-painted flowers scattered all over the walls, a bed covered with a floral duvet and drapes with stitched flowers framing a view of the enclosed garden—the one with the famed statue of Aphrodite. As an added touch, the orchid Amelia had selected for her was sitting on the nightstand. "So, this is it," he said. "Like it?"

"I like it well enough." She walked to a corner desk and grabbed a few sheets of paper. "I read the screenplay and made notes."

Julian took the few pieces of hotel stationery from her hands and inspected them. "I should've thought twice before asking a writer to read anything."

She snatched the pages from him. "It's a good thing. I'm excited!"

"But are you hungry?" he asked, hoping for a diversion. "Ready for dinner?"

"Ready! I'll grab my purse."

She headed over to the dresser and dabbed perfume on the insides of her wrists. The gesture was so intimate, Julian felt privileged to watch it.

"Nina," he said.

She tossed him a look over her shoulder. He forgot what he wanted to say.

"Yes?"

"Uh… Right. Bring your notes. It's early. We can talk over drinks."

"Ah!" She folded the pages into a tiny clutch purse. "Now you're talking my love language."

They were seated at the hotel bar with a half hour ahead of them. When Francisco and his date arrived, they'd have the dining room to themselves—Julian had seen to it. Who knew how many first dates and birthday dinners were canceled to accommodate him? Only he wasn't too worried about it, not if it meant guaranteeing quiet time with Nina… and Francisco, too.

Their reflection was splashed against the mirrored wall. Seated like this, facing each other, dressed as they were, Julian couldn't deny it: they were one *smoking*-hot couple. Not that appearances mattered for anything. Still, it was hard to ignore the truth.

Hands shaking, she pulled her notes from her bag and smoothed them on the onyx bar top. "You wrote *Midnight Sun*," Nina said. "There's nothing you can say to convince me otherwise."

He paused, took a sip of his gin and tonic. "What makes you say that?"

Julian had taken precautions to send her an unmarked copy. He'd wanted her honest opinion.

"Every character sounds like you," she said.

He winced and reached for his drink again.

"Don't look so worried. I told you I liked it."

He thumbed through her notes open on the onyx bar top. "So, what's all this?"

"Just some notes." She sat up straight and crossed her legs. The slit of the skirt spread to reveal toned thighs. Julian's gaze skidded off the pages onto her lap. "Which role are you playing?"

Julian hesitated. Would she be disappointed when he told her? He wasn't the star of his own movie. He couldn't be. If he were going to salvage his career, he'd have to try new things. And he couldn't do that if a film's success rested on his name and image. That left him with supporting roles, which meant his star would dim. Not the one on Hollywood Boulevard, thankfully. That one was set in concrete.

"I play Luke."

"The con artist? Oh, God… I love him!"

In that moment, Julian loved her.

"That scene when he drives Amanda home from the party is so tender," she said. "I'm glad the lead is a woman. That was a good choice."

"Is the dialogue *that* terrible?"

"Actors need lines. Good delivery isn't enough. It has to be on the page. I learned that from my mother."

She was so brilliant; Julian couldn't get over it. When she picked up her dirty martini, he reached out and toyed with the gold bracelet at her wrist. She brought the glass to her lips, her eyes on him, her expression dark. If he didn't know better, he'd swear that she was making up her mind about him. God, he liked his chances!

"Julian! There you are!"

Francisco was early. Nina turned to the voice and recognized the actor. In his motorized chair, he looked sharp in a dark blue suit. She slipped off the bar stool and floated over to him. "Francisco Cortes! What an honor!"

Frank beamed up at her. He had not lost his matinee-idol looks: deep tan, chiseled jaw, trim beard and sterling silver hair. Julian approached and introduced her properly. "Frank, this is Nina Taylor. Nina is a very talented writer and a friend."

"Nina, I'm familiar with your work."

"Really?"

She seemed completely flabbergasted. Did she not understand the reach and importance of her work?

"Oh, yes," Frank said. "I caught your mother on stage once. Brilliant performance! And you know we actors love to read about ourselves. That can't be helped."

"Well, I loved you in *The Longest Day*. That might be my favorite movie of all time."

Francisco laughed. "Have I interrupted something? I arrived early, I know."

"Don't be ridiculous," Julian said. "You honor us."

Grace joined them. She and Francisco went way back, and she was his date for the evening. They took off ahead of them, Grace leading the way to the dining room. Nina and Julian followed.

"You weren't that excited to meet me," Julian said, speaking low so only Nina would hear. The added precaution wasn't necessary. Frank and Grace were enthralled with each other.

Nina did nothing to conceal her joy at his petty display of jealousy. "Francisco Cortes isn't disrupting my vacation plans."

"You didn't know any of my films."

"None of your films were featured at the Tribeca Film Festival," she said. "I can't be blamed for that."

"Is Grace single?" he asked. "See how Frank is looking at her?"

"Lucky woman!" Nina exclaimed.

"Go on and twist the knife," he said.

She laughed and slipped her hand in his.

The dining room was an intimate setting with sloped ceilings and shell-inlaid walls that gleamed in flickering candlelight. He'd seen it earlier in the day. Tonight, he had the pleasure of seeing it through Nina's wide eyes. She never held back, and he loved that about her.

A grand table was set for four. After a pleasant meal, Grace left them to talk business. Frank got straight to it.

"I'd like to talk about the script. It needs tightening up."

"Let me guess," Julian said. "The dialogue."

"Bingo!" Frank said with a snap of his fingers. "That gives me such hope. I thought you were going to give me a hard time."

"It's too late for that. Nina beat you to the punch."

Francisco turned to Nina. "You agree?"

"It needs some dusting up. Otherwise, it's perfect."

No…she was perfect. Her support meant even more to him than she could imagine.

"So, you've agreed to take on a rewrite?" Frank asked.

"Me? No!" Nina looked to Julian in panic. "I'm not a screenplay writer. You know that, right?"

"But you're a writer," Julian said.

"And a damn fine one," Frank added.

"Yes, but— Thanks, but— No."

Julian hoped she didn't feel ambushed. That wasn't his intention. He hadn't thought the script needed any help, but he wasn't so stubborn to refuse it. Why take their chances with a script doctor? Nina would be perfect for the job.

"Welcome to Hollywood," Frank said to her. "Nobody knows anything and we're all just winging it."

Julian couldn't dispute that. If he'd waited around for someone to proclaim him an actor, he would have never had the balls to audition for any role.

"I'll give you my notes. How about that?"

Julian studied her for a while. She was blinking so fast, it was certainly to hold back tears. What could be holding her back? She'd claimed to be excited about the project. All at once, the pieces snapped together in Julian's mind. Why would she want to work with him? She was a respected artist. His legacy was synonymous with mud. With that realization blooming inside him, he turned away from her.

"We'll leave it at that," Frank said. "You must be busy, working on other projects."

"If you don't mind," Nina said, rising to her feet. "I'm going to the ladies' room."

Julian immediately stood to help her with her chair. She rested a hand on his arm and eased him back into his seat. "I'll be right back."

He watched her go. It took a while for him to notice that Frank was staring at him. "God help you, my man! You're in love with that woman."

"No way!" Julian protested. "We've only just met."

"What difference does that make?" Frank asked.

Julian pushed away his dessert plate. "What's going on with you and Grace? Is that love?"

"Maybe? Who knows?"

"You ought to." Frank seemed to know enough to comment on his state of affairs. Shouldn't he be more self-aware?

"Here's what I know," Frank said. "Do the work, find someone to clean up the script and I'll direct. But I have one other request."

Julian was at the edge of his seat. All this talk of love had derailed him. This was the conversation he wanted to have with Frank. "I'm listening."

"You assist me in every way. When we wrap this thing up, I want you to have the tools and know-how to do this on your own. No more shopping around for someone to direct the thing that you've conceived in your imagination. I understand that you need a push, a pat on the back, someone to believe in you, and I'm willing to step into the role. And it's exciting. I'll admit it. But after this, I'm done. And you've got a career ahead of you. *Comprende?*"

"Understood!"

So this was what paying it forward looked and felt like? If so, he'd have to give it a go, because it felt damn good. He reached across the table and shook Frank's hand. "Thanks, man. I don't know what else to say."

"Say you're ready to get to work. I don't believe in wasting time."

Julian was more than ready. And all he had was time.

# Ten

Nina locked herself in the ladies' room. With the scent of lavender swirling in the air and a gold toilet, it was as good a place as any for a meltdown. She lowered the toilet seat and sat down.

Why had she turned down such an awesome opportunity? She loved the material and had great ideas on how to improve it. Julian was open to criticism, which meant he'd be easy enough to work with. Plus, he really needed the help. Over dinner, she'd noticed how nervous he was. Francisco's opinion mattered to him. It wasn't every day that she got the chance to collaborate with people so committed to their work. Lastly, she needed the work. Her inbox wasn't exactly crammed with offers. What was holding her back?

Her agent was going to kill her if she ever found out.

"Nina? Are you in there?"

It was Julian. How long had she been spinning her wheels in this restroom? Long enough that Julian had had to lead a search party. She strained to make her voice chipper. "I'll be right out!"

"What are you doing in there?" His voice was low and muffled, as if he were speaking into the thickness of the door.

"What do you think?" To make her point, she stood and flushed the toilet that didn't need flushing.

"I don't know," Julian said. "My guess is that you're breathing into a paper bag."

Nina did not gratify him with a response. Having flushed, she made a production of washing her hands, splashing water.

His next guess wasn't any better. "Crying into a towel?"

"Oh, God!"

She twisted the gold faucets shut, dried her hands and yanked open the bathroom door. Julian was leaning against the frame. His relaxed posture suggested that he would have waited there all night. And he was so handsome. All that muscle fitted in an immaculate suit. All that smooth brown skin, turned golden by his time in the sun. All the sparkle and intensity in those endless brown eyes. She could barely stand it.

"I'm not having a panic attack, if that's what you're thinking."

"Good," he said. "May I come in?"

This request coming from anyone else would have been bizarre. For whatever reason, she and Julian had skipped the awkward getting-to-know-you phase and were at the point of holding secret meetings in public restrooms.

"Did you leave Francisco alone at the table?" Nina asked.

"He's gone," he said. "He called it a night."

Nina stepped aside and let him in. The generous restroom contracted in size. She eased down onto a tufted bench under a gold-framed mirror. He stood before her, looking down at her upturned face with concern. Why did she feel so exposed in his gaze?

"Julian, I'm okay. Really." She sat up straighter. "I wasn't expecting your offer, that's all."

"I'm sorry," he said. "I shouldn't have assumed you'd want to work with me."

"What do you mean by that?"

His face was clouded. "Like you said, it's not your area of expertise."

For whatever reason, Nina didn't believe his explanation. Julian was holding back from her, and the feeling disturbed her more than was reasonable. "Why wouldn't I want to work with you? You're a big Hollywood star."

"I'm a big liability."

"Julian!" Nina rose to confront him. "What are you talking about? I'd love to work with you."

"Because you split your time between libraries and film festivals, you may not know that my reputation isn't the best."

"I don't split my time—" Nina paused, took a breath. "And you're being dramatic. So your movie tanked. So what?"

"It's not just that."

"I know," Nina said, waving her hands to brush the whole ugly business away. "There was a boycott and everything. And I'm sure you're not blameless, but you are not who those people say you are. You're not."

Emotion colored his face, prompting Nina to wonder about Julian's carefree facade.

"Then why were you so quick to say no?"

"Because I suck at fiction!" Julian pushed out a dry laugh. She grabbed his shoulders to force him to listen. "I've been writing all my life, and the memoir is my only successful project. My editor turned down a collection of short stories just this week. I'd feel more comfortable if you hired a professional to do this job."

He removed her hands from his shoulders and held them between his. "Would a professional care as much as you do?"

"Who cares? Nothing is better than competence."

Julian's voice was level. "I care a great deal."

They stood like that for a long time, her hands in his, their eyes locked. Julian's quiet confidence transferred onto her. Turning him down was the sensible thing to do, but would she regret it? Yes. Yes, she would. Certainty surged inside her. She was going to do it. She was going to jump into the deep. Only this time she was fully aware of the risk.

"Okay. I'll do it."

Julian asked her to repeat her words, as if he couldn't believe what he'd just heard.

"I'll do it," Nina said. "I'll take a chance. So long as you keep in mind that I've never done this type of work before."

"You're in good company," he said. "Neither have I. But if you want to come aboard this sinking ship, I'll be more than happy to have you."

Nina planted her hands on her hips. "Permission to come aboard, sailor."

"Permission granted."

He flashed a grin so infectious that she couldn't help but grin back. And then she snapped out of it. This was a negotiation, damn it! "I don't work for free."

"I wouldn't expect you to," Julian said.

"My agent will be in touch."

"We'll work something out," he said. "You won't be disappointed."

"One last thing," she said. "If at any point you're not happy with my work, please let me know."

"I'll be straightforward with you," he said. "But unhappy? I don't see it."

"Okay…" Nina said. What was left to cover?

"Now would be a good time to tell you that Frank signed on to be our director."

"Julian!" Nina bolted forward to draw him into an ungainly hug. "That's great! I'm so excited for you."

"For us." He held her close. "He's your director, too."

His breath fanned her cheek. Nina pulled back to look up at him. Those deep brown eyes… That flared nose… Those full lips… All within reach. *I'll do it. I'll take a chance.* As tall as she stood in her heels, she was not tall enough. She placed her hands on his shoulders one more time and, eyes half-closed, she tilted her head back, asking, *imploring*, for a kiss.

The kiss never came.

There was a knock on the door. Nina sprang away from him. If they were caught together in a public bathroom, social media would go nuts. Julian brought a finger to his lips and gestured for her to be quiet.

"Busy here!" he called out in a smooth voice.

A woman's steely tone drilled through the door. "Sir, this is the ladies' room!"

"You might want to rethink your gender norms, ma'am!"

An indignant cry, the staccato click-clack of heels, then blissful silence. Nina collapsed with laughter. Good thing Julian was there to catch her.

"I bet she's headed straight to the complaint desk," he said.

"With good reason. You shamed her and called her ma'am!"

"I'll step out first," he said. "Come find me in the courtyard."

The courtyard was dark except for the light from a few lanterns and a silver disk of a moon. Nina found Julian walking in circles, pausing only to smooth back his hair. When he saw her, he straightened his shoulders and pasted a smile on his face. Nina wasn't duped. Why did he look so conflicted?

Once she'd decided that she wanted him, she hadn't stopped to consider whether the feeling was mutual. Did he…not want this? Nina could address the matter in a straightforward way. Yet she opted to play coy instead. Because that always worked. "Hey," she said, taking a step forward. "We have a few things to celebrate tonight. Let's order champagne."

"Did you want me to kiss you in there?"

Oh, God! Why couldn't he let her play coy? "Yeah… about that… Did you not want to?"

"I had to be sure," he said. "You remember saying you didn't want to sleep with me, right?"

"When did I say that?"

"The first night we slept together—or shared a bed, I should say."

"Oh?" Nina replayed the tape in her mind. He couldn't hold that against her! She was bent out of shape that night. "Nothing after drowning really counts."

"Nina, I'm the mistake women make after a few drinks at a party. I don't want to be something you regret."

"That's not possible."

"Kiss My Ass" video notwithstanding, he was a good person. No amount of mean tweets and mean-spirited magazine articles was going to change her opinion of him. He was the man who dived into a pool, fully dressed, to rescue her after she'd spent the afternoon tossing back vodka shots. That man was the real MVP.

"I'm the woman who has never taken a guy home after a couple of drinks. Not ever." He arched his brows as though impressed. She immediately set him straight. "I don't say this to brag. It's not fun. I overthink and overanalyze everything and everyone."

"So, what's your take on us?"

"Well…here I am in Miami, in this gorgeous mansion. By some strange twist of fate, I met a man. He makes me feel like a goddess, but I wish he'd stop treating me like one, because I'm ready to be reckless and toss caution out the stained glass windows."

His grin broke like the dawn of a new day. "I'm your guy. Reckless behavior is my specialty."

Nina rushed to him, grabbed him by the lapel of his exquisite blazer and drew his mouth to hers. This time, he crushed her with his kiss. She reciprocated, exploring his mouth, taking his moans deep into her own. As the night breeze brushed her bare back, Nina was reminded of where they were: out in the open, perilously exposed. That feeling of being watched returned, and it was all but confirmed by the sound of footsteps in the courtyard. Julian didn't miss it, either. He groaned in frustration and pulled away to look around. Nina shivered, already missing his touch. She froze when she heard him say, "Hey there, Pete. Still on the clock?"

Pete! Why was he lurking around?

"On my way out, Mr. Knight," the driver replied. "Good evening, Ms. Taylor."

"Good night, Pete."

Nina grabbed Julian's arm and led him along the shadows of the cloisters toward the elevator. They passed the door to the bell tower. Julian pushed on the iron handle, and the heavy wood door swung open to a narrow stairwell with steep steps winding up to the top. Nina shot him a warning look. "Not in these shoes."

He glanced down at her delicate heels. "Thought you were ready to be reckless."

"I did say that, didn't I?"

Julian drew her into the stairwell and shut the door behind them. He hunched low before her and ran his hands along her calves. His fingers found and worked diligently to loosen the many buckles and straps of her sandals. Then he eased them off and tossed them aside. When he was done, he looked up at her. "Race you to the top."

"I don't think—"

He charged the stairs before she could dissuade him.

"Hey!" Nina cried. Her competitive nature kicked in, and she might have caught up to him if she hadn't stopped to gather her shoes before giving chase, then stopped midway to catch her breath. Julian stood waiting at the top of the stairs, hands in his pockets, a slice of moonlight adding extra sparkle to his cocky smile. She glared at him, and he laughed—the laugh of a man who had everything going for him. Nina vowed that he would have the absolute best sex of his life tonight.

"Come on," he said. "You're not dizzy, are you?"

"I'm fine. Thanks." Nina reached the landing and, panting still, ignored his outstretched hand. She stole a moment to take in her surroundings—a circular space with a bleached wood floor and a steepled ceiling. The metal bell swung from an arch facing the courtyard. A built-in bench hugged the walls.

"It's so beautiful," she said, in a whisper.

"Absolutely." He came to stand behind her. "But there's a chance we may be admiring different views."

He swept her braid away from her neck and pressed his lips on each knot of her spine. Her back to Julian's chest, she shivered in his arms. He threaded a hand through the slit of her dress and brushed her inner thigh. She covered his hands with hers and inched it higher. When his fingers brushed between her legs, meeting the wet silky fabric, Nina's back arched, and a moan escaped her. He cupped her face and drew her back for a deeper, more intimate kiss before pulling back.

"Here's my dilemma," he said, speaking softly. "I want to take you up to bed *and* I want to take you right here."

Those options were not mutually exclusive as far as Nina was concerned. She swiveled around to face him. "Can't you do both?"

"Sorry." He kissed the corner of her mouth. "I hate to disappoint, but I'm not prepared."

"Is that all?"

Nina slipped out of his embrace and searched around in the semidarkness for where she might have dropped her small purse. It was clear across the floor. She picked it up and pulled out a square foil packet from the zippered pocket. "Problem solved."

He smiled wickedly. "If you were hoping to get lucky tonight, I hope it was with me."

"Don't flatter yourself. I've kept one in every purse since college."

"I love a girl with a plan."

She made her way back to him on tiptoe, holding up the packet within two fingers. "Women have plans. Girls have hopes and wishes."

Julian's expression darkened as he focused on her. "Scrap your plans. Tell me what you wish for."

That was easy. She didn't have to mull it over. She had wanted to see him naked from the day they'd met. "Take your clothes off."

He took her hand and brought her wrist to his lips. "Please and thank you go a long way, Nina."

"All right," she said, her pulse skipping. "Take your clothes off, *please*."

Julian shrugged out of his impeccable dinner jacket and started working on the buttons of his shirt. She watched as the layers came off, revealing the broad shoulders, the narrow waist, the ripples of his abdomen and the sculpted thighs. He worked hard at maintaining his body and ought to be lavished with praise and adulation for it. Only Nina was limited and could only offer sarcasm.

"Wow!" she exclaimed when his boxers joined the heap of clothing. "It doesn't take much to get you naked, JL."

"I believe the words you're searching for are *thank you*."

Nina wrapped her arms around his neck and whispered her thanks in his ear.

"Now," he said. "One good turn deserves another."

If she had one wish remaining, it would be for her dress to miraculously fall away. Caught up in his kiss, she fumbled with the mini buttons and searched around for the zipper. Julian broke away abruptly. "Oh, for God's sake, woman!"

His hands went straight to a hidden zipper of the skirt. It was as if the man had studied the pattern of her dress all night. With a few adept moves, he had it rising over her head. Then he stood back, his gaze sweeping over her body. She was all but naked except for a pair of fine silk panties. The ocean breeze on her hot skin raised goose bumps. "So bloody beautiful," he murmured before scooping her up and laying her on the banquette.

Somehow, in the tight space, they managed to remain intertwined, kissing, touching, exploring. Nina had never craved anyone's touch as much as his. When she could not take a second longer, Nina took his face in her hands. Between harsh intakes of breaths, she said, "Let's just…do this fast…and…take our time later…upstairs."

He raised himself on an elbow and looked down at her, his eyes teasing. "A woman with a plan…"

"I plan, you execute… Sound good?"

"Not really." He plucked the foil packet from her hand and sat up with his back against the cement wall. He got busy, ripping a corner of the packet and extracting the condom. "We do this together or not at all."

"I love a man with principles," Nina said, teasing, and inched closer to loosen his hair tie. She ran her fingers playfully through his thick waves. A lock of hair tumbled over his forehead. She leaned in and took his earlobe between her teeth and tugged.

He drew her onto his lap. "Come to me, baby."

She loved how solid he felt in her arms, loved the steady drumming of his heart. Her own pulse was erratic, her heart skipping wildly. The kiss she gave him was just as wild. He tilted her backward to some degree and fit himself inside her. Nina went rigid at first. Then warmth spread through her, and she relaxed in his arms. She dug her fingers in his hair, breathed him in, tasted him and moved with him. And then they took off, driving faster, harder, until they reached a climax that left her shattered. Nina collapsed against him, certain that he would collect her scattered pieces and keep her safe.

*Journal Entry*

*The sense of urgency is gone when we finally stumble into the suite and strip away our fussy dinner clothes once and for all. I fall into bed; the silky sheets feel delicious. Julian locks the door and joins me, kneeling at the foot of the bed. He takes hold of my hips and drags me to him. Aching with anticipation, I grab a pillow, anything to anchor me. "Hold on to me," he says in a low voice that makes me shudder. I reach for him and dig my fingers into his shoulders. When our eyes meet, the mix of turmoil and tenderness in his scares me. I know this thing with Julian is going to undo me. It may well break me. I know it and want it anyway.*

# Eleven

Julian assisted Nina down the stone steps leading to the sidewalk and for a while they stood still, fingers linked, in the flow of pedestrian traffic. He grinned down at her. He could not stop grinning. All day it was as if he were walking on clouds.

"Just us?" she said. "No driver or entourage?"

"Just us."

"Are you sure you can get away with this?"

"I can get away with a whole lot. Haven't you noticed?"

The bell tolled the hour, and all the memories of the night before came tumbling back, every wicked thing they'd done in the tower. By the look on Nina's face, he was sure her thoughts mirrored his.

"Let's go," he said. "The sooner we're done with dinner, the sooner we can revisit the tower. But if you need an entourage, I can get Pete to drive us."

"No, thanks," she said. "To be honest, I find Pete strange. Don't you?"

"He's all right. Only trying to get a day's work in."

Julian slipped an arm around her waist and got them moving in the direction of the restaurant.

"No…" She leaned into him. "My instincts aren't wrong. You should be careful around him."

He didn't question her instincts, but everyone in his orbit was bound to act strange at some point. It was only one of the many downsides of fame. And one complaint to management could get the man fired.

"I should be careful around *you*," he said. "You look dangerously good tonight."

If he couldn't address her concerns, the best he could do was lighten the mood. His strategy worked. She broke away. The straps of her short cotton sundress fell off her shoulders. "Then maybe you should keep your distance."

That was the one thing Julian did not have the strength to do. He chased after her and pinned her to him. "I'll keep my eye on Pete," he said. "I promise."

"Thanks," she said. "Now feed me."

The hotel concierge had recommended Ocra, a trendy Jamaican restaurant on Tenth Street well within walking distance from Sand Castle. There was no stuffy maître d' to contend with, only a friendly hostess who tripped on her words when Julian and Nina entered. The manager, a jovial man named Cyril, took over her duties. Grinning from ear to ear, he led them to a private table in the back of the restaurant. They were stopped along the way by patrons leaping out of their chairs, requesting selfies or just a hug. Julian obliged them, doling out hugs and posing for photos without once letting go of Nina's hand.

"Sorry about that," Cyril said when they finally reached their table. "You're Jamaica's favorite son."

Julian stood aside so Nina could slide into the booth. "I think Usain Bolt has that honor."

"He's never eaten here, and tonight you honor us." He handed Nina a menu with a little bow. "Welcome to Ocra, miss."

She smiled, looking amused at all the fuss. "Thank you."

Cyril left them to study the menu. Julian slid to her side of the booth.

The white flared skirt barely reached her midthigh. He reached down and nudged it higher.

"Stop it," she said, her eyes on the menu. "You'll have us thrown out for indecency."

"Impossible." Julian lowered his head and tugged at her ear with his teeth. "I'm the island's favorite son."

"Second only to Usain Bolt."

"I'll take it," Julian said. "What looks good?"

"Everything! I'd like to try this."

She pointed to a cocktail on the beverage menu: the Smoke Show. It was a mix of mescal, agave and smoked bell pepper.

"Really? I would have pegged you for a cranberry vodka girl."

"I told you, caution is out the window."

"I love the sound of that."

They kissed. It started light and deepened quickly. He pulled away, frustrated and out of breath. They were one click away from starring in another viral video. She reached for her water glass and took a gulp. He did the same.

Julian had missed her, having spent the day at Frank's house, which was now, for all intents and purposes, ground zero. Frank's contacts in the business surpassed Julian's. By the end of the day, they were in talks with an independent production company, fleshing out a distribution deal. They'd discussed casting at length, which brought him to a pressing topic he wanted to discuss with Nina. He would have brought it up the minute he'd gotten back to Sand Castle, only he'd found Nina stretched out on the floor in cutoff denim shorts and a halter top. The printed manuscript was strewn out on the antique rug with notes in the margin.

"Don't touch anything," she said. "I gave it a closer read. I need to get into the characters' heads."

He walked over to her, sidestepping the pages like so many land mines. She rolled onto her back, a satisfied look on her face.

"I'd like to get in those shorts," he said, kneeling low to rub her flat belly.

"Not until you feed me," she said. "I've been snacking on granola bars all day."

"Want to get out of here?"

"Sure," she said. "But I've run out of fancy dresses. I only packed two, the one I drowned in and the one you made a mess of last night."

There was a blotch of blue ink on her cheek. He rubbed it away with the pad of his thumb. "No fancy dress. No problem."

By the time her cocktail was served, Julian had still not mustered the courage to share his news. He didn't want anything to sour their evening.

"I'd like to try the jerk chicken, the jerk corn and maybe a side of peas and rice," she said. "How about you?"

"The oxtail," he said without consulting the menu. No self-respecting Jamaican joint would lack an oxtail dish.

"But you're vegetarian!" she protested.

"Mostly vegetarian," he said. "After the night I had, I could eat anything."

She shut the menu and sent it sliding across the wood-plank table. "Really? My night was pretty tame."

She was joking, he knew it, but his pride took a blow. "You're younger than me by a few years, with way more stamina."

"No," she said with a crooked smile. "Your stamina is second only to Usain Bolt."

"What do you know about Bolt's stamina?"

"Only what I've seen on TV."

The manager returned to take their orders and to present them with an assortment of appetizers—a sample of the house's *likkle* plates. But as soon as he was gone, Nina pressed a kiss on Julian's cheek and whispered, "You're second to no one." Julian could not be prouder if he won a gold medal.

"I have to tell you something," he said.

"Yes?" she said, eyeing the platter of plantain bites, ackee rolls and salt-fish fritters. He thought he'd lost her, but after she bit into a fritter, moaned, rolled her eyes and broke into a happy dance, she reminded him that he had something to tell her.

"We had a discussion about casting today, Frank and I."

"You're still playing Luke, right?"

"Definitely."

The role in question was the lead: heiress Amanda King. Years ago, he'd offered it to Bettina. When he mentioned it to Frank, he took to the idea and wouldn't let it go. This left Julian the unenviable task of pushing back without coming off as a colossal jerk. "She won't work with me."

"Is it that bad between you two?"

It wasn't that bad, but it wasn't good. "Picture working with any one of your ex-wives?"

Frank had ignored his question and enlisted an impartial arbitrator. He got Karen Butler of B Plus Casting on the phone.

Karen was known in the industry for an open approach to casting actors in parts. As an African American actor whose prospects had dried up soon after she hit forty, Karen had started her agency with an aim to keeping underrepresented actors employed. Julian felt sure she wouldn't advocate for Bettina, but she did.

"I haven't read the script, so I can't say that she's right for the part you have in mind," Karen said. "But working together on a meaningful project would go a long way to shore up goodwill. You need that right now."

"She's not interested in helping me," Julian said.

Karen had a different take. "She'd be helping herself. I know on good authority that she doesn't have many offers in the pipeline. The controversy damaged both of you—no offense."

"None taken."

Julian had agreed to offer her the part. A phone call wasn't going to do it. Tomorrow he was flying out to Georgia, where Bettina was filming her television series, to offer her the part in person. First, he wanted to know how Nina felt about it.

"Frank thinks Bettina Ford would be right for the part of Amanda."

"Ah." She fell back against the cushion of the leather banquette. "What about you? What do you think?"

"I think she'd do a good job," Julian said. "I've always thought so. We've discussed it in the past. Even though I don't think she'll want the job, I should at least run it by her."

"What if she says yes?"

Her interest in the food had waned, which was unfortunate, because he knew she was hungry. He should have waited to tell her. Now he had no choice but to go all in. "You know about Betty and me, right? How things ended?"

It might have been his imagination, but Nina flinched when he mentioned Bettina by her nickname.

"I know what I read. I'd rather hear it from you."

As with everything, it started with a social media post. In this case, it was a tweet. He pulled it up and handed Nina the phone. She read it, grimaced and returned his phone.

Julian had it memorized. *When your so-called action-hero boyfriend is too limp to stand up for you, it's time to move on. #Bye.*

"Betty deleted it a half hour later, but the harm was done. Our breakup was announced on the news. Rather than overwork our publicists, we just went for it. We were done."

"Did you stand up for her?" she asked.

"I had it out with the director. I even threatened to bail on promotion." His answer seemed to ease Nina's concerns, but Julian didn't want to leave her with any misconceptions. "I stood up for her because she was my girlfriend, not because I cared about the big-picture implications of cutting her role out of the film. That came later."

"I get that you're not the most enlightened of your species, Julian. But you're not an ogre, either. You can stop beating yourself up already."

Julian wanted to believe her, but somehow she only saw the good in him. Her judgment had to be skewed.

"It's time you distinguish yourself from the balloon animal they've made you into."

She wasn't wrong. At some level, he believed every word printed about him. He let it define him, and to some degree he let it hold him back. It had almost stopped him from pursuing Nina, whom he considered a serious artist. It was unlikely one prickly tweet would damage her career.

"Today I focused on your character," Nina said, switching topics. "His lines have to be memorable."

"Going forward, should I sleep with all my screenwriters?" he wondered aloud. "No one's given a damn until this point."

"You could try," she said, her tone serious. "Why not?"

"I was being cheeky. You know that, right?"

"I wasn't."

He picked up a fritter and bit into it. He loved that she didn't cringe at his cringe-worthy jokes.

"If you want me to work extra hard, you'll have to motivate me," she said. "We have four nights left."

He nearly choked on the fritter. "Only four?"

She gave him a funny look. "Vacation is over."

"I thought you'd stay. Since you're working with us and everything."

"I can write from anywhere," she said with a shrug. "Might as well do it from my desk at home."

The strap of her dress finally fell over her narrow shoulder, but he was too distracted to care. Her dismissive tone unnerved him. "If that's true, you can stay and write here."

"No." She was firm. "I need my laptop and its stand, my wrist brace, special noise-canceling headphones, leggings and cozy slippers."

The waiter cleared the table and served their main dishes while Julian fumed. He was not going to let a pair of cozy slippers get between him and Nina. "Couldn't we have all of that shipped from Amazon?"

"No!" she objected. "I need *my* things. And I need clothes. These are my vacation clothes. There's not much to them."

"I like your vacation clothes," he said, tugging at the strap of her sundress.

She slapped his hand away. "We have to eat our food before it gets cold or Cyril will be insulted."

"I can't have that."

Julian picked up his utensils and attacked his oxtail without tasting it. He had no explanation for it, but the thought of her leaving filled him with dread. She probably had a full life to return to. He was asking for too much. Come to think of it, he hadn't asked for anything at all. Maybe he should try.

Julian laid down his fork and knife. "Stay with me. Don't you want to?"

She swallowed hard, although she hadn't been eating for a while. "It's not that simple."

"I can make it simple."

Having her stuff shipped was no big deal. If she needed to fly to New York and take care of things, he could arrange that, too. Needless to say, she didn't have to worry about running a tab at Sand Castle. He'd take care of it. There were no logistical problems that money couldn't solve. He didn't want to put it so bluntly, but that was the truth.

Her grip tightened on her fork. "I don't want to discuss this anymore."

They finished their meal in near silence and walked back

to the hotel. The usual group of tourists had gathered out-side the hotel gates, cell phones in hand. Julian signaled one of the guards to assist them, but he took the lead, shielding Nina. She hooked a finger through a loop of his jeans and did not let go, following him to the lift. When the doors slid shut, she swiveled around and buried his face in his chest. Julian held her close. He finally tasted relief.

She slipped her arms around his waist. "Ask me again tomorrow. Okay?"

"Sorry. I don't think I can relive the trauma."

"Just do it, please."

"Why?" He smoothed her hair. "Do you need time to overthink it?"

"Something like that."

Julian did not her ask again. Instead, the next morning, he inquired about something less incendiary.

"The left one is larger than the right?"

She curled up to him. "Yup!"

"I'm left-handed, so that's perfect." To prove his point, he cupped her left breast with his left hand. It fit perfectly.

"You're left-handed?" she asked.

"I am. Is that a deal breaker?"

"Only for my right breast."

"Don't worry," he said. "I got it covered."

He bit down on her right nipple and sucked until he heard her moan. Every day should start like this, except it was already lunchtime. They'd slept in. Sunlight burst through the stained glass windows, fighting its way into their co-coon. And he was hungry.

She reached down and cupped him between the legs, startling him. "Are these a matching set?"

"Don't, Nina," he warned. "You'll wake up the Knight."

"Wait! What?" She pulled away from him and sat up on her knees. "Is that what you call it?"

"It suits him, don't you think? He's honorable and brave."

"Brave?" She laughed. "He bravely goes where no man—"

He pinched her chin between his thumb and index finger and pulled her in for a kiss. "Silly woman."

"Is he dependable?" she asked.

"Rain or shine, gets the job done."

"Maybe we shouldn't talk about him as if he's not in the room."

Julian agreed. "His ego is pretty fragile."

"Why? He's such a tall, proud soldier."

"A knight. Please don't mess with his title." He reached for the room service menu on the bedside table. "Breakfast?"

"Yes, please." She tossed aside the crumpled bedsheet and knelt between his legs. "I could eat."

He closed his eyes. His last coherent thought was that he must be the luckiest bastard in the world.

# Twelve

Nina was curled up in the wide bed, listening to the sounds of Julian in the shower, when her phone rang. It was on the nightstand next to Julian's two mobile phones and his array of chargers. Seeing their devices lumped together like that bothered her. It looked to her as if they were becoming a couple. Rattled, she reached for her phone and answered without first checking the caller ID. "Hello."

"Hey, Nina? It's me. Checking in again."

"Valerie?"

"Yes," she said. "I was in the neighborhood and decided to stop by your hotel."

"Excuse me?" Nina stammered.

"You're here, right? Staying at the Sand Castle."

"Yes."

"Well, I'm downstairs. In the courtyard. Are you free to chat?"

Nina sat up and drew the blanket over her bare legs. There was no question her cousin had seen the photos and read the blog posts. Her identity was no longer a mystery, and her social media accounts were clogged with mentions. No doubt Valerie wanted to check in on the state of her mental health. Was it out of character for Nina to hook up with a high-profile movie star? Absolutely. Was it any of her cousin's business? Absolutely not. But Nina hadn't grown up in a tight-knit nuclear family, and she was fuzzy on the rules. What was the best way to deal with an interfering but well-meaning cousin without coming off as rude?

Nina lowered the phone to her bare chest and took a

few sharp breaths to calm down. It didn't work. Through clenched teeth, she said, "I'll be right down."

Ten minutes later, Nina came down the grand stairway in the same frilly dress she'd worn out to dinner the night before. Valerie Pierre, a lawyer, looked polished in a blue pantsuit. A curvy woman with deep brown skin, she wore her hair in a cropped Afro. She stood by the fountain, scrolling on her phone. Nina hadn't seen her since her mother's funeral. Valerie was the only relative on her father's side of the family who had bothered to show up. The others sent flowers, food and money. For that reason, she couldn't kick her to the curb—as much as she wanted to.

"Hey there," Nina said with an awkward wave.

"Nina!"

Valerie rushed over and pulled her into a hug. Her genuine warmth melted away Nina's icy irritation. They ended up at a table on the terrace with coffee and pastries.

"Don't worry," Valerie said, eyeing her from behind her large glasses. "I'll be out of your hair soon. I have to get back to work."

"There's no rush. It'll be great to catch up."

Valerie pursed her lips. "Yeah. I'm just going to jump right in."

Nina gave her a blank smile. "What do you mean?"

"Okay. So, last night, I was clicking around the web for reviews of *Thunder III*. Patrick wanted to stream it, but I'd heard some negative things."

Nina smirked at the mention of Valerie's husband. It was like Julian had said—women rarely owned up to liking the films. It was always a boyfriend or husband. Men did the same with dance or baking competition shows. It was always the girlfriend or wife who made them tune in every week.

She handed Nina her phone. "Then I stumble on this."

Nina pinched the screen to zoom in on the offensive

content. A website had put together a slideshow of her and Julian's courtship in chronological order under the headline, *Love Him or Hate Him, JL Knight Heats Things Up in Miami.*

Photo #1: *JLK and Nina Taylor\* on a balcony at Sand Castle gaze into each other's eyes behind a veil of summer rain. #Meetcute?*

Photo #2: *JLK dives into a pool—fully dressed— to rescue his girl. #RescueMeJLK*

Photo #3: *JLK assists his lady friend into a waiting car, his hand dangerously close to her ass. #PDA*

Photo #4: *JLK kisses his woman under the stars. #TrueLoveKiss*

(\*Nina Taylor is an author. Her memoir, *Back-stage Diva*, debuted at number seventeen on the *NYT* bestseller list.)

The last photo was of her and Julian's first kiss. It was the one photo of the bunch that truly upset her. She would have liked to keep that moment private. The sneaky photographer had caught an intimate moment. That night she had suspected they were being watched, and now she had proof. It *had* to have been Pete. He was the only one lurking around that night.

"Those photos are misleading." Nina tried to rationalize the irrational. "He did rescue me and we went out a few times, but there's nothing to that kiss and—"

Valerie reached across the table and squeezed her hand. "I'm not here to pry. But this is a whole lot of drama and I'm concerned, that's all."

"We're working together." Nina regretted the words almost immediately. Had Julian expected her to keep it confidential?

Valerie made a face. "Working on what? Not another *Thunder* movie!"

"I'm not at liberty to say. And please don't tell anyone."

"Nina," Valerie said gravely, "that guy hooks up with every one of his costars. Don't you keep up with this stuff?"

Nina realized that her smart-girl image, her large-and-in-charge persona, was a liability. Valerie couldn't imagine her having a vacation fling or even having fun. Any outlandish behavior on her part, any bit of drama, had to be a cry for help.

"Scratch that," Valerie said. "Your sex life is none of my business. Just make sure any contract you sign is airtight. The last woman he worked with got cut from his movie. And they were engaged, too."

"They were *not* engaged." For whatever reason, Nina was eager to clarify this point.

"Wait," Valerie said, looking past Nina's shoulder. "Is that him?"

A quick glance in the direction that Valerie had hinted at confirmed that it was in fact Julian and he was making his way toward their table. As always, the sight of him thrilled her. He looked fresh in his usual T-shirt and jeans. Her gaze fell to the travel bag slung over his shoulder, and she recalled that he was flying to Atlanta to speak with Bettina. Nina took a sip of coffee to cure a sudden headache.

"Heading out to the airport," he said. "Thought I'd say goodbye."

"And I'd like to say hello." Valerie popped up and introduced herself. "Hi! I'm Valerie Pierre, Nina's cousin."

"Nice to meet you. I didn't know Nina had family in Miami."

He went on to ask her where she lived and what she did for a living. And for a while they chatted like old friends. Valerie was obviously starstruck. Her bright eyes, overly broad smile and unbridled laughter were dead giveaways. Nina was baffled. How quickly the ice had thawed! Considering Valerie's low opinion of Julian, this was an astonishing 180.

When the time came to say goodbye, Nina caught the

hesitation in Julian's eyes. He made no attempt to hug or kiss her, no doubt dissuaded by her stiff body language. He waved, and she waved back. Once he was out of her sight, it was all Nina could do to keep from chasing after him.

She'd played this wrong, waffling in front of her cousin like that. Julian wasn't much older than her, but it was likely he'd matured past the need to play games. Except she was genuinely freaking out. Despite photo slideshows proving the contrary, she'd enjoyed their relative privacy. This hotel was their safe haven. She wasn't ready to answer questions about their relationship.

Valerie settled back in her seat. "So…that's Julian."

Nina nodded slowly. "That's Julian."

"I like him. He seems cool."

Nina was so relieved that she broke out in a cold sweat. It scared her how badly she wanted Valerie to like him, to differentiate the man in the crappy movie from the man she was sharing a bed with. At the same time, it saddened Nina that she needed outside validation.

"The rumors are true," Nina blurted. "Everything you've read about us is true. We're…" She searched for an elegant term and came up short. "We're hooking up."

"I hope so!" Valerie said. "Imagine coming all this way for an intervention and have nothing to intervene in. Do you know how much it costs to park on Ocean Drive?"

Nina wondered why an intervention was even required. "Is it so crazy what I'm doing?"

Valerie fixed her with her amber eyes. "Honestly? Yes. But just because it's crazy doesn't mean you shouldn't do it. Life is short. You'll need an exit strategy, though. Do you have one?"

Nina stared into her empty coffee cup. Sooner or later, she and Julian would part ways and return to their respective worlds. That wasn't so much a strategy as the charted course of a doomed voyage.

# Thirteen

Julian stood watching Bettina tumble into bed with a much younger man—younger than him, anyway. The guy was shirtless, hairless and slim. Bettina wore a white towel around her torso. In a moment or so, it would fall away. But this being Hollywood, nothing was as it appeared. Bettina was playing the role of Jennifer Duncan, a prosecutor who, for whatever reason, was sleeping with a key witness in a high-profile case. The man who played her lover was Pierce Alexander, an acclaimed film actor gunning for an Emmy. Finally, they weren't on a Hollywood back lot, but a soundstage in Atlanta.

Bettina and Pierce kissed with abandon until the director yelled, "Cut!"

Bettina pulled herself up and darted a look his way, her face tight with frustration. She raised an index finger. *One sec.*

Julian shrugged. *Take your time.*

He missed being in a long-term relationship. He loved the shorthand couples shared, even when it was passive-aggressive as hell.

Bettina and her costar huddled with the director for a few minutes, then she hobbled over in fuzzy slippers. Her red hair was damp and brushed away from her face. Her eye makeup was artfully smudged, and her freckles were double the actual amount. This was her third season playing Jennifer Duncan, a civil servant who managed to live in great style on a state government salary.

"Thanks for meeting me here," she said. "Can't do lunch.

We don't have Pierce for long, so we'll be working through the day."

Julian cocked his head, a nice way of saying. *Screw Pierce.* Seeing her on set with the actor had triggered a jolt of jealousy. But it wasn't fresh emotion, just something warmed up from the past, and he knew it.

"How about later? Come to the hotel. We'll have a drink at the bar."

Bettina searched his face with those clever green eyes. "A rendezvous at a hotel bar? That's not what exes do."

That wasn't what he was proposing. He simply didn't want to offer her a job while on the set of her current job. "I'm clear on that."

Julian's palms were sweating. He shoved his hands in his back pockets and thrust out his chest. Bettina caught the gesture and laughed. "You're nervous! Could you come out with it? I don't have all day."

He came out with it. "Betty, where do you stand on us working together again?"

"You and me?"

"Yes."

"Christ, no!" She recoiled from him. "Haven't we been through enough?"

The director called out her name and held up five fingers. "Got it!" she fired back and turned to Julian. "Just curious. What project did you have in mind?"

*"Midnight Sun."*

She laughed again, her bare shoulders bobbing. More freckles had been painted there, too. "Your *pet* project?"

He waited for the barb to lose its sting. They were regressing. It was starting to feel like old times. Except this tense exchange wasn't about her choice of restaurant or his pile of clothes on the bathroom floor. This concerned their careers and everything they'd worked so hard to achieve. Bettina would be phenomenal in the role of Amanda King.

He'd written the role with her in mind. But this project was supposed to mark a fresh start. How could they move forward if they were forever in each other's way?

"Sorry," she said. "That came out wrong."

The apology threw Julian off the path he was heading down. He stared at her without understanding. Bettina *never* apologized; at best she shared the blame.

"Don't look so shocked. I'm working on myself."

For the year that they'd been apart, Julian had been working on himself, too. But he'd been so close to walking out on Bettina just now, which was his MO. The theatrical exit was a signature move. Also, he had a tendency to be pushy. He could no longer deny that he'd been pushy with Nina. He'd pushed her into accepting to work on the script and again, last night, he'd pushed her to agree to stay. It had to stop. His bullishness stemmed from fear of losing her. He was sure they were at the start of something significant, but they needed time.

The director shouted, "Actors on set!"

Bettina snapped to attention. "You've got to go, Julian. The next scene is a closed set."

He played his last card. "I don't know if this makes a difference, but Francisco Cortes is directing."

Bettina was walking away backward and came close to knocking over a piece of lighting equipment. She stopped short. "For real?"

"I wouldn't make it up."

"Quiet on set!" the director bellowed.

Bettina waved goodbye and went back to work. A makeup artist approached her and began dabbing her forehead with a sponge. Julian exited the brick building at end of an alley lined with similarly bland buildings. The sky was the color of ash, and rain made the sidewalk slick. The driver sprang out of the car with an umbrella, but Julian was quick to slide into the back seat unassisted.

"To the W, Mr. Knight?"

"No. The airport."

Just as the car pulled away from the curb, he caught sight of Bettina, yanking on a robe as she stepped out of the building. Julian asked the driver to wait and rolled down the window. "What is it?"

She shielded her eyes from the sting of rain. "Send me the script. I can't promise anything, but I'll read it."

"I can't ask for more," Julian said. "Now get back inside. Pierce is waiting."

She gave him the finger. He blew her a kiss.

Nina spent the rest of the day working on the script. In the evening, she took her journal to the garden. She was greeted by the smell of freshly cut grass and nothing else. She had expected to find Grace enjoying a glass of wine, but the garden was empty. She paid respects to the goddess Aphrodite, plopped down in a rattan chair and flipped open her journal, picking up where she'd left off.

*"You look lonely in there."*

*"You mean peaceful. I'm at peace in here."*

*"Well...we can't have that."*

*Julian climbs into the tub. Water splashes everywhere, creating puddles on the marble floor. I give him my expert Goldilocks assessment. "This tub is too small!"*

*"Feels just right to me."*

*Our wet hands grab for each other, and his feels just right in mine. I fit him inside me. His moan is just a rumble in his chest. He nudges a lock of damp hair away from my ear and murmurs, "I could drown in you."*

*I'm drowning already. He cradles me, lifts me, but I refuse to be rescued—not this time, not again.*

Nina tucked the pen between the pages. The memory overwhelmed her. Thoughts of Julian had tugged at her all day. She hated the way they'd left things—without even a hug goodbye. He hadn't called all day; it was quiet on all fronts. She would have welcomed anything—a briefly worded text or simply a thumbs-up emoji. Plus, the larger question still loomed. Was she staying or leaving or what? He hadn't asked. After spending the day with Bettina, would he have a change of heart?

"Good evening, Ms. Taylor."

Grace arrived, looking more somber than a woman swinging an ice bucket fitted with a glistening bottle of wine had any right to be.

"Your Grace," Nina said with a little bow. "What do you have for us this evening?"

"A fine prosecco."

"Perfect."

Grace set down the bucket and two stemless champagne flutes. Nina wondered if she was always prepared for company or if she was expecting someone in particular. Either way, she accepted a glass of the sparkling wine.

Grace took her glass to her lips, sipped from it and let out a soft sigh. *"Qué rico."*

It truly was a rich experience: the warm evening, the wine, the fragrant garden, the mansion gleaming like polished ivory against the darkening sky. "Can you believe this house once belonged to a single family?" Nina said.

"I can," Grace said. "It belongs to my family now."

Nina jerked forward, and drops of prosecco flew onto her lap. "You own this hotel?"

"My father does. I run the day-to-day operations."

No wonder Grace carried herself like the grande dame of the château! It all made sense. But it didn't explain Grace's chronic dissatisfaction. Wealth, position and beauty—she'd inherited the trifecta. What exactly was her problem?

Voices rose in the courtyard, a chorus of "Welcome back, Mr. Knight!"

The hotel staff loved Julian. He was always polite and greeted everyone by name. Nina bolted her rear end to her chair. She would not dart out of the garden and tackle him. For one thing, she would not give Grace the satisfaction.

In the end, it was Grace that offered her an out. "Any dinner plans tonight? It's later than you may think. Shouldn't you be getting ready?"

"You're right." Nina stood up. "I should get going."

"Enjoy dinner, Ms. Taylor."

"Thank you. Enjoy your night, Grace."

Julian was on the grand staircase, scaling the stairs by two. Nina had to sprint to catch up to him. When he left with an overnight bag, she worried that she might have to spend a night without him, which would be a first since arriving in Miami. The idea had terrified her. "Hey!" she called out. "You're back!"

He didn't hide his delight in seeing her, drawing her to him for a kiss. Nina stiffened only because she was aware of Pete entering the courtyard. He had likely picked Julian up from the airport. He went over to the front desk and just lingered there. But even Pete couldn't distract her for too long. She shook off her worries and relaxed into Julian's kiss. Let the world see. Let them post about it. And when their relationship came to its inevitable end, let them tweet up a storm. This time together in Miami could be all they'd ever have, and she didn't want to ruin it with doubts and fears. She was going to live it fully.

"I need a shower before dinner," he said. "Want to come up with me to Paradise?"

"You mean Oasis."

"I said what I said. It's paradise with you."

"Fine!" Nina cried, as if she weren't elated beyond words. "I'll grab a few things."

Arm in arm, they made their way up the winding stairs. "Enjoyed your day?" he asked.

"It was productive."

In truth, her day hadn't been as productive as Nina would have liked. She'd wasted a good chunk of time scrolling through photos of JL and Bettina in happier times. They made a handsome couple; there was no denying it. His dark good looks contrasted with her pale beauty. On the red carpet, they flashed matching smiles. With each swipe, jealousy had churned in her chest.

"How was your trip? Did she say yes?"

"She didn't say no."

They'd reached her door. "If she says yes, I'll make sure she has killer lines."

She had little doubt Bettina would accept the role of Amanda King—it was that good.

He wrapped his arms around her and planted a kiss in the curve of her neck. "How are you so lovely and generous?"

Nina unlocked the door and switched on the lights. Julian abandoned her for her bed, stretching out with a sigh of contentment. Nina watched him from the foot of the bed. He likely sensed her looming over him. "Did you forget the plan? Go on. Grab what you need."

"Yeah. Right." She went into the bathroom and blindly stuffed a few toiletries into a case.

"You okay?" Julian called out from the bedroom.

"I'm fine!"

She wasn't, of course, and couldn't explain why. A minute ago, she was joy personified. She returned to the bedroom and grabbed her travel tote bag from the armoire.

"Are you sure about that?" Julian asked. He was propped

up on one elbow, watching her. "Did I say something wrong?"

"Yeah!" she said, awakening to the truth. "I'm not lovely or generous."

"You're not?"

"No! I'm jealous."

He sat up, all of a sudden alert, bright-eyed, engaged. "Tell me more."

"I spent the day looking at—" She bit down on her lower lip, thinking it might be best to keep the crazy details to herself. "I was worried that you two—" Was there any way to talk about this without sounding like a complete basket case?

"You were worried that Bettina and I would take one look at each other and fall back in love?"

"Something like that."

He reached out to her, wrapped his hand around her wrist and tugged her close. She stood between his parted knees. "It was nothing like that. I promise you. We spoke for all of ten minutes. Then I left and headed straight back to the airport. I spent the day at the lounge, waiting for clearance to fly. I didn't want to waste any of the few nights we have left."

Nina's heart was hammering in her chest. "Ask me again."

A spark of hope brightened his expression. "Have you had enough time to think it through? I don't want to rush you."

Nina took his face in her hands and ran her fingers along the angles. Stubble pricked her fingertips. "Just ask me."

He took her wrist to his lips. "Stay. Please."

He wasn't asking. He was pleading. Her response was a plea as well. She circled her arms around his neck and slid onto his lap. "Hold me. Don't let me go."

# Fourteen

Nina had long forgotten that disastrous commercial flight to Miami, and the delays and inconveniences that came standard with flying coach, when she boarded the private jet chartered to take her home. And now, at cruising altitude, sitting across from a handsome movie star, sipping espresso from a porcelain cup, a cashmere throw on her lap and no packets of peanuts or granola bars anywhere in sight, Nina wondered if she'd won some cosmic lottery. It was a good thing that clawing anxiety kept things in perspective. *Too good to be true is no good at all*, her mother used to say.

They were leaving Miami to spend the night at her tiny New York apartment. When Julian had offered to fly her home and back, she'd said yes before she had a chance to think it through. Her place lacked the comforts he was accustomed to—specifically, room service, fluffy white towels and housekeeping. Her apartment was a mess. Her plants had likely withered in her absence, and there was a high chance that leftover takeout was rotting in her fridge.

There was no time to worry about it during the drive into the city. She and Julian read lines in the back seat of the town car as the driver zipped through tunnels only to slow to a crawl as traffic picked up.

"'Day. Pool. Amanda floats on her back,'" Julian said, reading from his copy of the script. "'The man who spent the night approaches, fully dressed, and tells her that he's leaving. Amanda swims to the pool's edge.

"'Man says, "This was fun, babe. Let's do this again soon."'"

"'Amanda says, "Sure. You have my number."'"

Nina shook her head. "No…"

"You don't like it?"

"I hate it." Not every one of Amanda's lines had to be a zinger, but they couldn't fall flat, either. She jotted a few notes before reading aloud to him.

"'Man says, "Gotta go, babe. Let's do this again soon." Amanda, flirting, splashes him with water, and says, "But not too soon. Okay?"'"

Nina checked Julian's reaction. He stared down at the words on the page, his jaw tight. "It's a small change that does two things," she said. "This is the opening scene, and it ought to show Amanda's cocky playfulness. Plus, it wraps up this story. The audience won't expect to see this guy again."

"Brilliant," Julian murmured. "You're such a natural, Nina."

Nina thought of all the hours she'd spent at the breakfast table, spooning cereal into her mouth and reading her mother's scripts. It was paying off.

"I should have asked for more money."

"Too late. The contract is signed," he said. "Come here and I'll make up the difference."

She released her seat belt and would have climbed onto his lap if the driver hadn't pulled up to her building.

Julian was looking out the window, assessing her tidy redbrick building on Manhattan's Lower East Side. Nina didn't wait for the driver. She pushed open the door and climbed out. The sounds of the city swirled around her. No loud, drunken tourists or reggaeton blasting from convertibles here—only the sounds of the punishing pursuit of ambition. However temporary, it was good to be home.

Nina froze at the sight of a pink upholstered couch sitting on the curb. She recognized it instantly, having spent many evenings curled up on it, drinking wine and binge-watching nineties-era sitcoms. It belonged to her friend and neighbor, decor fanatic Laetitia. What was it doing on the curb? If her friend had grown tired of it, Nina would have gladly taken it off her hands.

As Julian tipped the driver, Nina pulled out her phone, snapped a photo of the couch and sent it to Laetitia. Within seconds, her friend called, shouting, "What in the world?"

"You tell me."

"Freaking Ted! He's moving out and being a colossal jerk about it."

Ted was moving out? Hell yeah! He'd always been a colossal jerk. It had taken Laetitia this long to figure it out. But still, what was the couch doing on the curb? "Is he tossing out your stuff?"

"He bought it for me as a birthday gift," Laetitia whispered. She was at work and probably hiding in a bathroom stall for some privacy. "He knows how much I love it."

A woman walking a dog tore off her earbuds and lunged toward the couch. Before she could thank her lucky stars, Nina chased her away. "Back away from the couch, lady!" Both the woman and her cocker spaniel growled at Nina and pranced off.

On the phone Laetitia was freaking out. "Don't let anyone take my Jonathan Adler!"

"Okay, Laeti, but I can't watch over it all day."

In her frustration, Nina turned to Julian. He stood leaning against the town car, arms folded, watching her with eyes sparkling with amusement. Nina lowered the phone and got him up to speed. "It's a Jonathan Adler, and it's beautiful."

He laughed and looked up at the hazy sky. "I appreciate the irony of my having to point this out, but this is a classic example of first-world problems."

"Julian! We don't have time for your musings."

"What do you want to do? Take it to your apartment?" He walked over to the couch, grabbed an armrest and lifted it with one hand. "It's not too heavy. I could use some help, though."

Nina swooned. Her very own action hero! Calm and composed and proposing solutions that actually made sense.

The driver offered his assistance. "I used to be a mover back in the day."

"Good," Julian said. "I'll make it worth your while."

Nina raised the phone to her ear. "Don't worry, Laeti. We have a plan."

"Who's the man with the voice like honey?" Laetitia asked.

"That's not important. We'll take it up to my place and—"

"No! Take it straight to mine! Ted is still there. I'll call him and straighten this out."

Nina was grateful. Her apartment would be cramped enough with Julian in it. She didn't need a large pink couch clogging up the foyer. Only this meant she'd have to confront the rabid ex-boyfriend. Anything for a friend, right? She would do it out of the kindness of her heart. "Hey, Laeti? You owe me big-time."

"Anything. I'll do your laundry if you want me to."

"I'm thinking dinner and drinks when I get back."

"Get back from where? You just got back."

"Can't get into it now! I'll fill you in later."

Nina ended the call and addressed her troops. "Okay, guys. We're taking it up to the third floor, apartment 3C. I'll hold the service elevator."

"Nice building," Julian observed as he carried his end of the couch through the lobby.

Holding the elevator as promised, Nina tried to see the space through the eyes of a millionaire movie star. It was well lit and clean. The frosted glass and gold accents did very little to elevate the plain design. "I'm sure you've lived in much nicer places."

"I have." He looked at her for a bit as if gauging if he should say more. Those quiet eyes always got to her. "But I've also lived in my car, so make what you want out of that."

Nina clutched the pair of bolster pillows to her chest. Why was she still struggling to see Julian as an ordinary person? She kept tripping over the same low wire. He was not an action hero or a movie star. He was just a guy who didn't hesitate to help lift a friend's couch off the curb.

He and the driver tried out different ways to fit the couch into the elevator until they got it right. On the ride up, he asked if Laetitia was a good friend of hers.

"Good enough," she said. "We binged an entire season of *Riverside Rescue* on this." Nina patted the couch standing upright between them. "That makes it worth saving, don't you think?"

Julian looked doubtful. "That's one opinion."

They reached the third floor. After some maneuvering, he and the driver moved the couch into the hall. She led them to Laetitia's door then swiveled around to give Julian a pointed look. "There's probably going to be some drama. I'll handle it."

"Whatever you say."

He backed away and leaned against the wall. Nina knocked on the apartment door. It wasn't locked and swung open. Ted looked up from a pile of boxes stacked like a pyramid where the couch should have been.

"Laetitia called," he said flatly. "Sorry for your wasted effort, but you're not bringing that thing in here. It's my couch. I bought it. I tossed it out. There's no law against it."

Judge Judy would have laughed that argument out of small claims court. "It was a gift, Ted."

"Mind your own business," Ted said. "And shut the door on your way out."

Nina was prepared for a little bit of back-and-forth, but not this stonewalling. At a loss, she turned to Julian. She hated to be the girl who got her boyfriend to fight her battles, but Julian wasn't her boyfriend, so it didn't count. He responded to her silent plea with a wink. "Guess we'll do it my way."

She nodded and went to stand next to the driver, who, to his credit, had not lost his professional composure. Julian didn't move. He stayed as he was, leaning against the wall, and called out to Ted, "How do you want to do this?"

Gone were the accent and any gentlemanly manners. He'd transformed into his on-screen persona. Nina hated to admit it, but it was hot.

"Hey, Nina!" Ted said, waving a duct tape dispenser. "Where'd you get this impersonator? Vegas?"

Julian pushed off the wall and crowded the doorway. "I'm bringing in this couch. It would be a mistake to try to stop me. And if it lands on the curb again, I'll know. We won't be far." He turned to Nina. "Where's your apartment?"

"Ted knows," Nina said. "I'm down the hall. Apartment 3D."

Julian slipped out of character, a mischievous grin spreading across his face. "Three D? Really? Will we need special glasses?"

The man was a child! "Ha-ha! Three D! So funny! Could you wrap this up, please?"

He turned to Ted and resumed his admonishment. "Look. If I have to carry this couch, or anything else, back up here, you and I will have a problem."

Ted's reaction was staggered. He pinned a blank stare on Julian, puffed out his chest, rolled his hands into fists and stretched to his full height. It was comical to watch.

Julian could snap the stockbroker in two, but Nina knew he wouldn't.

"Are we going to have a problem, Ted?" Julian asked.

Ted deflated. "To hell with it. I don't care."

"Good man."

After Laetitia's couch was back in its place and the driver well compensated, Nina welcomed Julian to her apartment. She liked her place. It was small, a studio, but it didn't lack character. The wood parquet floors were beautiful. The living area was bright thanks to tall windows with immediate views of the tops of oak trees and a row of redbrick buildings farther down the street. Julian walked around in circles, commenting on framed photographs and book collections. Nina did not need 3D glasses to see him in all his complexity. He was a beautiful man, but he was more than that. He was smart, funny, generous, insightful and fair. He was tender, gentle, understanding… She saw him, and he *was* beautiful.

"Goldie, what are you overthinking now?"

He came to stand before her, hands low on his hips. Apparently, he didn't need special glasses to see her, either.

"I'm *thinking* this feels just right."

Julian wrapped her in his arms. It was everything and it was not enough. Nina needed to feel his skin against hers. She stepped back, unbuckled her jeans and shimmied to better push the stiff denim over her hips.

"What are you doing?" he asked.

"We're home," she said. "Time to slip into something more comfortable."

*Journal Entry*

*"May I taste?"*

*I nod, because the words won't come. He presses me against the door and hunches low. I readily hook*

*a knee over his shoulder, but when his tongue meets
my tender skin, I'm not prepared for the rush... I have
to tug at his hair to keep from crying out.*

*We haven't made it to the bed.*

# Fifteen

Cozy in her bed, limbs intertwined, Julian and Nina got back to work. Nina seemed giddy to be reunited with her laptop. She had hugged it to her chest and spun around like Maria in the opening credits of *The Sound of Music*. And now she leaned on his shoulder as they scrolled through actor profiles, looking to round out the cast. Julian was partial to a French actor, Vincent Gabriel, winner of a César and a BAFTA, to play the role of Luke's accomplice. If he were honest, Vincent would probably shine in the role of Luke—if he weren't hogging it for himself. Nina was a foreign film buff, and she melted at the mention of Vincent's name.

Julian pulled away from her. "What was that?"

"What was what?"

"You sighed."

"You're imagining things."

"Do you sigh at the mention of my name?" he asked.

"I've cried out your name at three in the morning," Nina said. "What more do you want?"

"More!"

She tossed her copy of the script to the floor. Its pages were bloodied with red ink. "Sorry. I don't have much more to give."

"Not sure I believe that, Goldie. I'll have to double my efforts tonight."

He reached for his phone to check the time. It was 10:35 p.m. and he had two missed calls—from a studio executive in California.

* * *

Eleven p.m. Julian was still on the phone, arguing with the executive. The production company was backing out from its agreement to fund *Midnight Sun*.

"You hired an unknown to revise the script and Francisco Cortes to direct. There's a stable of hotshot directors to choose from, and you went with Cortes."

"Frank has a vision—"

"I'm sure he does. He's not the right person to direct this film."

Julian was pacing a hole into Nina's wood floors. "I won't drop him."

"We're not asking you to. We're pulling funding from the film, and we wish you luck."

"You're making a mistake."

"Sorry, Knight. It's done."

Straightaway, Julian got Frank on the phone. Frank answered on the hundredth ring, his voice raspy. "At this hour it better be important."

"Spring Pictures dropped us."

"For what reason?"

Julian hesitated. "It doesn't matter."

"How much were they in for?"

"Half the budget."

Frank fell quiet, and Julian did, too. They were screwed, and they both knew it. Funding from an established production house would lend the film clout. What the hell were they going to do now?

Frank had the answer. "I'll put up the money."

"Don't do this."

"I've always wanted to produce. If we stick to our budget, we can manage. And I can bring in some very rich people who've been dying to get into the movie business."

Julian went weak with relief and leaned against Nina's breakfast bar. She was folding clothes into her suitcase, pretending not to eavesdrop. He hoped she hadn't overheard the producer taking him to task for hiring her. It was the one decision he would not overturn. He needed her. They worked well together. More than that, she made work fun and challenging. He did not need Hollywood's seal of approval on this.

"I have one condition."

Julian ran a hand through his hair. "You and your bloody conditions, Frank."

"I come aboard as a coproducer and you take the reins."

"I don't follow."

"This is your movie to direct. You know it."

"Like hell I do."

"Trust me, Julian," Frank said. "I know this business. It runs on stories. This is *your* comeback story, not mine. Julian Knight writes and directs his first feature film. How does that sound?"

It sounded so good, Julian's chest ached, but assuming the role of director scared him to death. The best directors he'd worked with were creative geniuses. That wasn't him.

"I know you can do it," Frank said. "And I know you *want* to do it. Take a chance. What do you have to lose?"

"Your money."

"There's more to life than money."

This paternal side to Francisco Cortes was endearing. "Do you have kids, Frank?"

"More than a few." He laughed. "Can you tell?"

Julian made up his mind. He'd do it under one condition. "I'm not acting in a film I'm directing. We'd have to find someone to play the part of Luke."

He had to draw the line somewhere. As the writer, director and producer, all the trappings of a vanity project were present and accounted for. Besides, he wouldn't have the time. He had two monumental tasks ahead: one, to deliver a film on time and on budget, and two, to coax subtle and nuanced performances from the cast. The second goal was arguably the most important. His acting skills were limited, and this film was so different from anything he'd ever been involved in. He'd never had an acting job that didn't involve a gun as a prop.

"Agreed," Frank said. "But that's a question for another day. I'm going back to sleep."

"Did I wake you, Dad?"

"I'll tell you what I tell my kids, Julian. Unless you're calling from jail, don't call me after 10:00 p.m."

"Gotcha."

Julian slid his phone across the countertop and pressed his forehead against the cool granite. "Nina," he groaned. "I need your loving."

"I've got something better." She walked into the kitchen, pulled a bottle out of the freezer and grabbed a couple glasses from the cupboard. "What was all that about?"

"The studio dropped us. Frank is producing. I'm directing and dropping the role of Luke." He looked down at the glass she put before him. "I'm going to need more vodka than this."

She splashed more Grey Goose in his glass. "I don't know. Sounds perfect to me. Everything is shaking into place."

*This woman...* In an oversize concert T-shirt and fuzzy slippers, hair in a topknot, she was at ease in her home. That overall glow was the result of his handiwork, and he was proud of it. The T-shirt, though, was a relic from the past. He'd asked if she was a fan of Bruce Springsteen. Although she was a fan, she confessed that the T-shirt belonged to an ex.

"Since everyone seems to be expanding their roles, maybe I should, too."

"Would you like to try acting? We could find you a role."

"No, Julian," she said. "I'm not a performer. I'm a storyteller."

She spoke with the confidence of a lifetime of soul searching, pen to paper, first filling countless pretty diaries with locks, then spiral-bound notebooks and now leather-bound journals. Julian admired this about her above all.

"You hired me to patch up the dialogue, but I could do more with the material if you trust me."

"Do what you want with it. I trust you more than myself." He had rushed to reassure her, only now he was curious as to what she had in mind. "What are your thoughts?"

"The Amanda story arc needs an overhaul."

"Overhaul?" He'd expected a tweak here and there, not an overhaul. "Are you sure?"

"She's either rebelling against her father, competing with her brother or reacting to Luke. She needs an arc independent of the men in her life."

"How about you write a monologue to address this?"

She rolled her eyes at him. "You'd have her stand on a mountain and preach the gospel of feminism?"

"I see your point." Amanda was the lead, and he wanted her role to be as strong as possible. He wouldn't want to be accused of failing another female character. On the other hand, there was a risk that pulling on one thread could unravel the whole story. "You think it's possible to undertake a massive overhaul with our time constraints?"

"I'll work within the frame of the story," she said. "Nothing else has to change. I know your vision, and I respect it."

"It's still a lot of work. I'd have to bring you on as a partner and give you on-screen credit. That's how it works with original screenplays."

She fidgeted with a matching salt and pepper shaker set. Julian wished she didn't look so nervous. He'd agree to anything if it meant they could work together. Their long discussions into the night, debating ideas, meant something to him. That was a revelation to him. He'd been so protective of this project in the past.

"Screenplay by Julian L. Knight and Nina Taylor," he said. "Don't you like the sound of that?"

"Please don't think I'm trying to hijack your project."

"I don't," he said. "You, on the other hand, may want to overthink this. Do you *really* want your name linked to mine?"

A crease forged between her brows. "Why wouldn't I?"

Julian's gaze fell to the counter, catching the flecks of gold in the earth-toned granite. "I don't expect the critics will be lining up to applaud my efforts. They're going to trash it."

She inched closer to him. Their heads were nearly touching. "Not if it's good. They may never gush over it, but they can't trash it if it's good."

He kissed the tip of her nose. "Is it…good?"

She twisted her lips to one side. "As it is? Pretty good."

That wasn't good enough. "If we partner up, I'd have to pay you more."

"I'm not in it for money."

Julian sipped his vodka. "You're more principled than I am."

He wasn't expecting to make any money from his first film. Breaking even and a few positive reviews were the best he could hope for. He considered it an investment, a way to reset his image and establish himself as a serious filmmaker.

She took his glass from him, raised it to her lips and sipped, her expression vacant. "I went to Miami to fulfill one of my mother's dreams. Doing this sort of work fulfills one of my own."

It made sense. She loved cinema. She loved writing. Here was a chance to combine those two loves.

She took another sip and set the glass down. "You know what?"

"What?"

"I'm in it for money, too. I want to partner with you, and I want to get paid. This *is* a business."

Now they were on the same page. "I think we're going to work well together."

Her lips curled in the sort of smile she saved just for him. "How would you feel if I stuck around during production? I'd love to see the director at work."

"Is it okay if the director rests his head on your lap when he's losing his grip?"

She circled the breakfast bar and hugged him from behind, resting her cheek on the space between his shoulder blades. "Don't worry. You can do this."

"*We* can do this." Did he have to remind her that she was in this up to her teeth?

"Yeah, yeah," she said, and returned to her packing.

Julian followed her into the bathroom. It was a decent size by New York standards. It did not compare to the marble and brass sanctuary they'd left behind. There was only one sink, and the walk-in shower wouldn't fit two. It had rained earlier, and the streetlights bled into the small water-stained window.

"Are you almost done packing?" he asked.

"Nowhere close." She opened the medicine cabinet and pulled out an assortment of vials and jars. "You keep me busy, Mr. Knight."

"Would you like to stay one more night? There's no rush."

"You...wouldn't mind?"

"Not at all." Spending time away from the hotel was good for them. It took them out of the fantasy and put them squarely in real life. "Plus, I should keep an eye on Ted."

"Someone has to," she said. Earlier, she'd showed him

a social media post that had them both in stitches. *Is that #JLK hauling a pink couch into my BFF's building...or am I still drunk?*

"So, it's settled."

She opened a drawer and pulled out a strip of Trojans. "Should I pack these, too?"

"Sure." Julian reached out and tugged at her T-shirt. "Consider leaving this behind, and any other of your former lovers' clothing."

"But the cotton is so soft!" she protested.

He gathered the hem of the tee and gently tugged it over her head. Her past lovers could choke on their misery. Those breasts, those hips, that body and all that soft skin were his.

She touched the tip of a finger to his chin. "I love the way you look at me."

"I'm not thinking loving thoughts," he warned.

"Good." She ripped off a condom packet from the strip. He tried to take it from her, but she was too quick. "Oh, please. Allow me."

Earlier, they'd played and teased each other. This time, Julian cut out the superfluous. His desire filled him with urgent need. He slid her thin panties down to her ankles then turned her around. She tilted forward, pressing her palms to the wall.

They really did work well together.

# Sixteen

The simplest and most pleasurable way to rouse Nina from sleep was to press kisses to the back of her knees. It was daybreak in Miami, and the lavish hotel room was cloaked in shadows. Julian leaned over Nina's sleeping body and rubbed his chin, rough with stubble, into the softness of her thigh until she stirred and lifted her head off the pillow. Her eyes shone black in the darkness. Groggy still, she extended a hand, an invitation. "Come back to bed."

He was tempted, but he had other plans for her. "Let's go for a swim."

She raised herself on one elbow. "Now?"

"Trust me. You'll like this."

She kicked back the sheets, murmuring something about being too sleepy to argue. Minutes later, she came out of the bathroom in a simple black bikini. She reached for a silk tunic draped over the back of an armchair. "Ready."

"Are you sure that's all you'll need?"

"Oh, right." She found her flip-flops and slipped them on.

"We're going to stay awhile," he said.

She went into the bathroom for a bottle of sunscreen. "Okay. Ready."

Julian crossed the room to retrieve her weekender bag hanging from a peg in the closet and tossed it to her. "You'll need a change of clothes."

"Oh!" She brightened. "You should have said so." She did a quick job of packing. "Almost done."

Julian watched as she darted from the nightstand to the writing desk. Then with a sigh of frustration, she grabbed her purse and dumped the contents on the bench at the foot of the bed.

Julian checked his watch. He wanted to head out early. "What are you looking for?"

"My…um…nothing…" Although she'd stopped fretting, her brown eyes betrayed her worry. "It's not important."

"If it's not important, forget it. Let's go!"

Pete brought the car around. Julian raised the partition between the front and back seats as he had started to do whenever Nina was in the car. Two hours later, they pulled up to mile marker thirty-three on the Overseas Highway. Julian had reserved a simple boat, a twenty-foot Sportcraft with a Bimini top. He extended a hand to help her aboard. She turned to him, her face flush with delight. "Julian, where are you taking me?"

"I'll be honest. I have no idea."

"Do you know how to drive this?"

He laughed. "Just climb aboard."

Julian didn't have a final destination in mind. He was motivated by the need to escape the hotel. They'd been back in Miami for weeks now and, in a way, Sand Castle was home. Since their return, they had fallen into an easy rhythm, starting the day with conference calls with their financiers, production team or casting agent. Afterward, they parted ways. She stayed in, chained to her writing desk, wrist braces in place. He left to scout locations, approve props or hold auditions. Evenings, after dinner, they lingered at the table. Nina would give him her honest opinion on everything from costumes to set design.

Everything was shaking into place, just as she'd said. Nina had turned in a brilliant script, elevating his basic story to a richer and more nuanced one. Bettina signed on for the part of Amanda and went so far as to recommend Pierce Alexander for the role of Luke.

"Anything you'd like to tell me about you and Pierce?" he'd asked Bettina.

"Anything you'd like to tell me about the woman you've been photographed with all over Miami?"

"I can tell you this—the rumors are true."

"You won't find any rumors about Pierce and me. We're discreet."

"I'm happy for you, Betty."

Julian was just about happy for everyone—full stop. He was a barrel of joy, his work life and private life running on all cylinders. But at the moment, he and his lady needed a break.

After they'd sailed out a mile or so, Julian chose to drop anchor over a reef bathed in turquoise waters. Nina stood on deck, taking in the view. Her black hair was in her signature braid. Tendrils broke free and played in the breeze. He slipped off the hair tie at the end and loosed the three sections. Her hair broke into cascading waves down her back. He thanked God that his camera was at hand. He asked her to stand still and snapped a few photos, although he'd never forget how she looked standing there in the fresh morning light.

She leaned over the rail. "Think we can dive off?"

"I expect you to, my little mermaid."

"I don't know if you picked up on this, but I'm not a world-class swimmer."

She stripped off her silk tunic, revealing taut toffee-brown skin. Julian dropped the camera and reached for her. He toyed with the ties of her bikini bottom. "May I?"

She slapped his hand away. "What if they see us?"

"Who?" He struggled to spot a single sign of human life in any direction.

"I don't know. Pete or some photographer lurking somewhere."

At this point, Julian couldn't just chalk her concerns to paranoia. He had taken extra precautions with this outing and had not provided Pete, or anyone, with an advance itinerary. "We've left Pete on land." He tested the clasp of the bra. "Shouldn't we free these beauties? They've been cooped up for so long. They need the sun."

She tossed her head back and laughed. Her large black sunglasses slipped out of her hair and tumbled onto the deck floor. "They're not cooped up. They're fine!"

In order to convince her, Julian would have to put skin in the game. He stepped out of his shorts and dived head-first into the water. He braced himself for the frigid bite of the Pacific, except the bay was warm and welcoming. He broke the surface in time to catch Nina slipping off her bikini top. She dived in after him, the breeze making a sail out of her loose hair.

Julian swam over and caught up with her beneath the surface. While his hands explored her slick body, he closed his mouth on one of her tight nipples. He sucked hard until a faint plea escaped her. Then he kissed her full lips.

When he broke away, she splashed him with water. "Happy now?"

Julian turned his face up to the sun. "I may die of happiness!"

She giggled. "I love you when you're like this."

"Like what?" he asked, swimming circles around her.

"Playful, wild, sexy."

"Yeah?" What he said next surprised them both. "I think I love you, period."

Nina stared at him, blinking. Drops of water clung to her long lashes. She was stunningly beautiful. Julian took a deep breath, pacing himself before he did something crazy like propose marriage.

She swam to him and wrapped her limbs around his body like an octopus, gripping tight. He held her close and they bobbed in the water, the sun hard on their shoulders. She whispered in his ear, "You only think you do?"

Looking for a way to avoid the question, he kissed the spot where a vein pulsed at her neck.

She shivered despite the heat. "Let me know when you're sure. Okay?"

He slipped a hand into her bikini bottom. "Let me know when you're close."

They were going to do playful, wild and sexy things all day. That was the plan.

Nina was overwhelmed with emotion. When she felt like this (but when had she ever felt like this?), the impulse to write was strong. Only, she could not find her journal. It had been missing for weeks. She was pretty sure she'd left it in New York. But what to do in the meantime? She was so methodical and hated to start a new journal before filling the pages of an old one.

They stopped for a late lunch at a seafood shack. The place was nearly empty. Over conch fritters and beer, they talked awhile. When Julian left for the men's room, Nina borrowed a pen from the waitress and jotted on the back of a paper menu.

*Journal Entry*
  *It's love. It's love. It's love.*

# Seventeen

On the first day of October, Julian gathered the full cast at Sand Castle for the first read-through. With Grace's blessing, they'd taken over the hotel. She gave them permission to film a total of five scenes on-site and to use the cigar room for rehearsals and meetings through preproduction. The offer, however, wasn't without conditions. Frank had promised to throw a blowout wrap party on-site.

The cigar room, or Knight's Landing, as Nina called it, was fitted with a long buffet table to accommodate the cast and production staff. Julian stood at the head of the table to welcome them all. Before he uttered a word, he glanced down at Nina, seated to his right, and she nodded her encouragement. They'd been on this journey together since the start. She might be the only person in the room who saw through his mask of self-confidence, and that was saying something considering an ex-girlfriend was present.

Julian cleared his throat. "Everyone, welcome to our first table read."

The cinematographer, who had flown in from New Hampshire a few days early to "get some fishing in," raised his hand. Eyeing the custom humidors built into the walls, he said, "Will you be handing out cigars at the end of the day?"

Everyone laughed, and the ice wall of tension rising in him shattered. Every person at the table was a seasoned professional. If he could trust them and the process—if he could trust himself—things might work out.

"My writing partner, Nina, and I have a clear vision for this film, and we hope it's one you share. We've labored over every word and, for that reason, I ask that you keep to the script as much as possible. Outside that, as a director, I'm interested in the choices you'll make to bring these characters to life. Pierce, thank you for playing our charismatic con man. You're the man for the job." More laughter erupted. "And, Bettina…" Julian turned to face the woman who had shaped his past and who had a role in his future. But no sooner than he'd said her name, the general mood flattened. It was all the proof he needed to confirm his suspicions. Everyone, excluding Nina, doubted they could work together. He had to address those doubts head-on. "There's no one else I would have wanted to play Amanda. You were my first and only choice. I thank you for trusting me."

All eyes were on Bettina now. She never wasted an opportunity to shine. Addressing the room, she said, "Guys, you may not know this, but Julian and I have a bit of history." Her words were met with the low rumble of laughter. "I can vouch for him. We're in capable hands. Plus we've got a great script. And let's be honest, shooting in Miami isn't exactly a hardship. So, let's do this. Okay?"

Julian met and kept her gaze for a brief moment, hoping to communicate his gratitude. She lowered her eyes and studied her impeccably manicured nails, code that she was ready to move on. Julian clasped his hands together. "We've got twenty-eight days to wrap this up. Let's do this."

He lowered himself in his seat and straightaway reached for Nina's hand under the table. She mingled her fingers with his. As things stood, Julian was hopeful that he and Bettina would crack on and get the job done. But he was certain that he and Nina had a future.

Julian flipped open his copy of the script. "'Day. Pool. Amanda floats on her back. The man who spent the night approaches, fully dressed, and tells her that he's leaving. Amanda swims to the pool's edge.'"

The actor read his lines. "'Gotta go, babe. Let's do this again soon.'"

Bettina read hers with the perfect mix of flirtatiousness and arrogance. "'But not too soon. Okay?'"

At the first break, Nina had excused herself and left the room. When she didn't return, Julian delayed starting up again and went after her. Something about her rod-stiff posture when she'd walked out made him worry. He found her sitting alone in the garden, silently sobbing. He rushed to her.

"What's the matter, love?" he said, kneeling before her. "Why are you crying?"

She spoke through her hands. "I'm not crying."

"Then what's all this?"

"I don't know."

He pried her hands away from her face and lifted her chin to inspect her face. Her brown eyes were dry, but he wasn't reassured. She might not be crying, but she certainly was trembling. He cupped her face and kissed her eyelids. Her eyelashes fluttered against his lips.

"Tell me what's wrong," he whispered.

"That was a lot," she said.

"The table read? You don't think it's going well?"

"No!" She wrapped her arms around his neck. "It's going great, better than I could have imagined."

He stroked her hair. "Then what is it?"

"I've never experienced anything like this," she said. "A lot of the time it's just me alone with my computer and the voices in my head. Today it felt like I belonged to something, and I...don't know."

"Oh, love. Come here." He gathered her trembling body in his arms. He'd never seen her this way, and it tore him up. "You belong."

She belonged to him, but he couldn't say that without freaking her out.

"Sorry." She extracted herself from his embrace. "I didn't expect to get so emotional."

"Don't worry. I understand."

He pulled her up to her feet. She looked up at him, a glint of pride in her yes. "You were good in there," she said. "Really good."

"I may just be the next Scorsese."

"Oh, God! Help me!"

She was her playful self again, and Julian exhaled with relief. His world had spun off its axis just now. He didn't care if he had a room full of people waiting—he would have taken all the time in the world to get her to smile again.

She raised herself on the tips of her toes and kissed him. "Thank you."

"No, love, no." Julian buried his face in her hair. She smelled sweeter than any flower in the garden. "Thank you. Thank you. Thank you."

# Eighteen

A mid-October tropical storm caused *Midnight Sun* to wrap a day late. But once Julian had called it a wrap late on a Thursday afternoon, it was a party. The cast, crew and friends they'd made during the shoot gathered by the pool. The hotel staff was prepared, marching out with mini-bottles of Piper-Heidsieck fitted with straws and cigars for anyone who cared to smoke. The rollout happened under Grace's hawkish eye, her mouth gathered in a tight frown.

Nina approached her. "You must be happy to have us out of your hair soon."

Julian had booked the entire hotel, filling every room with the cast and heads of each creative department in order to have the privacy and freedom needed to film. Pretty soon the caravan would clear out. Nina was feeling anxious about it. She and Julian had not discussed the future. They'd been too busy. During filming, she'd stepped in as the script manager, making sure the actors kept to their lines and monitoring for lapses in continuity. This had given her a front seat to all the action. It had been an exhilarating experience, but it was over. So now what?

"Not really," Grace said.

"Are you saying you'll miss us?" Nina exclaimed. "Don't get sentimental on me now!"

"I would never." She folded her arms across her chest. "I'm nearing the end of an era. It's going to be an adjustment."

Nina felt sure there was more Grace wanted to say, but she was trapped in her role of mistress of the manor. "Come with me."

Grace slipped her a sharp glance. "Where to?"

"Let's go for a walk."

"Impossible. I'm working."

"This place runs itself. Come out for a walk with me. When was the last time you've been to the beach? And it's just across the street!"

Grace grunted, and Nina took it as a yes. She swiped two minibottles of champagne off a tray, threaded an arm around Grace's and dragged her all the way to the front gates.

"We'll be right back," Nina said to the guards.

"And if we're not, send for me," Grace added.

As soon as they made it across Ocean Drive, Grace Guzman loosened up. She slipped off her tailored cherry-red jacket. Nina had no trouble convincing her to kick off her stilettos, and together they trekked across the sand toward the shore. It was sunset, and the surf roared at their feet.

"Give me that bottle," Grace said.

"Yes, ma'am." Nina handed her a minibottle and raised her own. "Cheers?"

"I have nothing to be cheery about," she said flatly. *"¡Salud!"*

Nina decided to ask the question that had been burning inside her for months now. "Exactly what is your problem?"

"Men are my problem," she said. "My divorce is final, and my father has decided to sell the hotel."

"You're selling the Sand Castle?" Nina cried. "Why?"

"We love it, but it's a money pit. I'm going to have a hard time letting go."

So much made sense now. The way they'd catered to Julian *and* his cast *and* his crew *and* tolerated the imposed inconvenience of hours of filming, it all finally made sense. No wonder she'd kicked Nina out of the Oasis the instant a Hollywood star came calling. The hotel needed the business.

"Sorry about the divorce," Nina said, ashamed for having skipped over such a seismic life event in the first place.

"Actually, I'll drink to that." Grace raised her bottle. "Cheers!"

"That's the spirit." She wished that she and Grace had met under different circumstances. They might've become friends. She had one more question. She was pushing it, but the bubbly made her bold. "Do you think you and Francisco Cortes could be a thing?"

"I don't need a *thing*," Grace said. "Not right now."

"But you could use some company," Nina said. "Who will drink with you in the garden when I'm gone?"

"How about you and Mr. Knight?"

"What about us?" She turned to face the ocean. So much for being bold.

"I'm sorry. As a rule, I don't comment on the hotel guests' private affairs."

"It's okay. That's why I brought you out here. You can forget your rules."

"I'll say this—people come to Miami to fool around. It rarely means anything. Usually, it ends with regret."

The truth roared in Nina's ears as loud as the surf. She and Julian were not fooling around. If their affair ended tomorrow, she would not regret one sun-filled day, one night spent in his arms. But she did not want it to end. Today was particularly tough, because what were they celebrating if not the end?

"Now I've made you cry!" Grace cursed. "I should have stuck to the rules."

"Am I crying?" Nina wiped her cheeks with the back of her hand.

"I was going to say that you two look like the real deal. I've seen enough nonsense to know the difference."

Hope crashed into Nina with the force of the waves. Validation from an impartial and dispassionate observer such as Grace was priceless. It meant that she hadn't imagined this grand love affair. It wasn't all in her head. And what a relief! She was so in love with Julian, so wildly in love with him, she could not stand to lose him.

Nina couldn't overthink her present predicament. Grace was smiling at her, and it was distracting as hell. It was the first time the woman had smiled at her with genuine warmth, and it was luminous. If she weren't careful, she might fall in love with Grace.

When they got back to Sand Castle, she and Grace parted ways. The manager hurried off to her office, and Nina set out to find Julian. The party was unraveling. Bettina and Pierce had slipped away earlier with a bottle of champagne. Everyone else was slumped on lounge beds, partied out. Julian, however, had not lost steam. He stood with a foot propped up on a chair, telling a story to a captive audience. Seeing him this loose and animated made her realize just how much pressure he must have been under these past months.

She approached, and he drew her close and dipped her into a mock Hollywood kiss. Nina played along, swooning like a screen siren. Then he gazed into her eyes. "I think we're done here."

Nina knew what he meant, but wished he'd phrased it differently. She didn't protest when he carried her off to the elevator.

"To think I hated this tin can when I first got here," he said. "Look how handy it's been. Do you remember the first time we did this?"

"I coughed up on your shirt."

"And I was completely charmed." He squeezed her tighter. "It must be this house. It has powers."

"Grace's family will be selling it soon. Maybe you should buy, rename the place Knight's Landing."

"I love this house, but I don't ever want to be here without you."

The elevator stopped, and the doors slid open. Julian carried her to the door, over the threshold and into the bedroom. He dropped her unceremoniously on the bed and plopped down alongside her. He would break any bed he owned; Nina was sure of it.

Nina rolled onto her side and raked her fingers through his hair. Eyes shut, expression soft, his profile remained strong and defined—the not-so-classic matinee idol. She was not a performer, but she would gladly play the role of his screen siren. There really wasn't much she wouldn't do for him. That included tossing her pride aside and opening up to him. "I have to tell you something."

Eyes closed, he said, "What's that, love?"

Nina called to the angels of the fresco for strength one last time. "I may be in love with you."

He slid her a look, eyes brimming with equal parts affection and amusement. She'd hedged and he knew it. "Want to tell me when you're sure?"

Her answer was buried somewhere deep in her kiss.

# Nineteen

What was next for them?

The question kept Julian up well after Nina had fallen asleep, her cheek pressed to his chest. When she breathed, her breasts pressed into his ribs. Gradually his breathing synced with hers. In every way they were one, except they lived on opposite coasts.

Last night they'd cleared one hurdle—their feelings for each other were more or less clear. Where were they going to live? He was making plans to return to California in a week to get on with editing. Would she come? Maybe she could be persuaded to fly out with him. She could write anywhere; wasn't that what she'd said? His house on the Hills wasn't as romantic as this old mansion that had become their home, but it offered plenty of space for her to spread out pages on the floor, and the view from his desk was inspiring.

Julian's phone buzzed on the nightstand, and the screen glowed green in the night. He ignored it. He was too comfortable, and he didn't want to wake Nina. Then the damn thing buzzed again and again and again. Nina moaned in her sleep and rolled onto her back. He snatched the phone and tapped on the screen to silence it. It was two in the morning, and he had a missed call from his publicist and five text messages from Kat.

Julian tossed back the duvet and swung his legs over the edge of the bed, his insides twisting with apprehension. He'd been on a high! Wrapping the movie on time if not on budget, earning the respect of the actors and the crew, collaborating with Frank—these were all things he was proud of. Getting to share the experience with the woman he loved was a surprise gift that he wasn't sure he deserved. He was willing to go to the ends to defend this newfound happiness. He remembered his life before, and he wasn't going back.

He took the phone into the bathroom, and instead of wasting time scrolling through the messages, he called Kat. She answered straightaway.

"Hey. What's going on?"

"Didn't you read my texts?"

"No. I was asleep."

"Is *she* with you?"

It was too late to play these games. "What are you getting at?"

"We need to speak privately."

"It's all clear, just talk to me."

"All right. Nina Taylor kept detailed notes of your time together. Were you aware?"

"She's a writer."

"Intimate notes, Julian."

He breathed out through a fisted hand, forcing his brain to work. He tried coming up with the worst-case scenario. "She keeps a diary."

"To later publish as books."

"That's not why she does it."

Nina had hated the experience of publishing a memoir—that much he knew. She was reluctant to write another. Besides, she didn't have to. Screenwriting credits on your résumé had a way of widening your options.

"I'm looking at her bio. She's a memoirist. That's it. Sure, she used to work at a magazine, but that was a long time ago."

"Why are you looking at her bio? What happened?"

His temper flared so rarely, but everything about this conversation was pissing him off.

"An excerpt of her diary was published on Celebrity-Soup.com."

He processed this, the gears of his brain grinding painfully slowly. "How did it get out?"

"No one knows for sure, but I need you to consider that she leaked it."

"She didn't."

"How do you know?"

"I know."

An excerpt of her diary had been published on a gossip site. That was all they knew so far. But Julian knew how this worked. They would need someone to blame, someone to cast as a villain.

"Julian, you don't know this woman. She's wiggled her way into your life, and now she's writing about it. You didn't make her sign anything. She'll probably get a book deal."

"Kat." His voice cut into the silence of the bathroom. "Be careful what you say about Nina."

"If I crossed a line, I'm sorry."

"I don't need an apology. I need you to understand that she is not some random woman who wiggled her way into anything."

He'd lured Nina into his world, a world populated with paparazzi and gossip columnists. He would shield her anyway he could. She wasn't an attention seeker. She was a writer, a thinker and a private person. He would not let anyone insult or degrade her.

"Read the excerpt and see for yourself," Kat said. "I sent you the link."

"Thanks, Kat," he mumbled. "Sorry I jumped down your throat."

"Let's talk again in the morning with cooler heads."

Julian ended the call. He scrolled his messages until he found the link to the website post. The title alone turned his stomach sour. *One Hot Knight in Miami.* Once again, his private life was served up for entertainment. He scrolled down and started reading. The words jumped at him. *"May I taste?"* Julian heard the tap on the bathroom door, but he couldn't stop reading. *When his tongue meets my tender skin, I'm not prepared for the rush... We haven't made it to the bed.*

Intimate details.

# Twenty

Nina was alone in bed. She was sure of it even before she opened her eyes to heavy darkness. Julian was in the bathroom arguing with someone over the phone. When silence settled in, she slipped out of bed and tapped on the bathroom door. No answer. She called out his name. Nothing. She opened the door a crack. "Everything okay?"

He was staring intently at his phone, and when he looked up at her, the glow from the small screen gave him an eerie look.

"Julian, what's the matter?"

He handed her the phone. "Explain this to me."

"Explain what?"

She glanced at the screen, more concerned with the tight set of his jaw than any clandestine photo or provocative tweet. But she recognized the words as her own. *He presses me against the door and hunches low.* "What's this?"

"An excerpt from your journal."

Nina felt a tightening in her gut. She was going to be sick.

"How did it end up online?" he asked.

"I don't know!" she cried. "You tell me!"

"Did you leak it?" Those four words sent Nina reeling. She smacked his phone onto the counter and backed out of the doorway. He followed her into the bedroom. His voice was low when he asked the follow-up question. "Did they pay you?"

Each word was a blow, and he wouldn't shut up.

"I need to hear you say it. Then we'll figure out what to do."

She switched on the lights in the bedroom to better confront him. "You think I sold our story for money?"

"I don't. But since we don't have a confidentiality agreement, I have to ask."

"A confidentiality agreement?"

"I know. It sounds terrible, but it's more common than you'd think."

On the first day they'd met, they'd hashed out an agreement. She'd promised not to write about him or anything that happened between them. She reminded him of her promise. His silence told her that it wasn't enough. There was nothing he could add to or subtract from the equation to change the value of this revelation. Her promise, her *word*, was not enough.

Alarm bells were ringing in the back of her head. She would not waste her breath trying to reassure Julian. She had to look out for herself. Someone had stolen her diary. How did they get it? Who had it now? How many people were reading, sharing and tweeting her words at this moment?

She paced around the room. Soon Julian was doing the same. They circled each other.

"Where's the notebook?" he said. "Let's see it."

She opened the nightstand and desk drawers, hoping her journal would magically appear. "It's not here. To be honest, it's been missing for weeks."

He faced her. "Your notebook is missing? And you said nothing?"

"I asked the front desk if anyone had returned a missing journal. To be honest, I figured it would turn up."

"Let me understand. You kept a detailed record of everything we said and did together and took no measures to protect it?"

Her breath was coming hard and fast. Legal agreements and records... Who was this man? "We're talking about a *diary*, a place for my private thoughts. With or without any mention of you, I would have protected it. My diaries are private. I don't share them with anyone."

"Except you do," he said. "You turn them into books."

Nina's anger snapped. "Get out."

"Calm down. We can talk this through."

"I *am* calm. And I want you out."

"Where do you want me to go? It's the middle of the night."

"There's a pullout couch in the other room," she said. "Don't worry. It's comfortable."

Julian leaned against a chest of drawers. He'd gone pale under his honey-brown complexion. Nina turned away. Although he had hurt her, she could not bear to see him in pain. This was their first fight, and each blow had proven to be fatal.

The Uber driver hummed to the tune on the radio. John Legend was crooning about everlasting love over the speakers. Nina wished she could rip the radio out of the dashboard and toss it out the window. She was living proof that love was dead.

"How far is it?" she asked.

"It's way out by the zoo, so…yeah."

This meant nothing to Nina. "Okay."

"Good thing the roads are clear."

It was five in the morning. Nina had been up all night. With Julian banished to the other room, she packed, disentangled her phone charger from his and stuffed her makeup and important things in her tote bag. A quick text to Valerie and she had someplace to crash until she figured out her next step. The important thing was to slip out of Sand Castle undetected. She'd left Julian a note. It didn't say much.

The driver tapped her fingers on the steering wheel. She had long, elegant fingers and wore a princess-cut dia-

mond on her left hand. Maybe love wasn't dead after all.
She glanced at Nina and suggested she take a nap. It was a
tempting suggestion, but bad things happened when passengers dozed off in public transportation. However, pretending to nap meant that the driver could go back to humming
love songs and Nina could fold into herself and mope undisturbed.

She reclined her seat but did not close her eyes. If she
did, she'd relive the night's events. She kept her eyes locked
on the tangled ribbon of highway. The minutes ticked away,
and her eyes went dry from the strain. Despite her efforts,
the unwelcome memories surfaced anyway and she relived
it all.

It was close to six when Nina arrived at her cousin's
town house. Valerie lived with her husband in a tidy gated
community. The porch lights were on, and she was waiting
at the door. Valerie inspected her, eyes wide with concern.
"Are you okay?" she asked. "What happened?"

"We had a fight. It's over."

"It's over after one fight?"

Nina massaged her temples. She did not want to be rude,
but she really did not want to talk about it.

"You look exhausted," Valerie said. "I'll take you upstairs."

The guest bedroom was, funny enough, a home office
with a daybed pushed up against a wall. Nina stumbled onto
the bed, and the enormity of what she'd lost came crushing on her. She wanted to howl with grief, but Valerie, in
her pajamas and fuzzy slippers, hair tied back with a silk
scarf, kept shuffling in and out of the room. She brought
in a glass of water, a bottle of painkillers and a weighted
blanket. Her cousin was an excellent hostess.

"Get some sleep," she said. "I took the day off. We can
talk later."

"Why are you so nice?"

Valerie paused, a hand on the doorknob. "Excuse me?"

Nina sat up. "I've been nothing but standoffish with you…even bitchy. I keep hoping you'll take the hint, and you never do."

Valerie's face crumpled. Without makeup, she looked far younger than her twenty-nine years. "It's a long story."

Nina shrugged. "I'd like to hear it."

Valerie shut the door and took a seat at the neat Ikea desk. Nina had instantly recognized it. She'd had a similar one a few years back. "My favorite uncle, *your* father, died when I was seven."

Nina was nine when her father had died in a car wreck. She hadn't known that her absentee parent was anyone's favorite anything. She hadn't known much about him period. Her mother had been in her thirties when she got pregnant and not at all interested in settling down.

"On the drive back from the funeral, my parents were talking. They said he'd wasted his life. He was handsome and charming—a so-called ladies' man. But as you know, he never worked a day in his life."

"Yeah. I heard." Nina looked down at her knuckles, embarrassed on her cousin's behalf. Her father's inability to hold a job was one of the reasons her mother had refused to take him seriously. When Nina was old enough, she'd explained that her father had been a fling and nothing more. "Someone to have a good time with."

"It was the first time, at least to my recollection, that my parents ever mentioned you by name. My cousin Nina."

Nina's heart filled with a sort of ache that she had long thought extinct. Why did she have to pry? What good was it to revive these old ghosts?

"My mom went on and on about how beautiful you were. My dad thought my uncle was a loser for not raising his daughter. According to my folks, he didn't like to be around your mom because they'd fight—"

"About money," Nina blurted. "Yeah. I know."

It was true her parents had fought about money, late child support payments in particular. Then her dad had died prematurely, leaving her mother to make do. Although money was tight, Nina had not wanted for anything—ever. And by the time she'd started middle school, her mother's career had picked up. "Do you pity me? Is that it?"

"Oh, no! It's the opposite!" Valerie moved off the chair and onto the daybed next to Nina. "My parents talked about you like some beautiful girl in New York City. In my mind, you were Eloise living at the Plaza. I wanted us to be best friends."

Nina pressed a palm to her forehead. For her, it had been the opposite experience. Her father's big, boisterous family, with their Caribbean accents and traditions and foods, were an exclusive club to which she'd been barred access. She had never wanted to have anything to do with them. Valerie shuffled out of the room and returned with a box of tissues.

"Where are your parents now?" Nina asked.

"Port-au-Prince. They live there six months out of the year."

The older generation was now out of the picture. Here was Valerie, singlehandedly trying to repair the past and reshape the future. Nina couldn't let her do it alone. "Thanks for the tissues. I'm going to wallow now."

"Gotcha." Valerie rose to her feet. The sound of water rushing through pipes made the town house hum. Valerie's husband was likely getting ready for work. What was his name again? Oh, yes. Patrick. "The weighted blanket will help with that. It's a comfort. Trust me."

Nina wondered what Valerie would have to wallow about then stopped herself before she went down that route once again. She'd made that mistake with Grace. Everybody, no matter how rich, successful, stylish and attractive, had something to wallow about.

After Valerie left, Nina crawled under the blanket with the box of tissues, wholly determined to soak the pillows with tears.

Nina stayed through the weekend, which meant she spent two days in her blanket fort, wiping tears and blowing her nose into wads of tissue. It helped that in her haste to escape the hotel, she'd inadvertently grabbed one of Julian's T-shirts. She clung to it like Linus to a blanket. Now and again, she raised it to her nose, inhaling his clean scent, and she was in his arms again. Everything she loved about him surrounding her, except his massive trust issues and his disloyal little heart.

She was caught in an infinity loop of heartache and humiliation. It was one thing to have her heart broken and yet another to be exposed to public ridicule at the same time. The one person who could possibly understand was the jerk who'd smashed her heart in the first place.

On Sunday, Nina had no choice but to crawl out of her cave. It was Patrick's thirty-fifth birthday, and Valerie had organized a little gathering. Since Nina had been hiding out in the man's home office for days, she figured she owed it to him to shower, dress, brush her hair and wish him a happy birthday. In the morning, she was flying back to New York.

At the moment, she had a few more solid hours of blanket-fort time ahead. She wiggled around and settled in. Just as she got comfortable, Valerie burst into her room, carrying a laptop.

"Julian made a statement. Check this out."

Nina's heart took off in wild gallop. He'd made a statement! What was there to say? She shoved off the blanket and joined Valerie at the desk. Her cousin was clicking around the web, trying to pull up a *Miami Herald* article without first having to subscribe to the paper, join an email list or take a survey.

"Okay. Here goes… Wait. Okay. Damn it! Buffering."

A video was downloading at a snail's pace. Nina watched the screen in terror. The slow Wi-Fi was criminal, but as much as she was eager for the video to load, she wasn't prepared to see Julian again—not even on a computer screen.

"Has he tried to reach out to you?" Valerie asked while they waited.

That was anyone's guess. "I haven't checked my phone."

She'd left it on airplane mode and buried it in the bottom of a bag. Nina had needed to go dark. She could not handle the onslaught of messages that had flooded her inboxes. Her social media mentions had exploded. Last she'd checked her phone, #1HOTKNIGHT and #1KNIGHTSTAND were trending and every troll in the world agreed that she stood to gain the most from the scandal. After her agent had called with an offer from an editor to buy the rights to the "hot Knight story," she'd had no choice but to go dark.

"Okay. Here we go!" Valerie said.

A brief intro and there he was, standing in the hotel's courtyard. The fountain splashed and gurgled just a few feet away. He wore his usual T-shirt and tailored jacket combo, eyes hidden behind sunglasses.

Nina yearned for him. She couldn't help it. The sight of him would always move her this way.

"We're here today in Miami Beach with actor JL Knight," the reporter said. "Mr. Knight, you are certainly no stranger to scandal. Let's get to the heart of it. Who is Nina Taylor? Did you know her long?"

Julian looked straight to camera to deliver his answer. "Nina Taylor is an acquaintance, someone that I met and worked with here in Miami. The publication of her diary was a violation of privacy. We will pursue legal action."

"Thank you, Mr. Knight."

End of video.

Nina edged Valerie aside and refreshed the web page. "Is that it? That can't be it."

"That's it," Valerie said.

"An acquaintance?" Nina uttered. "Did he just call me an acquaintance?"

Valerie dismissed this. "His publicist probably drafted that statement. A lot of celebrities have their publicists handle their breakups. It's less complicated that way."

The room expanded and contracted around Nina. Julian's statement was factually accurate. They were acquaintances. They'd met and worked together in Miami. They'd kissed in the moonlight, napped in the sun, swum naked in the bay and made love through the night, but that didn't change the facts. If she'd been anything more than an acquaintance, he would have known that she could have never betrayed him for professional advancement.

"Here's my take," Valerie said. "This was damage control. Nothing more."

Nina left the room and stumbled down the hall to the bathroom. Julian would have called her on this—she did have a habit of hiding out in bathrooms—but she couldn't count on Julian to save her from herself anymore. He was an acquaintance. Someone that she'd met and worked with in Miami. Nothing more.

# Twenty-One

By four in the afternoon, the two-story town house was filled with the scent of fried onions, fried plantains and fried pork. Valerie's mother-in-law and other close family members had arrived early to help out in the kitchen and set up for the party. Nina's bedroom window overlooked the back patio. Patrick and his friends gathered there, nursing glasses of amber liquor or bottles of beer. Laughter, chatter and riotous *kompa* music drifted to the second floor.

Nina looked longingly down at the tableau. This was everything that she had been deprived of growing up. She had long wished to belong to a clan of some sort. And this was without a doubt a gathering of a clan. Valerie was extending an invitation, but was it too late?

*Do I fit in?*

She was itching to reach for a pen and write the words down. The sad thing was, she didn't trust herself with a journal—not anymore. Julian was right about one point. When it suited her, when it was convenient, she *did* sell her private thoughts for profit. If she hadn't given in to the childish need to "Dear Diary" every life event, she could have spared herself a lot of pain over the years.

Valerie brought her a cup of tea. "I told *ma belle-mère* that you had a migraine and, she sent up ginger tea. She doesn't believe in pills. It's only weird because she's a pharmacist."

Nina set the hot cup of tea on the windowsill. "Give me a sec and I'll head down with you. I'm starting to feel like the disturbed woman in the attic up here by myself."

\* \* \*

Nina studied her reflection in her compact mirror and winced. She swiped on lip gloss to liven up her complexion, but that was a lot to expect from a fifteen-dollar tube of goo. The doorbell rang and, a moment later, a child let out a bloodcurdling scream. Nina startled and dropped the lip gloss wand. Next thing, she and Valerie had joined a stampede toward the front door. They rushed down the stairs but only made it as far as the landing. The foyer was cramped, everyone straining to catch a glimpse at whoever was on the other side of the screen door. There was one word on everybody's lips: *"Thunder!"*

Nina wished a bolt of lightning would strike her dead.

Valerie turned to her, eyes bright. "It's Julian!"

Nina gripped her cousin's arm. "How did he know where to find me?"

"I don't know!"

The birthday boy, already a little drunk, had some insight. "He called the house and asked if he could come by!"

"And you said yes?" Nina said.

Patrick was a smart, attractive man. He had a quick smile and poreless chocolate-brown skin. Otherwise, he was a guy's guy and proved it with his next words. "JL Knight calls and says he wants to come over on my birthday and you expect me to say no? Get outta here!"

"He's not here to see you!" Valerie scoffed and turned to Nina. "Don't look so grim. He's probably here to grovel."

"I don't want him to grovel."

The look her cousin gave her left no room for misinterpretation. "Now I know you're full of it."

"It won't change anything."

"It's a start," Valerie said. "He grovels a bit, and then you work something out, come to an understanding."

Valerie's mother-in-law came out of the kitchen brandishing a massive wooden pestle. She elbowed her way through the crowd and proceeded to question the intruder. Nina ordered Patrick to call back his mother. She didn't want Julian pummeled to death with a wooden pestle. Her concern amused Valerie. "Let the groveling begin!"

If he groveled, they could work something out, come to an understanding. That was the rule. Except Julian wasn't groveling, not even a little bit.

Valerie had finally let him in, apologizing for the raucous welcome. "Sorry! My family is extra." And there he was, standing in the tight foyer, looming over everyone, her tall, dark and handsome movie star.

After Patrick gushed over him and they snapped the obligatory photo, Valerie led them to a quiet seating area on the second floor so they could talk in peace. They settled on opposite ends of an upholstered bench. He looked like a dream in a blue button-down shirt, his hair slicked back. He had no right to look so good when she felt and looked as if she were living a nightmare.

"Sorry for crashing your party," he said to Valerie.

"Don't be ridiculous," Valerie said smoothly. "You've made my husband's year. Anything to eat or drink? We've got plenty of food."

"No. Thank you," Julian said. "I won't be staying long."

He wasn't staying long. Drive-by groveling? Did that count for anything?

"Let me know if you change your mind," Valerie said.

Nina's gaze stayed with Valerie as she headed down the stairs. What she would give if her cousin could stay and arbitrate. Julian was as stiff as a stick figure. He sat tilted forward, elbows on knees and fingers in a steeple under his chin. Silence pulsed around them. She felt sure it echoed the beat of her heart.

"How are you doing?" he asked.

"I'm flying home tomorrow." That wasn't the answer to his question, but that was all she had to say.

He nodded as if processing her words. Then he very slowly opened the messenger bag that he'd dropped at his feet and pulled out her journal. The pages were waterlogged and the red leather cover had new scuff marks.

Relief shot through her. "Oh, God! Where did you find it?"

"Grace found it in the garden." He flipped it open. "Someone ripped out a few pages before tossing it in the bushes."

He handed her the journal. She opened it on her lap and ran her finger along the frayed edges of the missing pages. "What sort of person does this?"

"The sort of person that is Pete. He was caught on camera."

Nausea rolled through her. "I *warned* you about him."

"I know," he said quietly. "And I'm sorry. That's why I'm here. I could have had it shipped to you, but I needed to look you in the eye and tell you how sorry I am. Pete was working with that website, feeding them information and tipping off their photographers, and I overlooked the obvious signs. I just didn't want to cost a working man his job if it wasn't true."

Did this count as groveling? Nina wasn't sure.

"The only reason they did this to you was to get to me," he said. "They used you, and I'm sorry for the hurt and embarrassment."

*They* may have caused her great embarrassment; only *he* had hurt her.

Nina tightened her grip on the journal. "I saw your statement. I don't want to take legal action. I just want this story to go away."

"I understand."

He rose from the bench and picked up the bag. "If I have any more information, can I call you? Will you answer?"

Nina swallowed past the pit in her throat and nodded. He stared at her awhile, looking as if he had more to say but finally deciding against it. "Okay, Nina. Take care."

She nodded again and turned to stare at a framed painting of a rowboat. She could not bear to watch him leave.

# Twenty-Two

After Julian made a discreet exit, Valerie joined her upstairs. "How did it go?"

Nina struggled to come up with an answer that simple question. "He didn't grovel."

Valerie plopped down on the bench next to her. "Maybe your standards are too high. Nobody said he had to bend the knee."

"An apology would have been nice."

"He didn't apologize? For anything?"

"He said he was sorry."

"Okay. That sounds like an apology."

"But it wasn't!" Nina blinked, her tears near. "He apologized for the wrong thing."

Valerie looked genuinely confused. "You're not making sense."

"He kept going on about what *they*'d done to me. The driver who stole my diary…the website that published it. It was all their fault. He was sorry that *they* hurt me."

The light in Valerie's eyes dimmed as her hopes for a happy ending died. "He doesn't get it."

"No! He doesn't!" Nina cried, but she was happy that her cousin did.

The next day, Nina flew home. She sat cramped in a middle seat, staring at the minuscule television screen. Meg Ryan was falling in love (again) with Tom Hanks. The actress opened wide blue eyes, filled with hope, and Nina wanted to punch the screen. The journal on her lap wasn't the one Julian had returned. As a parting gift, Valerie had unearthed her father's notebooks and offered them to her in a bundle wrapped in ribbon. Each notebook was inscribed with his name in ink: Raymond Pierre. Nina treasured them. She was not a fool for filling up diaries; she was carrying on a family tradition.

It was a relief to return to her quiet apartment. And it did not take long for her to resume her quiet life with its routines: mornings at the gym, writing sprints, cooking, some television and on occasion drinks with Laetitia. It was the best she could stitch together. She'd been banned from the creative carnival of which Julian was the center. So now she lived the low-key life of an exile. Her sleepless nights were more comfortable in her own bed, but her sense of loss did not lessen with time. Most mornings, she woke up confused to find that Julian wasn't within arm's reach. Then she'd go on with her day, her heart heavy, as if filled with slush. At night, she missed his overwhelming presence, the way he filled whatever bedroom they shared with laughter. She missed the sound of his voice.

And days stretched into weeks.

The paperback edition of her memoir steadily climbed the bestseller lists. Requests for interviews and appearances poured in. Only now she was known as *that* Nina Taylor—a virtually unknown author whose career had skyrocketed after she slept with an action star and wrote about it. To the dismay of her publisher, she turned down every interview request, but that only seemed to add to her mystique.

She had no idea how Julian was doing, and that was a sort of torture. The one time she'd googled him, she'd stumbled upon this gem: *If you thought JLK was a "Wham! Bam!" type of lover, think again! Diary excerpts paint a portrait of a sensitive and intuitive man. Men and women alike are clamoring for a piece of that action. The actor could not be reached for comment.*

\* \* \*

On a chilly Saturday morning in January, Nina and Laetitia, bundled in parkas, trekked back home from spin
class. They spotted a woman on their stoop, frantically
pressing the buzzer.

"Looks like there's going to be some drama!" Laetitia said.

"Bet you anything that it's Carl in 3F," Nina said. "He's
so messy."

"I know! Right?"

Laetitia sprinted forward. She was a decade older than
Nina. Her sloppy breakup with Ted (an episode only referred to as TEDx) had done her good. Aggressive self-care
was working wonders. Her inky-black hair was glossy and
her olive complexion glowed. She was once again her up-
beat self—and as nosy as ever. She hopped up the steps,
pausing on the landing to peek over the woman's shoulder.
Nina caught her friend's startled expression and stopped to
study the petite blonde more closely. She suddenly looked
uncannily familiar.

"Don't waste your time," Laetitia said. "No one is in 3D."

The woman whirled to face Laetitia. "Why? Did she
move out?"

"Depends. Who's asking?"

"Katia Wells," she replied. "I'm looking for Nina Taylor. Do you know where she is?"

"I'm right here."

She narrowed her eyes at Nina. "Ah! There you are.
That's a relief!"

Nina's body stiffened under the down-filled parka, and
it had nothing to do with the biting chill in the air. "Is Julian with you?"

"No. Just me," she said. "Is this a bad time? I hoped we
could grab coffee."

* * *

Moments later, Nina sat across from Katia at a bar-height table at a Starbucks, stirring sugar into an almond-milk macchiato. Katia lifted the lid of her cup and blew on the foam, in no apparent hurry to explain herself. Why had she shown up at her door? What was so urgent? Had Julian sent her?

"I owe you an apology," Katia said.

That was not what Nina expected to hear. As far as she knew, she had no beef with Katia Wells. "What for?"

"I misjudged you," she said. "I thought you'd leaked your diary. I was sure of it."

Not. This. Again. "Why would I do that?"

"Why do people do anything?" Katia fit the lid over the rim of her cup with a snap. "For money or attention or both."

This was absurd. Who, in their right mind, would want this kind of attention?

"You had your chance to capitalize on the scandal, and you didn't," Katia said. "No talk-show interviews. No book deals."

Nina grabbed a packet of sugar and squeezed it between her palms. "You didn't have to fly across the country to tell me that. I'm sure there's a Hallmark card that fits the bill."

"I didn't fly across the country to apologize. Thought it would be a nice way to break the ice, that's all."

Nina had ice in her veins. There wasn't much Katia could say to warm her disposition. Plus, she wasn't the finest of diplomats; it was time this woman got to the point. "Did Julian send you?"

"No!" Katia was emphatic. "He doesn't know I'm here."

Nina prayed disappointment wasn't oozing from her pores. Julian hadn't sent her because Julian had moved on. If she could only accept that maybe she could move on as well.

"As the head of publicity for Knight Films, I'm here to set up press for the New York premiere in April."

Nina couldn't suppress a jolt of excitement. "A premiere? Already?"

"Yup! It's an exciting time for us. *Midnight Sun* is getting good buzz. We've decided on a limited release—New York and LA."

Nina had flinched at Katia's use of the collective *us* and *we*, and now she was desperate to end this meeting. "What do you want from me, exactly?"

Katia took a long sip of her soy latte, a reminder that Nina's macchiato was cooling fast. "I'm here to coax you out of hiding."

"Coax me out of what?"

"Hiding," Katia said. "Here's how I see it. You're a woman, and you're sexual. You wrote about a meaningful encounter with a man. There's no shame in that."

"You make it sound like I'm cowering in shame. I'm not."

Nina was very strategically staying above the fray. She wasn't making public appearances, but she wasn't sequestered in her apartment, either. She'd resumed her routines, picking up freelance editorial work and tinkering with creative projects of her own. The problem was the "routine" part. Life with Julian had been anything but mundane. Bright and fun, every day had been an indulgence.

"You are—kind of—and I can tell you it's not a good look. You should speak up."

"Why?" Just a second ago Katia was praising her for *not* speaking up. What was she missing here?

"To help the movie. Okay?" Katia spoke with caustic impatience, as if she couldn't believe she had to explain this to a seasoned professional. "Right now, this movie release is covered under your big shadow. You're the elephant in the room. You—"

"Okay. Stop." Nina couldn't hear one more cliché. "I've done my part. I've stayed away from press and—"

"And it's only made things more awkward. You need to speak up."

"You mean throw myself to the wolves."

"No one is asking for a blood sacrifice," Katia said. "Don't forget, this is your film, too. It's in your best interest to promote it."

How could she? She had a scarlet letter pinned to her lapel. "It's not a good idea."

"I get your concerns," Katia said. "But listen. The one thing I know is PR. How do you think I got this job? Up until now I was Julian's capable assistant. I had to rebrand myself, and so do you."

This conversation couldn't get more LA if they tried. "I think with time all of this will go away."

"No! You have to be proactive. Unless you want to be known as #sexgoddess for the rest of your life."

"Hashtag what?" Nina came close to knocking over her coffee. She moved her cup out of the way with a shaky hand.

"Don't you google yourself?"

"No," Nina said. "I'm not insane."

"Well, #sexgoddess is what you're known as these days. Way better than #famewhore, in my opinion."

Nina drummed the tabletop with her fingertips. "Awesome…just awesome."

"I know. It sucks. It all sucks."

It sucked that Katia was right. Nina had been hiding. She wanted nothing more than to crawl into a hole, or her apartment, and die. She'd had a hand in the making of this scandal and was deeply embarrassed about it. How could she have been so careless as to leaving her diary in a public garden? Once again, her published words had caused a loved one pain.

"Come out and support the film," Katia said. "The Miami Film Festival in March is a good place to start. You won't have to talk to the press. If you show up to the director's Q&A event, I'll make sure your photo gets to the press."

"Will Julian be there?"

"Of course. He's the director."

Nina reached for her coat hanging on the back of her chair. She was suddenly feeling cold in this hot and cramped coffee shop.

"I'm sorry things didn't work out between you two, but he's worked so hard on this. You more than anyone should know that. If you ever cared for him—"

"I love him!"

Katia grabbed the table as if a quake had hit. The words had exploded from Nina. She didn't *care* for him. She loved him. Nina loved Julian Knight, and she couldn't carry that truth around like a concealed weapon anymore. Was Julian worthy of her love? That was a separate issue.

"Sorry, Katia," she said. It wasn't fair to unload on her. "I didn't mean to scare you."

Katia raised her hands to her head and massaged her temples. "Ugh! I promised I wouldn't meddle."

"That's surprising. All you've done is meddle."

"Clearly, I'm good at it." She laughed, nervous. "I can't speak for my boss's feelings, obviously. I can say that he hasn't been the same since Miami. I've seen him low before, but this is different."

Nina didn't like the idea of Julian feeling low. A part of her was comforted by the idea that he was out in the world, making it a better place through sheer charisma and joy.

"I want to talk to him," Nina said. "Ask him to call me."

"I can't do that. He doesn't know I'm here."

Nina grabbed her keys off the table. "Fine."

"Wait!" Katia cried. "Let me see what I can do."

Katia whipped out her phone and stepped outside to place the call. Nina dropped her keys, shed off her heavy coat and finally took a sip of coffee.

# Twenty-Three

Kat called early on a Saturday morning while Julian, in the company of Wasabi, was sprawled on his couch, watching *Jules and Jim*. He was working his way down the list of Nina's favorite classic films. This was his new weekend ritual, and he was serious about it. He would have normally let voice mail pick up, except Kat was away, setting up the press junket for the New York release. This was new territory for her, and she might have questions. He didn't expect her to have a convoluted story to tell involving Nina.

After months of tortuous silence, a demand. Nina was *demanding* that he call her. As if he had to be forced into it and that he hadn't tried a thousand times. The thought of hearing her voice again…

"Alright," he said.

"You're not mad?" Kat stammered. "You asked me not to meddle, and I clearly am."

He'd write her a bonus check for this. "How about this? Don't bring it up again and I won't."

"Gotcha."

"Is she with you? May I speak with her?"

"Give it thirty minutes, okay? We're at a crowded coffee shop."

"Okay."

*Thirty minutes.* Julian lifted Wasabi off his chest and got up to shower and shave. He always wanted to look good for her, even on a call. With ten minutes left to go, he wandered out to the yard. He needed a clear head. What did she want to say to him? What would he say to her?

He and Rosie had resumed their weekly meetings at the gazebo. She thought he was wrong for letting go of the #sexgoddess—as Nina was referred to on Twitter.

"It's the best thing for her," he'd said to Rosie.

"How do you figure?"

"No one would have ripped and sold pages of her diary if she were not writing about me. I can't ignore that."

When Julian had finally cooled down and read the entire published excerpt, he was moved to tears. Her heart beat in every line. He couldn't imagine the embarrassment it must have caused her, still caused her to this day. She was a serious writer, and they'd made her a hashtag. It infuriated him that they'd reduced her to a cartoon character. That was his fault.

Rosie toyed with the plastic lighter in her hand. A weak flame blossomed then failed with each flick of her thumb. "Julian, life is not cinema."

At the mention of his name, Julian snapped to attention. To Rosie he'd always been JL Knight. This departure from the norm was remarkable. "I'm aware."

"You don't get to run around, bark orders and blow things up. You have to talk to her, and you have to listen to what she has to say." Then she added, wryly, "You're not really a knight, you know."

He could not get Rosie's words out of his head. That conversation had nudged the boulder sealing his reasons in place. Nina had walked out, but he'd stayed away to protect her privacy, dignity and reputation. That's what he told himself. Or, possibly, he'd blown it all up because it was easier that way.

With five minutes left, Julian went back inside and straight to the kitchen. He filled his trusty electric kettle, the one that he'd purchased the week he arrived in America. Soon the sound of gurgling water was the only sound. His house, his *life*, was devastatingly quiet. Julian couldn't wait a second longer. He grabbed his phone and dialed her number.

"Nina?"

"Hi."

Julian closed his eyes. Every emotion that she had ever stirred in him hit him all at once. "You wanted to speak with me."

"Yes."

Her tone was guarded, and it killed him. They'd always been so free with each other.

"It's time I write about the whole missing-diary episode."

Now this was a surprise. "Did Kat put you up to this?"

"No." The one syllable dropped in the space between them. "It's something I need to do."

"Why?" He couldn't understand. Why would she want to throw more red meat to the wolves?

"I've been silent all these months, and I want my voice back."

"I understand, but I'm worried—"

"You don't understand," she said. "I've been labeled everything from a slutty opportunist to a sex goddess. I need to define who I am."

Julian ran his palm over his face. Fearful of making a bad situation worse, he opted to shut up.

"If you think my goal is to sell more books or somehow keep this story alive—"

"I don't think that!" Julian protested. How could *she* think that?

"For a minute there, you did."

Julian stared out the window, blind to the view. He was only now coming to grips with how much his earlier suspicions had hurt her. How much *he* had hurt her.

"It'll probably be a blog post or an op-ed," she said,

continuing as if she hadn't just gutted him. "I won't accept compensation."

Steam gushed out of the kettle with a hiss. He yanked the power cord out of the socket to quickly silence it. "I don't care about any of that."

"You may not, but everybody else does."

"Nina..." Since when did they care about what people thought? He did not recognize the people they'd become.

"One more thing," she said, hastily. "Katia thinks I should attend the Miami Film Festival. She said it would help if we present a united front. What do you think?"

None of his thoughts had anything to do with the film. He thought he'd messed up. The harm he'd caused was irreversible. He'd lost his lover and his friend, and nothing would ever make up for it. But Nina was waiting for an answer to her question. "I'd love to see you in Miami."

"All right," she said. "See you in Miami."

Three days later, Kat called with the news that Nina had published a blog post on the feminist website *Feminine-Plural*. For once she was too late. Nina had sent him a copy of the post the night before. That didn't stop him from spending his day at his desk, refreshing the website until the byline popped up in red print: *Her Name is Nina Taylor.*

*Dear fans, followers and inquiring minds of all stripes:*

*Thank you for your interest in the #1HOTKNIGHT affair.*

*If you're not familiar with the scandal, I will get you up to speed. Last fall, my diary fell into the hands of an unscrupulous individual who ripped out a few pages and sold them to a gossip website. Those of you who've read the excerpt know more about my sex life than I'd be willing to share with my closest friends.*

*The story begins in July. While on holiday in Miami, I met action movie star JL Knight. Our courtship got off to an unusual start. Day 1: We agreed to share a hotel suite. Day 2: He dived into a pool to save me. Day 3: We went on an excursion with his former landlady. Day 4: He kissed me in the moonlight.*

*Don't take my word for it. There are photos documenting it all.*

*This love story should have remained a closed-bedroom-door romance. Instead, readers have been offered an explicit account of our most intimate encounter. My intention here is not to fill the few remaining cracks in your imagination. But since this is a story, and I'm a storyteller by nature, I would like to take this opportunity to flesh out the main characters, provide some context and backstory.*

*My name is Nina Taylor. The man who became my hero, friend, lover and creative partner is Julian Leroy Knight.*

*I am a writer. I've kept a diary since childhood. My journals have always been the guardian of my secrets. I've published a couple in the form of a memoir. However, that was a very different experience. I had control over the material and the process. Also, I had an editor to prune out the excess exclamation points and overabundance of clichés.*

*Julian is an actor, writer and filmmaker. He trusted me to read and revise the script he had spent years working on. We bonded over the written word. It is disheartening that words—my written words—caused so much havoc.*

*How this love story ends is none of your concern.*

*Over the next few weeks, I will be actively promoting* Midnight Sun *alongside my friend, director Julian Knight, and the countless other creative pro-*

*fessionals who brought the film to life. Should we
meet along the way, ask me about the creative process. I'd love to share. Ask me about my private life
and I'll have no problem putting you in your place.*
    *Thank you and be well.*

The following day, Julian met with Kat for lunch at her
favorite French bistro in West Hollywood. Kat was her
usual chatty self. Julian was sullen. Nina's words pursued
him, unsettled him. *Friend. Lover. Creative partner.* How
had he managed to lose all of that?

Kat was full of praise for Nina. "Mark my words. She
is now and for all time a feminist icon." She squeezed a
lemon into her iced tea. "Right up there with Rosa Parks."

Julian raised his eyes from the menu. "Don't bring Rosa
Parks into this."

"Why aren't you happier?" Kat said. "She masterfully
rebranded you as an artist. JL Knight is dead. You are now
Julian Knight, a triple threat—actor, writer and director."

"I don't care about that." Julian knew how insane that
sounded, because it was all he'd cared about up to this point.
"I betrayed her and let her down."

Kat reached for her glass of iced tea, knocking her designer sunglasses clear off the table. Their waiter retrieved
them, set a breadbasket on their table and took their order.
But Julian knew Kat well enough to know when she was
hiding something.

"Anything you want to tell me?" he asked once the
waiter had left.

Her blue gaze skidded away. Julian crossed his arms and
waited. Finally, she turned to him, composed. "It's my fault
you two split up. I called in the middle of the night with all
my theories and wouldn't drop it. What's wrong with me?"

"You were looking out for a friend," he said. "But I knew

what I had with Nina. It was real, and I should never have been swayed."

"She loves you, you know."

Julian lowered his head and pinched the bridge of his nose, as if that simple gesture could keep him from falling apart. "But she hates me, too."

"That's to be expected," Kat said. "I'll say this—the woman I got a glimpse of in Miami last summer was not the woman I met with in New York. She tried to hide it, but she looked sad, dejected and disappointed as hell that you weren't traveling with me."

Sad? Dejected? He thought she'd be better off without him, but his better-off theory was proving to be bull. A guttural moan escaped him. "I want her back so badly. I don't want to go on like this. I don't think I can."

"Moaning to me about it won't get the job done, Knight."

He composed himself. "I need a strategy."

"Yeah, you do."

Julian grabbed a piece of crusty bread and tore it in half. It was going to take a heck of a lot of groveling and the mother of grand gestures to get Nina to consider forgiving him. "Would you mind helping me?"

She passed him the butter. "Thought you didn't want me to meddle."

"Does it make you uncomfortable? It's not exactly your job."

"Julian, we're friends!" she cried. "If I wanted to win someone back—or just get back at someone—I'd enlist you."

"And I'd say yes."

"Good," Kat said. "Now that we got that straightened out, let's strategize."

# Twenty-Four

*Miami Beach, Florida*

This was his night and she would play fair, but she reserved the right to be pissed.

Nina sprayed perfume on her wrists and slammed the delicate bottle on the marble vanity. One last glance in the bathroom mirror, and she was out the door.

During the ride from the hotel to the Fillmore theater, she repeated her mantra: *He's nothing to me. I'm over him.* It had been months since she'd laid eyes on Julian, but she was prepared. In the weeks leading up to the film festival, she'd built a sturdy emotional dam to keep her anger and resentment at bay. *I'm ready*, she thought. However, when the car pulled up to the red carpet and she spotted him standing there, elegant in a smoke-gray suit and sunglasses, she understood that she could never be ready.

There he was, her midnight sun.

He held open the car door. Nina looked up at his face, because she could never pass an opportunity to gaze at him. Her trained eye saw the man beneath the veneer. He looked fragile, as if he'd been shattered and pieced back together. His extended hand trembled slightly. She accepted it without hesitation. He squeezed tight, sending shivers racing up her bare arms, before helping her out of the car. Nina repeated her mantra, more frantically this time: *I'm over him. He's nothing to me.*

Under a hailstorm of flashing cameras, he stole a moment to whisper his thanks. "I can't tell you how much I appreciate this."

"I'm here to support the film," she whispered back. "We didn't work so hard for it to fail."

This movie was as much her own as anyone else's. She was proud to come out and support it. And with any creative project, she wanted it to be a smash hit.

"Whatever your reasons, I'm grateful you're here."

He pivoted and smiled for the remote pool of photographers sectioned off with velvet ropes. Nina was not the natural showman that Julian was proving to be. Her posture was stiff and her smile wobbly. She blamed her frayed nerves. It wasn't easy to face the cameras after all that she'd been through. Her weak knees had nothing to do with how close they were standing or his hand on the small of her back.

After what seemed like an eternity, Katia escorted her off the carpet. Bettina and Pierce had arrived, and it was time for her to yield her spot. "You did great. Now grab a glass a champagne and relax."

Valerie was waiting in the lobby. Nina's cousin was her plus-one for the event. Perceptive as always, Valerie hadn't missed a thing. "You two look amazing together, and, honestly, it's time for you to kiss and make up."

Nina kissed her cheek in greeting instead. "Shut up and show me to the concession stand."

With champagne, popcorn and gourmet snacks, they entered the packed auditorium. An usher escorted them to the front row, where Nina was reunited with Francisco and Grace, who appeared to be on a date.

*Midnight Sun* was a gorgeous film. Nina lost herself in the world that she'd had a hand in creating. From the opening scene with Bettina in a white bikini, floating on her back in that magnificent pool, to the end credits with Pierce driving into a citrus-hued sunset in a stolen white

Camaro, frame for frame, the film was art in motion. The performances were as strong as the setting, and the audience rewarded the actors with a standing ovation. Julian was welcomed on stage for the director's Q&A to thunderous applause. He glowed with pride. Nina was bursting with love. She loved Francisco for having insisted he step up and direct. She loved the actors for their dedication. And she loved the audience for their warm reception.

Julian took a seat in a director's chair next to the evening's host, tall and lean and gorgeous. *He is nothing to me.*

Valerie nudged her in the ribs. "Relax! And quit glaring at the guy."

Nina could not relax. "Why does he look so good? It's distracting."

"How about you, #sexgoddess?" Valerie said, teasing. "Let me guess. Your trusty LBD was at the cleaners, so you grabbed a Grecian gown."

Nina had borrowed a play from her mother's book: face your critics looking like a star. She'd headed straight to Fifth Avenue and enlisted an in-house stylist at Saks to help find the right dress: "I'm going to an event and I'm not sure what kind of reception I'll get."

"Sounds like you're venturing into shark-infested waters."

"Something like that. I need to look devastatingly beautiful. Can you help me?"

"Darling, that's my expertise."

The gauzy one-shoulder dress she wore was the first he'd put her in, but they'd kept coming back to it again and again. She appreciated the way it hugged her figure, but the pleats and folds made it easy to wear. To complete the look, the stylist had insisted on gold accessories. And to save a trip to a hair salon and stave off Miami's humidity, Nina wore her hair in a long French braid.

"Ladies and gentlemen," the host said, "please welcome Julian L. Knight."

There was a fresh round of applause. Julian smiled and waved, but his gaze swept the front row until his eyes locked with hers. Nina's aggravation dissipated. Briefly, they were alone in the packed auditorium. Nina nodded her encouragement. All those nights they'd stayed up working on the script and those long days on set, she'd been with him almost from the start. She was with him now. They might never ride off into the sunset together, but she was on his side.

"Mr. Knight, you are better known as Thunder. From action hero to movie director, that's quite a leap. How did you go about it?"

"First I'd like to thank you for having me. I love Miami Beach, and I'm happy to be back."

The audience cooed at his words. They loved him and Nina loved them for loving him—although, to be sure, she still hated him.

"To answer your question, the story idea came to me a long time ago. I spent years working on it, but I could only take it so far. I had to wait for the right people to come into my life. People like your hometown hero, Francisco Cortes, whom I consider a mentor and father figure at this point." He paused for applause. Francisco twisted around in his chair and blew kisses to his fans. Grace looked proud and... for the first time ever, surly Grace Guzman looked happy. She also looked devastatingly chic in a black Versace dress, but that was classic Grace.

"I'm lucky enough to count my neighbor's nanny as one of my dearest friends," Julian continued. "At the right moment, she gave me the push I needed."

"Your neighbor's nanny!" the host exclaimed. "Are you comfortable sharing their name?"

"Absolutely. Rosie Parker." Julian scanned the audience.

"Where are you, Rosie? Stand up and let the people see you."

A petite brunette stood from the second row and waved like Queen Elizabeth to great cheers. Nina dabbed away tears from the corners of her eyes. She'd never met Rosie, but had heard all about her. Some might be surprised that Julian would rather befriend the rich neighbor's nanny than the neighbor himself, but not Nina. He had such an open, generous heart. Not a pretentious bone in his hunky body.

"As someone who has followed your career in the press," the host said, "it sounds like you've grown a lot."

Julian nodded. "You could say that."

"Anyone else you'd like to thank publicly tonight?"

"Nina Taylor."

"Your cowriter?" the host asked, as if there were any doubt.

Nina had stiffened at the sound of her name. Should she stand and wave, too? Or could she slink under her chair? Soon, though, the theater went dark and the curtain rose. The movie screen lit up with a still image of her on the rooftop deck at Sand Castle, her linen shirtdress billowing in the breeze. It was the first photo he had taken of her. *I want you to see what I see.* That morning he had sent her a copy of the script; both their love affair and creative partnership had begun.

In the next photo, she was standing in the boat that Julian had chartered, staring at the turquoise sea. The sky was bursting with oranges and pinks, almost as if in celebration of a love they had not yet declared.

The photos that followed were candid shots taken by the cinematographer during production. She and Julian reading off the same script, walking around the set hand in hand, talking with the crew, laughing at jokes long forgotten, dancing at the wrap party.

When the lights flickered on, Julian stood alone on stage,

looking down at her. Nina gripped the armrests, torn in two by terror and tenderness. He raised the microphone to his lips, and his smooth voice filled the theater. "You published your response, and now it's my turn."

*Oh, no...* She raised a hand to her forehead to shield her face. She did not want photographers capturing the moment she at long last came undone.

"Nina, you are my creative partner, my muse and my best friend. The night I lost you, I was more concerned with protecting my reputation than the woman I loved. It pains me to admit it, but that's the awful truth. After you left, I didn't think you could ever forgive me, or that I even deserved forgiveness."

What was he doing? Hadn't he read her blog post? She'd been firm on keeping the public out of their affairs. He'd had every opportunity to speak with her. She did not want to have this conversation in a room full of strangers. "Julian, please," she said. "Don't do this."

"Goldie, let me say this one last thing."

He'd managed to turn a nickname that she despised into a sweet endearment. Damn him for weaponizing every tender memory! What was he trying to do? Rip her heart out of her chest?

"I betrayed you. And by staying away, I know I must have hurt you. All I wanted was to protect you—"

Someone heckled from deep within the audience. "Dump him, honey! He doesn't love you! This is all for show!"

Fueled by outrage, Nina jetted to her feet and faced the assembly. This was not the audience participation part of the show. "You don't know him! Mind your business!"

The response came lightning fast. "He made it our business!"

Nina couldn't argue against that. This grand romantic gesture wasn't worth their privacy. She swiveled around to take it up with Julian. Come to think of it, this did have all the trappings of a stunt. If he pulled a ring from his pocket and dropped to one knee, she would punch him in the face. Only Julian did not appear fazed by any of this. He laughed at the heckler. "I love this woman, and I don't care who knows."

Oh, God! That laugh! She remembered the first time she'd heard it in the courtyard at Sand Castle, the day their eyes had met and she'd lost all good sense. This was her man. She loved him. There was no denying it.

"Just kiss and make up already!" Valerie cried. "This is killing me!"

Nina turned to confront her, but found her cousin, Grace and Francisco all beaming up at her encouragingly. She was reminded of what Grace had said the first night they'd talked: for some people, it takes a village.

She took one step toward the stage, one step toward Julian. His eyes were bright with emotion, and no force in the world could keep the words locked inside her. "I love you, Julian Knight. Okay? Happy? I love you! I don't want to live without you. Now, please stop trying to protect me from things. I hate it."

The assembly erupted in bravos and cheers. Julian dropped the microphone and smoothly leaped off the stage like the action star he absolutely was. He drew her into his arms and kissed her. They kissed as if a roomful of people were not watching, as if photographers weren't snapping photos like mad. He cupped her face and kissed her tenderly, lovingly, until Nina was out of breath and out of words to express her love. Then he released her, stepped away, pulled a ring out of his pocket and sank down on one knee.

Nina didn't hear the crowd gasp. All the world faded to black.

# Epilogue

"We're here on the red carpet with the *it* couple of the moment, Nina Taylor and Julian Knight. Welcome and congratulations on your engagement!"

"Thank you."

"Thanks."

"Julian, *Midnight Sun* is in the running for some of the night's top awards, including best director, best actress in a leading role and best original screenplay."

"Don't forget best cinematography."

"How could I forget? The film is so visually arresting! So, tell our viewers, how do you feel tonight?"

"Incredibly proud of the work and of the people who came together to make art. It is an awesome feeling."

"Nina Taylor, this is your first award season as a nominee. What is going through your mind?"

"I'm a little emotional. It was my mother's dream to walk the red carpet—and here I am!"

"Your mother was an actress."

"That's right. She's in my heart tonight, but it's wonderful to share billing with Julian. He thrust me into this. It's his job to see me through."

"Such a beautiful partnership! But speaking of partnerships, Bettina Ford credits you, Julian, for her breakthrough performance. What are your thoughts?"

"Bettina is a force of nature. She did not need any help from me."

"Nina, how do you plan to celebrate if you win?"

"As soon as the festivities are over, we fly back to

Miami, where we plan to decompress. And by that I mean start working on the next project."

"What about wedding plans? Can you share anything about that?"

"Sorry. That's off-limits."

"No doubt! Well…best of luck you two, for tonight and forever."

*July 5. Julian Knight and Nina Taylor were wed last night in Miami Beach, Florida. The couple tied the knot at the hotel formerly known as Sand Castle. They exchanged vows poolside in front of fifty of their loved ones. Thereafter, the groom offered his bride the keys to the mansion as a wedding gift. They now have plenty of space to display the multiple awards won for their first collaborative effort,* Midnight Sun.
—Vanities

\* \* \* \* \*

# INTIMATE
# NEGOTIATIONS

## NICKI NIGHT

This book is dedicated to my husband and best friend,
Les, for showing me what love feels like
every single day.

Lord! Thank You for bringing me through this one
more time. Let the glory be all Yours! I love writing
and I'm so blessed to be able to indulge this joy.
I want to thank everyone who inspires me just for being
who they are. Thank you to Glenda Howard, Stacy
Boyd and the entire Desire team. Thank you to my
fellow writing cronies who keep me inspired, Zuri Day,
Lutishia Lovely, Tiffany L. Warren, Victoria
Christopher Murray, ReShonda Tate Billingsley, Leslie
Elle Wright, Sheryl Lister, Brenda Jackson, Beverly
Jenkins, Donna Hill and so many more. To my
heartbeats, Big Les, Little Les, Milan and Laila, you are
my life. To my siblings, cousins, besties, readers,
maniacs and book club buddies nationwide, thank you
for being on this journey with me! Where would I be
without your support? Like I said before, I dunno!
You all rock!

# One

"Well…better luck next time." Seth Sanders's tone was cool, almost frigid, and devoid of any concern.

Zoe Baldwin saw Seth's lips form into a smirk. He was gloating. She held her expression, hoping her true feelings didn't best her and spread across her entire face. "Yep." She offered a tight smile. "Next time," she said and then turned her attention to her computer. Chest up, back erect and eyes straight forward, she dismissed him.

She was done talking, even though she really wanted to lash out with stronger words. But she didn't want to come across as the bitter employee who didn't get the promotion. Yet, she *was* bitter. This was the second time she'd been overlooked, the second time an employee she trained was now getting the title she deserved, and Seth was instrumental in both incidences. Zoe couldn't prove it, but deep inside, she knew it.

Seth lingered for a moment before walking away. At his exit, Zoe felt the threat of tears sting her eyes. She grabbed her cell phone and headed to the ladies' room. Going into the farthest stall, she bowed her head and let the tears fall. She hated that anger caused her to cry. Crying made her feel weak.

Zoe took a few deep breaths and then stood straight. She swallowed hard, pushing down other rising emotions. She closed her eyes, inhaled slowly and exhaled as much frustration as she could.

Seth's actions were nothing short of retaliation. She'd been one of the few women at Bowman Advisors who'd rejected his advances. She didn't care if he was the son of a board member. Seth was slick. He never made another pass at her but tried every single day to be just annoying enough to make her miserable at work. Most times she successfully ignored his childish behavior. But now he was standing in the way of her moving up the ladder. She didn't have enough evidence to actually prove it—yet.

Zoe took another deep breath and released it with conviction. Either Seth had to go, or she would. Her mentor had once told her that sometimes bosses fired employees but other times, employees fired their bosses. It was time to fire Seth.

She exited the stall, tucked her cell phone under her arm and washed her hands. She grabbed tissues from the box on the sink and dabbed her eyes. Studying her image in the mirror, she stared directly into her own doe-like eyes that matched her mother's, drawing strength from inside.

Zoe put a smile on her face. If she could handle the challenges of the life she lived, she could certainly handle the Seths of the world. With new conviction, she left the bathroom and dialed Willena Williams. Tough, brilliant and well respected, Willena was an icon in the finance industry. She was also one of Zoe's professors from grad school and had become her most trusted mentor.

"Good morning, Zoe." Willena's singsong voice was full and strong. It was one quality that allowed her to move a room full of people to silence or action. Zoe pictured her at her desk, the large office, the wall of windows behind her. She could see Willena in one of her tailored suits and her salt-and-pepper tresses cut low in the back and swinging over her left eye in the front. "Have a good weekend, my dear?"

"I did, but today…not so good. Can you do lunch?"

"Oh…lunch won't work but I can meet you for dinner. I haven't been to Smith's in a while. I could use a good steak."

"That would be perfect, Willena. Six o'clock?"

"Let's do five thirty."

"Great. See you then."

"Ta-ta for now" was Willena's signature sign-off. She even closed text messages with it, using TTFN.

Zoe headed back into the office feeling a tad better. She watched Seth eyeing her in his normal squinted fashion as she made her way to her cubicle. Zoe hoped the day went by quickly so she could get to her dinner with Willena.

Despite Seth's nagging presence, it did. The second the clock on her computer struck five, she shut it down, grabbed her purse and headed out the door. Again, Seth eyed her entire departure.

Maneuvering through the throngs of New York City's after-work crowd, Zoe walked at a brisk pace, the pace and rhythm that matched the soul of the city. It came automatically when she hit those streets. After a quick subway ride, she reached the restaurant with minutes to spare. Willena walked up seconds after her and in no time, they were being seated.

"Blue. Neat please, my dear?" Willena said to the waiter, asking for her usual Johnnie Walker Blue straight with no ice even before the server had a chance to place the menus in front of them. "And she'll have…" She paused for Zoe.

"I'll have Riesling, please," Zoe added.

"Uh!" Willena held up a finger just as the waiter was about to turn away. "Your best Riesling, thank you."

One day, Zoe would drink scotch like Willena, no ice, no chaser. Willena's drink choice was an indicator of the type of woman she was: aged, refined, hard and smooth at the same time, and of course no-nonsense. For now, Zoe was a white wine kind of woman.

"How's it all going, my dear?" Willena buttered a warm piece of bread from the basket on the table and took a bite.

"Okay." Zoe toyed with her bread, turning it over in her hand.

"Just okay? How's the family?"

"All are well. Stable. And yours?"

Willena had no husband or children to speak of. She'd

been married to her work for more than twenty-five years, managing to maintain a few boyfriends along the way. She'd turned down her share of proposals. Instead, she was the proud, wealthy aunt who spoiled her tribe of nieces and nephews. "My nephew chose Harvard. Following in his auntie's footsteps. I'm so proud."

"That's great news! I know that makes you super happy."

"It certainly does."

Willena leaned aside for the waiter to place their beverages on the table. They took a moment to order appetizers and entrées.

"Now," Willena said, bringing the focus back to their reason for meeting once the waiter left with their selections. "What's going on at work?"

"I was passed over for a promotion—again."

"Hmm."

"This time stung worse than the last. I mean, at least the last time, I chucked it up to fair game. But this time, it feels…personal. Like sabotage. It's like they don't want me to move up in this company."

"Mmm-hmm." Willena nodded. Her lack of dialogue always propelled Zoe to talk more.

"Seth seemed happy that I didn't get the promotion." Zoe told her about their exchange this morning. "He's so inappropriate at times. I'm going to file a complaint, but I want to make sure the timing is right. I don't want to look like a sore loser." She took a deep breath, feeling the need to calm herself. "He takes joy in bugging me. I'm qualified. I deserve this."

Willena chimed in with a hummed response here and a nod there as Zoe continued to vent until their food arrived.

"You know that company is home base for the 'old boys' club,'" Willena said at last. "I think it's noble that you figured all you had to do was work hard and then you'd be rewarded." She shook her head. "Not there. If you don't have an in with the right executive or you're not family to one of the board, your chances of making it up the ladder are slim. But you knew that." She huffed. "You got what you needed from them. When other companies see them on your résumé, they'll take notice. It's time."

Willena bowed her head silently over her meal for a quick grace. Her gesture reminded Zoe that she should do the same. Her mother would have reprimanded her had she picked up a fork without giving thanks first.

"You need to move on," Willena said when she looked up. "What's your plan?"

A plan. Good question. Zoe hadn't quite thought of one. She just knew it was time to move on. Hopefully she'd get a better salary. "I need a plan," she admitted.

"Yes. Spontaneity is best preserved for romance. Planning is imperative in business. We don't want to make rash or careless decisions about our career choices. Think about where you see yourself in the next few years and make sure your next steps are ones that get you closer to that goal."

Zoe was glad she'd called Willena. She rarely volunteered her wisdom, but since Zoe had shared her situation, Willena had managed to give her the most thought-provoking advice in just a few words.

"In the meantime, I have a few friends in a few places." Willena always referred to her vast network of professionals with nonchalance. "You know Blackwell Wealth Management, right?"

"Of course."

"They're expanding. I'll ask Bill what the deal is over there. There may be an opportunity coming up with them. I'll keep you posted."

"I'd really appreciate that."

"In the meantime, work on your plan and send it to me. We'll see what the possibilities are for you."

Zoe nodded. Suddenly she felt lighter. Seth wasn't going to stand in her way of becoming all she was destined to be.

Just because he didn't want to promote her didn't mean she wouldn't achieve her own career advancement.

"Now, about that love life!" Willena watched Zoe curiously with a raised brow.

Zoe threw her head back and laughed. "Willena! I'm fine."

"You have to have a *little* fun, honey."

"Mmm, this salmon is delicious!" Zoe tried to hold her smile back as she wrapped her mouth around a forkful and closed her eyes. When she opened her eyes again, Willena was still giving her the same raised-brow expression.

Zoe laughed again. She had no answer for Willena. She wasn't sure when she would ever be able to answer *that* question.

# Two

"I just had the worst interview ever." Ethan palmed his forehead and sighed. "This guy was so arrogant you would have thought he was interviewing me to be his boss."

"Wow. Sounds like you've had some crappy candidates lately. I guess that vice president position is going to be mine after all?" his brother Carter teased him over the phone.

"I didn't say that. Don't go printing new business cards yet, bro. I've got three more interviews lined up for today alone! That VP job is mine."

"Wanna put a wager on it?"

"Nothing like a little friendly competition. What would you like to bet?"

Carter hummed. "Let's see. How about something really humiliating?"

"Ha! Don't do that to yourself. I'd hate to laugh at your pain when I win, but I will."

Carter laughed. "You mean when I win. Let me think…"

Ethan pictured Carter tapping his fingers on his desk while he thought.

"I got it!" Carter spit his words out so fast they startled Ethan.

"Okay. Whatcha got?"

"The loser buys the winner a brand-new set of Callaway irons."

"Ooo-wee!" Ethan sang. "That's a nice set of clubs. I could use those to beat you on the green again. Let's throw in a new golf cart, too."

"Aww. You want to buy me a cart, too?"

"Nope, it'll be you dipping into your savings for me. And I want my cart customized with some torque. Then I can ride over to your house with my irons just to hand you my business card with my new title."

"Um…excuse me… Mr. Blackwell."

Ethan's head snapped up. He noticed his assistant standing in the entrance to his office. "Yes, Bella?" Once the branch manager was hired, Bella would become the new office manager at that location.

"Your next candidate has arrived. A Ms.—" Bella looked down at the papers in her hand "—Baldwin. Zoe Baldwin."

"Okay. Give me two minutes and send her in."

"Will do, sir."

Bella left and Ethan returned to his call. "My next interviewee is here. Let's hope this one is better than the last one. I'll catch up with you later."

"Cool! And good luck. I'll send you some pictures of the clubs I want when you lose this bet."

"Ha! Later, big brother." Ethan ended the call and popped a mint in his mouth.

He wasn't exactly looking forward to the string of interviews ahead of him. The past few days of meeting with potential candidates to run the new branches of Blackwell Wealth Management in his territory had proven to be a bit exhausting. He and Carter had already swapped some interesting interview stories since their father put them to the task of expanding the company.

They were charged with opening several branches in each of their territories. Ethan was responsible for all of Long Island from the Cross Island Parkway to Montauk. Carter's territory included the five boroughs of New York City, and their colleague Dillon Chambers was responsible for expansion in Westchester County. Each held the position of regional director, and depending on how well they fared in the first six months, one of them would be selected to become the new vice president for the combined territories.

The position came with an impressive salary, new bonus structure and a corner office with a spectacular view of

Lower Manhattan. And now that they had a bet going, Ethan or Carter would also end up with a whole new set of high-end golf clubs and a brand-new golf cart to go along with their bragging rights.

"Ready, sir?" Bella was at his door again.

"Yes, thank you. Send her in." Ethan closed his eyes for a quick moment and took a deep breath. *Please let her be normal.*

"Good morning, Mr. Blackwell."

The woman's voice went right through him. Ethan looked up. He stood slowly. Instinctively, he extended his hand at the vision approaching him. She was gorgeous. Gorgeous enough for him to have to actually think of the appropriate response to her *good morning.*

"Um. Yes. Good morning, Ms…"

"Baldwin. Zoe Baldwin."

"Yes." Ethan shook her hand and then put his hands in his trouser pockets.

Ms. Baldwin stood awkwardly for a moment. The silence between them suddenly rang in Ethan's ears like an alarm.

"Please. Sit." He gathered himself. "Do you have a copy of your résumé with you?"

"Yes, I do." She handed it to him. Ethan looked to see if she had a ring on her finger. She didn't.

"Great." He took the résumé from her and began looking it over, scanning the words but not reading a thing.

He had already decided he couldn't possibly hire this woman as his branch manager. One look at her and he barely remembered his name. Protocol and decorum abandoned him. This wasn't good. He was a professional. A professional that was accustomed to beautiful women, at that.

"Mmm-hmm." He pretended to take in the skills and credentials listed in the document. It could have been written in Greek for all he knew. He cleared his throat and focused harder, finally taking in her qualifications. Impressive. A few more moments passed.

Ethan placed the résumé down in front of him and sat back. "Why Blackwell Wealth Management?"

"Your history over the past decade has been quite impressive, despite a few hiccups here and there," she began. "You seemed to have responded quite well to the challenges you've faced and instead of just surviving, you thrive as a company. You have a record of unprecedented growth, yet you've managed sustainability extremely well, as well as double-digit growth."

Zoe seemed to warm to her topic, exuding calm and ease as she spoke. "Financial media used to have you on the one-to-watch but now list you as one of the best companies to trust your assets with and work for. Your employees and your clients rate you well. That reputation doesn't come by chance or good luck, but by great people leading great teams and lots of hard work."

She lifted her chin. "I'm a hardworking team player and a good learner with proficiency in the areas you're seeking. I'm also well-educated and smart enough to interact with amazing mentors who are extremely knowledgeable, well connected and instrumental in helping me navigate my career. I'm also very ambitious and believe I can truly be an asset to the company by helping you reach your goals. I'm looking forward to joining a solid team and continuing to develop and grow in this field, and I believe Blackwell is a great place to make that happen."

Zoe ended her response with a confident smile. Confidence. Not smugness.

Ethan almost didn't know what else to ask. She'd said all the right things. He wanted to shout, *You're hired*. Instead, he nodded, reviewed her résumé further and asked a few pointed questions about the different positions she'd held.

Each response was better than the last. Ethan was truly impressed. He could already see her leading a branch and possibly even taking on his role once he was promoted to vice president. Smart *and* beautiful. So what *was* wrong with her?

"Do you have any questions for me, Ms. Baldwin?"

"Yes. I have a few. With rumors stirring about a potential recession, what is Blackwell's strategy for protecting the interests of the company, your employees and clients, as well as their assets?"

*Whoa! She's good.* "That's a great question."

Ethan went on to speak to the organization's strategic goals and explain why despite the rumors of a recession, this was also the right time for the company to expand.

Zoe took notes as he spoke and asked a few more poignant and thought-provoking questions. As her lips moved, Ethan found that he needed to concentrate to focus on her words. He shifted in his seat several times to keep from staring. The last thing he wanted to do was come across as inappropriate or make Zoe feel uncomfortable.

Ethan was sure one of the challenges she had referenced was the sexual harassment issue they had dealt with a few years back. Blackwell had addressed the report immediately, taken a strong stance against harassment and implemented changes to avoid future cases, but not before the media had gotten a hold of the news and published several scathing headlines. It took some time for the company to recover from that stain. They'd put in the necessary work to ensure their employees' safety and rebuild their brand.

Ethan answered her last question about the next steps in the hiring process. When she confirmed that she had no more questions, he stood. "Impressive. If you're selected to advance to the next round of interviews, we'll be in touch."

"Thank you, Mr. Blackwell. I hope to hear from you soon. I'm excited about the opportunity to work for Blackwell Wealth Management and truly believe this would be a mutually beneficial fit."

Ethan smiled. Again, she'd said the right thing. "Thank you, Ms. Baldwin." He held out his hand. When he touched her, her palm felt as soft as he remembered from the top of the interview. He let go quickly and nodded. She turned to leave, and Ethan tried his best not to watch her walk out. Setting his focus on his desk, he shuffled papers aimlessly. When she exited, he plopped back into his chair.

Ethan sighed. She was the best candidate by far. But how could he hire a woman he could barely take his eyes off of? She was bound to be some kind of trouble.

He looked at his clock. He had fifteen minutes before his next interview. He made a few notes on her résumé and put it aside before checking to see who was scheduled to come next. Ethan went to the LinkedIn profile of the next candidate to look at their picture. He couldn't be thrown off by another stunning beauty.

Suddenly he laughed. It started as a chuckle. He laughed harder. He chided himself for his ridiculous behavior and chuckled more at how Carter would joke when he shared this with him.

With several more minutes to spare, he decided to check messages. He still needed a distraction. Zoe Baldwin dominated his thoughts. When he opened his email, her name was already at the top of his inbox. He clicked and read her email, thanking him for taking the time to meet with her and consider her for the position. She reiterated a few key points from the interview and wrote that she hoped to hear from him soon. She closed with a line about being grateful to her mentor, Ms. Willena Williams, for making her aware of the opportunity.

Smart woman. Mentioning that a respected professional like Willena Williams was your mentor could never hurt. Between that and the quick follow-up thank-you note, Zoe Baldwin was racking up points.

Perhaps, Ethan would have to figure out how to work alongside a beautiful woman that made him struggle to keep focus. He was an experienced man. Most of all, he was a professional. But there was something about Zoe Baldwin that would test him. He could feel it.

He thought a moment longer. He needed the right team in place to guarantee a win. Zoe could definitely be an asset.

This was his chance. He had to impress his father and get that promotion. Carter had an advantage that Ethan didn't have. Ethan had much more to prove to their *father* than Carter ever did.

# Three

Zoe was on her fifth outfit. The four others she'd tried on were strewn across her bed. Twisting side to side in the mirror, she shook her head before removing her suit jacket yet again. She tossed that one across the bed, too, removed her pants and threw those on top of the pile.

She chuckled and told herself that her outfit mattered because it was her first day, that she needed to make a great impression and she wanted to look very professional. Some of it was true but the real reason she wanted to look her best was because of her new boss.

Zoe had to admit, Ethan Blackwell was one of the most handsome men she'd ever laid her eyes on. She wasn't trying to entice, but she wanted to look great.

There was something about Ethan. He was smart, confident, and sex appeal oozed from him. Her second interview with him had gone smoother than the first. She'd been determined to land the job, but she'd still felt like she had been crushing on him after she left his office the second time. For the next few days, he'd randomly shown up in her thoughts. When he'd called to offer her the job, the thought of being around him on a daily basis had almost made her weak in her knees.

Having never been boy crazy, she laughed at herself now. Why in the world did she feel like she was in high school, crushing on the cute popular boy? The truth was, while she had done her homework on the company, she had also done some research about her new boss. He was well respected and gave back to the community. He and his brother Carter were bachelors. They were also Blackwells, which meant that they were from a different world. Theirs was filled with privilege and pedigree. The only window she had into that exclusive world was her clients in financial management. And Zoe made sure they knew few details of her modest background.

She grabbed the navy blue pantsuit from the pile on her bed and put it back on with a soft pink blouse and matching belt. She slipped her stockinged feet into a pair of smart-looking navy pumps. With gold stud earrings and a link necklace to complete her look, she was ready for her first day of work at Blackwell Wealth Management. Assessing her choice in the mirror one last time, Zoe sighed.

"Let's do this, girl," she said to her reflection.

She pulled her designer tote over one shoulder and picked up her car keys. Unlike her last job, her new commute would require no more than a fifteen-minute car ride. Parking in the lot near her office was plentiful. No longer would she have to fight the rush-hour crowds on the commuter rail-road and subway for an hour and a half to get to downtown Manhattan. Besides her impressive new salary, this was one of the best benefits of her new job. Well, that and having a ridiculously handsome boss to look at every day.

That was all Ethan was going to be for her: something nice to look at. Dating her boss was out of the question. She'd seen too many people's careers fumble for dating on the job—especially due to dating bosses. Zoe also knew that after a few weeks of working alongside Ethan, she'd get used to him and his good looks would no longer matter.

For now, looking forward to seeing him every day was sure to make work interesting. Besides, a man like Ethan had to have his pick of beautiful women on a daily basis. Zoe could imagine he probably had several that he was prob-ably seeing all at once—perhaps enough ladies vying for his attention that he could pick one for every night of the month without repeating. She was also certain that those women probably came from similar backgrounds—a perfect one filled with enormous wealth and privilege. Zoe had neither and she was fine with that.

Before walking out the door, she popped a pod in her coffee maker and filled one of her spillproof travel mugs with her favorite dark roast and added a touch of French vanilla creamer. Instead of wearing a light jacket, she wrapped a pashmina around her neck to protect herself against the cool autumn air. Her blazer was enough to guard her from the slight chill.

"He's probably arrogant," she said to her reflection in her rearview mirror as she put her car in Reverse and pulled out of her designated parking spot at her town house complex.

"Arrogant and entitled," she continued assessing him, "from a model, privileged two-parent household."

The women at the job would probably make her sick from their pining after him. That alone would make her want to steer clear of any man. She could already imagine the hushed talk of him throughout the office. She would never be party to that. Taking in discreet glances of him would be enough for her. She appreciated good-looking men but was never one to *need* a man.

Zoe's favorite playlist blasted through the car's Bluetooth system. She nodded to the rhythm as she navigated traffic along some of Nassau County's busiest streets. The commute took longer than the fifteen minutes she'd estimated and she was glad she'd decided to give herself just over a half hour to get to work. It was all the time she needed to get her mind ready for her first day.

This branch manager position had everything she wanted and needed. The compensation package was the best she'd ever received. She would soon have a fairly large team to manage and was ready for the challenge. She'd gleaned her management style from what she believed were the best characteristics of the bosses she'd worked under. She looked forward to being a fair, firm and motivating leader.

Her thoughts carried her all the way to the office. She

maneuvered her car into one of the spots designated for Blackwell Wealth Management and headed inside.

Bella, the new office manager, guided Zoe to the office she would occupy. It was slightly smaller than Ethan's over-size corner office and situated right next to his.

Outside of her office, Zoe took in the modern company space with its open floor plan, crisp white workspaces and a common area that also served as a kitchen. Any wall that wasn't full of windows held abstract artwork with bright pops of color. Her eyes scanned the rows of empty cubicles that she would help fill over the next couple of weeks. She was excited about the task of having a hand in building the team.

Just as Bella finished helping her set up her laptop, they heard footsteps. Butterflies fluttered in Zoe's belly. Before she saw his face, before she heard his voice, she felt him. Ethan had arrived and set off the butterflies.

Moments later, he appeared in the frame of her office door, looking like a work of art himself. She tried not to but couldn't help taking him in slowly, savoring every inch of him that filled out the tailor-made suit, from his Italian designer shoes to the starched white shirt. From his perfect jaw line to his pearly white teeth, full lips and bright smile.

She sat rigidly to keep from shuddering. *Soon enough.* One day soon, he wouldn't have this effect on her. She'd be so familiar with him, she wouldn't notice how gorgeous he was. For now, she'd have to manage her response to him. How rare for her.

"Good morning, ladies," he greeted.

"Morning." Zoe gave him a quick nod and set her eyes back on the computer screen, looking at nothing in particular.

"Good morning, Mr. Blackwell," Bella said.

Ethan wagged his finger. "I told you to call me Ethan."

"Oh. Yes. Ethan. Good morning, Ethan."

"Zoe." Ethan didn't call her name in any special way, yet

it still felt like he summoned her musically. "I hope you're getting all set up just fine. How about we meet up in about an hour after you've had a little more time to get settled?"

"Sure, Mr. Bl—" Zoe paused abruptly when Ethan raised his brows and tilted his head. "I mean, sure, Ethan."

"That's better. We're a team around here."

"Yes. Of course," Zoe replied.

"Good." Ethan looked at his watch. It sparkled from clear across the room. "See you in an hour."

Zoe smiled and nodded.

After another thirty minutes with Bella, she was all set up. When Bella exited her office, Zoe sat back to take things in. Eventually, she stood, walked over to check out her view overlooking the lot and beautiful landscaping of the business park.

She closed her eyes and sighed. The flutters died down, but she wondered how she'd survive working in such close proximity to this man. One way or another, she'd figure it out. She needed her job.

# Four

Ethan walked into the headquarters of Blackwell Wealth Management in Lower Manhattan with positive, excited energy coursing through his veins. The first phase of their expansion plan was now complete. He, Carter and their colleague Dillon Chambers had each identified three locations to open branches in their respective territories and hired branch managers they believed were perfect fits for getting their new offices off the ground.

His mind quickly switched to Zoe and he tried, yet again, to push thoughts of her from the forefront of his mind.

Today was the day that their teams would come together for the first of their monthly management meetings at the company's main office on Wall Street. Ethan was proud of his picks for branch managers. Zoe, Jasmine and Brian all came with stellar credentials and had already begun to prove their worth.

His stride exuded the confidence he felt about being the one to come out on top of this expansion. Admittedly, it wasn't just the prospect of expansion that excited Ethan. Today he would see Zoe for the first time in a few days. With him managing several locations, he didn't get to see her on a daily basis. On the days he didn't visit her office, he thought about her often. But that was the most he could do.

As beautiful as she was, Zoe was an employee and that made her off-limits. Blackwell Wealth Management had strict rules against employee dating, and their father, William Blackwell, known to most as Bill, held his sons to an even higher standard. The company had narrowly survived sexual harassment charges from a former employee that had tainted the company's reputation for a time. They'd worked hard to overcome that past and rebuild their reputation to the point where they were recognized as one of the best places to work several years in a row now. Bill had recently graced the cover of one of the industry's most popular financial magazines because of their accomplishments and new expansion.

"Ethan."

Ethan paused just at the entrance to the conference room. "What's up?"

Carter's stride morphed into a light jog until he caught up with Ethan.

The brothers slapped hands and hugged. "You ready for me to be your boss?" Carter asked.

"Nope." Ethan shook his head. "Because that's not going to happen. This win is all mine!" Both men laughed and headed into the conference room.

A continental breakfast, coffee urns and an array of waters and juices lined the back of the room.

"Coffee?" Ethan gestured toward the food.

Carter nodded. "Looking forward to meeting your team," he said.

"Yes, I've got some great people. They're already executing. I think it's going to go well. What about yours?"

"I'm excited about what they bring to the table. We're off to a good start."

Ethan wondered briefly if he should volunteer any information about Zoe or keep his thoughts to himself.

"Ethan…" Carter called. "You with me, bro? What's on your mind?"

"Ah…nothing."

"You zoned out on me for a sec. Having reservations?"

Ethan looked at the door to the conference room to make sure no one else was coming in. "There's this one manager I hired." He lowered his voice. "Wait until you see her. Her résumé is great but to say she's a beauty is a gross understatement."

Carter's eyes widened. "And?"

"And nothing. I'm just saying she's gorgeous. I'd never do anything to jeopardize the company, but I will admit, the first couple of days weren't easy." Ethan sighed. "It took lots of concentration for me to stay focused. It's all good now but wait until you see her. You'll understand what I'm talking about. Even more than being beautiful, she's smart and she's got amazing ideas. She's probably my best pick. I can already tell that her branch will do well."

"Understood. I can't wait to see her. Beauty and brains. Perfect combination. I'm sure you're keeping your hands clean when it comes to her."

"Absolutely." Ethan waved off Carter's concern. "She's amazing to look at, but I'm a professional."

"And much more by the book than I'll ever be. Ha!" Carter laughed.

"You're right about that," Ethan agreed with a chuckle. What Carter had said was true. Since they were teens, Carter had always been a bit more rebellious. Ethan, on the other hand, avoided upsetting his father at all costs. The relationships they shared with their dad were different. Ethan had always been cautious, and for good reason.

He heard footsteps and both he and Carter looked toward the door.

Zoe stuck her head in tentatively. "Good morning, Ethan." She stepped into the room. "I was just about to ask if I was in the right place until I saw you."

"You're in the right place." Ethan turned to Carter. The two exchanged a quick, knowing look. Ethan knew Carter agreed that Zoe was as stunning as he'd claimed. He and Carter met her halfway into the room. "This is Zoe Baldwin, branch manager for the Garden City office. Zoe, this is my brother Carter Blackwell, regional director for the outer boroughs."

Carter held out his hand. "Pleasure to meet you, Zoe. Too bad you're on the losing team."

Zoe's eyes widened and she looked from Ethan to Carter.

"You wish." Ethan moved Carter out of the way. "Hungry?" he asked Zoe.

"Um." Zoe's eyes were still on Carter.

"He's a joker and unfortunately, not all that funny. Worst thing is he's also delusional, thinking that his territory has a chance of beating our numbers in the first six months. He owes me a new set of irons when he loses."

Understanding spread across Zoe's face. "Oh! I see." She laughed with Carter. "Good thing I never lose." She dropped her bag on an empty seat and headed toward the refreshments.

Carter's laughter ceased abruptly. "I like her confidence," he admitted.

When she came back with her coffee, the three of them engaged in small talk for the next several minutes until Bill, Dillon, Blackwell's executive team and the rest of their branch managers arrived. When Zoe wasn't paying attention, Carter looked at Ethan and discreetly raised his brows. He was impressed. Ethan knew they'd talk more about her later.

"Morning, morning, morning!" Bill's big voice filled the room.

Ethan stiffened at the sound of his father's booming voice, then forced himself to relax—a habit he hadn't managed to break since he was a teenager. The jovial mood had broken; it was time to get to business.

After rounds of introductions, the executive team, which included Ethan and Carter's oldest brother, Lincoln, welcomed the new branch managers and began taking them through various components of the company's strategic plan. The senior vice president of Human Resources provided them with an uplifting account of how the company's most important commodity wasn't the strength of their portfolio, but the value of their employees. The room felt energized. Everyone seemed enthusiastic about working together to meet the firm's goals.

A few incentives were offered to stir up some fun, healthy competition between the regions; for example, the office with the best numbers after the first six months would be awarded a catered breakfast and lunch sponsored by the other two offices.

Zoe looked across the table, capturing Carter's attention with a fierce, competitive gaze. With two fingers, she pointed at her own eyes and then turned those fingers around at him as if to say, *I'm watching you.*

Carter threw his head back and laughed, prompting others in the room to look around. But Zoe simply glanced at Ethan, nodded and mouthed, *We've got this.*

The meeting adjourned and everyone enjoyed a tasty catered lunch. Carter and Zoe's competitive banter painted the atmosphere colorfully, but still kept things friendly for all of the managers. By the end of lunch, the entire team had begun to bond in spite of their respective territories.

It had been a good morning for Ethan. He was excited to present his team but was most proud of the way Zoe had fit right into the Blackwell fold. He was impressed by the way she handled Carter's personality, meeting him toe-to-toe for every joke he tossed her way. Brian and Jasmine, the managers of Ethan's other locations, did well also, but of course Zoe monopolized his attention. Ethan hoped it wasn't too obvious.

The regional directors stayed behind once all the branch managers were dismissed, and Ethan and Carter went out for coffee.

Carter placed their cups of dark roast on the small bistro table at the coffee shop closest to their headquarters. "I like her."

"Who, Zoe?" Ethan asked as if Carter could have been talking about anyone else.

"No, J.Lo," Carter teased. "Of course I'm talking about Zoe."

Ethan shook his head. "Yeah" was all he said.

"She *is* gorgeous." Carter nodded slowly. "Smart, got spunk and a sense of humor. She seems like she can really hold her own."

"Yeah," Ethan said again. He realized he was smiling and sipped his coffee.

"Be careful, brother."

"What?" He reared his head back. "I can handle myself around beautiful women. I'm a professional." He had every intention of being a respectable boss. There was too much at stake otherwise.

"Mmm-hmm." Carter sipped his coffee but kept his eyes on Ethan. "Like I said, be careful."

# Five

Zoe snatched her cell phone off the side table and jabbed her finger on the screen to stop the annoying chimes of her alarm. Not having the strength to put it back, she dropped the phone on the couch beside her, let her head fall against the cushion, closed her eyes and sighed. The sun had yet to rise, but if she was going to make it to work anywhere near on time, she had to get up immediately. She groaned and rubbed her neck. It hurt from sleeping in such an awkward position on the couch.

Zoe looked around the dark room and didn't see her sister Shena. She grunted, then tried to muster enough energy to get herself up off the couch.

"You're awake?"

The sound of her mother's voice startled her. Zoe watched Laura Baldwin struggle down the narrow staircase, holding the banister with both hands. Her cane dangled from under one arm.

"Hey, Ma." Zoe walked over to help her mother with the last few steps.

"Did you sleep at all?" her mother asked.

"A little."

Laura groaned. "Hardly a wink." She scanned the room. "Where is she?" she asked, referring to Shena.

"I don't know." Zoe looked around and saw that Shena's boots and sweater were no longer in the chair by the window. "She was gone when I woke up. She'll turn up," Zoe said, trying to reassure her mother. They'd been here before with Shena. She never stayed away long. Sometimes it took hours, and, unfortunately, sometimes it took a few days, but she'd always come back home.

Laura shook her head and huffed. "You have time for a little breakfast?" She started toward the kitchen.

Zoe didn't want to leave her mother, but it was too early to start taking time off from her job. She certainly didn't feel like divulging her family drama to her new boss. "I really need to get home so I can get dressed for work. Are you going in?" she asked, hoping that Laura, too, was going to work.

Being in the office would take her mother's mind off Shena instead of her sitting at home waiting by the door and the phone. Despite her mother only being in her fifties, Zoe wished she could retire early. Life hadn't been easy for them and the wear and tear showed all over her mother's body. The near-crippling car accident a few years back hadn't helped either.

"Yeah," Laura finally said after a few moments of silence. "I need to go in. Got too much to do." She paused, leaning on her walking stick with one hand on her hip. "I've tried everything. I feel so helpless." She raked her hand over her head. "I don't know what else to do."

"I know, Ma. You can't blame yourself or Shena's condition. All we can do is support her."

"If she would just stay on the medicine they give her…" Laura knit her lips together, took a deep breath and let it out with a sharp huff.

"Yeah." Zoe shrugged. "There would be fewer…" She paused trying to find the right word. She settled on "episodes" to describe Shena's hysterical state from the night before.

After days of not taking her medication, Shena seemed to have come undone and Laura had called Zoe over to help with her sister. It was their routine. Shena would take her medicine for a while, feel better and stop. Eventually, she'd have some kind of major depressive episode. They weren't sure what had sparked this current episode but believed it had something to do with recent issues with her boyfriend.

It was well into the night before they'd been able to calm Shena down. But now she was gone. When she disappeared, there was no telling whether she'd return in a few hours or a few days. And Laura and Zoe would worry the entire time.

Zoe grabbed her purse and jacket from the sofa and kissed her mother. "Call me if you hear from her and I'll do the same, okay?"

"Yes. Let me know when you've made it to work."

"Okay." Zoe made it outside and tamped down her emotions. Dealing with her sister's illness was painful and exhausting. She knew that the pain she felt could never match that of her mother. That was why Zoe never hesitated to drop everything and come when called. Besides, she loved her younger sister. Caring for her was the closest she'd ever come to being a mother herself.

Zoe started the ignition but sat in the car for several moments before driving through the predawn blackness. It seemed to serve as a metaphor for what her family was dealing with right now. Hadn't they been told it was always darkest before the dawn? Was there a dawn for her sister's condition?

Zoe headed home. Even after a shower and a light breakfast, she was still tired. She made a quick coffee stop on her way to the office. It was a café Americano kind of morning. Her regular medium roast or chai latte wasn't going to do. She ordered the largest size they had and drank as much from the steaming cup as she could by the time she pulled into the parking lot at the office. Her day felt as if it had been long already. The rest of the day would be full of meetings, including an early one with her boss, and she had to be alert.

"Morning!" Bella was especially chipper this morning.

Zoe forced a smile that she hoped matched the brightness of Bella's. "Good morning, Bella."

As she stepped farther in the office, she could tell that Ethan was already in. She'd been hoping to arrive before him to prepare for their meeting and muster up some more energy.

Zoe dipped into her office and closed the door behind her. She checked in with her mom to see if she'd heard from Shena. Of course she hadn't. After that, she gathered the résumés of the potential candidates she wanted to share with Ethan during their meeting.

There was a soft knock on her office door. Zoe cleared her throat, forced her lips into a smile and spoke through it. Feigning a cheerfulness she didn't feel in her heart, she sang, "Come in!"

"Hey!" A fresh wind seemed to accompany Ethan into her office. Like Bella, he was obviously in a great mood. Zoe held her smile. "Good morning. Did you have a good weekend?" he asked.

"Yes, I did, thanks. And you?" Zoe swallowed hard as she allowed her smile to fade.

"Great!" He sat in one of the chairs positioned in front of her desk. "Yes, me, too." He went on to describe a fun-sounding gathering he'd attended with his family to celebrate his grandfather's birthday. The details of the festivities seemed so lavish and filled with grandeur; nothing like the modest gatherings she had with her mother and sister.

Zoe pasted on her smile before she spoke. "That sounds nice."

Ethan paused, taking her in pensively. She squirmed a bit under the intensity of his gaze. It felt like she was being sized up.

"You okay?" he asked.

"Oh, yes, I'm…fine. I'm fine." Why had she said *fine* twice?

Ethan tilted his head with a measure of skepticism. "You sure?"

"Sure." She chuckled a little. "Yes, I'm sure. It sounds like you have a lovely family. A big one, too."

He analyzed her another moment before responding.

"Yes. Huge. Tons of cousins on both sides." He proudly shared a bit more about his large, close-knit family.

As he spoke, Zoe pictured them all dressed elegantly in their opulent environment. The image was perfect in her mind: everyone with erect posture looking refined against the picturesque backdrop of the clubhouse he described at the golf course where they'd held the festivities.

It was all far from what she was used to. She hardly knew opulence before going away to college and working in Finance. In school, she'd met girls with more wealth than she could have ever imagined. And the financial industry had given her a taste of what that life was like through co-workers and clients. She admired it from a distance but had never craved it for herself.

Zoe was particularly proud of what she'd accomplished in her career, which afforded her a very different lifestyle than how she'd grown up. She loved her stylishly decorated yet modest townhome and was especially happy to be able to help her mother make ends meet. Occasionally, she'd treated her mom and sister to nice dinners at great restaurants and even some beach vacations over the past few years. She was responsible for her mother's very first ride on an airplane. That gave her so much joy.

"Enough about my family," Ethan said, pressing his palms flat on her desk. Zoe realized that she had tuned him out and hoped he hadn't noticed. "Well." He hauled himself up from the chair. "Ready when you are. We can meet in my office or the conference room, whichever you prefer."

"Either is fine for me."

Ethan started to walk out but turned back toward her. "And you're sure you're okay?"

"Yes. Really. Just a little tired. My weekend was…a bit exhausting. Not as fun as yours, though."

"Okay." He shrugged. "See you in about—" he looked at his watch "—ten minutes?"

"Your office?" Zoe confirmed in the most cheerful tone she could manage.

"Yes."

She watched him walk out and for once was glad to see him go. Much too soon to divulge any of her family's drama. Would there ever be a time where she'd feel comfortable speaking about that with Ethan?

She began gathering the things she needed for her meeting with Ethan when her phone rang. She was about to send it to voice mail until she saw that it was her sister's number.

"Shena!" Zoe tried not to sound frantic. Closing her office door, she lowered her voice before asking, "Where are you?"

"Home." Shena's voice was so small that it made Zoe's heart tighten. She knew her sister was in a bad way.

"Who's there with you?"

"No one. Mom went to work, I think."

Zoe sighed. "Yes. She did." Now that she knew where her sister was, she felt a little better. Shena's bipolar condition was a never-ending matter, but she was home safe for now. "I'll be there after work so we can talk, okay?"

"Yeah." Shena's voice sounded small again.

"I've got to get to work. See you later."

"Bye."

Zoe hung up feeling more like Shena's mother than her sister. She stood straight, took in a deep breath and let it out slowly before heading to Ethan's office for their meeting.

With her sister dominating her thoughts, it helped Zoe not to focus on his good looks. She didn't have to try hard to concentrate in his presence this morning. And the mention of his lavish lifestyle helped her determine that aside from work, their realities were really far apart. There wasn't much they could possibly have in common. She needed to remember that.

# Six

Ethan tapped the steering wheel to the beat of an old-school R & B song on the radio. He couldn't help but smile as he made his way toward Zoe's house to pick her up.

She'd called to inform him that she'd woken up to a flat tire and would be late getting to the investment conference they were scheduled to attend in downtown Brooklyn. Immediately, Ethan had offered to pick her up along the way. He called his other two branch managers and asked if they wanted to carpool, as well, but they were already on the road. At least he'd attempted to both make Zoe feel comfortable and quiet any potential whispers about the two of them riding in together.

Ethan pulled up to her town house and texted her to let her know he'd arrived. Minutes later, she emerged from her door in a well-fitting gray skirt suit, yellow blouse and matching pumps.

He loved her sense of style. She always managed a professional yet sexy appearance with a touch of something unexpected. He hadn't seen many people pair colors the way she had, and that gray and yellow made her glow. He watched her intently until she pulled the passenger door open. He was glad he'd chosen to drive one of his sportier cars.

"Morning!" Zoe's voice rang in his ear like a melody.

"Morning." Ethan smiled and waited until she was buckled in before pulling off.

"Thanks so much for offering me a ride. I didn't want to put you out of your way, but it seemed to be the only option for me to avoid getting there late." She sighed. "At first, I was going to just change the tire but realized my rim was bent really bad. I guess that pothole I hit on my way home from my mother's house last night did more damage than I expected."

Ethan's brow furrowed when she mentioned changing the tire. He didn't want to come across as a jerk that didn't expect women to be able to do the same things as men. He thought about his words before speaking. "I like that you change tires." That was the truth. He was intrigued.

"Change tires, change oil. It takes a few major skills to be a girl these days."

"Impressive." Ethan raised a brow and trained his eyes on the road. He liked Zoe even more.

"My mom made sure of it. She wanted her girls to be okay living independently."

"Smart tree makes for a smart apple."

"Did you just call me an apple?"

"I think I did just call you an apple." The sound of their laughter filled the car. Ethan enjoyed her humor and decided he could listen to her laugh all day.

"What other interesting skills do you have?" Once the words left his lips, he realized they could seem rather suggestive.

Zoe looked over at him. He could feel the heat of her watching him.

"Okay. That didn't sound right but you have to know I had the purest of intentions," he said after several moments passed.

She grinned at him. "It's a good thing I know you're a gentleman."

"Glad my reputation preceded that comment," he said dryly.

"To answer your question, I own a great drill set, know how to shoot... What else? Oh! My sister and I spent a few years doing karate. The community center offered free classes for the youth in our neighborhood. We were the only girls. Somehow my mom found pink karate uniforms and insisted that our instructor allow us to wear them."

"Wow. So you can fight, shoot and fix cars? If I had a type I think that would be it—a pink-gi-wearing, karate-fighting, gun-toting, car-fixing, hole-drilling apple."

Zoe laughed hard. Ethan imagined that if beauty had a sound, her laugh would be it.

"Where did you learn to shoot?"

"My uncle lived deep in the country down in South Carolina. He hunted, and taught us when my sister and I went down during the summer. What about you? What are your special skills?"

Zoe's question sounded as suggestive as his had. Ethan swallowed before responding. His mind veered into naughty territory and he had to rein his thoughts in. Though he couldn't act on it, he couldn't deny her effect on him.

He finally answered, "I collect cars. It's one of my hobbies. My parents said I've been obsessed with them since I was a kid. You know those little Matchbox cars and Hot Wheels? Yeah, I had hundreds of them growing up. Every birthday, every Christmas, all I asked for was more cars. I had special cases for them and everything. My mom said that by the time I was three, I was calling out the makes and models on the cars that passed us on the highway. I even memorized license plate numbers."

"Seriously! Wow. How many cars do you own?"

"Five."

Zoe's eyes bulged. "Five? What kinds? Makes and models!" she added.

"This one," he said, referencing the top-of-the-line BMW coupe they rode in. "My convertible is an Aston Martin, the Bentley is an SUV, the Silverado is my pickup." Ethan noticed Zoe nod knowingly as she counted on her fingers. "Then there's my favorite baby, the coal-black 1969 Mustang." He was sure his pride was evident as he described his last vehicle.

"No kidding? Mustangs are my favorite. 1969? Ah! That must be a beauty."

"You like old cars?"

"Love them! You restored it yourself?"

Ethan would have driven the Mustang had he known she would have loved that one. But he often reserved that for special drives. "Yep. But I probably spend more time cleaning it than driving it. I only take her out on special occasions."

"Okay. What else?" she asked. Her voice was melodic.

"What else what?" Ethan asked.

"What else don't I know about you?"

Zoe obviously didn't know her effect on him but he couldn't possibly say that. "I did a little karate when I was a kid, too. Nothing major. My dad, brothers and I are big golfers. Other than that, you can say I'm pretty adventurous."

"Oh? What kinds of adventures?"

"Anything that gets the adrenaline flowing and makes the heart pump a little faster. You know, like fast cars and things like skydiving and four-wheeling."

Zoe smiled. "Skydiving and four-wheeling sounds like fun. The height of my adrenaline-rush ventures would probably include the big roller coasters at Six Flags. Oh, I did go zip-lining once. That made my stomach do flips but I liked it." She chuckled and shook her head.

Ethan was enjoying their conversation. He wanted to hear more. Communicating had come easy for the two of them from the start. He hadn't expected that ease to transfer into playful banter but was glad it had. For once, he wasn't annoyed at the dense rush-hour traffic crawling across the Belt Parkway. He could have stayed in the car laughing and getting to know Zoe all day.

The more she talked about herself, the more intrigued he became. They talked about everything from their backgrounds to work to dreams to politics. Zoe had strong opinions on the latter. They debated current events and shared their favorite shows to binge watch. Ethan was a fan of older shows like *Law & Order* and *Criminal Minds*. Zoe could tolerate those but was a bigger fan of newer series like the ones on Netflix.

It took well over an hour and a half to reach the hotel where the conference was being held. Had it not been for the heavy traffic, they could have made it there in a half hour. New York had its own brand of rush hour painted with impatience, colorful language from angry drivers, aggressive maneuvers and obnoxious horn blowing. Despite the long drive, Ethan felt like they'd arrived too soon. His time of having Zoe all to himself was over. Suddenly he looked forward to the evening drive. Traffic would be just as bad, if not worse, but having Zoe in the car with him would make it all worthwhile.

By the time they arrived, they'd bonded. Ethan couldn't lie. He liked Zoe—a lot. She was incredibly sexy, and he was definitely attracted to her. But she was his employee, which made her off-limits. The most they could be was good friends.

He wished he had met her under different circumstances. Everything about her was refreshing—her conversation, wit, intelligence, style—everything. And the fact that she could change a tire and loved Mustangs gave her bonus points. He hadn't met a woman quite like her before.

There was an undercurrent of strength, resilience and grit about Zoe that he found captivating. That had been missing in the women he'd dated before. Ethan hadn't known how attractive those qualities were until now.

He maneuvered the car into the parking garage under the hotel where the conference was being held. There was a lot more to Zoe than what met the eye. It was all nicely arranged in a beautiful, smart, feminine package. He would have to exercise some special restraint to focus throughout this conference. His curiosity had been seriously piqued.

Once the car was handed over to a valet, they headed

for the elevator. Reaching for the call button at the same time, their hands brushed one another's. Both paused and smiled awkwardly.

Something electrifying generated from the area her hand had touched and traveled up the length of his entire arm. Ethan swallowed hard and cleared his throat. He knew he hadn't imagined that feeling and wondered if Zoe felt the same thing.

It was going to be a long day.

# Seven

As Zoe and Ethan approached the registration table inside the luxury hotel, she tried to shake off the heat that still lingered from being so close to him during their car ride. And that car of his… She'd never been inside a vehicle with that magnitude of luxury. She'd been super proud of her sporty Acura. It was an upgrade for her and had all the premium features. But Ethan's BMW was made for driving.

She loved cars. Despite the potholes that New Yorkers knew all too well, their ride today had been extremely smooth. At times she could have been convinced that the vehicle hadn't actually touched the road. The seats had enveloped her in soft leather. The music had filled the interior with a crispness that had made her feel like the singers could have been sitting in the back seat.

Reflecting on their conversation, Zoe didn't know why she felt so comfortable chatting it up with Ethan. He was so easy to talk to—and fun. She enjoyed his sense of humor, and the way he tapped into hers carried their jokes even further.

They checked in, received their badges and were directed to the great ballroom for breakfast before the conference started. Ethan led them to a table with a sign that displayed their company name. She looked up and smiled when she saw the Blackwell Wealth Management logo flash across the large screens flanking the small stage and podium. She was proud that Blackwell had been one of the sponsors at the conference.

Zoe found a seat and put down her bag. She spotted Jasmine, waved and pointed toward their reserved table. She looked around for Ethan, but he seemed to have disappeared.

The room buzzed with energy. Well-dressed finance professionals from all across the metropolitan area were in attendance. Zoe spotted a few familiar faces as she made her way toward the buffet. She hadn't made many friends in the industry, so she didn't go out of her way to say hello to anyone she recognized. She'd greet them once they were in closer proximity. Her old boss, Seth, popped into her mind and she hope she didn't see him. She stepped into the buffet line and picked up a plate.

"Look who we have here."

At the sound of Seth's voice, all the warmth she'd settled into on her ride to the conference dissipated instantly. Zoe closed her eyes, held her plate with both hands and breathed deeply. She wished she hadn't thought of him and blamed herself for conjuring up his presence. Slowly, she turned around. He was immediately behind her in line. Way too close for her liking.

"Seth." She nodded coolly.

"How's the new gig?" His eyes washed over her from head to toe.

"Great. It's great." She offered a tight smile and turned to focus on the eggs and bacon she put on her plate.

"Glad to hear it."

Zoe decided to choose her selections quickly so she could get back to her table and as far from Seth as possible. "Good seeing you," she lied evenly.

"Yeah. It's good seeing you, too." He stepped uncomfortably close to her. His tone made her look his way. A sly smile eased across his face. Was he trying to flirt with her or intimidate her? "Tell me, did you file that complaint because you didn't get the promotion?"

Zoe just blinked a few times before narrowing her eyes at him. Anger crept up her spine. She filed the complaint because of his inappropriate behavior but it wasn't taken seriously. Seth's behavior persisted. After getting passed over for the second promotion she knew that leaving the company would be inevitable.

Seth reared his head back and dismissed her concern with a wave. "I'm not mad. You were upset. I get it." He stepped in even closer, eliminating any space between them. Zoe stepped back. He smirked. "Maybe if you had been a bit more—" he seemed to search for a word "—friendlier with me, one of those promotions could have been yours."

She gritted her teeth, whipped around and walked away. It was the best she could do without causing a scene.

"We should have lunch one day," he said to her retreating back. She kept walking.

She marched back to the table with steam rising inside of her. She saw that more of the Blackwell team had arrived and she willed herself to calm down. She greeted Bill and Carter, who were standing nearby holding court with Ethan and a few others from Blackwell's headquarters. They greeted her warmly.

She could have sworn she saw Carter pass Ethan a quick look. She couldn't read it but wondered what was behind it. Did it have something to do with her? She shook off that thought. They were brothers. It could have been anything.

Zoe headed to the Blackwell table and took her seat. She began to dig into her breakfast but found she'd lost her appetite.

"I'm not sure if you heard me," Seth said, startling her. She hadn't realized that he had walked up behind her. "I'd like to do…lunch sometime soon. I hope you're not harboring any hard feelings about, you know, from our work together."

This guy was unbelievable. Zoe pulled in her bottom lip before rising slowly. "Seth." She wanted to tell him to leave her alone but chose other words instead. "No." She forced a smile. "No hard feelings. In fact, I should thank you. Standing in the way of me getting ahead actually helped me to spread my wings. Now I have a dream job with amazing people, making so much more money. So don't worry. I'm doing just fine. And no, I don't think we should do lunch. Thank you!" She tilted her head and gave him a satisfied smile.

Seth opened his mouth but didn't speak. He recovered quickly. "Fine. That's great."

She folded her arms and tilted her head, almost daring him to say more.

"Well. How about instead of lunch, dinner would be even better?" He lowered his voice. "I've always been attracted to—" he quickly looked around, then drew closer, forcing her to move back "—women like you."

Zoe's eyebrows furrowed. "Women like me?"

Seth's slick smile returned. "Yeah. You know, from the other side of the fence, the tracks, whatever. You women of color got sass and I like it. What do you say? We don't work together anymore. It can't hurt."

Zoe felt like her temperature had risen by ten degrees in that singular moment. She pointed her finger close to his nose and opened her mouth to douse him with some of the sass he liked so much.

"Ethan Blackwell, of Blackwell Wealth Management." Ethan broke into that moment like a whip. He held his hand out to Seth. "And you are?" He carefully placed his hand on Zoe's lower back.

Zoe closed her mouth, thankful for his sharp interruption. How had he known she needed someone to step in at just that time?

For a brief second, Seth just looked at him. "Ah. Seth Sanders." He took his eyes off Ethan for a moment, looked at Zoe, then back at Ethan. "Um. Good to meet you." He didn't bother to say what company he worked for. "See you around, Zoe." His departure was swift.

Zoe huffed, crossed her arms again and shook her head.

"Old boyfriend?"

"Ugh! No. Former jerk of a boss from my last job. Part of the reason I left."

"Lucky me. I should have thanked him instead of running him off. Does he know what he lost?" Ethan picked up one of the water glasses on the table and sipped it.

Zoe let her arms drop to her sides. "I doubt it. It's hard for him to see around his own ego."

"Oh. One of those. You okay now?"

"Thanks for bailing me out of that."

"You looked like you were about to blow. Between the pursed lips and the finger you almost poked his eye out with, I knew he wasn't a welcome guest. I hope I wasn't being too forward by placing my hand on your back. I wasn't trying to be inappropriate. I just wanted to help."

"No. I'm fine, and thanks again."

"Anytime."

He picked up another glass of ice water and handed it to Zoe. "It's the strongest drink I can muster at this time of the morning."

That made her smile. "Thanks." She took the glass and drank. It helped cool her down. Ethan didn't know it but coming to her rescue in the smooth way he had scored with her in a big way. She could still feel the imprint of his hand where he'd touched her back. It tingled deliciously.

An older gentleman with perfectly cropped gray hair, stark blue eyes, a strong jaw and perfect posture took to the podium in what Zoe determined to be an expensive blue custom-made suit. Turned out, he was the CEO of one of the largest global investment banking firms and on the boards of some major companies, according to his bio inside the conference pamphlet. He was a true Wall Street man who looked every bit of the part.

The gentleman welcomed the conference attendees, thanked the sponsors and delivered a brief state-of-the-industry address. After his speech, he announced that everyone should head to their breakout sessions.

Zoe's schedule included two full days of sessions, meetings, lunches, a dinner and a highly anticipated closing reception at the end of the second day. She wondered if she would be able to ride with Ethan again the next day since their team hadn't bothered booking a room at the host hotel. She wouldn't have time to take care of her bent rim and flat tire until after the conference. Missing any part of the conference was the last thing she wanted; this was the first time in her career that she'd been in a position high enough to participate in these kinds of events.

Zoe followed the rest of her team out of the ballroom to her first session, which was led by a Robert Richford, the CEO of a company providing similar services as Blackwell.

Zoe headed toward the door as the session came to a close. She wanted to compliment the presenter for how much she'd learned but by the time she got to the front of the room, he'd been flanked by people waiting to speak with him. She waited, assuming he'd be a great person to connect with and follow.

When she reached the front of the line, she held out her hand to Robert. "Zoe Baldwin," she said.

"You're part of the Blackwell team, right?" he asked.

"Yes," she said, smiling.

"I thought so. I saw you with them earlier. I hear they're expanding," Robert continued, friendly and interested.

"Yes. I manage one of the Long Island branches."

"Oh really? That's great. Who's your regional director?"

"Ethan Blackwell."

"Right. Yes. Well, here's my card." Robert handed Zoe a card from a designer case. "Perhaps we should have coffee sometime soon. Talk shop. Do some good old-fashioned networking. I promise I won't try to steal you from Blackwell." He chuckled.

"That would be amazing," she said enthusiastically. "I know you must be a busy man. Let me know your schedule and I'll work mine around it."

"Will do." He smiled, nodded and addressed the next person in line.

There was something oddly familiar about Robert, now that she'd spoken with him up close. Zoe wondered what had made him suggest coffee with her specifically, yet she was happy that he had. Willena had always told her that networking was important. Zoe needed to do it more often.

She continued to the next session where Blackwell was slated for a presentation on managing change. The panel was led by the senior Mr. Blackwell, along with Carter, Dillon and Ethan.

Zoe and her team watched intently as the three of them shared their knowledge of market trends and the best ways to navigate the ever-changing environment of the industry. She was especially impressed with Ethan's savvy style of communication. Both he and Carter were witty and elicited a few chuckles from the audience, but Ethan had a certain charm that really pulled people in. As she listened to all of them, her chest swelled with pride for simply being part of the Blackwell team, but she did have one burning question.

Zoe raised her hand. Ethan looked her way. She could have sworn she saw him attempting to hide a smile. She locked eyes with him briefly.

"My question is with regards to diversity, specifically when it comes to women. While I truly believe each and every one of you are brilliant and appreciate the knowledge you have shared, looking at your all-male panel does raise the concern about how our industry looks when it comes to opportunities for women at the top. Can you tell me what changes you see with the roles of women in this industry?"

Several women in the audience applauded her question.

Zoe looked directly at Ethan, and that smile he'd seemed to be hiding eased across his lips.

"I'd love to answer that." Bill raised his index finger.

"Thank you, Mr. Blackwell."

Bill went on to answer Zoe's question in the most favorable way, first speaking to the fact that despite what the presentation of the panelists may suggest, Blackwell's ratio of men to women was just about fifty percent. He further explained some of the major changes across the industry to ensure that they were operating in the most equitable fashion and spoke of the value and expertise that the women on his team brought to the firm.

"Speaking of which, Ms. Baldwin, I think you should join us up here the next time we lead a panel. We can truly show the value that the women and men of Blackwell bring."

"I'd like that, Mr. Blackwell. Thank you for answering my question."

"I'd like to echo my father's comments," Ethan began, "and add that we've worked hard to ensure that we're pulling the best possible talent from the most diverse pool possible. It takes all perspectives to ensure that a company can truly meet the needs of clients and thrive. Diversity shouldn't be an item on an organization's list to check off. It should be imbedded in the DNA of the organization because it impacts every area of a successful business, especially the bottom line."

A proud smile spread across Zoe's face this time. Blackwell was so unlike her last company. She glanced around to see if Seth was in the room. He wasn't, and she actually wished he had been to hear what Ethan had just said. Once again, Ethan scored more points with her. Not that she was counting.

Once the panel ended, people flooded the front of the room to speak with Dillon and the Blackwell men. *The Blackwell men.* They must have made Mrs. Blackwell and the rest of their huge family so proud. Based on Zoe's conversations with Ethan, family seemed to be everything to him. She was sure they had their issues, but on the surface, they appeared to be a perfect bunch.

She intentionally hadn't mentioned much at all about her

sister and mother during the family-centered parts of their conversation during the car ride to the conference.

Zoe looked toward the front of the room. Lots of attendees still milled about, speaking to the Blackwell men. She took notice of the posture of some of the women as they addressed Carter, Dillon and especially Ethan. Some of their body language was a bit flirtatious. A twinge of jealousy hit her and she literally shook her head in an attempt to shake it off. She had no reason to be jealous of the attention women lavished on Ethan.

Zoe pulled out her schedule, checked in with her fellow branch managers and headed off to her next session. As much as she convinced herself how crazy it was to feel jealous, she wasn't interested in standing around watching women pine over Ethan. She walked out of the room, wondering how many of them suggested "lunch or dinner" with him.

She acknowledged to herself that she was being ridiculous. Ethan was nothing more than her boss. That was all he would ever be.

# Eight

"I heard you boys did a good job on the panel at the conference the other day," Ethan's mom, Lydia, said as she sat gracefully at the end of the large dining table. A feast fit for a king's court was spread before them.

She had baked a ham and made stuffed fish, basmati rice infused with fresh herbs, and roasted green beans. Since their children had become adults, Bill had been trying to encourage her to allow someone else to cook for them, but she enjoyed it too much to put it in someone else's hands—especially when it came to cooking for her family.

Bill sat on the opposite end of the table. Between them, their son Lincoln, his wife, Britney, and their two young children, Ava and Logan, occupied one side while Ethan, Carter and their younger sister, Ivy, sat on the other. Even though Ivy was just two years younger than Ethan, they still emphasized the word *little* when they spoke of their younger sister.

Carter had invited his woman of the month—a curvy lawyer named Edison Wells, with honey-colored hair and skin the color of a blanched almond. To everyone else's surprise, this was the second family dinner that Edison had attended.

Today was one of their family Sunday dinners. Once their children had graduated from college and become adults, Bill and Lydia had declared a family day rather than see less of them. Despite their schedules, the entire family came together for dinner on the first Sunday of every month. Until now, Carter had never brought the same "friend" to dinner twice. Everyone around the table was especially tickled.

"Who mentioned that? Was it Dad?" Carter teased his

mother regarding her comment about them doing well at the conference. "I'm glad you told us, Ma. Otherwise we may have never known." He chuckled. "You know Dad isn't one to dole out too much praise."

Bill was known for being stern and didn't shell out compliments often, lest his boys become complacent. He was different with his daughter, Ivy. He complimented her and his lovely wife every chance he got.

"Yeah," Lincoln added. "Dad can be stingy with the accolades."

Each sibling laughed except Ethan. He simply placed a forkful of his mother's delicious salmon in his mouth. Bill's lack of acknowledgment was something for his brothers to tease their dad about on a regular basis. It touched Ethan differently. For him, the subject wasn't so light. Ethan wanted his dad's approval. He wasn't needy at all, but his father's affirmation was extremely important to him.

"Okay, okay." Bill wiped his mouth with a cloth napkin. "Let's not make this Tease Bill Sunday. You're all doing a wonderful job. Okay. Is that better?"

"Bill!" Lydia admonished. She turned to her sons with a smile. "You know your father means well. He's just set in his ways and wants you to continue to reach high. Right, Bill?"

Bill playfully lifted a brow. "Could be."

Lincoln and Carter teased their father a bit more, and he dismissively waved his hand at their banter. Light laughter flitted around the table. Ethan still hadn't joined in any of the jokes.

"Yeah, but it would be nice to hear something affirming from you every now and then." Ethan's expression was stoic. His tone even.

The laughter subsided. Lydia sighed. Bill cleared his throat and the other siblings said nothing.

"Dad. It's just good to know when we have the big man's approval," Lincoln added in what appeared to be an attempt to break the thickening silence.

"I see." Bill's tone was flat.

"Okay, family. It's time for dessert. I made a pecan pie," Lydia announced. She stood and clasped her hands together.

"Yes! I guess I'll have to run that extra mile tomorrow morning," Ivy said. "I'm having a piece of this pie."

"I get the first slice. I'm the oldest." Lincoln raised his hand.

"I'm the youngest," Ivy challenged.

"No!" Logan, Lincoln's son, wagged his little finger. "Ava's the youngest." He pointed to his four-year-old sister and then jabbed his own chest. "And then me!" he said and giggled.

Laughter rose around the table again.

"He has a point," Britney said. "And since I'm their mom and I have to feed them, I should get my piece first along with them."

"Yeah, right!" Carter called out.

"Ha! Nice try, Brit," Ivy said.

"Didn't work, huh?" Britney shrugged and grinned.

Ethan laughed that time but was still a bit affected by the jokes around Bill withholding praise from his boys. He understood his father, but his way never sat well with Ethan. Then again, his situation with his father was different.

"Dessert is served," Lydia announced, placing the pie on the table.

"You only made one!" Ivy frowned. "What're the rest of them going to have?"

"Girl! I don't know where you put all this food." Lydia plopped back into her seat and sniffed. "Metabolism must be on one thousand."

"Yeah. She burns a lot of calories running—" Carter paused for effect "—her mouth!" He looked at his niece and nephew with a cheesy smile, then threw his head back and howled. The two children snickered.

Ivy tossed a napkin at him. "If that's the case, you should be the smallest person in the room but then again—" she turned to the kids "—how would his body hold up that huge head of his?"

Ava and Logan covered their mouths with their little hands and giggled harder.

Ivy winked at them and blew an air kiss to her brother. Carter acted as if he caught it. "Which one of you want this kiss from auntie?" he asked.

"Meeee!" both kids yelled, raising their hands.

"Ivy, we need another one," Carter said.

She kissed her hand and together she and Carter tossed the imaginary kisses at the kids, who pretended to catch them and slap them on their cheeks. The sweet moment elicited more than a few *awws*.

Together, the family dug into the pecan pie. Moans of pleasure rolled around the table as they ate. Once dessert was finished, everyone helped clear the table. The women took to the sitting room and the men headed toward the sliding doors to go onto the deck for their usual after-dinner boy talk.

Bill slowed, gently tugging Ethan's arm. Ethan turned and looked into his father's face. Bill looked pensive.

"What's up, Pop?"

Bill looked around Ethan to make sure his other sons had made it out onto the deck. "I've been meaning to speak to you about something. Come."

Ethan followed his father into the study.

"I noticed how you touched Zoe's back at the conference the other day," Bill began. "The gesture seemed rather... familiar."

Ethan shifted on his feet. He'd only thought about the possible implications of placing his hand on Zoe's back after it was done. His intention had just been to rescue Zoe from a guy who was making her uncomfortable. He cleared his throat and continued to listen.

"You're not involved with this woman, are you?" Bill's eyes narrowed.

"No!" Ethan said quickly. "No, Dad."

Bill sighed. "I don't have to remind you about the situation we dealt with before."

"No, Dad, I wouldn't put our company in jeopardy."

Bill looked disappointed. That bothered Ethan.

"It took a long time for us to overcome that situation. We have to continue to do the right thing by our employees." Bill raised his hands. "If you're involved with her in any way, it needs to stop immediately. If you're not, you have to be careful that your familiarity with this woman isn't misconstrued as any kind of inappropriate behavior."

Ethan felt a heavy sigh coming. He held his breath, not wanting to appear exasperated. He understood Bill's concern, and Ethan's feelings for Zoe made all of this much more complicated.

That sexual harassment claim had almost ruined Blackwell's reputation. Five years before, one of the male managers made a joke in poor judgment and a number of inappropriate comments that made several female team members uncomfortable. One brave woman filed a claim. The management at Blackwell responded immediately, launching an investigation, holding forums and ensuring that employees understood the company's strong stance against harassment. In the end the man apologized to all the women at the firm and was let go. However, due to the media exposure, the incident still caused a stain on the financial giant. It took a few years to clear their name.

"We're in the middle of a very critical expansion," Bill continued. "A problem like this could ruin everything. There's too much at stake here, our growth, our reputation, the culture we've worked so hard to rebuild." He placed a hand on Ethan's shoulder. "And possibly your chances at a promotion, son."

That last comment felt like a punch to Ethan's gut.

"I trust that you're capable of making good decisions.

I can trust you in this, right?" Bill looked directly into Ethan's eyes.

Ethan swallowed. Of course he didn't intend to cause any problems. "Yes, Dad. Of course you can trust me."

Bill patted Ethan's shoulder and nodded. "Good." The two men stood facing one another for several moments. Finally, Bill sighed and nodded. "Good," he said, as if he had more to say but had settled on repeating himself. "Let's go outside."

Ethan followed him through the sliding doors onto the deck for their usual conversation, cigars and scotch. Bill sparked the stone firepit to take the slight autumn chill out of the air.

It took a while for Ethan's tight disposition from their conversation to dissipate. After a while, he loosened up enough to enjoy sitting with his dad and brothers, talking about everything and nothing all the same. Sharp opinions on who would make it to the bowl game clashed. Ethan and Carter talked about how well their office expansions were doing and teased each other about what they would ask for when the other brother lost their personal bet.

When the sun had fully descended with a spectacular show of colors, Bill headed inside to watch TV with the ladies. Lincoln said his goodbyes, noting the need for him and Britney to get the kids home and into bed, leaving Ethan and Carter out on the porch, alone.

"You okay, bro?"

Carter's question caught Ethan off guard. "Me? Yeah. I'm fine."

Silence settled between them as they sipped from their glasses and puffed their cigars.

"If I tell you something," Carter said at last, "you have to promise to keep it to yourself."

Ethan looked at his brother with concern. "Of course. What's up?"

Carter took in a deep breath. "I don't know if I want to stay with the company."

Ethan's eyes widened. "I'm assuming you haven't said anything to Dad about this."

"Nope! You saw how unhappy he was when Lincoln decided to leave to do his own thing."

"Yes. He dreams of having his sons take over the business. What is it that you want to do instead?"

"I don't know. Just something different. I don't plan on leaving yet. I just know this is not what I want to do forever. It's been on my mind a lot lately."

The quiet of the night took over once again. After a while, Carter continued. "I don't know. Maybe it's a phase." He paused again. "Me wanting to leave doesn't mean I don't plan on beating you in this challenge," he said after a while.

"Aw. Your confidence is admirable." Ethan patted Carter's shoulder. "I hope you don't feel too bad when you lose." Both men laughed. Ethan needed that laugh.

"Anyway," Carter interrupted. "How are you doing?" He shifted in his chair and put his foot up on the ottoman. "I noticed you seemed a bit tight during dinner and when you and Dad finally came out onto the deck. You always get a little…you know…quiet when we talk about some of Dad's ways. Why does it bother you so much?"

Ethan was always ready for a good round of jokes but had never liked that his father didn't believe it was necessary to share his approval of his boys. He understood Bill's sternness and he loved his parents immensely, but he also knew something about them that his siblings didn't. He'd been warned never to tell a soul. Ethan and his siblings were close, and they had always shared everything—except this one secret. And it was because of this secret that Ethan desired Bill's approval the most.

"I don't know, man," he finally responded. "It's just important to me, I guess. It's hard for me to make light of."

"It's important to me, too, but despite that, we know how proud he is of us whether he says it or not."

"Of course. But it would still be nice to hear that directly from him."

"True." Carter nodded and sipped his scotch.

"Let's get to the subject on the forefront of everyone's mind." A Cheshire grin spread across Ethan's face. He looked back at the door to make sure no one was approaching. "So Edison made it to a second family dinner. Is she on her way to being my new sister-in-law?"

"Whoa, whoa. Been there… Well, almost," Carter said of the wedding that hadn't actually happened. "Not sure about going back. Edison and I are friends just having a good time. That's all."

"Cool. Just enjoying each other's company, huh?"

"Till the wheels blow off."

Ethan chuckled. "Uh-huh." Since the disastrous end to Carter's engagement a few years ago, he'd taken to running from love like he was being chased by a wild animal. He hadn't dated seriously in years and it wasn't due to a lack of options. However, it was nice to see him enjoying one woman's company even if it was short-lived.

Their conversation reminded Ethan about Zoe. He enjoyed her company a lot, too. He knew he shouldn't but Ethan wished for more time like that with her. The conversation never dulled. Even their periods of silence were comfortable. He cleared his throat. She penetrated his thoughts way too often. Maybe he needed to find someone else's company to enjoy so he could take his focus off Zoe. He couldn't be with her anyway.

He leaned toward Carter as if he had a grand secret to tell and asked, "Does your friend have a friend?"

"Ha! She has plenty of friends, but you wouldn't be interested."

Ethan reared his head back. "Why wouldn't I?"

Carter tossed him a skeptical stare.

Ethan held his hands up. "What?"

"One word... Zoe."

Ethan looked back at the door again. "What? Zoe! She's my employee," he said incredulously.

"And that doesn't seem to stop you from being sweet on her."

"Wh-what?" he stammered.

"You can fake it with your team, but I know you too well, brother. You've been sweet on her since the day she stepped into your office for her first interview. Not that you've done anything wrong," Carter assured him. "And before you ask, no, there aren't any rumors sliding around that I know of. I just know you. I see it as clear as a sunny day. It's in your eyes when you speak about her. The way you smile at the mention of her name. It's evident in the way you try to avoid her when everyone is around. You can fool them, boy, but you can't fool me."

Ethan closed his gaping mouth. There was nothing to say. He was close to all his siblings, but the tie between him and Carter was even more unbreakable. Now his father was suspicious, too. He thought back to their earlier conversation. Bill was right. There was too much at stake. Aside from his possible promotion, Ethan would hate to be the cause of something terrible happening to Blackwell's reputation at such a critical time. He needed to be more careful around Zoe.

"Yet she's untouchable," he said.

"It doesn't help that she's gorgeous." Carter smirked, looked out over the massive yard and took another sip of his drink.

Ethan chuckled before taking a sip of his own scotch. He sighed. What more could he say? Zoe was working her way into his system beyond his control. And she was totally off-limits.

# Nine

Zoe loved the city, but the energy and excitement of Manhattan came at a cost. After navigating the thick rush-hour crowds on the Long Island Rail Road and subway system for this month's management meeting, she was glad she no longer had to deal with that commute on a daily basis.

The weather reports predicted a storm would roll through the city late that evening, but strong winds had already begun to kick up. Wall Street ended abruptly at the Hudson River, and that coupled with the high winds added an unseasonable chill to the air.

Zoe held her coat tight at the neck. The wind beat her face and blew fiercely through her hair, giving her more to contend with as she pushed her way through downtown streets toward the headquarters for Blackwell Wealth Management. It was too early for scarves and gloves, but she wished she had put both on before leaving the house. If the winds were any stronger, she imagined they would pick her up and set her down a few yards back.

Their monthly management meetings usually lasted a full day, but Bill had already mentioned they were likely to end the meeting early to allow everyone to get home safely before the hurricane they'd been tracking would hit their area. Zoe had stocked her and her mother's refrigerators with anything and everything they could possibly need to ride out the storm. She looked forward to a cozy night and full weekend of wine, pajamas, movies and snacks.

She was glad her sister's health was stabilized. When she'd gone to speak with Shena at their mother's house that one night, she'd convinced Shena to get back on her medicine. Shena agreed and had been doing well since. Hopefully it would last. Maybe Zoe would even have Shena join her, or she'd go to her mother's house and spend her movie-watching, pajama-wearing weekend with them. The day was just starting. She had plenty of time to decide.

Braving the increasing winds, Zoe made it into the office fifteen minutes early. She checked in with Security and headed up the twenty flights to Blackwell's offices.

Some of the team had already arrived. Her colleagues stood around the conference room in clusters of two and three, gnawing on fruit and bagels. The smell of fresh-brewed coffee scented the air, and her stomach growled.

"Stand down!" She swatted her belly playfully before placing her coat and bag in a seat next to her fellow branch manager, Jasmine.

Jasmine stopped chewing and chuckled into her hand. "I felt the same way," she said. "I was starving by the time I got here."

"I actually had a fistfight with the wind," Zoe joked. She gestured at her windblown hair. "Obviously I lost."

"Ha!" Jasmine laughed. "It still looks better than mine." She pointed to her own head. It wasn't bad, but it wasn't the perfectly coiffed style she normally wore.

"Be right back." Zoe spun around and headed to the bathroom to assess the damage done to her hair. She finger-combed some of it back into place, freshened her lipstick and washed her hands before returning to the conference room.

She headed to the array of pastries on the console in the back of the conference room. Choosing a sesame bagel, she dug out the bready center and filled it with cream cheese. Then she made herself a steaming cup of coffee and fla-vored it with a creamer. She took a long, slow sniff. The French vanilla creamer made her mouth water.

After a bite and a sip, she moaned. "Jazz," she began, shortening Jasmine's name, "either this is the best darn bagel and coffee I've ever had or I'm hungry as *heck*!"

"I promise you're hungry as heck, but enjoy nonetheless," Jasmine said.

The women laughed just as Ethan and Carter walked through the doors. Zoe sat a little straighter, noting the impact of his presence on her every single time. She would sit straighter, smile harder, smooth her hair into place even if it wasn't mussed. She'd check her teeth for lipstick stains. His presence kept her on guard whether she admitted it or not. She just hoped no one else noticed. Quickly, she tried to eject a sesame seed that had lodged its way into the small gap between her two front teeth before speaking.

"Morning!" Carter sang.

"Good morning, everyone." Ethan's deep voice rolled through her like electrified molasses. It was sweet but still made her tingle.

Morning greetings sprang out across the room.

"Some wind out there, huh?" he acknowledged as he pulled off his overcoat and sat directly across from Zoe.

She would have preferred for him to sit next to her. It would have been easier not to have to look into his gorgeous face. Now she'd have to actively avoid looking at him. She had also caught him staring on several occasions.

Moments later, everyone else had arrived and settled into their seats with various combinations of breakfast foods on paper plates. Bill walked into the room, snatching all the attention. He was a distinguished-looking gentleman who carried himself with perfect posture. His stature exuded importance yet was still warm. Ethan was just like his father.

"Good morning, all, let's dig right in. We'll try to get you all out of here as soon as possible so you can go on home and get comfortable before this big storm sweeps in tonight. Dillon, let's start with your territory."

"Certainly, Bill." Dillon's team stood and made their way to the front of the room to report on their progress.

Carter's team went next and the reporting was rounded out by Ethan's. Carter led in number of new clients, but

Ethan's team was in the lead with the amount of assets acquired. Dillon was close behind on both.

There was so much to go over. Despite how swiftly they moved from one subject to another, the hours rolled on, and before they knew it, it was time for lunch. They jumped right into the next topics after lunch and planned to shorten some of the reports and presentations to let everyone start on their way home.

Suddenly, Bill's executive assistant, Monica, ran into the room to tell the team what was happening outside. At twenty stories off the ground in a sturdy steel-reinforced skyscraper, they were cushioned from the true impact of the elements. All they saw were gray skies and rain.

Bill switched one of the several flat screens from its usual financial channel to the breaking news Monica had told the group about. Everyone balked at what they saw.

The storm was hitting earlier, harder and faster than anyone had expected. Strong winds had already knocked out power lines in areas right outside and around the city. Several trains in the subway system were affected by the outages and were now dealing with signal problems. Large debris had been blown across the rails for some of the commuter trains. Zoe hoped she could get out of the city without any major delays.

Bill called the meeting to a close and told everyone to make their way home as best they could and to check in once they arrived. The group said quick goodbyes and headed out.

Jasmine, Brian, Zoe and Ethan, who were all headed to Long Island, agreed to travel to Penn Station together. Less than twenty minutes later, they arrived to find the station in a state of complete chaos, teeming with people waiting on trains and complaining of delays and cancellations. They navigated through the dense crowd as closely as possible, trying to find information on when their trains would depart to Long Island.

Jasmine found that her train was leaving in seven minutes. She hugged her coworkers and raced through the throngs of people toward her platform. Brian decided to head to his mother's house in Queens and jumped on a subway that was still operating. That left Ethan and Zoe to wait on information about their trains.

Zoe dialed Jasmine to make sure she'd boarded safely.

"I made it, but you won't believe how many people are on this train," Jasmine said breathlessly. "I'm squished against the door. A lot of folks couldn't get on and have to wait for the next one. What time is your train leaving?"

"Lucky you. I don't know what time my train will leave. They pushed the departure back. They keep changing the information. The signaling problems seem to be affecting more and more lines. Let me know when you get home, okay?"

"And you do the same," Jasmine replied.

"Look at this." Ethan held his phone out so Zoe could see what he was watching. He handed her one of his earbuds so she could hear over the noise in the station.

She watched and listened in awe as a weather situation like none she'd ever seen in all her days as a New Yorker played out before her. This was worse than the superstorm the city had experienced several years before.

Breaking news announced that the storm had in fact hit the tristate area well in advance of when they'd anticipated, bringing with it harsh elements and extreme winds. It had already dumped several inches of rain across New Jersey and was dumping just as much over New York City. It swept across the city with a swift vengeance. There was even talk of tornadoes touching down in some areas. The hurricane ravaged the area, uprooting trees, flooding homes and businesses and leaving thousands without power.

"Wow." All Zoe could do was shake her head. She and Ethan continued to wait for updates from the stations. For a long time, it didn't look like any trains were pulling out at all.

After she and Ethan had been waiting well over an hour and a departure time for her train still hadn't been posted, Zoe was beginning to believe she wasn't going to make it home. She called to check on her mother and sister. Fortunately they were safe in her mother's house.

"Keep us posted, honey. Let us know what's happening. Come here if it's easier for you than getting home."

"Thanks, Ma! I'll let you know."

Zoe ended her call and huffed. What if she couldn't get out of the city? She'd have to stay at a hotel. She didn't have any close friends in Manhattan.

She and Ethan listened to more news and continued checking the board for any updates on departures. Each time an announcement blared over the PA system, she prayed they would mention her train. Instead they announced more cancellations and delays.

"Any updates on your train?" she asked Ethan at last.

"No, but I'll be okay. I have an apartment here in the city if I can't get back home," he admitted. "I lived downtown while attending grad school and decided to keep the place after graduating. I go there sometimes after work or if I don't feel like heading to Long Island after hanging out late. You're welcome to stay there if you'd like. I don't keep the refrigerator or cabinets as well stocked as I do my home on Long Island but there's enough to get by."

"Thanks for the offer, but I'll figure something out." Zoe was grateful but didn't think staying at her good-looking boss's house was the best idea.

Her phone rang. It was Jasmine. "Hey. How's it going?"

"I can't hear you!" Jasmine said.

Zoe repeated herself more loudly. Penn Station was now filled to the brim with panicking riders worrying about getting home to kids and pets.

"I just got off the train." Jasmine was yelling into the

phone. "The parking lot is flooded. I've never seen anything like this before. I'm wading through water to get to my car now. How are you making out?"

Zoe huffed. "I'm still at Penn Station. Only a few trains left right after yours. Nothing else has moved since then. It's been well over an hour."

"Oh my goodness. What are you going to do? If they don't start letting trains through soon, you'll have to get a room, Zoe!"

"Ugh. What a nightmare. I'm hoping this passes through as quickly as it came."

"You and me both," Jasmine said.

"Text me when you're home safe."

"Okay. And you let me know if you make it home or end up staying in the city," Jasmine insisted.

"Will do." Zoe shook her head before adding, "Have a good weekend despite the weather."

"I prepared, so let's hope all goes well."

"Okay. Talk to you later." Zoe ended the call. She had to figure out her next move. "Ethan, you don't have to wait on me. If these trains don't start moving soon, I'll get a hotel for the night." She smiled at him. "I appreciate you making sure I'm okay, but I don't want to hold you up any longer. You could be warm, safe and dry in your apartment by now. Oh! And how'd your brother and father make out?"

"Don't worry about me," he insisted. "I want to make sure you're okay. I just spoke to Brian. He made it to his mother's house. Carter and Dad are fine. Carter jumped on the subway to his place in downtown Brooklyn and Dad made it across the Williamsburg Bridge just before it was shut down due to winds and flooding."

"The Williamsburg was shut down?" Zoe asked in disbelief. This truly was another superstorm.

"Yep. Can't believe it. The news said some subway stations were closed due to flooding, as well."

"Whoa." She shook her head. It seemed that she'd definitely have to spend the night in Manhattan. She looked around at the crowded train station. All she could see were tightly packed people for yards.

"Listen. You go ahead and try to make it to your apartment before you get stuck," she said again. "I'm going to head to one of these nearby hotels and get a room. I need to move quick before all these people start filling up the vacancies."

"It's fine. I want to make sure you're okay," he repeated.

The sincerity in his tone was touching. Despite her telling him she'd be fine on her own, she was glad he was staying with her. Not being able to get home was unsettling. She tried hard to keep it together.

A woman next to her was frantically crying into her cell phone about having no one to pick up her daughter from day care. It made Zoe want to cry with her. Poor woman. Poor child. Being stuck was bad enough. She couldn't imagine being stuck and unable to get to her children. She wanted to help the woman but what could she possibly do? They were in the same position.

Though Zoe had never suffered from the condition, she now understood what claustrophobia felt like. The air felt thick. She had to get out of that station so she could breathe.

Ethan was still by her side.

"Let's get out of here," she told him at last. "I need to find a room."

"Okay." He immediately grabbed her hand and led the way through the dense crowd of people in Penn Station.

Outside, the rain came down in sheets. Zoe pulled her umbrella from her bag, but the moment she opened it, the wind took it away. She watched in disbelief as it tumbled down Thirty-Fourth Street. The forceful winds threatened to treat her the same way.

"Come on." Ethan tugged, leading her by the arm.

The stoplight turned green and they headed across the street to the Hotel Pennsylvania. Cars lined up along Seventh Avenue as far as they could see. Windshield wipers swung rapidly, sending water into the air. Despite the short distance between the station and the hotel, Zoe and Ethan were drenched when they reached the lobby.

Zoe couldn't believe her ears when the woman at the registration desk said they were already out of rooms. Between the conference they were hosting and the people who'd booked rooms because they couldn't get out of the city, the hotel had no vacancies left.

"Let's go over here." Ethan led her across the lobby to a corner that wasn't overcome with people trying to stay dry. "Let's call some of the other hotels in the area. We can also try checking in online."

"That's a good idea. I'll call some and if you don't mind, can you check others online?"

"Sure." Ethan began swiping away at his cell phone.

Zoe was so grateful for his presence. She pulled up local hotels and began making calls. Each one said they were at capacity.

"This travel app seems to have a few vacancies." Ethan turned his phone around so she could see the display.

Zoe pulled up the same app on her phone and booked a room a few blocks away. Ethan headed back outside to hail a taxi. It took at least twenty minutes for an empty one to pass by. The hotel was just a few blocks north on Eighth Avenue, but it took another half hour to make it there. Had it not been for the ball-size raindrops, they could have walked and gotten there faster.

They finally arrived at the hotel only to be told they didn't have any rooms available.

"But I have a confirmation!" Zoe waved her phone in the air. Her last bit of patience departed. "What do you mean you can't accept the reservation?"

The exhausted woman behind the counter explained that the app had somehow allowed the booking in error because there were absolutely no vacancies left. She explained how to request money back from the app.

Zoe couldn't believe this was happening to her. Then she thought about all those people down in Penn Station, still hoping to make it home.

"Look, Zoe," Ethan said at last. "This is not working out. Just come to my place. You'll be safe there. We'll grab something to eat and wait this out for a bit. Hopefully the trains will be back on track in a few more hours."

"Thank you, Ethan, but I'd hate to impose."

Imposing wasn't the problem. While it was fun to secretly crush on him, being with him in his Manhattan bachelor pad was just too much.

"It's not a problem. Let's go."

"I don't know…"

"Then what are you going to do?" he asked. "If we stay out here any longer, we'll both get sick."

Zoe huffed. What was she going to do? She had been completely soaked from head to toe for a while now and had begun shivering. "Let me try a few more hotels."

"Sure," Ethan said. "Let's try a few more."

Zoe called hotels outside of the immediate area, hoping she would have a better chance booking a room. Some still didn't have vacancies and others just weren't able to promise her a room over the phone because of the volume of hopefuls filling their lobbies.

Reluctantly, Zoe turned to Ethan and threw her hands up. She felt defeated and wished she could blink and magically appear in her own living room. "I guess it's your place."

"Come on." He took her by the hand again and maneuvered out of the crowded hotel back into the heavy rain. "Let's hope we get a taxi faster this time."

The rain pelted them like darts. After a long while, they were finally able to get a taxi. The ride to SoHo took forever through flooded streets. Water ran down the windshield like someone was on top of the car pouring buckets over the glass.

Finally, they made it to Ethan's apartment building. Zoe was soaked down to her undergarments, her hair stuck to her face and her shoes squeaked when she walked across the lobby floor. But once she stepped inside his apartment, the beauty of it made her momentarily forget all she'd just waded through.

Ethan's place was stunning with an airy vibe. Dark wood floors made a striking contrast against stark white walls adorned with huge canvases of beautifully framed art. The stylish yet masculine decor brought together strong, dark colors against warm and creamy hues. Navy blue sofas held ivory pillows on one end and gray pillows on the other. The space opened to a kitchen with all of the cabinets and appliances aligning one wall and a massive granite-topped island setting the space apart from the living room. Next to the kitchen sat a dining table with places for six.

"Here. Let me take your coat," Ethan offered.

Zoe peeled it off and handed it to him. She felt a rush of coolness and hugged herself to ward off the chill. She looked up at the lofty exposed ceilings. Through the fully windowed wall, the storm looked like a beautiful but unsettling work of art. She took off her soggy shoes and walked around slowly.

"It's beautiful in here," she said finally.

"Thanks. I'll see if I can find you something dry to put on or at least get you some blankets. Then I'll see what I have in the freezer that I can defrost. There's probably not much more than water and butter in the fridge. I'm sure I have pasta and a few jars of sauce somewhere."

"Okay." Zoe heard him but never took her focus off of admiring the space.

Moments later, he emerged with a hoodie and sweats that were sure to be too large for her.

"You can change in that bedroom or the bathroom down there on the right." Ethan pointed.

Zoe released a heavy sigh. "Thanks, Ethan." She went into the bathroom, which was clad in marble from the ceiling to the floor. A floating vanity with a stone sink boasted contemporary faucets, making the small bathroom look like something straight out of a fancy hotel. She peeled off her wet clothes, leaving just her underwear, and put on the oversize sweats Ethan had given her. They were big, soft and dry and for that she was grateful.

She put her belongings in the spare room he'd offered, then headed back to the living area and found Ethan already changed.

She was used to him looking handsome in tailored suits, but Zoe wasn't ready for how rugged and sexy Ethan would be in simple sweats and a college T-shirt. His taut chest strained against the university's logo. The short sleeves exposed muscular arms wrapped in smooth brown skin. She watched his muscles shift and flex as he pulled food from the freezer. Not knowing what to do with herself, Zoe joined him in the kitchen.

"Can I help?" she asked pensively, not wanting to get too close. The pressure of being alone with him at his place was both stimulating and nerve-racking. Still, she'd had no choice, she reasoned.

"You like burgers and fries?" he asked. "I found some ground turkey in the freezer."

"Turkey works for me"

"Cool. No help needed. Why don't you find something on TV? I'll whip up one of my gourmet burgers for you. I found some good bread in the fridge."

Again she thought about how grateful she was that Ethan had waited with her. What would she have done if he'd gone home and left her alone at Penn Station? She might have ended up sleeping on a bench.

Zoe called her mother and sister to let them know she

was safe and had gone to a "friend's" house in the city to ride out the storm. They were glad to hear that she was okay.

She pointed the remote at the television and found a news station to get more updates on the weather. Hopefully she'd be able to head home in a few hours.

She glanced back at Ethan in the kitchen. He was humming as he patted out the burgers. She'd never been in an apartment like this before or with a man like him, and for just a moment, she allowed her imagination to roam. What would it be like to actually be the girlfriend of Ethan Blackwell?

# Ten

"What did you do to that burger?" Zoe asked, popping the last fry in her mouth. "That was amazing."

"Can't tell you." Ethan kept his eyes on the television with his feet comfortably propped on an ottoman.

Zoe gave him a sideways glance. Ethan laughed. She looked beautiful even when she shot him sketchy looks.

"I have to give you credit," she said. "It was great. I didn't peg you for a cook."

"You figured I was spoiled." He let the assumption hang in the air.

Zoe remained quiet. After several moments ticked away in silence, she offered up a puppy dog look. "Guilty as charged," she finally admitted.

"You do karate and change tires. I cook—among other things—*and* change tires."

Zoe shrugged. "I misjudged you."

"Yep. You did. Consider us even, though. I misjudged you, too. I was surprised you knew so much about cars."

"Surprise!" Zoe chuckled. It was like a soft melody.

He smiled. Not because of the funny way she'd said *surprise*, but because the sound of her laughter gave him a sense of joy.

Her perfectly plump lips made Ethan want to reach over and kiss her. Instead, he got up, took her empty plate, placed it on top of his and headed to the kitchen. "Want a refill on your iced tea?"

"Sure."

Ethan stayed in the kitchen longer than necessary. He had to put some distance between Zoe and himself. Being close to her was wreaking havoc on his will. Having her all to himself like this when she was completely off-limits was taking a toll on him.

He studied her for a quick moment as she took in the news. Her hair had dried some. Even his oversize clothing looked good on her. Her frizzy tresses and the sight of his clothes on her shapely body made his imagination run wild. Zoe looked a sexy mess.

After a while, he returned with the jug of iced tea and poured more in her cup, set the jug down and turned up the volume on the television. Updates on the train system would be a safe distraction.

"I need to—" Zoe turned to him to speak but stopped abruptly when she noticed him studying her. She cleared her throat "—let my mom know I'll be home later than I thought."

He smiled. "Sure." Then sat back and returned his focus to the news.

Zoe stood, grabbed her cell phone and called her mother. She paced the kitchen as she talked. From what Ethan overheard, her family seemed to be fine.

While she spoke to them, he reached for his phone and dialed 311, New York City's service line. He asked about transportation updates in an attempt to get more information for Zoe. To his surprise, Manhattan was completely cut off from the other boroughs. The bridges were shut down because of strong winds, and tunnels, stations and streets were flooded all over the metropolitan area. Sporadic power and out-of-order streetlights caused traffic debacles. Trees were down everywhere.

Ethan ended his call and turned up the volume on the TV. The mayor was declaring a state of emergency, and authorities encouraged everyone to stay inside until the storm passed. Soggy newscasters, out on location and covered by ineffective raincoats, reported on the extreme weather conditions as they were pelted by large raindrops and jostled by the wind. Their cameras showed scenes of people taking shelter inside restaurants and stores. Stranded commuters were packed in bus and train stations across the city.

Ethan looked out his lofty windows. A brooding darkness loomed across the sky. As if on cue, lightning flashed and thunder rolled, making Zoe flinch where she stood in the kitchen. Ethan wished he could hold her in his arms.

This storm didn't look like it was passing anytime soon. Even if it did, how soon would transportation get back up and running? Maybe the bridges would open first. He could drive Zoe home with the car he kept in the garage below the apartment building. But what about those flooded streets?

Zoe ended her call and came back to sit on the couch.

"I have good news and not so good news," Ethan began.

"Okay." She stretched the word with curiosity.

"Which do you want first?"

"Hit me with the bad news," she said, throwing up her hands. "It can't get much worse than it already is, can it?"

"Well…" Ethan sighed. "I don't think you're going to get home tonight."

She groaned. He shared the information he'd gathered from 311 and the news.

"This is horrible," she grumbled. "I never thought I'd see anything like this in New York again."

"I know. Me, too." A few moments of silence passed as they absorbed this reality.

"So what's the good news?" Zoe finally asked.

"You're welcome to say here for the night."

Zoe stiffened at once.

"If you're okay with it," he rushed. "I'm concerned that you won't get a room anywhere at this point." He sensed how uncomfortable this made her. As her boss, he understood. "You can sleep in the spare room. If the trains still aren't running in the morning, I can drive you home. I keep one of my cars here for when I stay over."

"You…" Zoe cleared her throat. "Are you sure you don't mind?"

"Do you have a better option?"

Zoe looked around as if she'd find a better option right there in the room. "I guess not."

"Besides food, we have Netflix, a deck of cards and a DVD player."

"Wait! A what? Who still has a DVD player?" Zoe's eyes widened and she chuckled.

"I do!" Ethan said confidently. "It's Blu-ray with Wi-Fi, Netflix, Amazon Prime and YouTube. Sometimes I want to watch movies that aren't on Netflix or Prime. I have a few old favorites that I can watch whenever I want to."

"Okay." She nodded approvingly. "Now that I think of it, that's not such a bad idea. I can't stand it when I want to watch something and can't find it on any of those services. You're a smart guy after all, Ethan."

"I am pretty smart." He stood, puffed his chest and strutted over to his bookshelf.

"You're hilarious, too."

He laughed, relaxed his posture and picked up a few DVDs, shuffling through them. "Come see if there's anything you want to watch."

Zoe hopped up from the couch and joined him as he sifted through his movie collection. She seemed more comfortable now. A bit cheery, even. He was glad. He didn't want her to feel uncomfortable. She might be off-limits, but he'd never deny enjoying her company. The fact that he was going to be able to continue enjoying her presence tonight made him smile. But misbehaving wasn't an option, no matter how kissable her lips looked.

"You have so many older movies," she commented.

Ethan reached for the movie she held, the first in the *Fast & Furious* franchise. "There's a new *Fast & Furious* movie coming this year. I can watch the entire series and get ready for the latest installment."

"I love that franchise," she confessed. "That's actually what I did before the latest *Avengers* movie came out. And you're right, I had to get creative in order to find some of the earlier movies." She paused a moment, tilting her head. "I think it might be time to buy myself a DVD player."

"See what I mean?" Ethan nodded.

They fell silent for a bit while Zoe went through the movie collection.

"So, did you decide on anything you'd like to watch?" he asked after she'd put a few aside.

"A few things. Let me narrow down my choices. Oh!" Her sudden excitement caught Ethan's attention. "*Avatar*! I loved that movie. Wanna watch that?"

He shrugged. "Let's do it."

Zoe handed him the movie, and he inserted it into the player, then made his way back to the couch with the remote.

"Something to drink before the movie starts?" he asked. "Truthfully, I don't have much more than some soda and several choice bottles of wine." Ethan thought for a moment. "Not sure if you're a scotch drinker. I do have some choice scotch and a nice bourbon."

Zoe chuckled. "I had a former boss who drank scotch. She said her father taught her to appreciate it and that resulted in her being respected by some of the most prominent businessmen in the world."

"It sounds crazy but it's true. A woman who knows and can handle a good scotch is one to be reckoned with."

Zoe chuckled. "You don't seem to have much in the way of regular food here, do you?"

"Guilty." He held his hands up. "I'm usually here to entertain so I never run out of spirits. Scotch or wine?"

"I'll start with wine," Zoe said.

"Okay. Red or white?"

"Red."

"Oh. Bold. I like it."

"Yes. It's even better with chocolate—especially dark chocolate."

"I definitely don't have any chocolate here."

"Didn't think so. Would have been nice."

Yes, Ethan thought as he selected a nice cab and poured her a glass. It would have been really nice to feed her chocolate between sips. But that wasn't what Zoe was there for. She wasn't his company to entertain in that way.

He wondered what it would be like to date a girl like her. She was nothing like any woman he'd ever been with. Of course they, too, had been smart, confident, ambitious, fashionable and so much more—just not in the way that Zoe was. She owned and exuded each adjective in ways he'd never seen before. Most women he knew wouldn't touch a tire, let alone change it. Zoe's confidence didn't border on conceit. She was sure and comfortable with who she was. Plain and simple. She was also sexy in a natural way. She didn't put sexy on like a cloak and try to convince the world of her appeal. She just was. Her appeal was effortless. That was what intrigued him most.

Ethan wondered why she didn't seem to have a boyfriend. He hadn't asked. Of course it would have been inappropriate since he was her boss, but he wanted to know. There was so much he wanted to know about Zoe, but he had to tread carefully.

"…Ethan?"

"Yes." He realized she'd called his name more than once. He poured himself a glass of wine and pushed away those thoughts.

"You're with me?"

"Yeah. Just thinking…that's all." He stopped there, unable to share more. "Ready." He held up the remote, his thumb hovering over the play button.

"Ready! I love this movie. Haven't seen it in so long."

"Here goes." He pushed the button. For the next two hours and forty-plus minutes, they remained enthralled in the decade-old blockbuster movie, polished off two more glasses of wine and munched on chips and a few other snacks that Ethan found hiding in his pantry.

The movie ended, leaving them in a limbo of awkward quiet. He looked at his watch. It was just past nine.

"Let's see what the news is saying about the storm now."

Ethan flipped to the news. They took in several moments of reporting from various stations, all of them saying the same thing. This storm was categorized as the most severe storm of the decade, and despite how much the city had prepared, New York just hadn't been ready for the resulting damage. And the storm wasn't over. The mayor detailed all that the city was doing to help residents navigate through this disaster. Most important for Ethan and Zoe, trains still weren't running and the bridges had yet to open. Zoe definitely wasn't getting home tonight.

Ethan muted the TV, quieting the bad news. He and Zoe sat back on the couch at the same time, looked at each other and acknowledged their twin behavior with a smile.

"Another movie?" he asked.

"Where are those cards you had? Ever play War?"

"War?" He scrunched his nose curiously.

"Yes. Get the cards. It's a little silly, but fun."

Ethan was much more of a poker player but was happy to indulge her. He got up from the couch and headed over to the same shelf that held his DVDs. When he returned, he handed her the cards. Zoe shuffled them.

"Okay. My sister and I used to play all the time when we were kids. We start with the same number of cards, keep them facedown and turn them over only when it's time to play a card. Whoever plays the highest card gets to take two cards that were already played and add them to their deck. If we play the same card, then we declare war, playing one card per word, 'I. Declare. War.'" She demonstrated, laying down three cards as she spoke. "Whoever plays the highest card on the word *war* takes all the cards played. You win by getting all the cards. Got it?"

"I think so." Ethan furrowed his brows.

"It's easier than it sounds. Come on." Zoe dealt the cards and taught him as they played.

Once he got the hang of it, he played more aggressively, raising the stakes. The intensity made both of them more competitive. They opened two more bottles of wine, adding to what they'd shared during the movie, loosening their tongues, evoking a more comfortable, uninhibited vibe between them.

"Ha! Got you that time." Ethan thrust both hands in the air after winning and boasted, "War."

"Beginner's luck."

"No luck. That's skill!"

"Really, Ethan? That would make sense if you could actually see what card you're playing. The cards are facedown when you pull them, silly."

She laughed at him, and he couldn't help but join in.

They played several more games, talking trash and mocking one another when they won, slamming down winning cards, grunting and groaning their losses, having unadulterated, tipsy fun.

Next, Zoe taught Ethan how to play a game called Spit—another two-player game that required quick thinking, coordination and speed. The wine they drank hindered all three, causing them to exude more laughter than skill.

A few games in, Zoe was in the lead. Ethan had repositioned himself to better grab the smaller stack of cards, but he still moved too slow and Zoe grabbed the stack. The larger pile was now Ethan's hand, bringing him closer to losing the game. Now they were down to their last play of the latest game.

Ethan sat leaning forward, ready to slam his hand down and claim his victory. He played several cards. Zoe slipped in and played a few from her hand. He watched intently, keeping an eye on how many cards she had left. She was down to two. If Zoe hit the empty spot first, she'd score another win. If Ethan beat her to it, he was back in the game and would have another chance. He readied his hand to hit the empty pile.

Zoe played her very last card.

Time seemed to move in slow motion.

She raised her hand. Ethan raised his. Both aimed for the empty spot, in a race to secure the win or get back in the game. Zoe's hand reach the floor a split second before Ethan's, and his hand landed on top of hers.

For a brief electrifying moment, all his senses converged. All he could feel was a pulsing sensation that shot through his hand on top of hers. In that millisecond, he felt how soft her skin was and wished he could continue touching her.

The moment was over as quickly as it began.

Zoe rapidly slid her hand from under his, jumped to her feet and thrust both arms triumphantly in the air. "I win again!" She rolled her arms in front of her in a Cabbage Patch dance, singing "I'm a winner" over and over again. She switched up her dance with some flossing and ended with a dab.

After her silly display, she plopped back down on the couch, and all Ethan could do was laugh. He wasn't used to losing but the sweet sound of her joy made him want to see her win every moment of every day. Her laugh seemed to erupt from the center of her core, and he loved the sound of it. Enjoying her glee, he watched her. Watched her plump lips part, framing a perfect set of teeth. Watched the sensual line of her neck as she threw her head back. Watched her tresses bounce as her shoulders shook. Watched her eyes sparkle with joy. He noticed her smooth, glowing skin.

His hand moved without instructions from his brain. He responded to a need that compelled him, and he gently touched her cheek with the backs of his fingers.

Zoe's laughter subsided. Her eyes locked with Ethan's. No words passed between them. None were needed; all the desire they'd tried to contain seemed to take over, pulling them to one another. Instinct took over. Inch by inch, they drew closer, mouths parted, ready for each other.

Ethan's eyes closed seconds before their lips connected, and electricity exploded inside of him. He wrapped his arms around her, and she placed her hands on his face, pulled him in and kissed him harder.

They kissed like they had been starved and their lips were the only thing that could satisfy their hunger. He didn't want to let her go. She clung to him as if she felt the same. They kissed until they had to stop just so they could breathe.

# Eleven

Zoe opened her eyes in time to glimpse the warm hues of the sunrise through floor-to-ceiling windows. She looked around and tried to blink the confusion away. Obviously, she wasn't at home. Where was she? It took a few moments to gather her wits about her. She looked around once more and remembered.

The memories appeared before her in flashes—breaking news, thunder, lightning, the *Avatar* movie, playing cards, wine and the kiss. Instinctively, she touched her lips, remembering how his lips on hers had taken her breath away. She had kissed her boss. Zoe closed her eyes. She shook her head. She'd kissed her boss and loved it! If she were honest with herself, she'd admit she wanted to do it all over again.

At that memory, Zoe closed her eyes and let her head fall back. She felt sluggish with a slight headache.

Lifting her head, she scanned the posh, spacious living area. She never had made it to that second bedroom. Nor had Ethan made it to his. He was sprawled out on the floor near the couch where Zoe slept. How much did they drink?

A hint of panic settled in. She had always been careful not to drink too much when she was with coworkers. That had proved to be a dangerous choice for colleagues in the past. She never wanted to have to take that walk of shame through the office after doing too much at a company event.

The spectacular colors of the sunrise caught her eye once more. Instead of panicking, Zoe decided to take the moment to enjoy watching the sun come up. With the position of Ethan's apartment and the height of his floor, the view was unhindered. She took a deep breath and simply watched.

Zoe was a born-and-bred New Yorker, yet she'd never seen a sunrise from this perspective.

The urge to relieve herself hit her fiercely. As quietly as possible, she slid off the couch, picked up her phone and tiptoed to the bathroom without waking Ethan. She thought about last night. She'd actually had a great time with him. The initial discomfort she'd felt about sharing such intimate space with her boss had passed as the night went on—with help from the wine, of course. She'd been warm, dry and safe. What more could she ask for?

Zoe wondered about all those people who had been stranded at the train and bus stations. What had happened to them? What about the parents who couldn't get to their children? She said a quick silent prayer for those impacted by the storm.

She stayed in the bathroom to check in on her mother and sister. She didn't want to wake Ethan with her conversation. "Hey, Ma. How are things going?"

"Not too bad, considering." Laura sighed. "Our lights went out last night."

"Ugh! Did they say when they will be back on?"

"No. How about you? Still in the city?"

"Yeah. Couldn't get out yesterday. No one was supposed to be on the roads. I'm hoping I can get home today."

"This is truly something, isn't it? I'm glad we went shopping before all this started."

"I'm glad, too. You have food. I would have been going nuts over here if you didn't."

"Thank God. When you get out of the city, don't worry about coming here," Laura insisted. "We're going to be fine. Go home and check your place. See if you have electricity. I've been listening to the radio all morning. The damage is bad. Power lines are down. Trees have fallen on cars and houses. And some of the train stations…whew! The news showed video of water flowing down the steps like someone was pouring out a jug. The commuter rails have flooding up to the platforms. You could actually see fish swimming in the tracks!"

"Wow!"

"I know."

For several moments, Zoe and her mother were simply silent, the only sound the two of them breathing. Zoe was glad that the worst of the damages her mother had experienced was a power outage.

"Okay, Ma. I'll let you know when I leave here."

"Keep me posted."

"Will do."

Zoe ended the call with her mother and dialed a neighbor. She wasn't particularly close with any of her neighbors, but they did look out for each other. Her neighbor said that, like Laura's area, their town house complex had lost power, and listed all the other damage the storm had done in their community. Zoe thought about all the food she'd have to toss because of the loss of electricity. She shook her head and decided to save that worry for when she got home.

She noticed that Ethan had left a folded towel, face cloth, toothbrush and travel-size bottle of mouthwash on a small shelf inside the bathroom. She freshened up, then walked back out to the living area to be greeted by the mouthwatering aroma of fine coffee. She could also smell a hint of vanilla. She didn't see Ethan, but she heard the faint sounds of a shower running behind his closed bedroom door.

Zoe headed to the kitchen and poured steaming coffee into a mug that Ethan had obviously set out for her. She topped it off with creamer and returned to the living room to get the latest updates on the news.

The storm had passed, but the city was still paralyzed due to the damage it had left in its wake. Bridges and tunnels were still closed. Businesses and residences alike were running on backup generators due to all the power lines that were down. Transformers had actually caught fire in the rain. It was going to take a while for the city to recover.

Zoe had no idea when she'd be able to make it home, but she tried to remain hopeful. She'd already survived one night in her boss's private domain.

Still, she hoped she didn't have to stay at Ethan's place another night. Besides not wanting to be an imposition, being this close to him challenged her ability to focus. She was used to seeing him in business attire. Seeing his taut body in a T-shirt and sweats with bare feet showed him in a whole different light, one that was laid-back, comfortable and incredibly sexy. Zoe had only hoped he hadn't caught her taking in his pecs and biceps. By contrast, she had on his clothes and was sure she looked a frumpy mess.

She had seen many sides of Ethan yesterday. She loved how he'd taken charge and insisted that she let him help her, all to ensure she'd be okay. Zoe had always loved a man keen enough to wield the right balance of humor, wit and consideration. They'd had fun last night. His playful and competitive demeanor teased her. His concern for her safety warmed her. His thoughtfulness moved her.

All of these things were reasons for her to get out of his place as soon as possible.

Zoe curled up on the couch, sipped from her coffee cup and refocused her attention on the news.

"Good morning."

Ethan's rich voice startled her. It sounded a bit lower than usual, causing a slight squiggle to curl down her back. She chalked it up to him being tired just like she was. She swallowed quickly. "Oh! Hey. Good morning." She tried to appear unaffected.

"I didn't mean to startle you. How's the coffee?"

She took another sip. "Delicious."

"Good."

Ethan walked into the kitchen, opened the refrigerator and pulled out eggs and a few other items. "I hope you like frittatas."

"I do."

"Good. There's not much more in here for breakfast. We can do that and some toast with water and coffee?"

"Sounds great to me."

Zoe watched as he worked his way around the large island, pulling out pans and preparing to cook. He had on a different T-shirt and sweats than the night before but looked just as sexy. His body boasted of a regular workout regimen. And even from the couch, he smelled fresh and amazing. She took in a long sniff. His oaky scent mixed with her French vanilla coffee was delightful.

"Can I help?" The words came out before she realized she'd offered. "You've already done so much. The least I could do is help with breakfast."

"Sure."

Zoe unfolded her legs, got up off the couch and joined him in the kitchen. In silence, they worked seamlessly together as if they'd cooked this way every day. She finished whipping the eggs while Ethan chopped veggies before tossing them into the hot frying pan. They had a rhythm and it worked well.

The only disruptions were the moments where they accidentally touched, causing tingling sensations to crawl over Zoe's skin. She hoped she was the only one to feel those tingles. She remembered their kiss and shivered, hoping he hadn't noticed.

It helped that he was off-limits. Zoe didn't mind crushing on Ethan; it made working with him fun. But she had never in a million years thought of acting on any of it. She loved and needed her job.

"It's still pretty bad out there but I'll be out of your hair today," she said, breaking the silence. "Thanks so much for putting me up last night."

"I saw the reports while I was getting dressed," Ethan said. "You still might not be able to get home today."

She sighed. "Yeah. But don't you worry. I'll be out of your hair either way."

"Zoe." The way Ethan called her name caused her breath to catch. His voice held so much concern. He turned to look at her and she almost couldn't stand the caring but penetrating way he looked at her. "It's dangerous out there. You're welcome to stay another night. Really, it's not a problem. And I have the room."

"Uh…um…" She cleared her throat. "You've done enough, Ethan. I appreciate it so much, but I need to try to get home and deal with what the storm left for me there."

He looked pensive for a quick moment. "Okay. I'll do what I can to help. If we can get across any of the bridges or through the tunnels, I'll drive you home. We can assess our options after we eat."

The two returned to silence and finished preparing the few items they had for breakfast. The frittatas were tasty and all they had to wash down the food was water and coffee. When they were done, Ethan made some calls to see about being able to get back to Long Island. He took a few of those calls in his room behind closed doors. Zoe wondered if he was speaking to a lady friend.

Unfortunately, a way home did not reveal itself. The roadways were still shut down, the trains weren't running yet and authorities were still assessing the damage. Cars were stuck in water along some of the major highways and downed lines made traveling through water dangerous. A number of people across the area had suffered electric shocks.

"What now?" Zoe asked once they'd cleaned up after breakfast.

"Movie?" Ethan took his coffee and plopped on the couch. He pointed the remote at the television.

"Or I could beat you in another game of cards."

"Ha!" Ethan threw his head back. "This time, I'll teach you a few games."

"Bring it on."

He grabbed the deck of cards and showed her a new game

that he and his siblings used to play, a game where players had to constantly call each other's bluffs.

"All right," he began. "It's called BS."

Zoe raised a brow and tilted her head to the side. "BS. As in bull—"

"Yep," Ethan interjected. "When you suspect your opponent of bluffing, you have to call out BS."

"Did your parents know you were playing this?"

"My grandmother taught it to us!"

Zoe laughed hard. "I like your grandma."

They played the game for the next hour or so and by the time they stopped for lunch, Zoe's belly hurt from laughing so much. Once she got the hang of the game, she bluffed a lot and Ethan called her out on her bluffing just as much.

At one point, he turned up the television and they got updates on the aftermath of the weather before picking another movie to watch.

He called a few local restaurants to see if any were open for them to order dinner. Fortunately a few were, and they ordered his favorite Asian takeout.

After spending the past twenty-four hours together in close quarters, the atmosphere between them had settled into a more comfortable existence. Zoe felt it in her posture. Ethan's feet rested on the ottoman in front of him. She folded her feet under her as she picked fresh popcorn from a bowl. They flowed between laughter and conversation with ease. Subjects that they'd been careful not to broach before became a familiar part of their dialogue. Zoe felt like she and Ethan had been old friends for years—almost.

He looked at her and cocked his head sideways.

Her hand paused midway as she was bringing a piece of popcorn to her mouth. "What?" she asked.

"So, why don't you have a boyfriend?"

Zoe shrugged. "I can't blame it all on men. I haven't always made a good girlfriend."

Ethan reared his head back. "What makes you say that?"

"It's what I've been told," she said, matter-of-fact. "More than once."

His eyes widened. "Wow."

She waved dismissively. "That doesn't bother me." She laughed. "Well, not anymore." She handed him the popcorn. He took the bowl and dug in. "I've been accused of acting—" she made air quotes "—like a man." She sniffed. "One said I was too ambitious because I paid more attention to my career and not enough to him. I guess that summed up what most of them felt and honestly, I just didn't know what to do with that. My career means a lot to me. I spend a lot of time focusing on it and then there's my family."

Zoe stopped talking. She wasn't ready to talk intimately about her family with Ethan. He didn't need to know about her family's battle with Shena's mental illness.

"Seems like selfishness on their part."

"Eh. Sometimes it was hard for me to balance both. I worked really hard on my past jobs to earn my bosses' respect and set myself up for potential promotions. Whenever I didn't get a promotion, it made me work harder to prove myself for the next time. In the process, my relationships suffered. I didn't mean for it to happen that way."

"You didn't have the right men."

Zoe looked at him curiously.

"They should have been supporting you and celebrating your determination instead of getting upset about you working hard to get somewhere."

That was how she felt, too, but she remained quiet. Ethan was the first man who had ever said anything like that to her. The others just complained about how little they got from her.

"In my opinion," he went on, "it's obvious that they were threatened by your potential."

"I guess." She tilted her head, thankful for his apparent appreciation of her ambition.

"I bet you weren't as bad a girlfriend as you thought."

His deep gaze made something shift inside of her. She swallowed and smiled. "Thanks, Ethan. I'll remember that."

"Their loss. Lucky me," he said, taking the empty bowl to the island. He came to sit near her on the couch.

"How are you lucky?"

"Your boss's failure to give you the chance you deserve is what led you to our company. You're definitely an asset— hardworking, brilliant, savvy, full of great ideas and you deliver. It's why I hired you. Someone would have to be blind not to see what you bring to the table."

A smile slowly spread across her face. Zoe felt her cheeks warm. It was almost as if he'd said he loved her. Her previous boss had never complimented her or praised her work. Not once. "Thank you, Ethan."

"I mean that."

The lights flickered and she yelped. "What was that?"

Ethan huffed and jumped up from the couch. "I hope it's not what I think it is."

The lights flickered again. She folded her knees to her chest, praying that the power wouldn't go completely out.

Suddenly they heard a thud and everything went black.

# Twelve

The only light in the apartment came from the dim evening sky. Soon, all they would have was the moonlight.

Ethan called Maintenance, who explained that flooding in the basement was causing sporadic outages in the building and the backup generator couldn't keep up. The only active lighting was the emergency lighting in the hallways.

Ethan had bought a loft in this particular building because of the older charm and larger room sizes, but it also meant it didn't have some of the latest technologies like newer structures did. The technician assured Ethan that help was on the way and that they would be working diligently to restore power to the building. This also meant they couldn't use the elevator, so they were stuck inside the building unless they wanted to walk up and down several flights of stairs. Until then, he and Zoe would have to remain in the dark.

Ethan groaned as he ended the call. He looked at his phone. Since he'd spent most of his time watching movies, playing cards and talking with Zoe, he still had pretty good battery life. He relayed the info from Maintenance to Zoe.

"Wow! What else could go wrong?"

"Hey, shh! Don't say that."

"You're right. Or the universe will show me what else could go wrong. My bad." She laughed.

"How's the battery in your phone?" he asked.

"Pretty good. Yours?"

"About eighty percent."

"I have my portable charger in my handbag, too. Do you have one here?"

"I don't." He huffed.

"What about candles? Do you have any around?"

Ethan pressed his lips together and thought for a moment. "I might." He'd used this place for entertaining plenty of women; he was bound to have a few candles inside a drawer somewhere. He checked the kitchen and linen closets and came back with a few. He lined them up on the kitchen island and pulled out a lighter.

"No!" Zoe held her hands up. "We still have a bit of sunlight. Let's wait until we really need them."

Ethan was grateful to still have her company. "See. Smart lady."

"Oh, Ethan," she said in an exaggerated tone. "Flattery will get you everywhere." They laughed, easing the intensity of the moment.

Ethan sat back down on the couch. The shadows and light from the descending sun cast her face in a mysterious glow. She looked even more beautiful.

"Where do you see yourself going after Blackwell?" he asked.

"Hmm." Zoe put her hand on her chin. "I'm hoping to be here for a while and learn as much as I can from you and your family. I'd love to make it to the C-suite one day."

They talked until the only light in the apartment came from a sliver of moonlight through the window and a few sporadically placed candles. Circumstances had created a romantic atmosphere that Ethan hadn't anticipated.

He fought to keep his focus on their conversation, but his attention kept drifting to her perfect silhouette. A time or two, perhaps three, they brushed against one another, unable to properly gauge their distance in the dim light. Each time, Ethan felt currents strong enough to light the room with his own fire surge along the places that she touched.

They talked and talked, familiarizing themselves with one another's life, getting comfortable in each other's presence. He asked question after question, eager to know things about Zoe that he hadn't known before. In spite of the inconvenience of the weather, he was secretly thankful for the time he was spending with her. It couldn't amount to much, but he enjoyed it nonetheless.

"What about you, Ethan? Why don't you have a girl-friend?" Zoe asked, tilting her head.

She'd brought the conversation back to that. "I did." Ethan sighed. "Like you, I've been accused of putting too much of my time and energy into work. We started working on the company's expansion a while back, way before we actually put any of our plans into action. I was working long days, spending weekends with my dad and the rest of the team strategizing and mapping things out. One afternoon, I decided I wanted to surprise my girlfriend and take her out, spend some time with her. I pulled up to her place and there was a man standing on her front steps. She opened the door, he swept her into his arms, kissed her and carried her inside. He used his foot to close the door."

"Oh! Ethan. I'm so sorry. What did you do?"

"I sat in the car fuming for a few moments before I realized that what we had was over long before that day. I got out of my car and used my key to get into her house. I followed their sounds toward her bedroom. The door was wide open. She obviously wasn't expecting me. I calmly walked in and said hello. She screamed. The two of them jumped out of the bed, covering their naked bodies with the sheets. It was obvious they hadn't wasted any time. Clothes were tossed across the floor from the door to the bed. I held up her key, placed it on the table next to her bed and walked out."

Zoe's eyes stretched wide. Her hand covered her mouth. "What did they do?"

"Nothing. They just watched me with their mouths wide open. I closed the front door, got in my car and went back to work."

"Oh my goodness, Ethan. That's terrible."

"Like I said, it was over way before it was officially over. The end was inevitable, so I wasn't totally surprised to see she had moved on to someone else. By the way, they're married now. Ha!"

"Whoa!"

Darkness had fully arrived, swallowing up the tense silence they fell into. Zoe reached over and touched Ethan's arm. "I'm so sorry about that. You're a catch. There's a woman out there that will appreciate the hardworking man that you are."

Ethan felt the electricity from her touch. He looked at her. "Of course," he said confidently. A smile eased across his lips and he took in her beauty; the candle's flickering light shimmered in her eyes. She looked radiant under the moonlight.

He imagined that the woman Zoe spoke of would be a lot like her. Despite all common sense, for a moment, he wished it could be her.

Her lips were perfect. Inviting. Ethan recalled the softness from their kiss. He wanted to kiss her again. The curve from her chin to her neck was the sexiest angle he'd ever set his eyes on. He recalled her confidence, and silly things like the fact that she could change tires. He didn't know many women like Zoe. The fact that it seemed like she didn't need a man at all intrigued him all the more.

She swallowed, and Ethan watched her neck shift in the soft light. Every maneuver came across as sensual. Her hand was still on his arm. He covered it with his hand. Electric sparks radiated in his palm.

Ethan took that hand and before he knew what he was doing, he kissed it. He found himself leaning toward her, and she drew closer to him. He felt controlled by an outside force, unable to resist the pull. She seemed compelled by the same force. His breath came in a rush.

They closed the space between them and paused once they were close enough to almost touch. They were still for a brief moment. Ethan contemplated the feel of her lips. He shouldn't. He wanted to. So badly. He fought the good fight against his will and lost.

Zoe reached out with her free hand and touched his face, pulling him closer. Closing the gap. Her caress ignited a fire that reasonable thoughts and common sense could not quench. Their lips connected.

Hers were so soft. Sweet but also salty from the popcorn. Perfect. Fireworks exploded in his head, danced and then consumed them both. The kiss was hot, deep, passionate and breathtaking. She moved closer and held his face with both her hands. Ethan wrapped his arms around her, pressing their bodies together.

The fire licked at them, sparking a hunger that refused to be doused. Their hands roamed every part of the other's body. All the restraint Ethan had exercised in her presence since the day he'd set eyes on her crumbled like a house made of cards. Desire scorched a hot path through him, and he felt his temperature rise. If he could trust his sense of touch, her body was blazing as much as his.

He couldn't get enough. He pulled his mouth from Zoe's long enough to take a breath, lacing her face with loving pecks before taking her lips fully again. They shifted positions, never truly disconnecting from each other, her body stretching out under his, her hands furiously exploring any area she could reach.

Ethan was careful not to apply too much pressure as he held himself over her. He could feel his erection strain against his sweats, pressing against her. Aware of how his desire surged over him, he reluctantly ended the kiss.

Several beats ticked by as the hastened rhythm of their thumping hearts slowed. Their chests rose and fell in the same declining tempo.

Ethan stared into her eyes. He could see the rawness of her longing. Zoe licked her kiss-swollen lips and he wanted to feel them again but resisted. He pushed himself up and sat back on the couch and tried to catch his breath. He fought to remove himself from her the way magnets fought to connect.

Zoe sat up beside him. She took his hand in hers, breathing just as hard. Neither of them spoke. Together they sat there in the dark.

What had he just done?

# Thirteen

Forget butterflies, something deeper fluttered in Zoe's stomach. Ethan—no, her *boss* had just kissed the breath out of her and all she could think about was kissing him again and again. She could see the inquiries behind his eyes. She knew that, like her, he was pondering what they'd just done.

She had just kissed her boss—again! She should have felt worse about it but didn't. It felt too good. Zoe felt like she was floating when his lips touched hers. She couldn't stop thinking about it after. Her mind had told her not to do it, but with one touch of his hand, she couldn't resist. She wanted more. Much more.

She put her hand back on his face, knowing he would understand the gesture as an invitation. He looked into her eyes and nodded. The air in her lungs swirled. She was breathless at the mere thought of tasting his lips once again. Hunger rose in her, and their lips met again. The same urgency flared again, an all-consuming, desperate fire.

Caresses turned into tugs and pulls. Longing blazed a hot trail from her center up to her chest. Ethan pulled back from their intense kiss and stared into her eyes again as if seeking more permission. She gave it to him by rising up to kiss him.

"You're so beautiful," he said, breaking the kiss again to catch some air. "Tell me if you want me to stop." He spoke without taking his lips off of hers.

She kissed him back, meeting his increased tension with her own.

"Should I stop?" he asked, his voice a breathless whisper. "Tell me to stop." He kissed her deeply, and she moaned.

"I will if you want me to. Tell me what you want," he said hoarsely, and Zoe felt the rumble of his voice in her belly.

"You," she said without fully breaking their kiss. He gave her an intense look, and she nodded. "I want you, Ethan. If you'll have me."

"I want you, Zoe, as long as it's all right with you."

"Yes." Her voice was soft and filled with desire even to her own ears.

Zoe didn't want to think about him being her boss. She didn't want to think about what tomorrow would bring. She no longer cared about not being at home. All that mattered in that moment was being with Ethan. Their attraction for one another was obvious and had been for quite a while. Since they'd arrived at his place the evening before, the chemistry between them had turned into smoke rising, becoming more dense as the hours passed. Now it practically suffocated them. It couldn't be ignored. Denying it hadn't worked.

Zoe had dreamed of this. They were two experienced, grown, consenting adults. She decided not to expect much after this night. It would be their one night together.

"Just this one night," she said, convinced that was all she needed to quench the hunger she held for him.

"Just this one night," Ethan repeated.

"That's it," she confirmed.

"If that's what you want."

Instead of a verbal response, Zoe placed both hands on either side of his face and pulled him to her. After another passionate kiss, she lifted her shirt over her head. Ethan helped her out of the rest of her clothes and she helped him in the same way.

Fully naked, they admired each other, feeling and touching as if they were handling exquisite works of art. Taking their time, they held each other close, skin to searing skin.

Ethan explored every crevice of her body with adoration,

kissing her here and there. She was sure that the moisture from each kiss evaporated immediately from the heat of her body. The more he took his time getting to know her body, the more she wanted to feel him inside of her.

He lifted her from the couch and carried her to the large kitchen island. There, he laid her on her back, kissed and caressed her some more, then buried his face between her thighs and took her into his mouth.

The sensation of his warm tongue made her arch her back, and a moan rose from her core and up her throat. Zoe clawed the smooth surface of the granite countertop, unable to actually grasp anything. She writhed. The pleasure was intense, almost too much to handle but far too good to stop. Her body began convulsing. She grabbed the back of his head, pulled him closer to her. The rhythm of his tongue quickened. She wriggled against his skillful licks, strategic nibbles and powerful sucking as he coaxed the orgasm from her.

Her release was explosive, matching the magnitude of an earthquake, the highest possible rating on the Richter scale. Her back came off the cool countertop, and she heard herself howl. Her muscles clenched, and Ethan cajoled the rest of her climax out of her, suckling and teasing.

She relished the powerful force until she could stand it no longer. She pushed him away, aftershocks rippling through her, and lay in a fetal position until the delectable spasms subsided.

Ethan planted sweet kisses along her side until her body calmed. Then he kissed her, letting Zoe taste herself.

Before she could fully catch her breath, he pulled himself away from her long enough to shield himself with protection. Picking her up from the counter, he carried her to the nearest wall and set her on his erection. Zoe's eyes squeezed shut when he filled her. He grunted beneath her, and she lifted her head to the ceiling with an answering groan. Ethan nibbled at her exposed neck as he plunged in and out of her. Zoe braced against the wall, matching his pace.

She couldn't remember being made love to with such intensity. She opened her eyes; she had to see Ethan in this moment.

He must have felt her looking at him. His eyes opened, and his expression was one of sincere delight. Their gazes locked without breaking their rhythm, hearts pounding, breathing heavy, eyes penetrating. Zoe licked her lips; the deep eye contact intensified the sensations.

She groaned again, helpless, as another climax rose within her, and her head rolled back. She felt herself tighten around him. Ethan moaned and his rhythm quickened.

They moved together, faster and faster, and Zoe's body gave in to the pleasure. Shock waves spread through her, reaching every extremity. She hummed through her release.

Ethan growled, and then his body shook against hers. Wrapping his arms around her, he held on tight as if he would drift away otherwise. They stayed that way with her back against the wall until he was soft enough to slip from her.

Ethan carried her to the bedroom. Gently, he laid her across the bed, climbed in and spooned himself against her back, his arm around her waist. The only noise in the dark room was their breathing slowly returning to a normal pace.

After a while, he asked softly, "Are you okay?"

"I'm fine." Instead of allowing an elephant to join them in the room, Zoe decided to head it off. "Thank you for tonight." She pondered how to express what she was thinking. "I mean, for everything. Thank you for everything… For yesterday and especially tonight." She chuckled. "And please, don't worry. I'm not the clingy type. I knew what I was doing here. I have no expectations. I wanted you just as bad as you wanted me. Monday morning, it will be business as usual. Cool?"

"What if I didn't want business as usual?"

Ethan's words shocked her. She turned to look at his face. He seemed serious. She formed her mouth to respond but nothing came out. For once in her life, Zoe wasn't sure what to say next.

# Fourteen

Ethan opened and closed all the cabinets and the refrigerator several times. He and Zoe had eaten most of the snacks. Now they were down to the condiments and the few frozen items left in his freezer, which did him no good this morning. After an unbelievable weekend of constant lovemaking, he was famished and was sure Zoe would wake up feeling the same way.

The last thing on their minds after the first time they'd made love was food. They'd satisfied each other's hunger in more delectable ways.

Finally he pulled half a loaf of bread from the refrigerator along with peanut butter and jelly. He knew Zoe didn't have nut allergies because she often kept some around her office to snack on. He toasted the bread a bit and made both of them sandwiches and then prepared two cups of coffee.

He returned to the bedroom to find the bed empty. He heard water running in the bathroom sink, so he placed the tray on one of the side tables and walked over to the window to take in the landscape. The view from the bedroom overlooking the East River was by far the best in the entire apartment.

Moments later, he heard the bathroom doorknob click. Zoe emerged, looking sex-worn and gorgeous as hell. She'd attempted to finger-comb her hair into place and was wearing nothing but her panties and one of his T-shirts. He was still in his underwear, as well. He sat on the side of the bed and patted the empty space next to him.

"I made breakfast," he said, pointing to the sandwiches.

"Peanut butter and jelly! How did you know?" Zoe laughed.

"Well, it was all we had left." His own words gave him pause. He'd said *we*. It came out comfortable and familiar, as if they'd been existing as *we* all along.

"Perfect! I love peanut butter and jelly sandwiches."

"Good. Shall we?" he asked. He picked up one plate and handed it to Zoe before taking his own sandwich in his hands.

He turned on the television as they ate. The news updated them on the latest since the storm hit on Friday. It was now Monday and many homes and businesses were still out of power. The bridges and tunnels were back in service, as well as a few subway lines. Others remained shut down due to flooding.

"I can finally get home and assess any damage," Zoe said. "My neighbor has been keeping me posted. The power is back on in some parts of the neighborhood, but it was still hard to get around because so many trees are down. Luckily my mom and sister are okay."

Ethan's phone rang. "Speaking of which. Excuse me, please." He stood and carried his phone conversation to the living room. It was Carter, and Ethan wasn't ready to reveal any details about his weekend with Zoe. "What's up?"

"It's all good," Carter said. "Did you see the email Dad sent? He wants to open up the offices on Wednesday."

"That's good. We have quite a bit of staff affected by the storm. This will give them a little time to get things in order before returning to work," Ethan said. "I'm going to ride out and check out my branches today. I hope we have power. I understand there are lots of trees down across Long Island. It got hit pretty hard. How are your locations?"

"Fortunately not too bad. Power outages are the worst of what we've seen."

"Good."

"You're still in the city?"

"Yeah. Like I said earlier, I'm heading back to Long Island today."

"How's your staff?"

Ethan looked back toward his bedroom. "Fine." He smiled. "I've been in touch with them. Some doing better than others but no major problems overall."

"Good. Mine, too."

Zoe sneezed and Ethan covered his phone, hoping Carter hadn't heard anything. "Okay, big brother," he said. "I'm going to jump in the shower and head to the island. I'll catch up with you later."

"Late start, huh?"

"Uh. Yeah." Ethan didn't offer an explanation. "Call me later?"

"Cool."

Ethan ended the call before Carter could say another word. He returned to the bedroom to find Zoe sitting where he'd left her. It appeared that she was on the phone with her mother. He picked up their empty plates and cups, taking them to the kitchen and giving her privacy for her conversation. He came back when he heard her say goodbye. He was hoping he could make love to her one more time before they both had to leave.

"Hey," he said, leaning on the door frame.

"Hey." She turned to face him and crossed her arms across her chest.

"Can we talk for a second?"

"Sure."

He sat on the bed next to her. "I enjoyed my time with you this weekend and I want you to know that I'd love to continue seeing you. I don't want this to get awkward. We don't have to make it anything serious and we can certainly keep this to ourselves. It was fun. You're fun. We had a good time together."

"Fun is one way of putting it," Zoe said. That made both of them laugh. "I don't want you to feel pressure to make sure that I'm okay. I'm a big girl. We knew what we were doing. We enjoyed it. We don't have to continue something we know can't work."

That stung. Ethan swallowed. He wasn't used to rejection of any kind. But he wasn't ready to let Zoe walk away. He searched his mind for the right words. "I like you. A lot. If I tell the whole truth, I've been attracted to you from the day you stepped foot into my office for your first interview. I've pushed that aside to remain professional, but after this weekend… I realize I don't want this to be over so soon."

Zoe blinked a few times. "Ethan." Her shoulders deflated. "You're my boss… I mean, don't get me wrong. You're incredibly attractive, which by the way, I noticed from that first interview, as well, but I wouldn't want to jeopardize anything. I like you, too, but I love my job. I don't want to lose it. I don't want to lose the respect of my colleagues. I mean… I—"

Ethan put a hand to her lips. "Let's just have fun. That's all I ask. When it no longer feels like fun, we stop. That's all. Like you said. We're adults. We set the boundaries. We stick to them. We enjoy ourselves in the meantime. And it would be our secret. I would never want to do anything to jeopardize your career or mine anyway." He looked at the crumpled sheets and then back at her. "You're gonna tell me you didn't enjoy yourself this weekend? Can you honestly say you don't want this?" His lips eased into a smirk.

Zoe chuckled, then sighed. "You're so bad, Ethan."

He raised his brow. "You want it?" He felt himself warming for her.

"Ethan! You're making this so hard."

"It doesn't have to be. It will be just between us. When the wheels fall off, we go back to the way things were. We are two mature, consenting adults. So what's it going to be?"

She drew in a long breath. She let it out slowly. Ethan knew the gears were churning inside her head, turning over all the possibilities, both good and bad. He held his breath, awaiting her response.

Zoe groaned. "I'd be lying if I said I didn't want to continue seeing you. I enjoy our time together." Zoe closed her eyes and took a long, slow breath. "I mean I really enjoy being with you. I just—I didn't want any of this to reflect on either of us in a bad way. My career is important to me…" Zoe paused again. She sighed. "Okay. Yes, I want this—"

"Shh." That was all Ethan needed to hear. She wanted this just as much as he did. He vowed to enjoy his time with her as much as possible, knowing that when it was over, their memories would be all they would have to hold on to.

He kissed her, deep, hard and long. Ethan felt his erection rise and he rolled on top of her so she could feel it, too. She slipped her hand into his underwear and massaged him to his fullness.

He moaned but ended their kiss with several soft pecks on her lips, then got up to retrieve protection from the nightstand drawer.

Zoe took it from him, tore it open and slowly rolled it over his erection. Ethan was more rigid than a rock. Climbing over her, he teased her with licks and pecks from her lips to her center until Zoe demanded he enter her. When he did, their eyes rolled back from sheer delight. Together they entertained several positions and rhythms, pleasing one another in all the ways they'd learned from each other in the past forty-eight hours.

Ethan had discovered the ways she liked to be touched and held. By now, he knew how to make her moan. Speaking sweetness in her ear made her moist, and he told her she was beautiful, used soft words to express how she made him feel. She talked back to him. Told him how good he felt to her, inside and out.

Ethan knew when she was getting close to climax. He could feel its ascent, knew how to ride her toward a powerful, body-trembling peak. Since he wasn't sure when he'd get to have her to himself again, he decided to prolong her pleasure.

He slowed his pace—let her catch her breath. Removing himself, he tasted her, bringing her close to that delicious moment with his tongue, and then stopped.

He entered her once more, taking slow, deliberate strokes, trying to give her ultimate bliss while keeping his own excitement at bay. It didn't help. She felt too good.

Grabbing his hips, Zoe pulled him deeper into her. She tightened her walls around his erection until he couldn't stand the pressure anymore. Ethan exploded. So did she. His heart raced, and she panted. His skin tightened, and she held him tight. His muscles spasmed, and she trembled under him. He collapsed. She did, too.

Spent. Happy. Ready for what was next, they lay in each other's arms.

Zoe had become his enchanting little secret. One he would hold on to as long as he could.

# Fifteen

Since Zoe returned home, she'd been plowing through an endless list of to-dos. The first was to check in on her mother and sister. Laura had sounded quite tired when they'd spoken on the phone before Zoe left Ethan's house, yet she had insisted that Zoe go and take care of her own home first. Fortunately the power was back on and Zoe wouldn't have to navigate her town house without electricity.

Ethan had taken her home and come inside briefly. The rank smell of her kitchen garbage had been an unpleasant greeting, having sat there since Friday morning and it now being Monday afternoon. Ethan helped her get rid of all the garbage and the spoiled food in her refrigerator. After that, he insisted on helping her with her car, but she convinced him that she would call roadside assistance, so Ethan eventually left.

She spent the rest of her afternoon cleaning her house. Despite how much she had to do, thoughts of Ethan kept invading her mind.

Despite the severity of the storm, being with him had felt like a vacation—an erotic fantasy lived out loud. Zoe remembered how good he'd made her feel and shivered involuntarily.

That was just it. Ethan was like a fantasy. An indulgent, sensual fantasy. Being with him made her feel like she was starring in a silly romantic comedy or some fairy tale. He was a charming prince—wealthy, worldly and well-rounded. Zoe was the regular girl getting swept off her feet.

But it was so much more than just an opportune moment brought on by being trapped in his apartment. She felt it. Zoe was smitten. Ethan was a man unlike anyone she'd ever dated before. They came from two totally different leagues.

She shook her head as she stacked the last of her bottled waters from her pantry in her fridge. What was she thinking? She couldn't date this man. He was her boss. Why had she agreed to continue seeing him? Now that he wasn't around, she could think more clearly. There was no way she could go through with this.

She thought back to when she'd dated Langston in college. He'd come from a wealthy family just like Ethan's.

One weekend, he'd brought Zoe home to attend a family function. From the moment she'd stepped foot on his family's estate, she'd known she didn't belong. His haughty mother had confirmed that by openly wearing her disdain from the moment she'd said hello. The woman had stared at Zoe through narrowed eyes. Her lips had turned up as if she'd smelled something bad. Both his parents had asked a barrage of questions about her family background. Clearly her modest upbringings hadn't been good enough for their son. Before they'd left, Langston's parents had pulled him aside and denigrated her as if she weren't within earshot.

From that point on, she'd stayed clear of wealthy men. And since she was so protective of her family, she vowed to keep information about them to herself, as well.

She'd have to let Ethan know when he came into her branch this week. She both longed and dreaded to see him.

"Ugh!" she grunted. This was an impossible situation, but she knew what she had to do.

Zoe finished up at home and headed to her mother's house. The moment Laura opened the door, Zoe knew something wasn't right. Laura looked weary, and dark circles framed her eyes.

Concern filled Zoe. "What's wrong, Ma?" She didn't give her time to answer before she made her way into the house. "Where's Shena?" She looked around.

Laura shook her head. "Not in a good place."

Zoe gave her mother a quick kiss on the cheek and went in search of her sister. "Shena," she called.

There was no answer, but she heard feet shuffling over her head.

"Shena." Zoe climbed the stairs frantically, two steps at a time.

Shena was in her bedroom.

"Shena," Zoe called again softly. "Hey. You okay?"

Shena was pacing back and forth, grabbing handfuls of her hair. Tears streamed down her face. Her words were clipped and erratic. She wasn't making sense.

Zoe cautiously stepped into the room. "Wanna talk?"

"No! I don't want to talk to anyone! I can't. I don't wanna," Shena yelled and went back to her erratic speech.

"Come to my house. I could use your help." Zoe hoped she would agree. Laura needed a break.

Shena stopped pacing. "Why. Who's there?" she snapped.

"It will be just you and me, that's it. I'll make a nice salad. I know how much keeping your figure means to you." Zoe laughed, hoping Shena would, too. "Come on. I could use the company. Please."

Shena sat at the foot of the bed. For several moments, she remained silent. Zoe sighed in relief. Maybe she was going to be okay. Then suddenly, Shena burst into tears.

"Shena." Zoe inched closer and put her arms around her sister's shoulders. "Come with me."

Zoe expected Shena to protest, as she was clearly irritated, but she didn't. "Okay," she said instead in a childlike voice. "I'm so tired." Her voice was weak.

"I know. Pack a bag. We can stop for food along the way." Zoe prayed they'd get to her house without incident. When Shena was in a bad way, her behavior became extreme. At times she was overly giddy; at others she was highly agitated and irrational.

Shena shook her head. While she packed belongings, Zoe went down to tell their mother that she would be taking Shena with her. The Blackwell office was closed for one more day. Zoe didn't mind spending that time helping her mother and sister out. Plus, Shena liked being at Zoe's house. Maybe that could help ease her mood swings. Perhaps she could get to the bottom of what was going on with Shena's meds. With the way she was acting, Zoe was convinced that Shena hadn't been taking them like she said she was.

Once they'd gotten everything together, Zoe asked Shena if she'd packed her medicine.

"No. I don't have anymore. I don't need them anyway."

Zoe wanted to scold her sister, ask her what she was thinking. Instead, she sucked in a deep breath. There was no use going there now. Shena wasn't in the right frame of mind. Zoe knew she'd have to make an appointment, go to the doctor with her sister and make sure she got a new prescription. She'd done it all before.

During the car ride back to Zoe's, Shena said nothing. That gave Zoe space to think, and despite how much was on her mind, Ethan popped up.

She couldn't stop thinking of him. This situation confirmed that continuing to see him wasn't a good idea. What would happen once he got a glimpse into her reality? Would he still be so smitten?

At home, she and Shena ate the food they'd picked up along the way. Shena still said very little. A while later, she lay across the couch and slept like a rock.

Zoe covered her with a throw and headed to her room. In the bathroom, she looked in the mirror. She could see the weariness from lack of rest in her own eyes. She and Ethan hadn't done much sleeping.

And her mind was back on him. Some thoughts made her core flutter, others scared her.

"What. Are. You. Doing?" she said aloud.

This all felt good. In fact it felt amazing and adventurous and forbidden and of course fun, but it had to stop. How long would they be able to hide their affair? Someone was bound to find out. He'd be in major trouble. It would embarrass his family. She'd be out of a job. Plain and simple. Despite how it felt—how she felt—despite how much fun they had and could potentially have, it was up to Zoe to shut it down.

She decided to tell him when he came to her branch this week. She even went over a few scenarios in her head. She wasn't going to waste any time. The very next time he set foot in her branch, she was going to ask him to her office and explain why they couldn't go on like this.

Zoe arrived at her office extra early on Thursday. Nervous energy coursed through her veins, putting her on edge. Although they'd texted one another, Zoe hadn't laid eyes on Ethan since he had dropped her off at her place on Monday afternoon. A part of her couldn't wait to see his gorgeous face. On the other hand, she just wanted to hurry and speak with him so they could both move on.

Instead of going in on Wednesday, she took an extra day off to visit the doctor's office with Shena to make sure she was set up with the right medicine. She even went to the pharmacy with her to pick up her prescription and made her take the first pill right in front of her. With Shena taken care of without incident, and their mother getting some well-needed rest, there wasn't much left to distract Zoe from thinking of Ethan. And he appeared in her thoughts constantly.

At her desk, she turned on her computer but failed to take in any of the information she scanned in her emails. She sat back and rubbed her temples. "Focus, girl."

She went back to an email from one of the other branch managers who'd had to stay out another day due to home repairs from the storm. She tried to read a few more, but still unable to concentrate, she got up and paced.

She couldn't eject Ethan from her thoughts, so she contemplated the words she would use to let him know they had to end this…this…whatever they were doing before Zoe got hurt.

She practiced letting him down easy, explaining why it made sense to call it quits. She'd even dressed more conservatively than she ever had since she started working at Blackwell: a basic black suit, a black-and-white blouse with a bow at the neck and practical black pumps. "Nothing to see here," she joked, mimicking a police officer.

Zoe's door was closed, but she could hear the chatter of her staff as they arrived for the workday. When Ethan came into the branch, he usually didn't arrive before ten in the morning. She looked at the set of clocks on her wall depicting several time zones. The flat screen on her office wall, always tuned to her favorite financial news network, confirmed that it was just after nine o'clock. She had time.

The moment that thought left her mind she heard his voice.

Her body stiffened. He had arrived.

Three light taps at her door. Instead of answering, Zoe remained still. He tapped again.

"Zoe," Ethan called through the door. His voice went right through her as always.

"One moment." Zoe punched the air twice and huffed. Then she stood tall, straightened her suit jacket and swallowed. She took calculated steps to the door.

"Hey, Ethan," she greeted as if all were cheery. "Come on in. I'm glad you're here early. I need to talk to you." She turned on her heel and headed toward her desk, wringing her hands.

"Cool." Ethan closed the door behind him. She heard the lock click.

Before she could make it to her desk, Ethan caught up with her, took her by the arm and gently turned her around and kissed her. The kiss was wild and passionate. It felt forbidden.

"Mm. I've missed that," he whispered.

The sweet way he spoke made her knees wobble. Before she could respond, he kissed her again. She welcomed the deep kiss without protest. He pulled her close to him, and Zoe thought she would melt from the heat of their bodies together.

When he softened back, she had to catch her breath. She touched her kiss-swollen lips. Ethan's touch made her weak.

"Ethan." She found her voice, scolding him with the way she said his name.

"Don't worry, I locked your door." He planted a series of pecks on her lips before letting her go. He sat in the chair across from her desk.

Zoe needed a few seconds to gather herself. This wasn't going as she'd planned. Finally she sat. "Ethan," she said evenly.

"Wait!" He held his hand up. "Do you know who Leah Cartwright is? What do you think about her?"

"Of course I know who she is. I think she's amazing. Why?"

"Good. Would you like to meet her?"

"Wait. What?" Zoe was confused. "What are you talking about, Ethan?"

"I thought you would. She's coming to the Barclays this weekend to speak and sign her new book. A friend dropped some VIP tickets in my lap. We can meet her backstage after the event."

Zoe's mouth dropped. She admired Leah Cartwright immensely. She had never been the fangirl type but Leah Cartwright was…different. She was Zoe's favorite motivational speaker. Zoe had watched her talk show when it was still on the air and had read all of her books. She'd always wanted to attend one of Leah's live appearances. When she'd heard that Leah was coming to New York, she'd wanted to attend but the tickets had cost hundreds of dollars. As much as Zoe loved Leah, she wasn't willing to sell off stock to see her.

But what Ethan had offered was different. Not only

would Zoe get to see her, she would be able to actually meet her. She was going to meet Leah Cartwright in the flesh!

"Wait!" Zoe held her hand up. She couldn't let Ethan suck her in. She had to put a stop to this. "Ethan."

"What's wrong? I thought you'd like this. The opportunity came up and I thought of you, but if you don't want to go, it's fine. I'd still like to spend time with you this weekend. I have a few great places that I'd like to take you. All off the beaten path."

Zoe sighed. She wanted to spend time with him both on and off the beaten path. That was the truth.

She really liked him. What if she truly fell for him and all of a sudden, they had to end it all? By then she'd be in too deep. It would hurt more later. If she cut ties now, she could put the weekend behind her and accept the fact that they would never be together.

But just like him, she really wanted more. Zoe closed her eyes and shook her head.

"Zoe?" Ethan looked concerned.

"What are we getting into here, Ethan?"

"Just having fun, remember? But I don't want to push you." The light in his eyes dimmed a little. "Think about the event this weekend. Let me know. Okay?"

Zoe watched him walk out of her office. She dropped her head into her hands and groaned.

# Sixteen

Ethan was happy to get the call from Zoe about the Leah Cartwright event. There was something about Zoe; he didn't understand it himself, but he wasn't willing to just let it pass. Being with her felt good, even though he knew it was wrong.

He'd managed to keep his weekend with Zoe to himself so far and planned to keep things that way. That could present a problem down the line, but he wanted to see how far this could go. As long as he was careful, they would be fine.

Ethan's driver maneuvered along the streets of Zoe's neighborhood with ease now, but he knew that once they hit downtown Brooklyn, traffic would be a nightmare. He didn't feel like being bothered with congested streets and lack of parking, so he'd ordered a car to take them to the event and bring them back. First, they would have dinner at a friend's restaurant near Dumbo. It was an exclusive place off the beaten path. Ethan wasn't worried about running into Carter. He had called him earlier in the day to gauge his whereabouts for the evening.

The driver pulled up in front of Zoe's town house. Ethan stepped out, straightened his suit and walked to her door. After a few quick taps, the door opened, and Zoe filled the entrance with her gorgeous frame. She looked radiant in a touch more makeup than she normally wore to the office. Her hot pink lips were enticing. Her electric blue jumpsuit was stylish and the pink shoes and handbag finished her look in that well-put-together, unexpected way she always managed.

Ethan felt himself smile. "You look amazing."

"Thank you. Let me get my jacket."

Zoe went back in, grabbed her coat and met him back at

the door in no time. He reached for her hand as they walked to the car. She looked around and hesitated before placing her hand in his.

"There's no one around here we need to worry about," he said, realizing she was nervous. Prior to this, they had spent all their time together indoors.

"I guess." She shrugged.

Ethan stopped walking and faced her. "Thanks for coming. I'm glad you changed your mind. I promise this will be fun, and like I said, as soon as we're no longer having fun, we'll stop. No hard feelings."

"Ethan." Zoe paused. "What if the fun doesn't stop or we end up taking things further?"

"Yeah."

They stared at one another. Silence blossomed between them for a few long moments.

"We'll cross that bridge when we get there. Okay?" Ethan finally said. "We'll just shift our focus back to work. It will be our secret. No hard feelings. How hard could that be for two consenting adults?"

Zoe pressed her lips together. "Okay." She shook her head as if she needed to confirm what her mouth had just said with an action.

"But let's not think about that now. Let's just focus on the fun part."

Zoe nodded. "Okay," she said again.

"All in?" Ethan asked.

"All in," she replied.

At the exquisite French restaurant, Ethan greeted his friend Jacques. The host led them to a table overlooking the water.

"I forgot to ask," Ethan said to Zoe. "How's your family after the storm? Did they suffer any flooding or damage?"

He noticed that she looked away. A moment ticked by before she answered. "Fortunately—" she picked up her wineglass and sipped "—they're fine. No floods. No outages."

"Are you all close?"

"Yes. We're a small bunch."

Ethan changed the subject. Zoe didn't seem enthusiastic about that conversation. The waiter returned with their appetizers.

"Ready to order your entrées or would you like a little more time?" The waiter's French accent stitched his words together like a melody. Ethan smiled and listened carefully as Zoe placed her order. He wanted to know all about the things she liked.

"Ever been to Paris?" he asked her once the waiter left.

"No, but I like his accent." Her spirits seemed to lift, evidently liking this conversation better than the one about family. "It's on my bucket list. I want to set foot on the other six continents."

"I see. Which ones haven't you been to?"

"Outside of North America, I've only traveled to islands off the coast of South America. How many continents have you traveled to?"

"All but Antarctica."

"If I were to leave one out, that would be the one. It's probably too cold for my blood." Zoe laughed.

Ethan smiled. He liked the sound of her laugh. "What other areas are on your bucket list?"

"Just about everywhere," she admitted gamely. "London, Iceland, Scotland, Paris, Ethiopia, Italy, Greece, Tokyo, South Africa, Australia. You're going to have to pay me more money so I can get to some of these places."

"Ha!" Ethan leaned forward over the table. "I see where your bonus is going. If we win this competition with the other branches, we'll both have more to travel with."

"Speaking of which… I know we're not supposed to talk about work, but I have this great idea of doing a series of information sessions that I think will be helpful for current and prospective clients and it could also help bring in more business."

"Really?" He drew back. "Tell me more."

Zoe explained her idea in more detail. Ethan simply shook his head while she explained.

"Wow! That's brilliant."

"I believe it will set us apart from competitors both inside and outside of the company and show how we place a strong focus on service and value. The industry has changed so much." Zoe took a sip of her wine. "Lost that personal touch. I think people would like that."

Ethan pondered her idea. "I love it. Let's get started on that first thing Monday. Outline what these events would look like. We can get on a management call with the rest of the team and begin rolling these out branch by branch across our territory and see how it works."

"Don't tell Carter," she warned. "If this works, it will give us an advantage over the other regions and we'll win for sure."

"I like your thinking, Zoe."

They talked more over dinner about ways to boost business, each idea giving them more energy. He loved how passionate she was about business. Zoe constantly confirmed her worth. He'd picked the best.

But as much as he loved talking shop with her, he eventually turned the conversation back to the two of them. They could talk about business Monday through Friday from nine to five. This time he had with her tonight was personal. That was what Ethan wanted for this night—to get personal with Zoe.

Their dinner was as delectable as Ethan had anticipated. The moment they finished, he paid the bill, gave the waiter a hefty tip and together, he and Zoe jumped back into their waiting car and headed over to the Barclays. Ethan held her hand in the car. He wanted to do much more than that but kept his cool. Memories of the explosive times they'd shared in his bed invaded his thoughts. There was more to Zoe than great sex and he wanted to explore those things, too.

When they arrived, he helped her out of the car but purposely let go of her hand as they walked past the long, winding lines leading up to the main entrance and headed over to the VIP doorway. They were greeted politely and ushered right inside. Zoe kept a cool expression on her face, but he could tell she was excited.

Inside the suite, Ethan greeted his colleague Colin, a tall, muscular, bald gentleman with stark blue eyes. He pulled Ethan into a bear hug as his greeting.

"Colin, this is Zoe Baldwin," Ethan introduced them. "She runs the Garden City branch of Blackwell Wealth Management."

"It's great to meet you, Zoe." Colin offered her a firm handshake.

"It's great to meet you, too, Colin. Thanks for the invitation."

"Anytime." He patted the back of Ethan's shoulder with his large hand and repeated, "Anytime," with a warm smile. "We've got food, drinks, everything. Enjoy yourselves, and when this is all over, we'll go down and meet Mrs. Cartwright. Cool?"

"Cool," Ethan and Zoe said simultaneously.

Ethan watched Zoe look around at the impressive spread inside the suite. Gourmet finger foods lined one side of the suite. On the other side was an array of salads, crudités, desserts and wine and liquor. Inside a stainless steel refrigerator were more beverages of every kind. Ethan and Zoe ate, drank and mingled with the few other people Colin had invited to his suite until the program started.

When Leah Cartwright sauntered onstage, Zoe gave the revered speaker her undivided attention. Minutes into the presentation, it seemed like the only two people in the room were Zoe and Leah. Ethan watched Zoe's starry eyes as she took in every word that fell from Leah's mouth.

At the end, Zoe sighed. Ethan wondered if she had held her breath the entire hour and a half.

"I need a drink." Those were the first words that Zoe had spoken since the show started.

Ethan looked at her bright, excited eyes and chuckled. "You okay?"

"That was amazing. She's amazing. I need a drink so I can calm down a bit before meeting her." Zoe laughed at herself.

"At your service." He waved an arm like a server. "What would you like?"

"More red wine would be great."

"Be right back." He returned a few short moments later with two glasses of wine and sat back beside her. "I believe you enjoyed it, so tell me what you thought about it."

"Goodness!" Zoe shook her head as if trying to think of the right words. "She's so…so…real. Yeah. So real and down to earth. Like we could be friends. I could literally see sitting down and having dinner with her. She's brilliant. Just… This was incredible. Thanks again, Ethan."

"Yeah, she's pretty brilliant."

"And those boots! Woo. I need to find those. I mean, I probably can't afford them, but that wouldn't stop me from trying them on." Zoe laughed.

Ethan thought about finding those boots for her. Wondered if they would make her smile just as brightly as she did now.

"Everybody cool?" Colin's voice boomed through the suite.

A few yeses rang out. Others nodded their heads.

"Then let's go meet our guest of honor."

Ethan took Zoe by the hand and they followed Colin and their private escort to what looked like a lounge behind the scenes of the arena. Ethan watched Zoe's face as she scanned the room in search of Leah Cartwright and smiled deep in his core when Zoe's mouth dropped at the site of her. She closed it quickly enough.

Leah greeted everyone and thanked them all for coming. After a few sips of water, she took her place in front of a step-and-repeat and held brief conversations with people as she shook hands and took pictures.

When it was Zoe's turn, Ethan stepped aside so she could chat with Mrs. Cartwright. Their photographer took a few shots, then Zoe had Ethan take some with her phone. She waved him over to join in, but he politely declined. He would have loved to share in the moment but thought it was best that he avoid taking pictures at this juncture. Besides, he wanted to let Zoe fully enjoy her moment.

Leah and Zoe ended their brief time together with a few selfies. Leah wrapped Zoe in a gracious hug, sending her off with a smile that spread halfway around her face.

"This was amazing. I will never forget this day. Thanks again, Ethan."

"We have Colin to thank."

"You're right. But you could have brought anyone here with you tonight. You chose me. So…thank you." Zoe planted a sweet peck on his cheek. Despite the gesture seeming more friendly than sensual, a spark ignited in Ethan's belly.

The kiss awakened his desire for her. Simple touches from her made him weak. All evening, they had been careful to avoid any telling touches. But now she'd unleashed the passion he'd tried to keep behind his polished exterior. The air in the room seemed to have become warmer. He looked around to see if anyone was paying attention. No one appeared to notice.

"Ready to go?" he asked.

Her seductive gaze was sweltering. "Sure." It seemed that the same desire awakening in him was also awakening in her.

Ethan said a quick thank-you to Colin and called for the driver to meet them at the VIP access entrance. They entered the car as hastily as they had said their goodbyes. For the first few seconds, they stared at each other, and then broke out into laughter.

Their desire was now palpable, pulsing in the air like a heartbeat. Ethan held out his hand. Somehow, knowingly, Zoe reached for it and laced her fingers between his.

Ethan made sure the partition in the limo was up before pulling her toward him and capturing her mouth with his. Their hands explored one another's bodies, and they kissed themselves breathless, touching, caressing, roaming and grasping each other. Ethan felt himself grow rigid in his pants. He pulled away from her just long enough to catch his breath before going back for more. Her lips tasted like heaven. Her mouth felt like clouds. He wanted to be inside of her.

Totally unaware of how much time had passed, Ethan pulled himself away from Zoe and looked through the window when he felt the car roll to a stop. They had arrived at her complex. He huffed, trying to contain the sexual tension pent up inside of him. He didn't want the night to end but that would have to be Zoe's choice.

"You coming…inside?" she asked.

Ethan licked his lips instinctively. He didn't miss the innuendo. "As long as you want me to."

"Oh. I want you to."

Ethan didn't wait for the driver to exit the car and come around to the door. Instead, he shot out and was at Zoe's door in an instant.

"No worries, man." Ethan waved his hand. "I'm good. I'll call for a pickup when I'm ready. Thanks!" He took Zoe by the hand and the two made quick steps to her front door.

Inside her town house, their lips connected again. Zoe kicked the door closed with her foot, and Ethan turned the locks. Their lips never parted. She tugged at his shirt. He undid the buttons and she peeled it off his shoulders. Ethan unzipped her jumpsuit, sliding his fingers into her sleeves to maneuver it down her body. She stepped out of the outfit and removed his belt. Tearing, peeling and pulling, they relieved each other of their clothes and left them pooled at their feet.

Ethan stepped back, putting a few inches of space between them. His breath was ragged. He craved her but needed to admire her natural beauty. He took her in, feasting on her visually from head to toe. Zoe's body was magnificent—flawless to him. Maybe he was blinded by her beauty, but every time he had the honor of seeing her in her natural glory, he felt the same way. Even her imperfections were perfect.

Zoe looked at him in a similar way. He watched her gaze rake over him ravenously, then she reached one hand behind his neck and wrapped her other hand around his erection. She pulled him toward her, and Ethan went willingly.

Their kiss was wild, unbridled and hungry. He embraced her firmly and lifted her up off the floor. He carried her to the dining table, moved her stylish place settings out of the way and laid her down.

Zoe groaned before he even touched her body again. He trailed her sweet caramel skin with kisses from her lips to her knees. Zoe reached for him—he'd grown as rigid as stone—and guided him inside of her, forgoing the tease and getting straight to the point. A sound caught in her throat for the first of countless times that weekend.

Ethan didn't make it home that night.

Or the next.

# Seventeen

Ethan hadn't, as they say, rocked Zoe's world. He'd completely shifted her universe. She couldn't get enough of him. And he tried his best to give Zoe her fill. She'd spent so much time with him in recent weeks that she felt guilty about not spending as much time with her family.

This week, she'd taken some time off to be with her mother and sister. They were a trying few days, ending with Zoe taking Shena for a follow-up visit with her doctor. Zoe looked forward to Shena bouncing back from a manic high. One of the days had been so bad that Zoe had waited half the night for Shena to experience a moment where she could get through to her. Shena had cursed her sister, but Zoe had remained calm. She was committed to working with Shena through her ups and downs and holding her hand through it all.

Being away from work meant being away from Ethan. She communicated with him mostly by text when she was with her family. She missed him horribly. At management meetings or during his visits to her office, they avoided each other. Outside of work, they spent every night and weekend they possibly could together.

He stimulated every part of Zoe: her mind, her body, her heart… She had never dated a man like Ethan before. Her body had never hungered for a man's touch the way hers did for Ethan's. The sound of his lowered voice was enough to make her moist.

She chalked it all up to the forbidden nature of their relationship. That, she assumed, was what made their trysts so exciting.

They graduated from weekends in bed to exclusive romantic experiences, like when Ethan had a famous chef friend prepare an incredible meal at his restaurant on the only night they were closed. Most people had to wait weeks to get a reservation at that place, but they'd had the entire restaurant to themselves on a Monday night. After their meal, they'd danced to a playlist on Ethan's phone, then gone home and made love until dawn. Zoe had been giddy and exhausted the next morning at work.

She wished their "fun" could last forever. She hoped no one would become suspicious. Either way, she was going to enjoy as much of Ethan as possible for as long as she could. Hopefully it wouldn't hurt too much when they got to a point where it all had to end. If she were honest, she'd admit how much she cared about him. But being truthful about her feelings would never be enough.

Still, they grew closer in other ways, too. Being with Ethan so much, she realized how important it was for him to please his father. He worked harder than his brothers, but never seemed to feel like he could ever do enough. But as much as they talked, she never revealed the complete truth about her background or her sister's mental illness. Her life was such a contrast to Ethan's affluent, near-perfect lifestyle. How could they ever bring those two worlds together?

Zoe's cell phone rang at work, startling her. The sound pulled her focus from her inner thoughts. She'd almost forgotten where she was. She picked the phone up from her desk, tapped a key on her computer to bring it to life and said, "Hello."

"Hey." Ethan's voice made her heartbeat quicken.

"Hey, yourself."

"How's your mom doing?"

"Fine. Everyone is just fine," she said, feeling a bit guilty for the white lie she'd told him about her prior absence from work. Instead of telling him about her sister's episode, she'd said her mother wasn't feeling well and she needed to accompany her to a few doctor's appointments.

"That's good. I miss you."

Zoe looked around her office. The door was closed, and she was alone. No one could possibly hear Ethan on her phone. Overcautious. She chuckled at herself. "I miss you, too."

"If you'll let me, I'd like to take you on a little excursion. I want to show you a good time. Actually, I want to show you how much I miss you."

Zoe giggled. She wasn't sure how she'd allowed Ethan to reduce her to a giggling little girl. "Where?"

"It's a surprise."

"Okay, then. When?"

"Take off tonight. I'll pick you up this evening and have you back home by Sunday night."

She shook her head with a smile. "You're impossible. Where are we going?"

"Just somewhere to spend some time together. I'll help you pack to make sure you're dressed right."

"What?"

"Are you in?"

Zoe laughed, placed her elbow on her desk and her hand on her forehead. "Yes. I'm in."

"I'll be at your house at six sharp." He ended the call.

She looked at her phone and then at her computer screen. It would be six more hours before she got to see Ethan's handsome face, and she couldn't wait.

She took a deep breath. Ethan had stolen her focus and filled her with anticipation. How would she get through the rest of the day? She needed to concentrate in order to finish preparing for the next few information sessions. The idea she'd come up with a few weeks back while out with Ethan had proved to be extremely profitable. They'd held three reception-like sessions so far, offering clients and guests wine and refreshments. The results had been more solid relationships with existing clients and additional accounts with new clients.

Zoe took a quick break to clear her head, returned to her desk and got back to work. The second the clock turned to five, she was out the door. At six, she was on her couch, waiting for Ethan with a drink in one hand for her and another on the table for him. As always, he was right on time.

He knocked and she opened the door right away, handing him his drink. They kissed in between a few sips, then Ethan put his glass down and took her by the hand. Zoe followed his lead. Moments later they were in bed, showing each other how much they had missed one another. Afterward, they both collapsed in each other's arms, unable to move. She stayed put until the waves of pleasure rolling through her body subsided.

"We have to go!" Ethan groaned. Lazily, he pushed the tangled sheets aside and climbed out of bed. Reaching for Zoe, who shot him a puzzled look, he said, "Come on."

She groaned. Although she'd rather stay in bed, she peeled herself from the comfort of the cozy mattress. He grabbed her hand and led her to the shower. They made love there again but quickly.

Back in her room, he told her to pull out a suitcase and asked her to pack enough outfits for that night through to Sunday. Zoe was confused when he said to make sure she added a warm coat, scarf, gloves, boots and bathing suits to the bag.

An hour later, they were in a waiting room at JFK airport, preparing to board a private plane.

Zoe had never experienced anything like this before. There was coffee, refreshments and cushioned chairs in the waiting area. It was nothing like the crowds and hard plastic seats of the regular terminal.

Ethan held her hand as they cuddled in the comfortable seats. It was so different than when they went out locally, acting as if there were regular friends or work colleagues. She enjoyed being in his arms in public. She allowed herself to relax and take in yet another incredible experience at the hands of Ethan Blackwell. She could get used to letting a man take the lead and was surprised to realize that she trusted him enough to do so.

Zoe didn't realize she'd fallen asleep on his shoulder until he nudged her awake.

"It's time to go."

She followed Ethan along a pristine Jetway onto an airplane with a creamy-beige interior and cushioned leather couches along the walls. A few chairs faced one another at each end of the jet, with polished wood tables nestled between them. Their flight attendant greeted them with a warm smile, letting them know they could sit anywhere they wanted.

Ethan sat on one of the couches, pulling Zoe down beside him. Their attendant offered them drinks, brought them promptly, then disappeared behind one of the cream-colored walls.

Minutes later, Zoe could feel the plane taking off. Ethan put on soft music and sat back beside her.

"Now will you tell me where we're going?" she asked.

"One of the places on your bucket list."

Zoe sat up. "Are you kidding me?" She tried to think back to all the places she'd told him she wanted to visit. "Which one?"

"The closest one. Now get some rest. There won't be much sleeping after we land."

All she could do was shake her head in disbelief. At last, she rested on his shoulder again. What if she could be with Ethan forever?

"Welcome to Iceland."

Zoe squeezed her eyes, blinked and opened them slowly.

"We're here," she heard Ethan say.

Where was here? She had to get her bearings. Yawning, she recalled the airport terminal and getting on the plane with Ethan. Slowly she began to rise from the sofa. "I thought I was dreaming."

Ethan laughed. "That's a good thing. It's time to get off this bird."

She stood and stretched. Whatever he had planned, she was ready for it. These memories would be hers to cherish far beyond their time together. Thinking of the experiences they shared in this way made the inevitable end much less distressing.

Ethan had a car waiting for them outside.

"Are we really in Iceland?" Zoe had to confirm.

"Yep."

"Oh, my goodness, Ethan!"

"You said you wanted to visit. It was only a five-hour flight. Much closer than all the other places you mentioned. And close enough for a nice weekend getaway."

"And the flight."

"Courtesy of a friend. He owed me."

"Wow!" Zoe got in the car, a cushy luxury ride. She held Ethan's hand but stared out the window. There wasn't much to see this early in the morning, but she was too excited to turn away. She wanted to see everything possible. "Is this your first time here?" she asked.

"No but it will probably be my best."

"Why is that?"

"Because I'm here with you," Ethan said evenly.

Zoe pressed her lips together. "You're trying to butter me up."

"I'm serious."

She looked at him suspiciously. He didn't crack a smile. He seemed serious enough. She looked back out the window.

The four-star hotel was the epitome of luxury. After a quick check-in, they entered their room to find a space that rivaled the size of her entire town house. Clean lines, simple but elegant decor and large windows offered a plush and inviting feel. Zoe marveled at the view of the water below them and what appeared to be snow-capped mountains in the distance.

"What body of water is that?"

"It's the Blue Lagoon."

"Wait! What?" Zoe's eyes widened. "Seriously?"

"Yep. Hungry?"

"Ethan!" He was too nonchalant about all of this. Zoe wanted to burst into tiny little pieces with excitement. "Is that really the Blue Lagoon?" She pressed her forehead against the window. "Oh, my goodness. You have to be kidding me. I'm in Iceland. At a hotel. Overlooking the freaking Blue Lagoon and you're sitting here like we're in your apartment above the muddy East River. Ethan! This is incredible!" She leaped toward him seated on the couch, straddled him and planted kisses all over his face.

Ethan laughed.

"I can't believe you," she said at last.

"I love seeing you smile."

Zoe stared into his eyes. They seemed to sparkle. She kissed him again, this time on his lips. Passion rose inside of her. She was about to make love to Ethan Blackwell, in a room big enough to fit her entire town house, as they looked over the milky-blue water.

Ethan made love to her with care, with the beauty of the lagoon beckoning them through the bedroom window. Zoe woke a few hours later feeling like she was still living inside of a dream.

"Put your bathing suit on underneath your clothes but dress warm," Ethan instructed.

"Whatever you say, buddy." She was giddy again. She couldn't help it when he did things like this. Being with him felt like Christmas came at will. "Where is this journey starting?"

"The Secret Lagoon."

Zoe had never heard of the Secret Lagoon but squealed anyway. She did as he said and put on a bikini under her jeans, sweater and coat.

A shuttle picked them up at the hotel for some sightseeing before going to the lagoon. It drove them through some of the most breathtaking landscapes she'd ever seen in her life.

Zoe was amazed at how cool the weather was, but the lagoon was nonetheless hot and steamy. They stripped down to their swimwear.

Ethan stepped into the water and dunked his body until only his neck was above the water. Zoe took her time savoring the moment. Who knew if she'd ever have a chance like this again? She stepped in, one foot at a time. The sensation sent a cozy feeling over her. She put the other foot in and moaned. Slowly she descended deeper into the sultry water.

The cool weather had nothing on the warmth that wrapped around her as she dipped her body lower. It was like she had cloaked herself with a heated blanket.

Ethan watched her, waiting. She swam to him and kissed his lips, and he lay back to float, pulling her with him. The two frolicked in the hot spring like kids at a neighborhood pool. They swam, waded, soaked and floated for the better part of an hour. Zoe's stomach growled and she realized it had been quite a while since they'd eaten.

"Hungry?" she asked Ethan.

"Depends on what you're asking if I'm hungry for."

Zoe swatted at him playfully. "Naughty boy. That can be dessert. Right now, I need food."

Ethan led her out of the lagoon, and they dressed and ate at the nearby café. She fed him off her plate, and he licked her fingers seductively.

They moved on to the next part of their excursion, touring a volcano. Their weekend continued at that pace, a whirlwind of nonstop tours and activities. The only downtime they had was overnight, which they spent much of making love. By the time they got back to New York Sunday night, she and Ethan were exhausted. That didn't stop them from making love well into the night and falling asleep in each other's arms once more.

It was past midnight when Ethan rose to head home. Zoe didn't want him to leave. She knew his schedule for the week, and it was a hectic one; she wouldn't get to see him again until the managers' meeting in Manhattan on Thursday.

He said goodbye with a deep, passionate kiss. "Get some rest," he said before walking out the door.

Zoe missed him immediately. The void of his absence loomed over the bedroom.

She felt like she was living a real-life fantasy, but that wasn't what this was at all. This was a secret. Some would call it a dirty little secret. Zoe was having an affair with her boss. It was the stuff of scandalous television shows and novels. Some days it felt fun, mysterious and exciting. Others, like now, it felt...unfair. A part of her knew this could never be her real life. There was too much at stake. She could lose her job. Her income supported her family. Her mother would be so disappointed. What would her colleagues think of her? They'd lose respect for her. Despite all of that, the idea of their affair coming to an end was what she dreaded most.

Truth be told, Zoe cared for Ethan—deeply. She'd fallen deeper than she'd ever expected. There was so much to adore about him. He was witty, kind, intelligent and savvy. She loved how he commanded the attention of a room full of people. And yes, he was handsome beyond explanation with the taut body of an athlete. He knew how to have fun and most of all, he was considerate. Ethan listened to her, sifted through her words and held on to what he knew was important.

She hadn't realized how much that meant to her until now. She'd never dated a man as considerate as him before. In fact, she'd never dated a man like him at all.

Zoe didn't dare think that she loved Ethan just yet, but she could easily see herself falling in love with him if they didn't put an end to this soon. Either that or they'd get caught.

Which would be worse?

# Eighteen

"You're coming to the management meeting, right?" Carter asked.

"Of course. Why would you ask that?" Carter's comment caught Ethan off guard.

"You've been MIA a lot lately. I've barely gotten to speak to you. What's going on?"

"With me? Nothing. Just been busy."

"Busy with Zoe?" Carter asked. Accusation rang in his voice.

Ethan almost hit the brakes in the middle of the parkway. He tried to recover quickly and make sure his pause didn't last too long. "Why would you ask that?"

"Come on, bro. This is me. I know when something's up. You haven't been around. I stopped by your house last Saturday and your car was there, but you weren't. It was pretty late. I wanted to crash there after hanging out with this new lady. I called, you didn't answer and you didn't call me back until the next day. When you do get on the phone, you don't have much time to talk unless it's during the workday. I tried to get you a few times this weekend and your phone went straight to voice mail."

"What makes you think that has anything to do with Zoe?"

"From what I see… I think you're hooked. You're not hiding this well, bro."

"Don't be ridiculous, Carter. I know what I'm doing. Don't worry about me."

"If that's the case, why did Dad ask me about you and her after the last management meeting?"

Ethan's eyes widened. It felt like a brick fell in the pit of his stomach. "What?"

"Don't worry. I covered for you. I assured him that everything was good."

"Shit!"

"Just be careful. And listen, you don't have to hide anything from me. I've got your back."

"Thanks, Carter. I'll see you at the meeting."

Ethan felt like turning the car around, but it was too late. He had already reached Zoe's exit. They'd planned on riding into the city together for the meeting. Now he felt like that wasn't such a good idea. They definitely shouldn't come back together. He'd tell Zoe he needed to stay in Manhattan for more meetings and send her back by herself so they wouldn't be seen leaving together.

What had made his father ask Carter about them? Had Ethan done or said something that caused suspicion? He and Zoe had promised to enjoy one another until the fun stopped. And after his conversation with Carter, Ethan felt like the fun was suddenly coming to an abrupt end. He tried to think of anything that he'd done to raise suspicion. He and Zoe couldn't keep their hands off each other in private, but in public they were very careful—especially at work.

He pulled up in front of her house with a thousand questions trampling through his mind. He got out of his car and Zoe met him at her door as usual, yanking him inside by his tie. She wrapped her arms and legs around him and kissed his lips.

"I missed you." She planted pecks all over his face.

"I missed you, too." He couldn't keep the stress out of his voice.

Zoe stopped kissing him and studied his face. "What's wrong?" She put her feet back on the ground.

"Just work stress."

"Aren't we in the lead? The information sessions have been great for business."

"That's fine, but it's other stuff. Carter, Dillon and I have to meet with my dad after our management meeting this morning." Telling that lie stung. A knot tightened in the center of his chest. He hated not being truthful with Zoe.

"Oh. Poor baby. Just come back here after work and I'll help you feel better." She kissed him again.

"Yeah. I'll do that." He needed time to think. "Let's get going."

"Okay. Let me get my stuff." Zoe grabbed her keys and purse. Her cheerful demeanor was a stark contrast to Ethan's unsettled mood.

He forced a smile, trying to push back the stress taking over his mind. The ride to the city was mostly quiet. Giving him space for his mood, Zoe didn't speak much. Ethan appreciated that. Instead she focused on her phone, bobbed to the music on the radio and watched the city passing through her passenger window.

He felt bad for dampening their time together with his anxiety. He looked over at her staring out the window and took her by the hand. He didn't say anything, just held her hand. She squeezed his in return. He was grateful she didn't press him to talk because he needed time to find the right words to say.

The meeting began in its usual fashion; the team chatted over coffee, bagels, yogurt and fruit. Bill called everything to order and they went over the numbers for each territory. Ethan's team had a strong lead and they'd already planned to share their newest tactic for building the business with the rest of the branches.

All eyes were on Zoe as she spoke about the information sessions held by each branch in their region and the impact on business as a result.

"…and the feedback from our clients was overwhelmingly positive," she went on. "We asked them to complete surveys at the end of the sessions and via email. They all seemed to appreciate the face time with the advisors as well as the opportunity to network with other clients. They were happy to have been able to invite guests—many of whom became clients," she pointed out. "They also liked having a forum to learn about additional investment options and hear from guest speakers such as attorneys and tax professionals who were able to provide additional insight into their investment choices." She swept her gaze around the room confidently. "Overall, it's been a huge success with direct results to the bottom line for all of our branches. Oh, and something they all seemed to agree on is that we serve great food and wine."

Everyone chuckled and Zoe looked over to Jasmine, who picked up where she left off.

"A few even suggested a few good wines for upcoming sessions. Here's what else we learned…" Jasmine went on to speak about challenges that they were working through, such as the best methods for following up, obtaining feedback and determining the best days of the week to host the sessions.

Ethan was proud of his team. It was important for him to have the branch managers do the reporting for this initiative so they could get the spotlight. He was especially proud of Zoe, since this had been her innovative idea. He found himself staring at her as he thought of how much of an asset she'd become to the company.

When he glanced over at Carter, his brother was already staring at him. Carter discreetly raised a brow. Ethan sat back and sighed quietly.

He wanted the meeting to be over so he could think. Too many things swirled in his mind, making it hard to concentrate. He felt Carter looking at him and thought he felt his father's eyes on him, too.

Ethan was thinking too hard and making something out of nothing.

When the meeting finally ended, Ethan was ready to go. He'd almost forgotten about the lie he'd told Zoe earlier about meeting with Dillon, Carter and his dad. Like always, the meeting disbanded and the branch managers split off to chat. They had begun to bond and these meetings were the only times they really got to see one another at work. A group of them decided to get together for lunch before heading back to their respective offices.

Ethan stayed behind with Carter and his father. Dillon headed back to Westchester for a meeting with a big prospective client.

"Ethan. Can I talk to you?" Bill asked.

Ethan stilled at the sound of his father's voice. He swallowed hard and turned around. "Sure, Dad. What's up?"

"Carter. Give us a minute, please."

"No problem, Dad. Ethan, let me know when you're heading out so we can handle that."

"Yeah. Will do," Ethan replied. He and Carter had nothing to handle. That was code for *we'll talk after this*. If Bill wanted to speak with Ethan about anything that had to do with Zoe, he was going to need to talk to his brother afterward.

Carter left and Bill pointed to the chair next to the one he sat in at the head of the conference table. "Have a seat, son."

Bill's tone made Ethan's stomach clench. He sat down more slowly than usual and folded his hands on the table to keep them still.

"Is everything okay over in Long Island?" Bill asked at last.

"Of course. We're doing great! You heard our reports. I'm excited."

"That's not what I'm concerned about."

Ethan held his sigh. "What are you concerned about, Dad?"

"You and Zoe. Is there something going on between the two of you?"

Ethan felt the seconds ticking between his father's question and his answer. He wasn't a liar and he didn't want to add another lie to the ones he'd already told today.

It obviously took him too long to answer.

"Ethan." The disappointment in the way Bill said his name made Ethan pull in his bottom lip. He began gnawing on it. "We discussed this! You know how I feel about this kind of thing. We have strict policies in place for good reason. Blackwell can't afford to take another hit on our name if your little fling with this woman goes south. Do you remember the scrutiny we faced?" Bill sat back and huffed, slamming his hand against the table. "You're the last person in this company I would expect to have this conversation with. Twice! Are you willing to jeopardize everything? Even your title?" Bill stood.

His words stung but Ethan kept his gaze forward, refusing to look down.

Bill paced a moment and plopped back down in his chair. "She's not worth it! She's not even on your level." Those words made Ethan's jaw twitch. "You need to end this immediately."

"Um… I'm sorry."

Ethan and Bill turned abruptly at the sound of Zoe's voice.

"Please excuse my interruption," she said. "I left my files on the table."

From the change in her tone, Ethan knew she'd heard some of what his father had just said.

"Sure." Bill waved her in. "Come on in and get it." His smile seemed genuine enough, but Ethan knew his father. "Great presentation today."

"Thank you," Zoe said dryly. She cleared her throat and briskly walked to where she'd been sitting during the meeting, snatched her folder and headed out of the conference room just as fast. "Enjoy the rest of your day," she said without looking at either one of them.

Once she was gone, Ethan released the breath he'd been holding.

"I expect that you will handle this accordingly." Bill

stood again. This time he pulled his suit jacket together, signaling the end of this encounter.

"I understand. I wouldn't put the company in any jeopardy. Our reputation matters to me, as well." Ethan paused to contemplate his next comment. "Zoe is an exceptional employee and an amazing woman. She'd be a great fit for any man who would be lucky enough to gain her attention." He knew his father wouldn't like his response, but he couldn't let Bill's words about Zoe stand without defense.

Bill exhaled loudly. "Just take care of this. And do it without making Blackwell the next front-page feature or having our name plastered across every television station in the nation as breaking news. Good day, son." He snapped his suit jacket straight and stormed out of the conference room.

Ethan wanted to move but couldn't. He sat there with his mind ablaze with hot thoughts.

He was angry at how his father had put Zoe down. How he spoke of her not being on Ethan's level. He was angry at himself for losing control and letting things get this far. He was upset that he'd have to end things with Zoe.

How much of their conversation had she heard? Ethan knew she was upset. He'd seen it in her posture, in the cool way she'd entered and exited the room, in the standoffish way she'd told them to enjoy their day without looking at them.

What would their very next conversation be like? The fun was officially over, but could he really just let her go—now?

# Nineteen

When Zoe saw Ethan's number light up her cell phone again, she hesitated. He had been calling all afternoon and evening and she'd refused to answer. She'd figured a good night's sleep would help her find the words and strength to deal with what was coming but she woke in the morning feeling just as bad.

With a coffee cup in one hand and her cell phone in the other, she paced circles around her small kitchen. Finally, she paused and groaned. This was really happening. Why had she allowed it to go so far? Why had she fallen for him? She cursed the day she'd gone back to his apartment during the big storm. But she hadn't had a choice. Or had she?

Zoe grunted and put the phone down. She needed more time before she could speak to Ethan. He wasn't due to come to the office today so that would give her more time. Delaying the inevitable, she put her phone on vibrate. They had agreed that they would enjoy each other's company as long as it was possible. It had been easy to say and even easier to do. The hard part was now here—ending it all.

She had dated casually before, and when the novelty wore off, she and her former prospects had gone their own ways with no hard feelings. This was different. It felt different. Ethan was different.

Zoe knew it was time to walk away. She wondered if she actually could. She knew she didn't want to. What would it be like to work for Ethan now? And Bill. She'd heard what he'd said about her. She wasn't on their level. She already knew that. His family would never accept her. But Bill's words angered her. Who did he think he was?

Zoe plopped down in a kitchen chair and held her head in

both hands. Where had she and Ethan gone wrong? They'd been careful. Had they become too familiar with one another in front of people? This had been a bad idea from the start and now her heart was stirred into the mix. She hadn't spoken to Ethan yet, so nothing was official, but she already felt her heart breaking.

Sleep had evaded her the night before. Tossing and turning, she'd finally just gotten out of bed and showered. She still had at least two hours before she needed to be at work and her drive was no more than fifteen minutes.

With the extra time, despite the lack of any real appetite, she decided to fix some breakfast. Taking eggs, butter and bread from the refrigerator, she placed everything on the counter and pulled out a small frying pan. One egg and a slice of toast would do. She just needed something in her stomach. She heated the frying pan and added a pat of butter. She pulled out a slice of multigrain toast and placed it in the toaster. When she cracked the egg on the hot skillet, the scent of it rose to her nostrils and her stomach lurched.

"Ew! That egg must be bad," Zoe said to the empty room. She tossed it in the trash, cleaned the pan out and added more butter. She cracked a second egg into the pan, but immediately the scent made her gag. A wave of nausea came over her. She instinctively covered her mouth. "Ugh! That whole carton must be bad."

Zoe tossed the entire carton. Fortunately she had a new, fresh dozen. Again, she cleaned the frying pan and cracked another egg. Again, the scent assaulted her. She wretched, covered her mouth and ran to the bathroom just in time to vomit without making a complete mess.

Zoe cleaned herself up, brushed her teeth and went back to the kitchen. She tossed the second carton of eggs out and tried to remember how long ago she'd purchased them. That last carton wasn't a week old, there was no reason the eggs should have gone bad in that short amount of time. Suddenly she wished she hadn't thrown them all out; she could have taken them back to the supermarket.

She put away the butter and pulled out milk and cereal and grabbed a bowl from the cabinet. Out of habit, Zoe opened the carton of milk and sniffed. Immediately the scent turned her stomach. This time she couldn't make it to the bathroom. She threw up in the kitchen sink.

"What the hell!" She wiped her mouth with the back of her hand.

Zoe washed her hands and headed back to the bathroom to brush her teeth again. She glanced in the mirror and the possibility hit her. Slowly, she lowered the toothbrush.

" Could I be pregnant?" she wondered in disbelief. "I can't. Get." Her mouth fell open. She stood unmoving for several moments. "Pregnant," she finally finished.

Zoe knew it was supposed to be impossible. That's what her doctor had told her and her mother when she was just a freshman in college and suffered severe pelvic pains. She'd missed half a semester of school after having to get emergency surgery. Her condition had been described as some kind of common polycystic issue. The final blow had been delivered when the doctor had said that she would probably never be able to have children. Though she hadn't been ready to be a mother then, she'd cried for days over the inability to bear future children.

Zoe stood staring in the mirror, turning the question over and over in her mind. Could she be pregnant?

She finished up in the bathroom and emailed both Ethan and her office manager to let them know she would be late. She put this one on her sick mother. No one would question that. At first she thought of going to the local pharmacy to get a test, but thought better of that. She needed to know for sure. Zoe waited until her doctor's office opened and called to ask if she could come right away.

By ten that morning, Zoe heard words she never thought

she'd ever hear in her entire life. "Ms. Baldwin. Congratulations. You're pregnant!"

*Congratulations!* The word rang in her ears. She couldn't find a response.

The smile fell from the doctor's face. "There are options, Ms. B—"

"No. Um. Thank you. I won't be needing those options."

"Okay." The doctor sounded uncertain.

"I'm sorry. Dr. Brown. This is just a little unexpected, that's all. You know with my condition and all."

"Yes, I understand. But you know that the man upstairs always gets the final say."

Zoe offered up a weak smile. "Yes. He does." She cleared her throat before asking, "Um, how far am I?"

"Nine weeks. We're going to need to monitor this pregnancy very closely. We already know the potential for it being high risk. As you get further along, we'll see if you need to be placed on bed rest. Let's get you in for an appointment within the next week or so. Okay?" Dr. Brown's voice soothed her.

"Sure," Zoe said.

Dr. Brown patted her on her shoulder. "You'll be fine, Ms. Baldwin." She typed something in her tablet. "I'm sending over some prenatal vitamins to your pharmacy. Start taking them right away."

"Thanks, Doctor. I will."

"See you soon."

Zoe left Dr. Brown's office moving like a zombie. This was never supposed to happen. Yes, Ethan and she had gotten comfortable, or should she just call it careless. It only happened a time…or two. Most of the time they used protection. They'd never established themselves as being in a committed relationship. That was never the intention. But they knew they were only seeing each other.

*Pregnant.* The word played over and over in her mind.

A barrage of emotions fought to overshadow others. She

felt confused, angry, hurt, overwhelmed and, of all things, excited. Excited because she was going to actually have a baby. A baby that she had been told would never be possible. And because it was likely that it might never happen again, she had no choice. She had to have Ethan's baby.

# Twenty

"Ethan! What are you doing here?" Zoe scanned the block and then stepped back to let him inside her town house.

"You won't answer my calls or texts." Ethan brushed past her. He looked around her house as if he'd find clues to the questions that had been flooding his mind for the past three days. "Are you okay? Is your family all right?"

"I emailed you."

"About work." He breathed in slowly and let it out. "I've been trying to reach you for days. What's really going on, Zoe? I know you heard what my father said."

"My family is fine." Zoe turned around and headed to her kitchen. Ethan followed. "Thanks for asking."

"This is about my father, isn't it? I know. I'm sorry about that. He was wrong."

Zoe reached the counter and turned around. She shrugged. "We said we'd stay on this ride until it was no longer fun, right? Well, the ride is over, Ethan."

"That's it?" Ethan asked, feeling himself becoming agitated. He didn't like her nonchalance. "Just like that?"

"Just like that." She threw her hands up and let them fall against her sides. "What are we supposed to do? Ugh. We knew this would happen eventually."

He huffed, closed his eyes and took a moment to calm himself. "Is this what you really want?"

She looked away. "I don't have a choice, do I?" She held her hands up in surrender.

"Listen." Ethan massaged his temples. "I apologize for my father. He shouldn't have said those things. He's just worried about our company being dragged through the mud on possible harassment charges. He's disappointed in me, not you."

"Which is why we have no choice but to end this."

"I don't want this to end!" There. He'd said it.

Zoe sat down, lifted her head toward the ceiling and groaned. "Ethan," she said quietly. "We don't have a choice. I'd never do anything to jeopardize Blackwell. It's been the best work experience of my career. I love the team. I love the work. But…"

Ethan went to her. "But what?"

"This is not good." She looked up at him and shook her head. "I want to be respected by my colleagues for what I bring to the table. Not because I'm the boss's girlfriend. I want the respect of my boss and my boss's boss. Look how weird things have been since the meeting. If he knows about us, then who else knows? It will only be a matter of time before everyone knows. I don't want to be the subject of the juicy office gossip. I don't want to be the one everyone's talking about behind my back. I've worked so hard to prove myself in this industry. I can't believe I put all of that at risk."

"We'll be more careful and I'll deal with my father," Ethan promised. "Eventually he'll come around. I know what I want. Even he can't stand in the way of that."

"It's not the same. Your father was right." She lifted one shoulder in a half shrug. "We're two different people from two different worlds. It will be no big deal for you, but for me, this will always be associated with scandal. We knew what we were getting into. Now we have to deal with the consequences. We knew this day would come. Let's just cut our losses. Give me some time and I'll find another position."

"What? Now you want to quit?" Ethan took to pacing.

"Ethan!"

"No. Don't you think that's a bit much?"

"Ugh! You don't get it, do you?"

He stopped pacing abruptly. "Then tell me what I'm missing. So people found out that we were seeing each other. We're two consenting adults." His arms flailed.

"It was an affair. There's a difference."

"An affair?" he yelled. "Neither of us are married. There was no cheating involved."

"Then why were we hiding it? It was an office affair and no matter how you look at this, others will view it with a measure of scandal. I was screwing my boss!"

"Who cares what people think?"

Zoe shot to her feet. "I do! My last name isn't Blackwell. I won't get any pardons. My career path isn't guaranteed. My parents don't own the business. My career is on the line here," she said in a lower tone. "My reputation. My job. How I'm viewed by the executive officers will be shaped by this." She sat back down. "I can't believe I let this happen."

Ethan lowered to his knees so he could be face-to-face with her. "I understand. I'm sorry. But we shouldn't stop seeing each other because of what people might think. I care about what *we* think—about each other. I realize I have an advantage. I get that. But I still want to be with you."

Zoe shook her head. "I'm sorry, Ethan. There's more at stake here than you even know."

Ethan closed his eyes and inhaled.

Zoe's cell phone rang. He lifted himself from his knees and began pacing again while she went over to the counter where she'd left the phone.

"It's my mother. I have to take this." She answered, "Hey, Ma."

Ethan heard her gasp and paused to look at her.

"Oh, my God! Call 911, I'll meet you at the hospital. I'm on my way," Zoe said frantically. "Sorry, Ethan. I have to go." Worry covered her face, and she scurried to the front of the house.

Ethan wanted to ask what happened, but it wasn't his place. He wanted to offer his help but knew she'd refuse it.

"Everything okay? Is there anything I can help you with?" he asked anyway, following her.

"No. But thanks." Zoe grabbed her keys, opened the door and turned to him. "Ethan…" She stared into his eyes for a few beats. "I do care. But I can't do this. At least not this way. I'm sorry." She kissed his lips, closed her eyes. The kiss was soft. Slow. Final. She rested her cheek against his for just a moment. It felt like goodbye.

Ethan stepped out the front door and behind him Zoe locked up, then ran past him, got into her car and sped off. He watched her race down to the stop sign at the corner, pause for a brief moment and take off.

He was at a loss.

He was spoiled. Used to getting what he wanted. And he wanted Zoe.

He'd find a way to deal with his father. He hated to disappoint Bill. For all that man had done for him, he deserved Ethan's best. Torn, he fought between being faithful to his father and being faithful to his own heart.

But what difference did it make now, especially if Zoe wasn't willing to risk being with him?

# Twenty-One

Shena had had a seizure. The doctor said it was a side effect of the new medication that had been prescribed for her bipolar disorder. Zoe felt terrible for pushing her to try the new meds. She only wanted her sister to feel better. Now, after a frantic night in the emergency room, Shena was finally resting peacefully in the hospital bed with her mother and Zoe at her side.

Zoe hadn't been back home since she'd run out on Ethan the night before. She tiptoed from the hospital room and headed to the family lounge so she could text him. Exhausted, she flopped into one of the chairs and pulled out her phone.

Sorry I had to run out so quickly. It was a family emergency. All is well now, but I'll need another day off to handle a few things.

She hoped that would be enough. Next she texted the office manager, Bella, and told her about the family emergency. The only thing her coworkers knew was that Zoe had a sickly mother. Her true family dynamics weren't any of their business.

Her phone buzzed. She'd received a reply from Ethan.

Sorry to hear that. Glad all is well now. Take the time you need. Anything I can do to help?

Thanks and thanks for the offer. We will be fine.

OK. I'm here if you need me.

Zoe wasn't used to the cordial tone they were using in this exchange. Their familiar, playful nature filled with sexual innuendo was gone. It hurt. Bad.

But she knew she was making the right choice. She'd find a new job and raise her baby on her own. Neither she nor Ethan had signed up for that kind of commitment and she wasn't going to stand by and let his family speak ill of her or her child.

Zoe was no longer a nervous college student. She wasn't going to sit by and allow herself to be scorned by Ethan's parents for not growing up wealthy. She already knew how Bill felt about her. It would be one thing if it was just Ethan's father, but Bill was also her boss's boss. Work would become unbearable. If they found out about the pregnancy, their opinion of her would only get worse. She wouldn't subject herself to the Blackwells' judgment of her.

She'd never imagined being a single mom—or a mom at all. Her own mother had struggled all her life raising Zoe and Shena. With Zoe's finance career, she'd manage much better than her mother had been able to on a modest blue-collar salary.

And Zoe would cherish this baby like the miracle that he or she was. Of course, she would have preferred to raise a child under better circumstances.

A new job. Zoe hated to have to look for one. She loved working for Blackwell Wealth Management. Not to mention, she made more money working for them than she had her entire career. Hopefully she'd find a job with a great boss like Ethan and nothing like Seth.

Thinking about jobs made her go to LinkedIn. She checked her profile and noted changes she needed to make. She noticed that Robert Richford had just posted and remembered meeting him at the conference a few months back. She'd connected with him on the social media platform immediately afterward, of course, and with a few others from the conference, as well. His company, Richford

Financial, did similar work to Blackwell, with a few different options as to what they offered their clients.

Zoe went to his profile and wrote him a quick message about seeking opportunities with his firm. To her surprise, he responded right away.

Hi, Zoe, of course I remember you. I'd be happy to speak with you about opportunities here at Richford. Can you come by the office? Or perhaps we can meet for coffee or lunch sometime this week.

Zoe couldn't believe her luck. If she could land a job at Richford Financial, she wouldn't have to worry about hiding her pregnancy until something else came along. The sooner she could leave Blackwell, the better. She checked her work calendar on her phone.

Great. This week works. I have the most flexibility today. Otherwise Wednesday or Thursday would work.

Zoe hit Send and waited for his response. It didn't come as fast as the previous one. She put her phone down, got up and walked over to the window.

The family lounge looked out over the ambulance bay. Flashing lights colored the area. Zoe hugged herself against the coolness of the room and watched an emergency vehicle back up to the entrance. She couldn't see much else since the building blocked the rest of her view. Instead, she stared at the bright lights.

She placed a hand on her stomach. A baby. She was going to have a baby. Her mother would be the first person she'd tell when the time was right. She already knew this pregnancy would be risky, but she was willing to do whatever was necessary to ensure that her baby came out just fine.

Zoe's phone buzzed. She'd gotten a message back from Robert.

I could make today work as long as it's after 1 p.m.

She smiled.

2 pm is perfect. I can come to your office. See you then!

This was exactly what she needed.

Zoe went back to her sister's room. Her mother was stretching in the chair she'd slept in.

"Hey, Ma. I need to head home and get myself together for work. I have a meeting I have to get to this afternoon."

"Go ahead, honey. I'll call you if anything changes."

"Okay. I'll be back after my meeting." Zoe kissed her sister and her mother's forehead and headed home.

After making a few updates to her LinkedIn profile, she made similar changes to her résumé, and then called Willena to tell her about the opportunity.

"You want to leave Blackwell so soon?" Willena asked.

Zoe didn't want to go into the whole story but told Willena she'd explain more later. "I just wanted to get some insight about Richford before I meet with Robert. I didn't expect to be able to meet with him so quickly."

"It's a great company, but Blackwell is a better fit," Willena pointed out. "The company is expanding, and the opportunities there are endless. I think you should stay put, but it sounds like your mind is made up. Did something happen?"

Zoe closed her eyes and sighed. She decided to tell Willena the whole story. Willena had never judged her.

"Mmm-hmm," she said occasionally as Zoe spoke. "I see," she finally said. "A woman must do what a woman must do. Let me know how the interview goes. I'll call and put in a good word."

"Thank you so much, Willena. I'll call you as soon as I'm done."

Zoe ended the call and busied herself polishing her credentials until it was time to leave for her meeting with Richford Financial. She printed copies of her résumé and placed them in her bag.

The interior of Richford Financial was just as posh as Blackwell Wealth Management. Plaques of Robert featured in major finance magazines hung along the lobby walls.

Moments after Zoe arrived, she was called into his office.

"Good afternoon, Mr. Richford." Zoe reached her hand toward him.

"Good afternoon." Robert shook her hand. "Please, have a seat."

She discreetly scanned the space. Robert's office was the size of her living room at home.

"Good seeing you again," he said. "How are things over at Blackwell?"

"Actually not bad at all. There are a few changes coming down the pike and I thought it best to explore my options," she said casually. "I really want to plant my feet at a place where I can see myself staying and growing for a long time. I saw your recent post on LinkedIn and thought I should look into your firm. You've fared well in the market." Zoe didn't want to paint a bad picture of Blackwell but she couldn't say she was leaving because her secret affair with her boss had been exposed.

"Yes, we have," Robert agreed. "I see you've done your homework. So, tell me about yourself."

Zoe shared her work history, then Robert shared a bit about his career path, and the meeting turned more conversational. By the time their meeting was wrapping up, she felt like she'd been chatting with an old mentor.

"I like the way you think," Robert said at last. "I believe

you'd be a great addition to the Richford team if you're willing."

"Oh, I'm definitely willing." Zoe couldn't believe her luck. It normally took weeks of multiple interviews to land a job in her field.

"When can you start?"

"I believe it would be fair to give my job proper notice. Two weeks would do."

"Great."

In her excitement, Zoe almost forgot to mention the most important thing. "Oh. Mr. Richford. There's something I should tell you."

"What is it?" His brows creased with concern.

"Um. I'm expecting. You can't tell now, but I'm due this summer. I understand if you don't—"

Robert waved off her concern. "Fine. Your benefits will be in place way before then. Congratulations!"

"Oh. Thank you, Mr. Richford. I'm looking forward to getting started." Zoe was surprised that Robert expressed no resistance to her news.

"So am I," he said with a smile.

She closed out her meeting with him and headed back to the hospital. On the way, she called Willena to let her know how the interview went.

When Zoe got back to Shena's room, her sister was awake but groggy. Zoe sent her mother home to get some rest and stayed with Shena a few more hours. Things were moving forward. Not going the way she would have liked but going the way they had to.

Now she had to find a way to tell Ethan she would be leaving. Zoe felt her heart break all over again. She was doing the right thing. Right?

# Twenty-Two

Ethan tried to cleanse himself of his desire for Zoe, but it wasn't working. Her absence left gaping holes in his existence.

He was used to talking and texting with her numerous times throughout the day. They had been talking in the mornings on their way to work, continuing their banter through texts and chatting again on their way home. In the evenings, they would take turns making dinner at one another's house. Half the time, they would wake up together early the next morning and go home before heading into the office. They'd shared countless hours talking, laughing, playing cards and swapping business ideas.

Ethan had even used a few of her ideas to boost business. That was why their region was leading the company in client growth and market share. But all that had come to an abrupt end after the last management meeting.

His solution for filling her absence in his life was to work harder. However, longer hours weren't helping to fill the void. It didn't stop thoughts of Zoe from invading his mind and stealing his focus. He wanted her back.

His father had checked in with him several times about how he was "handling" the situation. Ethan was able to honestly say that he and Zoe were no longer seeing each other, but those words nearly choked him.

She avoided him at all costs. It helped some because seeing her and not being able to take her into his arms pained him. He spent as little time as possible at her office.

But today, he wouldn't be able to avoid visiting. Their branch was scheduled to meet to go over the latest numbers and prepare for another information session. Ethan had always prided himself on not allowing his emotions to interfere with business—until now.

He pulled into his designated spot in the parking lot and shut the car off. Instead of getting out, he sat back and took a deep breath, bracing himself for his encounter with Zoe.

It had been a few days since he'd last seen her. His visit to her home that evening hadn't gone well. And it had ended with her having to run out for a family emergency so he never got to finish their discussion. Since then, they'd spoken only about business. Zoe had made it clear that she wasn't interested in speaking about much more. Ethan understood her position; she didn't want to be the subject of watercooler talk.

He didn't care about people talking. He wanted to make her smile and laugh again. He craved her body and the way she made him feel in and out of bed. He longed to engage in one of their stimulating conversations over politics or the world of finance.

Ethan hadn't totally given up on them, but he felt he needed to give Zoe some space. He could only imagine how his father's words must have made her feel. But he wasn't convinced that all the things they'd shared in the past few months meant nothing to her. Walking away wasn't easy for him and he didn't believe it was any easier for her.

Finally removing the key from the ignition, Ethan pushed the car door open and headed toward the building. Inside the office, he greeted the staff as normal and headed straight for his office.

Zoe's door was closed when he passed by, and he didn't bother knocking like he normally would have. He continued to his office and shut the door behind him.

He opened his laptop, hit the power button and grabbed the television remote, pointing it to the flat screen on his wall. For the next few minutes, he took in some market updates before opening up a few documents that he would need for this meeting. The stock market had been experiencing a rough couple of days, and he knew each branch was fielding calls from clients with concerns about their investments. He added that to his agenda for the meeting. Going to his emails, his eyes scanned the words, but his brain failed to absorb any of what he read. Zoe had slipped into his thoughts again, stealing his ability to focus.

Ethan stood and walked to the window. Stuffing his hands in his pockets, he zeroed in on the intricate landscaping below. He anticipated and dreaded seeing Zoe. He looked at his watch. The meeting would start in less than fifteen minutes. He was going to need coffee.

He opened his door to head to the kitchen, and ran right into Zoe. Their bodies collided, causing the steaming coffee in her Blackwell mug to spill all over his blue shirt.

"Whoa!" Ethan jumped back, pulling his soaked shirt away from his chest. A few staff members sitting at their cubicles jumped to their feet.

Zoe's eyes widened. "I'm so sorry." She wiped at his soiled shirt. "I was coming to tell you that Carter was trying to reach you, but you weren't answering. He asked me to see if you were in the office. Is it hot? I'm so sorry. I have wipes in my office."

Ethan felt the burn of the hot coffee, but he was more aware of the concerned look in Zoe's eyes.

"I'm fine." He looked down at his shirt and then back at Zoe and the few faces that were still directed toward him. "Believe me, I'm fine." There was a large mocha-colored stain right in the center of his shirt.

"Come. I have wipes." Zoe turned toward her office.

Ethan followed her. She retrieved some wipes stashed in her desk and, pulling a few from the package, she started toward him. He closed her office door. She paused and stared at him.

"We have to talk," he said.

"Not now, Ethan."

"Then when? You've been avoiding me. I've tried to give

you space but we have to clear the air. We can't continue working like this."

Still holding the wipes, Zoe remained still. She closed her eyes and took several breaths. "Please, Ethan. Now is not a good time."

"Later. I can stop by. We need to settle this."

"Fine. Stop by later. You left a few things at the house anyway. You can pick those up."

That stung. He didn't want to remove his things from her house. It was nothing significant but removing anything that remained would be too final.

Ethan took slow steps toward her. He stopped, leaving only a few inches between them. He wanted to kiss her. To taste her sweet lips again. He wanted to pull her into his arms. What had she done to him? Why couldn't he just walk away?

They were close enough for him to feel her breath. Zoe didn't move. She seemed cemented in place. He watched her swallow. Watched her neck shift. She tucked her bottom lip into her mouth and gnawed.

Ethan took the wipes from her hands. They remained close. Inches apart. Being near her was electrifying. He wanted to touch her cheek, caress her face. He affected her; he could tell by the way her chest rose and fell now that he was so close. Her breathing changed, and she avoided his eyes.

He was glad there was still some impact. For him, that meant it wasn't over. All hope wasn't lost. He fought the urge to kiss her. He missed the feeling of her in his arms.

Zoe still hadn't spoken. She just stood there, breathing with more urgency.

"Tonight," Ethan said.

Zoe cleared her throat. "Tonight."

"Thank you." He leaned forward, compelled by a force, by his desire to be with her. His wet shirt sticking to him no longer mattered.

She didn't move, showed no sign of resistance.

Gently he placed his lips on hers. She didn't pull away, and Ethan kissed her. A soft peck. When he pulled back, her eyes were closed. "Tonight," he repeated.

Leaving with the wipes, he rubbed at the stains in his shirt on the way out. She hadn't resisted him. Tonight, perhaps they could make things right.

# Twenty-Three

Zoe checked her phone and ignored yet another text from Ethan. She had dodged him the night before. She just couldn't have handled seeing him after he'd kissed her in the office earlier that day. The kiss had made it hard for her to concentrate in her meetings. It had also entangled her thoughts into a jumbled mess. Zoe knew that she needed to face him sooner or later, but she had to buy some time. She'd meant to give him her letter of resignation, but couldn't bring herself to do that just yet either. None of this was easy.

She'd planned on making a clean break. Avoiding him was part of the process. But his kiss. That soft, sweet kiss had reminded her of how much she missed him. And now that she was sitting in the doctor's office with his baby growing inside of her, she definitely couldn't deal with him. She'd answer his texts when she got home.

Zoe looked at the couple sitting in the waiting room across from her. The woman took her husband's hand and placed it on her belly. "Feel that?" she asked.

The husband's face beamed. "Yep." He lowered his face to her stomach. "We're going to have to put you in football with a kick like that, buddy."

The two of them gushed over their baby. When he sat back, she rested her head on his shoulder, and they held hands.

The scene was sweet and intimate. Witnessing it made Zoe feel like an intruder. It also made her sad. Her story would never look like theirs. She was going to be a single mom.

She'd thought about not telling Ethan about the baby at all but figured she wouldn't be able to get away with that for too long. Unless she moved, she couldn't hide a baby forever. She'd tell him when the time was right, but she wouldn't dare expect anything from him. She'd show him and his family that she and her baby could manage without them. Bill wouldn't have to worry about her not being on their level. Based on the compensation outlined in the offer letter she'd received from Richford Financial, she could take care of her baby just fine by herself.

Another couple came in holding hands. Their excitement was written across their faces. This gentleman helped his very pregnant wife to her seat and supported her back as she sat carefully. He looked down and saw that her shoelace was untied. Without hesitation, he got on one knee and tied her shoe. Seeming grateful, she smiled, and he placed his arm around her neck when he sat next to her.

Zoe hadn't expected to feel so alone on this appointment. She wished things were different. Ethan could have been right there with her.

Truth be told, Zoe was scared. She'd heard all kinds of stories about being pregnant and she already knew her pregnancy wasn't going to be easy. Scar tissue from her surgery years ago posed a threat. Dr. Brown had used expressions like *monitor closely*, *high risk* and *possible bed rest*. She had no idea what all of that really entailed. She just knew this could be her only chance at bearing a child, so she had to take it.

Her need to have this baby didn't have to impact Ethan's life, so whenever she told him, she'd also let him know she didn't need him. He claimed he wanted to be with her, but would he still feel the same way when he found out she was pregnant?

Getting his employee pregnant during a secret affair certainly wouldn't fit into his family's perfect little setup. And Zoe could only imagine what his father would have to say about it. This was why she needed to leave Blackwell ASAP. It wasn't because she really wanted to go.

A nurse called Zoe's name, snatching her from her thoughts. She took one last look at the happy-looking couples before following the nurse into an examination room. The woman took her vitals and then gave her a paper gown and told her to undress. She assured her that the doctor would be with her soon and closed the door. Zoe flinched when the door shut. The small room seemed to close in on her.

Dr. Brown arrived a few minutes later. "Hey there, Ms. Baldwin. How are we doing this week?"

"All right. A little tired. I didn't get good sleep last night."

"We need to work on that. Baby is going to need you to get your rest."

The doctor examined her, and Zoe paid close attention in wide-eyed awe. This was all so new to her. She didn't really know what to expect.

"So far everything seems fine, Ms. Baldwin, but we're not going to take any chances. I'd like to see you every two to three weeks as opposed to monthly. When you hit your third trimester, I want to see you every week. Okay? Any questions for me?"

"Yes. Plenty. I don't even know where to start." Zoe released a nervous laugh.

"Start with the one that scares you most."

"Okay…" She unloaded all of her questions on Dr. Brown, who patiently listened and thoroughly answered, making her feel a little better. "And those vitamins you gave me," Zoe added, "they make me nauseous."

"Okay. I'll give you a new prescription. Make sure you're taking them after you've eaten. They don't do well on empty stomachs. I'll send it right over to your pharmacy. Anything else?"

"I think that's all for now."

"Well, congratulations again. To say this pregnancy is unexpected is an understatement. I imagine you two must be ecstatic. I can't wait until this little miracle bundle arrives."

Zoe forced a smile. "Yes. Me, too. Thanks."

Dr. Brown's comment brought Ethan to mind. Zoe doubted he'd be ecstatic.

She went straight to the pharmacy before going home. Back in the car, she opened her new prescription and took a look at the pills. They were huge. Zoe grunted. She hated taking pills, especially large ones. She tossed the bottle in her bag and started her car. Her phone chimed again. It was another text from Ethan. She'd read them at home.

She stepped inside her town house, placed her purse on the couch and went to the kitchen for crackers and water. She came back, plopped on the couch and turned on the television. She munched on a few crackers before popping one of her enormous vitamins and washing that and the crackers down with water.

This was one of the few nights that she hadn't planned to go by her mother's house. Shena had begun to do much better after her recent hospital stint, giving Zoe and her mother less to worry about.

Zoe realized she had dozed off when she heard the door-bell ring. Lack of sleep from the night before had caught up to her. She got up to answer the door, peeked out and saw that it was Ethan.

She braced herself a moment before opening the door. She'd avoided him last night. Tonight, she'd have to face him.

"Hello," Ethan greeted her cautiously.

"Hi, Ethan." Zoe stepped back.

"I texted you…a few times," he said, still standing in the entrance.

"I know."

"Can I come in?"

"Sure." Zoe turned and went back to the living room and sat on the couch. She muted the sound. "I'm sorry about your shirt."

"It was nothing my cleaners couldn't handle." Silence settled between them for a moment. "I'm sorry, too."

She shrugged. She knew Ethan was referring to the kiss. She couldn't really say she was sorry about that. She just couldn't let it happen again or she'd have to realign her thoughts once more.

"Can I sit?"

It wasn't until then that she noticed he was still standing. She shifted closer to the end of the couch, pushing up against her purse to could make room for him.

"We need to work this out," he said.

"I thought we did that."

"No. We didn't. You had an emergency and we never finished our conversation. How's your mother by the way?"

"She's fine. Thanks for asking." Zoe looked away from him.

Ethan held his hand up. "I know you were angry. I wanted to give you, and quite honestly me, as well, some time to think. We work together. You're a huge asset to the company. We need to be able to work together *and* I don't want to lose you. We can take this as slowly as you need to. Don't worry about my father. This is about you and me."

"Ethan." Zoe pressed her lips together. This was harder than she'd anticipated. "I took another job."

"You what?" He reared back. Hurt registered across his face. "Why?"

"Because. I needed to. I wanted to tell you before now. I'll email my official letter of resignation to you tomorrow. We don't have to worry about your father. Now we can both just move on."

Ethan opened his mouth, but no words came out. He blinked, looked around the room, then directed his gaze back at Zoe. He looked genuinely confused. "Why?"

"It was the best thing."

He blew out a sharp exhale. "Where?"

"Richford Financial."

Ethan's face morphed through several emotions right before Zoe's eyes. "Richford. Are you kidding me?"

"Yes. What's wrong with Richford?"

"Please. Whatever you do, don't go to Richford. Let's just work this out."

"I've already accepted the offer."

"This isn't happening." Ethan stood and paced with both hands on his hips. After a few laps, he sat back down and took both Zoe's hands into his.

His touch sent Zoe's emotions reeling once again. "Ethan, please don't do this."

"This is about more than Richford. If you're going to leave Blackwell, that's the last place I want you to go. But here's what I need to say." Ethan took a breath. "I don't want us to be a secret. You're not a fling to me or some scandalous office affair. I want to be with you. Tell me you don't have feelings for me."

Zoe dropped her head. She couldn't say she felt nothing. That lie wouldn't pass her lips. She lifted her head. Instead, she said, "I can't. I just can't do this. I'm sorry."

He looked to the ceiling and back at her. He still had her hands in his. Zoe fought back tears. She had to stand her ground.

"Okay." His voice was solemn. "Fine." He stood.

Zoe couldn't look at his face. His pain threatened to make her go back on what she'd decided. She stood also, knocking over her bag. She hated this. She felt awful.

Ethan's face changed as he stared at her bag. That painful looked changed into one of curiosity. He tilted his head. "What's that?" he asked, pointing near her feet.

Zoe looked down and noticed the contents of her purse had spilled beside it. The bottle of vitamins had rolled and stopped right at her foot. It was too late to mask the large Prenatal label on the bottle.

"Zoe, are you pregnant?"

Her mouth opened but instead of speaking, she clamped it shut.

"Zoe!" Ethan stepped closer to her. "Are. You. Pregnant?"

In a small voice, she answered, "Yes."

Ethan stepped back as if someone had pushed him. His breath became ragged. All the air seemed to have left the room at once. Zoe could hardly breathe herself.

"Don't worry, Ethan," she said in a rush. "I won't ask you for anything. Your father, your family won't have to be bothered with me or my child. We will be just fine."

"Your child?" His voice boomed. Zoe flinched. His voice lowered. "It's my child, too, isn't it?"

Zoe didn't answer right away.

"Isn't it?" he asked again.

"Yes." She instinctively hugged herself.

Ethan sat slowly—very slowly. "You were going to run off and have this baby by yourself? You weren't going to tell me?"

"Your family. I—"

"This has nothing to do with my family." He stood again and started pacing. "This is about us. Our relationship—and now our baby. And you thought it made sense to keep this from me? You're carrying my baby." He looked confused. Then he smiled. "I'm going to have a baby."

Zoe was confused by his reaction.

"How long have you known about this?"

Zoe groaned. "A few days."

Ethan shook his head. "Why?"

"Because we're not on the same level, okay?" Zoe couldn't help the tears. "I won't have my child being treated like an outcast because his own grandfather doesn't think his mother is good enough. We may not have as much as your family but my baby deserves to be loved and accepted. I don't come from a perfect family but that doesn't make us less than anyone." She stabbed the air with her index finger. "I won't have it." She couldn't catch her breath. "I know what rejection feels like and I'd rather raise my child alone than allow him to be treated like he's less than!" She felt the fresh sting of her father's abandonment.

"Zoe! Zoe! Zoe!"

He'd called her name three times before Zoe realized it. He wrapped his arms around her, and she cried into his chest.

"I would never let that happen to you or our baby either," he said. "I'd never let anyone mistreat our child. You think my family is perfect? We're not. Let me be the father our baby needs. Don't take that from me."

Zoe tried to speak through the tears. She wanted to believe him.

"Zoe, I care about you," he went on. "I have feelings for you—deep feelings for you. I can't believe that you don't feel the same. I knew it when I kissed you yesterday." He held her at arm's length and looked into her crying eyes. "Zoe. I love you. No one will ever hurt you or our baby. I'll make sure of that."

Zoe knew she was being emotional...but had she just heard him say that he loved her?

# Twenty-Four

Ethan was going to be a father. That single thought had consumed him from the moment he'd left Zoe's house the night before. The news excited and frightened him. He'd imagined a family—wife, a few kids. He hadn't been expecting to start one this soon, but what better woman to start one with? He wondered if he would be a good father.

Ethan was sure Zoe would make a great mom. He could go on for days about the great qualities she possessed. His child stood to inherit many of those same great characteristics. Zoe was smart, determined, beautiful, family oriented and even a bit stubborn. And thanks to her breakdown in front of him last night, Ethan understood her even more.

What Zoe didn't realize was that Ethan was much more like her than she knew. He knew the sting of rejection and abandonment as well as she did, which was why he was at Robert Richford's office this morning. Ethan hadn't bothered to call. He'd just shown up, wanting to catch Robert there.

"Good morning. I'm here to see Robert Richford," Ethan said to the woman in the posh reception area. Frosted glass framed in dark wood separated the area from the rest of the office. He strived to remain composed. Normally that wasn't an issue for him, but he had no idea how this meeting would go. The last time he'd approached Robert, years before, it hadn't gone the way he'd wanted it to.

"Good morning!" The woman's warm greeting and soothing voice generated an involuntary smile. "Is Mr. Richford expecting you?"

"No. But if you could please let him know that Ethan

Blackwell is here to see him and it's urgent, I'd appreciate it."

"Sure. Just give me one moment." The woman got up and disappeared through frosted double doors.

Ethan second-guessed his decision to come see Robert. Perhaps he should just leave. Immediately, he tossed that thought from his mind. He had waited long enough. This was the best time to have this conversation. He would leave once he got what he came for.

Moments later, the receptionist returned and invited Ethan to follow her across the office.

"Mr. Blackwell is here to see you," she said at an open door. She woman stepped aside, smiled and nodded at Ethan. "Good day to you, sir." She waved her hand for him to step into Robert's office.

"Thanks." Ethan walked inside. He looked around, taking in the multiple flat screens displaying various financial news channels. Robert's office looked as if an interior designer had decorated it. It was a cross between a presidential suite and a home draped in traditional elegance.

Robert stood behind a large mahogany desk. Two burgundy tufted-leather chairs faced it on the opposite side. Robert muted the TVs with a touch of a button. Silenced reporters from various financial news stations reported the status of the stock market.

Robert rounded his desk. "Ethan." He reached out to shake hands.

Ethan paused a moment before taking Robert's hand and shaking it. Instead of going back to his chair, Robert sat on the edge of the desk. He motioned for Ethan to sit.

"You look good," Robert said.

"I didn't come for the flattery, but thanks." Ethan's tone was a bit sharp. He inhaled to remain composed.

"What brings you here this morning, son?"

"Please don't call me that."

Robert raised his hands in surrender. "Sorry."

"Zoe Baldwin," Ethan said.

"What about her? I'm looking forward to having her join the team. Seems like she'll be a real asset."

Ethan paused for a moment pondering the right way to ask his question. "What made you hire her?"

Robert's brows furrowed. "She's a great candidate. Her résumé was impressive. Why?"

"You knew she worked for Blackwell, right?"

"Of course, but what does that have to do with anything?" Robert asked.

"Did she come to you or did you solicit her?"

Robert looked as if he were becoming annoyed with Ethan's line of questioning. "I'm not out here trying to poach on Blackwell's talent pool. What's this about, son?"

Ethan flinched inwardly when Robert said the word son. "Nothing. She's been an asset to the company. I'm sorry to see her go." Ethan hoped his response sufficed. He didn't want to appear defeated.

Robert nodded. "I see."

"I also have a few other questions," Ethan added. Robert raised a brow but didn't seem surprised. "I need to know."

Robert took a deep breath. "Now?"

"Yes. This is as good a time as any. I want to hear it from you. I was young when I came to you before and you refused to see me."

Robert lifted himself from the edge of the desk and put one hand in the pocket of his tailored slacks. "Have you spoken to your parents?"

"I deserve to hear the truth from you."

Robert walked toward a window and looked out. It took a few moments, but he finally spoke. "I was wrong. We both were. Perhaps we all were. It was a moment of weakness and horrible judgment."

Ethan waited for him to continue.

"We were friends...your mother, father and me. They started having issues and your mother had taken to com-

ing to me to discuss them. We had been friends even longer than your father and me. I was supposed to talk some
sense into your dad but instead I became emotionally attached to her. I was also going through problems with my
wife at the time. With the situation at hand and wild emotions, before we knew it, your mother and I had made the
biggest mistakes of our lives."

Robert paused and drew in a long breath. "My marriage
ended up in divorce. Your mother and father were lucky
enough to work things out. It was a long time before we
even acknowledged the reality that you could be mine. I
kept asking. I wanted to know."

Ethan listened intently. He'd only heard bits and pieces
of this story previously. Bill refused to address it, telling
Ethan that all he needed to know was that he was Bill's son
and that he loved him. His mother, Lydia, admitted the affair when Ethan approached her as a teen but refused to
speak more of it.

"It was years before I knew for sure," Robert went on.
"Before they admitted it to me. Since Bill and Lydia recon-
ciled, all he wanted was for me to stay away from them and
you. Somehow, we all thought it was better to leave things
alone. You knew Bill as your father. He was taking good
care of you. I had a new family of my own. We figured no
one would ever know anyway. That was until you came to
me. You were a teenager then." He sat down on the desk
again and paused longer this time. "I'd signed papers. You
were legally Bill's child. I couldn't say anything to you.
That's the only reason I sent you away that day. I dreaded
that and could only imagine how you must have felt."

"My mother told me," Ethan said. "I hounded her after
overhearing something my father said. That's when I started
snooping around. I found you. I understood enough to know
that Bill wasn't my real dad."

He felt something shift inside of him. All these years,
he'd believed that Robert had just rejected him, and now

he knew that wasn't the case. There was more to this story. He needed to speak to his father now.

"Thanks," Ethan said, standing. He had gotten what he'd come for. What more was there to say?

"Ethan," Robert called as he made his way to the door.

Ethan turned around.

"Why now?"

"I'm going to be a father."

Robert nodded. That seemed to be all the explanation he needed.

Ethan headed for the door again.

"Ethan," Robert called to his back. "For what it's worth, I may not have been able to show it, but I've always watched from the shadows. You'd make any father proud."

Ethan went back to his office. After work he drove to his parents' home. He'd timed his visit so that he would catch Bill just as he arrived home. He'd checked in with his mother on the way and knew she wouldn't be home. He wanted to speak with Bill alone.

Ethan pulled up behind his father just as Bill entered his three-car garage.

"Hey, son!" Bill waved as he got out of the car.

"We need to talk," Ethan said as he got out.

Bill paused. "Everything okay? Should I pour us a drink?" he said jokingly.

"Perhaps. It's about Robert Richford."

Bill lifted his brow and sighed. Slowly he closed his car door. "That."

"Yes, sir. That."

"Let's go into my office."

Ethan followed his father inside. His mother's stylish touch was all over their home. Even when she wasn't there, he could feel her presence. She was out tonight, as she often was, schmoozing on behalf of several nonprofit organizations where she served as a member of the board.

Bill filled two rocks glasses halfway with scotch. He handed one to Ethan and sat on a love seat.

"Can we get right to it?" Ethan wanted to save the small talk for another time.

"I forgave your mother," Bill said at once. "I loved her. Still love her with everything in me. We worked things out in our marriage and vowed to stick together from that point forward. Sticking with my wife, meant sticking with you— *our* son," Bill emphasized.

Ethan sipped his scotch. He looked at Bill, waiting for him to continue.

"I was building the business and wasn't around often at all. I imagine your mother got quite lonely. We had our issues," Bill admitted. "In the end, we didn't want to complicate things so we agreed that Robert would be completely removed from the picture."

"To save face."

Bill tilted his head. "You can say that." He leaned forward. "Ethan, you *are* my son. I never wanted you to feel any different than your brothers and sister."

"Yet, I always did."

Bill dropped his head but lifted it back up. "I'm sorry."

"I guess none of us are perfect, are we?"

It took a moment, but Bill finally nodded in agreement. "What made you bring this up now?"

"It's the right time." Ethan paused and considered his words. He knew that what he was about to say would hit his father hard. "Zoe is pregnant. She's no fling to me. No careless affair. I care about her—a lot. I want you to know and respect that."

Silence expanded between them.

Ethan was glad to get that off his chest. "We can talk more later. Right now, I have to go."

"Of course." Bill sighed, sat back and took another sip of his scotch.

Ethan wasn't sure how Bill was taking the news. His response didn't offer much in the way of how he felt.

"Thanks, Dad." Ethan held his hand out to his father.

Bill took it, but instead of shaking his hand, he got up and hugged Ethan. "I love you, son."

"I love you, too, Dad."

"And I respect your decision."

Ethan felt lighter than he had in days, possibly years. He left his father and headed straight for Zoe's house. There would be no covering up the fact that she was having his baby.

There was so much he'd suspected about the situation between his parents and his biological father but hadn't had confirmed until now. Many times he had tried to convince himself that none of it mattered. But it did, especially now that he was going to be a father himself.

He'd made several attempts to speak to his mother about it over the years, but it always seemed too difficult for her. Ethan hated the sadness that consumed her when he broached the subject. That trip he'd made to Robert's home as a young man had left him broken. When Robert had refused to speak to him, Ethan had taken on the armor of rejection. Though Bill had never really treated him differently than his siblings, knowing that he wasn't his biological father had still made Ethan feel like an outsider.

Bill didn't have to accept him, but he had. So Ethan felt obligated to be as little a burden to him as possible. That was where his desire to please his dad had come from.

How could Ethan have known that was an orchestrated arrangement? He sympathized with his mother. Somehow, he'd understood even as a teen the guilt that had taken hold of her. Until today, his mother was the only person he had spoken to about this.

These questions had lingered for years. However, becoming a father made it necessary to finally seek answers and Ethan was glad that he had. Knowing helped him understand himself. He needed that going into fatherhood.

He reached Zoe's house just as the sun was setting. She opened the door and stepped aside to let him in. Lifting on her toes, she greeted him with a cordial kiss on the cheek. It wasn't the passionate greeting he'd grown accustomed to, but it was warmer than the distant space they'd settled into over the past few days.

"I have some things I need to tell you," Ethan said. He took Zoe by the hand, led her to the living room and sat her down. He was pulling back the curtain on his own truth.

# Twenty-Five

Zoe couldn't believe what Ethan has just told her. She didn't even know how to respond. She guessed it was her own fault for thinking that the Blackwells were flawless just because they were wealthy. They were just like any other family. Perhaps even just like hers. She could see the pain in Ethan's eyes as he revealed family secrets that had plagued him for years. She also saw his relief in getting the information out in the open.

Zoe just listened as he spoke, not wanting to interrupt him. When he stopped, she waited several more moments to make sure he didn't have anything else to say. Then she hugged him.

She wrapped her arms around him and pulled him in tight, fighting back tears. He held her just as tight. They stayed that way, holding on to each other as if their lives depended on it. The embrace felt like therapy.

"So what now?" she said when she finally pulled away.

"If you'll have me," he began, "I say we proudly raise our baby. Stay in this together."

Ethan's words made her heart smile. But to make sure the air was truly clear of secrets, Zoe had some of her own to share.

"There are things that I should also tell you," she began.

"Tell me."

So Zoe told Ethan her truth, sharing the story of her own father walking out on her family when she and Shena were kids. The difference was, she'd never seen her father again. They'd received word that he'd died as a result of a work accident when she was in college. Unlike with Ethan, there'd been no kind of reconciliation. Zoe also shared Shena's condition with him and finally told him about how she'd thought she would never be able to have children.

"So we're having a miracle baby?"

Zoe threw her head back and laughed. "Yes." When their laughter died down, she continued, "We're a tight, loving bunch—my mom, my sister and me. We have our issues, our share of struggles. My family means the world to me. And I'm not ashamed of them."

"You shouldn't be." Ethan ran the back of his finger down her cheek.

"I guess the lesson here is that none of us are perfect," Zoe said.

"And I want to be imperfect with you." He kissed her. "And our baby. When I said I loved you the other night, I meant it."

Zoe blinked. Tears tickled her eyes. She'd realized how much she cared for Ethan in his absence. They'd spent months together, day and night. Ethan made her feel like no man had ever made her feel before. Being tough and trying to protect her heart and her child, she'd tried to fight those feelings. But when he'd said those words that night, she'd realized that she loved him, too.

"I love you, too, Ethan."

He grabbed her, wrapped his arms around her and kissed her deeply.

When he let go, Zoe touched her stomach, gazing down at it. "I still can't believe it. I'm hardly showing but I can't wait to feel my child."

"And both his parents will always be there for him."

Ethan's words touched her, but she couldn't resist. "His? Who said it will be a boy?" she teased.

"Boy, girl or frog. It doesn't matter to me. I'll be there. If it's a frog, we'll build a pond in the backyard and make sure it's got a nice pad. Get it?"

Zoe swatted Ethan playfully for the silly pun. She tried

not to laugh but did anyway. "Whose backyard are we building this lush lily pad in?"

"Ours!" Ethan declared. "We're in this thing together, right?"

Zoe looked at him with a raised brow. "Don't feel obligated to stick around because you knocked me up," she teased. Ethan's mouth dropped open. "As long as you'll have me," she said with a smile.

He smiled back. "I think I'd like to keep you around for a while."

Zoe laughed again and Ethan kissed her right in the middle of it. He pulled her close.

"We have to tell our families," he said, still holding Zoe in his arms."

"Yeah," she agreed.

"And we have to do it together," he added.

"Hmm. Yeah." Her mother and sister would be ecstatic. But despite what she now knew, she wasn't looking forward to having the conversation with Ethan's parents.

They kissed again. Ethan's lips on hers felt like healing to her soul.

He pulled back long enough to say breathlessly, "I've missed you."

Immediately she felt her body respond. "Show me how much." She let seduction sparkle in her eyes. She craved what she'd missed about him.

Ethan picked her up, carried her to bed, laid her down and showed her just how much he'd missed her.

Zoe had made it to twelve weeks. She sat in Dr. Brown's waiting room with Ethan at her side, holding her hand. There was so much about the moment that filled her up. She looked at the ceiling and blinked. She insisted on containing her emotions.

"Zoe Baldwin," the nurse called.

"That's me." She and Ethan rose and followed the nurse to an examination room.

Zoe watched him take in all the equipment in the room, still holding her hand. "Babe," she said at last. "I can't put on this gown if you don't let go of my hand."

"Oh. Right." He let go of her hand.

She laughed. Ethan had exhibited this nervous energy ever since he'd picked her up for the appointment. She thought it was cute. Zoe stepped out of her clothes and into the paper gown. Dr. Brown tapped lightly on the door just as Zoe slid onto the examination table.

"Come in."

"Good morning!" Dr. Brown's cheerful tone rang through the small room. She held her hand out to Ethan.

"I'm the proud dad," he said.

Zoe rolled her eyes and chuckled. "Good morning, Dr. Brown. This is my boyfriend, Ethan Blackwell."

"Nice to meet you, proud Dad." Dr. Brown shook his hand. "Have you ever seen an ultrasound before?"

"No. Never. I don't even know what that is," Ethan admitted.

Zoe smiled at his curious nature. She loved him more than she knew was possible.

"Well, you'll learn all about it today," Dr. Brown said.

For the rest of the quick visit, Zoe watched Ethan take everything in with a sense of awe. His face lit up at the gray-scale images of their baby moving around in her belly. He seemed enthralled at the thunderous sounds emanating from the sonogram. And at the end, when Dr. Brown cleaned the gel from Zoe's belly and left the room, Ethan wrapped his arms around Zoe before she could even get dressed.

"We're having a baby," he said as if the reality of it all had just sunk in.

His excitement warmed her heart. "And now we've been

cleared to share the news." That thought made her anxious but happy.

He kissed her, and she giggled and melted into his embrace. She hadn't imagined ever having a man like Ethan and certainly had never imagined having his child.

# Twenty-Six

$Z$oe was nervous. She could hardly take in the beautiful drive leading up to Ethan's parents' home. They'd passed several lavish estates and finally turned into a private driveway that was so inconspicuous she would have passed right by it if she hadn't been in the car with Ethan.

An expansive and sophisticated Colonial stretched out before them as they drove closer. The beige brick made the home look stately yet welcoming. Zoe gasped. She couldn't believe this was where they lived. By the time Ethan came to a stop, her leg was bouncing. She didn't know how the nervous energy would manifest next.

"Oh, my this is lovely," said Zoe's mother, Laura, from the back seat.

"Wow! It's huge," Shena said. She was having a good day. Zoe was happy about that.

Ethan exited the car and helped Laura and Shena out before taking Zoe's hand and leading her to the double entry doors.

The door opened before he could ring the bell.

"Hey, baby!" A short, caramel-skinned woman with salt-and-pepper hair opened the door and embraced him.

"Hey, Ma." Ethan hugged her and kissed her forehead. "This is Zoe." He presented her to his mother. "Zoe, this is my beautiful mother, Lydia."

"Let me see this gorgeous young woman." Lydia moved Ethan aside to take Zoe in. She scanned her from head to toe, then turned to Ethan with an approving nod. "You know how to pick 'em, babe!" Her laugh was more like a cackle. It was infectious, causing Zoe, Ethan, her mother and her sister to all laugh with her. Zoe liked her already.

"It's good meeting you, Mrs. Blackwell."

"Nice meeting you, honey. Come on in here." She held out her arms. Zoe stepped into her embrace.

"And you must be her mother," Lydia said after hugging Zoe. "I see where she gets her looks from."

Laura snickered. "Yes! You're looking pretty good yourself, young lady." Lydia had brought out the playful side of Laura, something Zoe hadn't seen in a while. She liked Lydia even more. "It's a pleasure to meet you, Lydia. My name is Laura. And this—" she turned around "—is my other daughter, Shena."

"The pleasure is mine." Lydia hugged Laura and Shena in turn. She ushered them all inside. Zoe gaped in awe at an elegant set of stairs winding its way up to the second floor. She had only seen homes like this in movies.

"Hey, Zoe!" Carter rounded the corner. He hugged her.

A tall gentleman who looked just like Ethan appeared just behind Carter. Zoe assumed he was their older brother, Lincoln. After him came a pretty, curvy woman with two kids at her legs. The way she lovingly clung to Lincoln gave Zoe the impression that she was probably his significant other. The huge diamond on her finger let her know that she was his wife.

Almost the entire family was gathered in the large two-story foyer, including Ethan's sister, Ivy. Lydia led the greetings, introducing everyone from both families. They all passed around hugs.

Bill was the last to enter the foyer. His brawny stature was intimidating, and his deep voice boomed when he spoke. Zoe found herself holding her breath when he approached her.

Zoe lifted her head to meet his gaze when he stood before her. She wouldn't stand down. Seconds ticked by and silence settled around them. Zoe was keenly aware that all eyes were on them.

Bill cracked first. A small smiled eased at the corners

of his lips and he narrowed one eye at her. She tried to hold her smile back and narrowed an eye back at him.

"Come here, young lady." He opened his arms wide. Zoe stepped in. His bear hug felt like the warmth of a summer day and she hugged him back.

"You don't scare me, old man," she teased.

Everyone laughed, and Bill released her. "Welcome to our home. We need you back on the Blackwell team," he said right away. "We can feel the impact of your departure already."

"Dad!" Ethan scolded.

"All right, all right. No business talk today." Bill leaned down closer to Zoe's ear and pretended to whisper. "We can talk about that later. I'll pay you more than Ethan did."

Laughter filled the grand home once again.

Lydia and Ivy led them to a large room with glass doors overlooking a spacious yard. Even with the barren trees and no flowers in bloom, the yard still seemed meticulously manicured. The men went out on the deck, the winter mild enough for jackets only. Lincoln's children ran around on the grass while the ladies talked inside.

Lydia handed out mimosas. "It's Sunday, so why not call it a brunch, and what's a brunch without mimosas," she said. "Enjoy. Our meal will be ready shortly."

Laura happily accepted. Zoe and Shena politely declined. Shena had been so much better at trying to stay well. Zoe was so proud of her sister.

"I heard you made quite an impact helping to grow your territory, Zoe," Lydia said. "Kudos to you." She held her flute in the air.

"Thank you, Ms. Lydia. We had a great leader and an amazing team."

"Oh, don't be modest, honey. I understand it was all you. Take your credit. It's a poor dog that can't wag its own tail."

"Oh. Well. Okay. Yes, ma'am. And thank you." Zoe chuckled.

Lydia winked at Laura before saying to Zoe, "I also understand that you overheard my husband say some things that weren't so nice."

Zoe paused as her glass was on its way to her mouth.

"Don't worry about him," Lydia went on. "He means well. Sometimes he forgets he came from a little town in South Carolina that most people never heard of. The day we met, he called me a sassy city girl. I told him he was nothing but a country bumpkin. It was love at first sight! Ha!" Lydia's laugh was sharp and jovial.

"Our first apartment could fit in this room." Lydia looked around. "But we made it work. We hit Wall Street with a strong sense of determination and an even stronger desire to make enough money to call our own shots. It took a little hard work, lots of struggle and even more luck. We climbed that corporate ladder together and set out to start our own business. I got out of the industry a few years ago. Finance can be grueling. I was over it." Lydia took a sip. "So don't let him fool you. He's a good man who wants the best for his children. He just needs to be reminded about where he came from every now and then."

A thin older woman entered the room. "Brunch is served."

"Thank you, Melanie," Lydia said. She walked over to the sliding doors, tapped and waved the men in. "Let's eat!"

The family gathered at a table large enough to fit all of them. Bill said grace and everyone dug into the delicious food. By the end of the meal, they had all eased into comfortable conversation.

Carter lifted his wineglass. "Let me be the first to say congratulations to Ethan for winning the competition. I have to give your team credit for building an incredible base out here on Long Island. You deserve your new position."

"Thanks," Ethan said with pride.

"Cheers!" the rest of the family chimed in.

"I'm proud of you, son," Bill added. "Congrats to the new vice president of Blackwell Wealth Management."

"Speech!" Ivy clinked her glass with a knife.

"All I have to say is," Ethan said dramatically, "Carter, where are my new irons?"

The family all laughed, knowing about the brothers' bet of a golf cart and a new set of premium clubs.

"It's on its way, bro," Carter said good-naturedly.

"No, really," Ethan said, a little more serious. "I want to say thank you to Carter for giving me a run for my money. You're a great businessman. Mom and Dad, thanks for teaching me all you know about building a business. You're the best mentors on and off the job. Zoe, thank you for bringing home the win. If it weren't for your great ideas, Carter's region might have kicked our butts! We couldn't have done it without you."

"Damn right! That position in my office is still open, Zoe," Carter joked.

"I'm good, Carter. Thanks," Zoe teased.

"I do have other announcements I'd like to make." Ethan looked at Zoe sitting by his side, and corrected himself. "That we'd like to make." He took her hand and pulled her closer.

"Dad, this will make you happy. In light of my promotion, Zoe has agreed to return to Blackwell and take on the position of vice president for the Long Island territory."

"That's my girl!" Bill raised a glass. "Welcome back. You sure are a tough negotiator and I like it!"

Zoe laughed. Lydia shook her head at her husband.

"You all may know," Ethan said, getting everyone's attention again. "Zoe and I have been seeing each other for quite some time. Well before anyone ever knew. We fell hard and fast for one another and built our relationship at the same time we built the Long Island offices. I'm happy to say that both our relationship and the company are thriving. We had some ups and downs and learned some valuable lessons in the process."

Ethan looked over at his mother and father. With smiles plastered on their faces, they nodded in agreement. "We realized that we're not perfect," he went on, "but we're perfect for each other."

Zoe rubbed his arm. "Perfectly imperfect," she said.

"Aww, how sweet," Ivy said. "Who is this guy and what did he do with my obnoxious brother?"

More laughter rang out around the table.

"It was important for us to have both our families here with us today to meet each other and hear our other special announcement," Zoe chimed in.

She zeroed in on her mother's face, ready to see her expression when they announced her pregnancy. Everyone else quieted and listened closely.

"Mom," Ethan said, nodding at her.

Lydia got up. She grinned and winked at Zoe and disappeared from the room.

Zoe was confused. They were supposed to announce the baby. What was Ethan up to?

Lydia returned with a large Tiffany box wrapped in their signature white ribbon. She placed it in front of Ethan. Zoe wondered what was in it. It clearly wasn't a ring box.

He handed the box to Zoe. She looked at it and back at him.

"Open it," he encouraged.

She opened the box and found a sterling silver rattle. She chuckled.

"We're…" Ethan started.

"…having a baby," Zoe finished with him.

Laura's eyes lit up. Lydia smiled hard, despite the fact that she obviously already knew.

Bill looked from Lydia to Ethan to Zoe before clapping. "A brand new Blackwell in the family! Congratulations." He beamed.

Laura and Shena got up to hug Zoe. Excited chatter buzzed around the table.

"One more thing," Ethan added. He got down on one knee next to Zoe and said, "Hopefully that will be two new Blackwells in the family." He picked up the box that the rattle was in and pulled out the most beautiful, radiant diamond ring Zoe had ever laid eyes on.

Her eyes watered. One hand flew to her mouth. "Ethan." Her voice was a tearful whisper.

"Zoe Baldwin. Please say that you'll be my wife."

"Oh, my goodness, Ethan. Yes. Yes. I will be your wife!" She wrapped her arms around Ethan and then kissed him all over his face.

They were in a room full of family members, but at that moment, the only two people in the world were Zoe and the man she was about to spend the rest of her life with.

* * * * *

# COMING SOON!

We really hope you enjoyed reading this book.
If you're looking for more romance, be sure to
head to the shops when new books are
available on

# Thursday 7th
# January

To see which titles are coming soon, please visit
**millsandboon.co.uk/nextmonth**